RITES AND WRONGS

RITES AND WRONGS

DEATH OF THE PARTY
BOOK 3

Kleggt

Podium

*Dedicated to my readers on Royal Road,
for the comments, encouragement,
and joining Sally on her journey.*

All rights reserved. No part of this publication may be reproduced, stored in a retrieval system, or transmitted in any form or by any means electronic, mechanical, photocopying, recording, or otherwise without prior written permission from Podium Publishing.

This is a work of fiction. Names, characters, places, and incidents are either products of the author's imagination or used fictitiously. Any resemblance to actual events, locales, or persons, living, dead, or undead, is entirely coincidental.

Copyright © 2025 by Kleggt

Cover design by Kart Studio

ISBN: 978-1-0394-6611-1

Published in 2025 by Podium Publishing
www.podiumentertainment.com

RITES AND WRONGS

CHAPTER ONE

Life of Slice

W arm morning light flooded through the window of the tavern, illuminating the plain bedroom. Sally groaned and tried to roll away from the beam currently burning her tired eyes, but just ended up slipping onto the floor instead. She rubbed at her eye sockets and tried to organize her mass of blonde hair.

"Too early to be morning already," she murmured. She sighed to herself and stood to stretch out her back. From the glowing STAR hovering above her wrist, she changed her clothes to black jeans and a shirt, with a red leather jacket. Black boots for walking on the sand.

Just because she was part zombie, it didn't mean she liked feeling half-dead in the mornings. She blamed Theo for that—and speaking of . . .

She walked around the room to the large metal coffin lying on the floor on the other side of the bed. With a swing of her boot, she kicked at it a couple of times.

The sound of metal grinding came as the lid shuffled off to the side, and the figure within loomed to a sitting position. His dark brown hair was a mess atop his pale face, and his crimson eyes were bleary.

"Morning, Theo!"

"Is it?" He groaned and held his head.

"Serves you right for staying up late grinding." She put her boot on the edge of his metal bed and leaned forward. "I'm off to have a coffee with Norah, so we can gossip about you and Humphrey." She grinned.

"Isn't that against the rules?" He plucked glasses from the side of his silk-lined coffin and put them on. "Want me to get the questing route sorted for later?"

"Please, pup. Gather the others and we'll meet you by the Temple?"

"Sure, it's a date then," he said with a grin.

Sally rolled her eyes and moved toward the door. "The only thing I'm hungry for is power. Oh, and human brains." She waved him off as she closed the door.

The Wastelands sure had changed in the time they had been in a quasi-coma. Even more so in the week since they had woken back up. At first, they drew plenty of glares and drawn swords from the Players who had never heard of or seen them before. Once they had been told of how the *Outsiders* had defeated the dragon, Ruben, to save the Wastes, they had been more accepted. Only took killing a handful of Players too.

She still received glances as she walked through the city—she was technically part Monster, after all. With the Party all together, they looked like a boss event made manifest. Theo was the only one also part Player; the rest were Unique Monsters in all but name. They had become a found family. Throughout all the trials and tribulations they had been through so far, they always had her back.

With a quick hop, she leaped into the walled garden of the cafe. Several round tables with chairs were dotted around the patio area, about half of them occupied by now slightly nervous patrons. Some of them were System-created, just fulfilling their routine, acting a role. Narrowing her eyes, she spotted Norah on the other side.

"Morning, Norah." She grinned as she approached. The Mummy looked radiant, despite being mostly covered by wrappings. She smiled and her bright yellow eyes lit up at seeing the zombie.

"Morning. How are you doing?" She gestured to the table where two coffees had already been ordered.

"Tired. I've been impatient to get to the next area." She cupped the warm mug. Pretending to enjoy drinking coffee was one of her newest favorite hobbies.

"Understandable, hun. Theo too, I bet?" Norah blew the steam from the top of her held cup.

"He was out most of the night farming for items. Relentless, that man." Sally pouted and looked out over the wall at all the people milling about. So many brains going to waste.

The Mummy had a grin across her face. "Regretting having his coffin in the same room?"

She snorted in response. "It's amusing. It's like being an old married couple. He can be annoying, but it's comforting having him in proximity. Even if there's nothing there, you know?"

Norah nodded. "Same for me and Humphrey, really. Undeath certainly changes how you think about relationships."

"Don't tell Humphrey . . ." Sally leaned across the table to whisper, "But I let Theo try to *bite* me."

The Mummy gasped. "Do tell?"

"It was terrible, worse than kissing." She stuck her tongue out to pretend to retch. "The media makes it look so romantic, but it was like having a medical procedure. I suppose it's the same as me not wanting to eat dead brains." Sally rolled her finger around the rim of her cup and sighed.

Norah watched her for a moment, a smile still on her bandaged face. "Enough of that, hun. What's really bothering you?"

Sally exhaled and sank in her chair. "Falling behind the curve, and knowing there are a lot of things going on in the third area. Nobody is answering my messages, but I know they're not dead." Her eyes narrowed. "Also, Lucius is hiding on the other side of the wall."

An emoji bubble appeared over the edge with a sweat drop within it. The figure of the Shade jumped up and waved his hands. Beneath the shadow of his black hood, his crimson eyes were wide with panic.

"No! Sorry, I came to find you and then it looked like you were in the middle of something, and I didn't want to interrupt, but then I was already here so it would look weird if I tried to walk away—"

"It's fine, Lucius." Sally rolled her eyes. "Your new outfit looks good on you."

"Thanks!" He stepped back so they could see his leather armor and cloak, now all in deep browns and black. A love heart emoji appeared beside his head.

It had taken them awhile to get the emotive and shadowy figure to open up and get more use out of some of his skills. He still held a little guilt over originally intending to betray them but had proved his loyalty ten times over since. If it weren't for the emoji bubbles, he would be the only one of them not overtly extra.

"Want to go find the other two? My hands are warm enough." She grinned and put the untouched coffee back on the table.

Norah shook her head with a smile. "So hard to keep you pinned down."

Sally jumped atop the chair and then onto the edge of the wall. "That's why they—*whoa!*" She wobbled, almost losing her balance, before a bandage shot from Norah's arm and held her up. "Thanks!" The zombie held out a hand to help the Mummy over the wall.

They dropped down beside the Shade, who had his arms crossed. "You both paid, right?"

"What's that mean?" Sally beamed, pushing her hair back from her face. "Norah, are you any good with hair? It seems to just grow based on my level rather than by any conventional means."

"It does look like it would get in the way, if it weren't usually matted back with blood, hun." The Mummy rubbed her wrapped chin. "I'll see what I can do when we get back later."

"Neat." Sally led them toward the Temple with a wide smile. Despite hoping they could get to Level Twenty in no time at all, apparently the System actively made it more difficult the higher you got. After the war against the dragon and the week of adventuring since, they had managed to get to Level Seventeen.

Their friend and now council member, Edward, had assured them that they would be able to travel to the third area at Level Eighteen. If they were willing to take the risk of being under-leveled, of course. She had no doubt they'd be able to handle it, given that they took down the dragon at Level Fourteen.

Two areas in the world saved and fixed, or at least as far as she considered. Unique Monsters that only had one life the same as Players, living in some kind of harmony among the System-created. The newer groups that had been dragged into this world knew no differently. There was still violence, sure—but at least things were more balanced between everyone who only had a single life here.

Now the third area had a conflict between two factions of Players over whether they should destroy or fix the System. Frankly, the destruction option seemed rather shortsighted, ignoring the fact that it was her original plan. If there was no way of ending the System and sending people back to where they had come from, then fixing it to be a more fair and genuine world they could live in was a close second best.

"There they are," Norah prompted her out of her runaway monologue.

The large plated figure of the Death Knight raised his hand in greeting, his skeletal face grinning as crimson flame rose from the back of his crown-like helmet. Theo stood in his black suit with a red vest, leaning against the wall of the tall Temple.

"Hope you didn't miss us too much." The Mummy wrapped her arms around the right arm of Humphrey.

"*Yes*." He grinned back. "Although it has hardly been an hour."

Theo tilted his head to look at the zombie through his crimson glasses. "How was pretending to drink coffee?"

"Hush, fangs." Sally kicked dusty sand at his slacks. "I know what you get up to with that mouth."

"Well." He stood up straight and brushed down his clothes. "Perhaps you'll be happy to hear we'll be splitting up for the leveling today."

She wrinkled up her face. "Not especially. Have you already picked teams?"

He shook his head and looked around the rest of the Party. "No, I figured we could just spend half an hour arguing among ourselves about it."

Sally leaned out to the side to catch the empty sockets of the Death Knight. "Classic Sally and Humphrey adventure?"

Theo smiled. "I knew that'd be your choice. The rest of us will group up too, then. You have elementals, we have giants."

"I can't eat elementals," she whined.

The vampire shrugged and went through his STAR to send them the coordinates. "You want to get to about 80 percent experience and then we'll meet up at the next point. There are some Level Twenty Elites near the coast. We'll grind them out for the level up."

Excitement burned in Sally's eyes. "Alright, let's get this started then."

CHAPTER TWO

In Her Element

Sally slid down the sand dune and stumbled, almost falling straight onto her face. She sighed and stretched out, glaring at their surroundings.

"I bet the others had a nice stone path to their Monsters," she grumbled.

Humphrey slowly stomped down beside her, his plated boots sinking into the sand and keeping him stable. "You don't think Theo would give you the easier task?"

"Theo knows I'm competent. He would have given himself the one that gives experience more efficiently, though." She rolled her eyes. "So, we have to deal with these." She gestured with her hand out at the elemental creatures roving around.

Seemingly made from random chunks of amber or gray stone and held together with nothing but magic and ill intent, the elementals moved back and forth in set patterns. They were perhaps the most dull and uninspired enemies Sally had faced so far. And to make matters worse, they probably didn't have brains that she could eat.

"It's like I'm being punished for something," she groaned.

"The next area is partially jungle." Humphrey grinned. "So it will be humid, but a welcome change of scenery."

Hopefully, it had dinosaurs. She had hoped the Wastelands did, but she hadn't seen any yet. She even pestered Archie before he had to leave, but the ginger cat was pretty tight-lipped. During the week she had wondered how the other two Archies were doing. The one in the fifth area must be pretty lonely given how unlikely it was that there were many Parties there, if any at all. Humphrey only had knowledge of the state of things from when the Architect had died.

"Let's get this started, I suppose." She unhooked a skull from her belt and withdrew her Skeleton Key. Theo had been a dweeb and farmed up a couple hundred normal daggers. Apparently, it tickled him that her bugged weapon ignored more defense with the more basic items she had. She knew he was envious, but he was already overpowered enough without allowing him to use it.

The Death Knight ran out toward the first elemental. The Monster turned as he approached and lashed out with a rock fist. Humphrey blocked and deflected it to the side with a metallic *clang*, as he spun with his greatsword to strike into the opponent's body, chipping the stone.

"Boring," Sally said with a sigh, and glared over at a second enemy. The skull burst into green flame as she lobbed it as *[Mortis Bomb]*. Where it struck the elemental, a dark green patch of energy burst around it, and four zombies began to crawl from the ground surrounding it.

If only her dagger was ranged. She drummed her fingers on the next skull on her belt. Maybe she could fashion a crossbow to fire it, and have it attached to a string to draw it back. No, that was pretty slow—and if she missed, she'd be out of luck.

She watched the head of one of her zombies burst like a watermelon as the elemental crushed it between floating chunks of rock. With a sigh, she tried to imagine which direction Theo would be adventuring, and she flipped off the dune-blocked horizon before running over to her undead.

A second one was almost torn in half by the time she got there, and she ducked the swing of stone. Their center had some kind of sphere of energy; perhaps the magical weak spot? She lunged with her dagger and struck it, and with a cracking *pop*, it vanished. The suspended stone pieces dropped to the floor immediately, almost taking her arm with them.

"Neat." She dusted herself down and turned to the Death Knight.

He was still in the throes of combat. Although he was strong, his sword was doing little but crack off parts of the creature to little effect. Likewise, despite taking a few hits himself, he showed no real damage, as his defenses and regeneration were simply too high.

"Hit them in the tummy!" she called out. It might be that Theo sent them here because she was able to kill them with one strike. A browbeating for later, perhaps. With a smile, she watched the Death Knight jab, striking the center magic of the elemental and destroying it.

"Kill count challenge?" He grinned back at her.

"You're on!" Tripping over the feet of one of her zombies, she ran off to the next Monster.

Although they were sparsely spread out, the number of elementals was dense enough and their respawn short enough that the pair of them could effectively almost constantly be fighting.

"Seventy-three." Humphrey grinned and placed the end of his sword into the sand.

"Huh?" Sally leaned over with hands on her knees, panting. Although she didn't need to breathe, something about running about in the sun for ages still tired her out. "Ah. We were meant to be counting?" She raised an eyebrow at the Death Knight.

"*Yes*. That's what . . . never mind." He deflated.

"Sorry, Humps. I got distracted." Sally stood up straight and stretched her back out. With *[Mortis Bomb]* not doing much damage, she hadn't bothered summoning more zombies, and after a brief accident, there was only one left. Said zombie was slowly working his way over to them from where she had left it behind.

"By what?" Humphrey narrowed his eye sockets out at the near empty expanse around them.

"Well, I thought I saw a lizard, but it turned out to be a dried bit of wood. That made me sad about the forest and how we haven't seen the goblins or Jackie for a whole year now. Then that made me think about babies—all the Players are adults, right? Even most of the System-created are. Are there pregnant Players in the world?" She tapped a finger on her mouth in thought. "Not that I'm judging, but the healthcare here is dire, and it's a dangerous place. Then I started wondering if the elementals had babies, and—"

"Alright, I understand. Now that I have part of the Architect's memories, I am able to answer some of those questions." He grinned and the flames at the back of his helm flickered.

"Yeah?" Her eyes widened.

"*Yes*."

They stood in silence for a moment, as Sally's eyes slowly narrowed into a glare. Just as Humphrey opened his skeletal mouth, a noise came from up atop the nearest dune.

"See, told you they were split up."

Five figures loomed over the sands. Five male Players, in a mixture of different gear to match whatever classes they had.

Sally folded her arms and scowled at them for interrupting her conversation. "What do you want?"

A dark-skinned man with bright eyes and brighter plate armor stepped forward and grinned at the pair. "Why? Is it not obvious?" His Party all had their weapons brandished or hands ready to cast a spell or ability.

"I'm not doing autographs right now." Sally rolled her eyes. "I'm working."

"There are some who accept your existence, but we believe you to be Monsters, and like all—"

"*Blah, blah,*" she interrupted. "Heard this so many times. How do you want to do this? Humphrey likes to duel one on one, but I'm good for either two-on-five or we can take turns or something?" A yawn escaped her mouth, but her stomach was starting to get excited.

A portly spellcaster with messy brown hair leaned in toward their spokesman. "They don't seem worried, Jake. Is this a good idea?"

"It's just bravado." He glared briefly at his comrade. "You'll both die either way." He shrugged.

Sally turned to the Death Knight. "Ah, Humps! This would be a neat time to show you my ultimate, right? You didn't see it last time. Too busy gawking at Norah, weren't you?"

"What? No, I . . ." He deflated. "Go ahead, I'll sit this one out."

She allowed herself a little fist pump. "Alright, we decided that I'll kill you all this time. One question first—did Theo send you?"

"Who?" The plated figure furrowed his brow. "We just received an anonymous message that . . ."

Sally punched Humphrey in his metal arm with a wide grin. "He's such a romantic. I really need to up my game." She furrowed her brow. "But what do you get a man who just grinds out whatever he wants himself?"

"Focus on the fight, Sally." Humphrey managed to look even more morose about having to sit out.

She snapped her fingers and looked up at them. They were still standing atop the dune, and she didn't feel much like running up it to stab them. Not being able to see levels or classes these days was also tiresome, but she could usually make a rough guess based on what armor they wore or weapon they held. A knight, a Ranger, a Wizard, a Cleric, and some other kind of Fighter. Maybe even a thief?

"I feel bad." She pouted at them. "You seem like a decent group to have gotten this far. I'll give you one chance to turn tail and let the System kill you some other time." She licked her lips. Sometimes, she was too selfless.

Their confidence seemed to wane slightly. Of course, the *Outsiders* reputation proceeded them. However, under the glare of their leader, they seemed to resolve that it was reasonable the five of them could take on one scrawny zombie.

The bow was raised, and the start of spells bloomed in the hands of the two spellcasters. She reasoned that the melee Players would try to maintain the high ground to allow their allies to pick her off. Their first mistake was putting the Ranger next to the Cleric.

Arrows were usually quickest, but this one wouldn't hit her.

[Escape Fate]

Her Level Seventeen skill had her vanish from the attack in a puff of dark smoke, four zombies taking her place instead. The System allowed her to jump twenty feet, assuming that in most cases *backward* would be the sensible option. But she could go in any direction. So she went forward.

Appearing in front of the Ranger, she lashed up at the shocked Cleric and rammed her dagger into the underside of his jaw. It was enough damage to meet the conditionals, so she used *[Eat Brains]*. A near instant skill when an enemy was on low health, it turned the process into something like taking a quick bite of an apple. Except a lot messier and more traumatic for those around her.

Temporarily empowered by the stats of the fallen, she leaped backward to avoid the swinging attack of the knight—a blaze of blue cutting through the air as she stumbled into the Ranger. As he attempted to draw a shortsword against her, she held a skull against his torso. *[Mortis Bomb]* engulfed him briefly in the green light, knocking him backward as more zombies crawled from the ground.

A shard of ice shot out from the Wizard, coring a hole through one of the fresh zombies as Sally weaved around them. The knight slashed out, anger in his eyes now. She kept backtracking along the ridge of the dune as he was focused solely on her. The thief had vanished, presumably going invisible for a surprise attack.

Both of them should be watching out for their spellcasters more.

She grinned as she used her zombies as a shield wall, watching as the dead Cleric rose from the ground and started off toward the messy haired man, who was now panicked and in shock at seeing their friend coming for them.

A rush of air and a burst of power came from behind her.

[Share Burden]

The thief's weapon stopped against her skin and two of her zombies exploded with blood, collapsing to the floor. She spun and grabbed his wrist, turning his arm away and then stabbing him in the gut with Skeleton Key. As he buckled, she kicked him down the dune, leaving a trail of blood against the hot sand as he rolled away.

"Looks like you're the only one left," she cooed toward the knight.

He paused and looked around. The Wizard had fallen to the undead Cleric, and the Ranger and thief were too wounded to contribute. When he turned back, his eyes were pure blazing fury. "You bitch!"

"I gave you a chance." She shrugged and pouted. "No need to be rude. You watching, Humps?"

The Death Knight nodded.

As the Player stalked toward her, his sword crackled with amber energy. A cooling wind whipped through the area.

"Oh, are we having an ultimate-off?" She winked. "Mine isn't ready yet. Could you wait?"

He drew back his sword, intending to let loose his power.

[Endless Dead]

"Phase one—a gal has to have some pals." Sally grinned as fifty zombies crawled up from the surrounding sand. She lowered herself into a crouch to hide among them.

The knight had no choice but to use his skill, and a giant arrow of burning energy shot out, immolating dozens of zombies as it flashed to where he had last seen her. He began backing away from the horde as they tried to close in on him, and a shield of blue enveloped his armor in a bubble, as a radiant light that pooled around his feet flared up.

"And then phase two—the actual skill." Her voice came out from somewhere among the dead.

[Quick Death]

CHAPTER THREE

Dine and Dash

The knight staggered back in shock. As one, every zombie in the area stopped their idle shambling or slow consumption of the fallen Players and turned to stare at him with their bright yellow eyes.

He ran, bursting through the side of the horde to stomp around on the soft sand, which slowed his movements. A buff of pale light flowed down his legs, and he increased to his normal sprinting speed.

Sally grinned widely, flame dancing in her red eyes. Watching him gain distance away from her and her zombie pals. Then she gave the unspoken command.

Together as a group, the gathered zombies moved after the escaping man. But not in a slow and awkward shamble . . . they *sprinted*. Exhibiting speed and mobility unlike their normal selves, the horde began enclosing on the fleeing knight.

She continued to watch. The man was fast, but with over thirty living corpses bearing down on him, he soon made a mistake and stumbled. As the first zombie eager for a taste of his flesh leaped into the air and knocked him to the ground, it was all over. With a smile, she turned and hopped to slide down the dune.

"Please . . . you—" the wounded thief began, before she stabbed him through the head and used *[Eat Brains]*.

"Always sours the meal when they beg." She wiped the gore from her mouth and sighed. "I gave them the chance and followed through with my word. That's fair, right?" She turned to the Death Knight and crossed her arms.

"In a manner of speaking, *yes*."

"It's more a shame that there are so many still against us," she continued, kicking some sand. "After all that we've done, some continue to see us as evil."

"Can't think of why," Humphrey said with a grin, as he watched the corpse of the thief stand up as a zombie. "Nice ultimate, though."

"It's not as flashy as Theo's, but being able to turn my slow pals into sprinting zombies for a few minutes is a pretty big deal." The other options at the time that had more pizzazz to them were either more situational or didn't fit the theme she was going for. Fast zombies were a whole new horror that was useful both for offense and defense—especially when her horde was larger.

"When you get to use [Zombie Apocalypse] again, then you will be unstoppable."

"Yeah." She smiled and tilted her head to the sky with her eyes closed. Even though it was over a year ago, it felt like two weeks given they had been in a coma. Summoning and controlling hundreds of undead had been amazing. The conditionals for the skill weren't met, and she was pretty sure that the System also had a hand in when she could use it as well. Given to her in error, it was essentially an invasion event rather than a normal ability, even greater than a boss ultimate.

She worked her jaw as all those proper nouns became harder to chew, the more of them her sentence became labored with.

"More elementals?" The Death Knight gestured back to the roving plain of boring rock Monsters.

"I have an even better idea," she said as her eyes twinkled.

A skull of flaming green shot across the courtyard and knocked the guard from the top of the parapet. Zombies rose from the ground in the area as the figure crunched against the stone ground.

"Huh, for some reason, I expected the ruins to be abandoned." She rubbed at her chin as her horde clambered around the buildings in search of the rest of the System-created. Sally kneeled beside one that hadn't turned yet. "Lizard people, but these are more like . . . iguanas? Or geckos?"

"They are reasonably weak." Humphrey wiped his sword off on his red cloak. "What is it you seek here?"

"Aww." She stood up as yellow light pooled into the large eyes of the fallen guard. "Don't tell me you've forgotten?"

The Death Knight paused, briefly panicked that he had forgotten some manner of anniversary or special occasion. "It's . . . your birthday?"

"No! Well, probably not. We were in a coma for a year, so I must have had one at some point, but I have no concept of time past three days either way, so . . . guess again."

He rubbed a plated finger against the side of his face, a metallic scratching in contrast to the groans and yells of combat as the zombies took the area.

She went through her Inventory and brought out a small piece of paper.

Holding it aloft, she cleared her throat to read it. "Within Walls, Lands Afar, Broken Ground, Crimson Mar."

"Ah!" He grinned widely as his helmet flame rose higher. "The secret note from back in the crypt."

"From when you chose to abandon your role as an Observer and saved my life." She grinned and stuffed the paper into her pocket. "Took me a little while to figure out where it could be, but I think this is it."

Humphrey looked around. Inside this small stone outpost of sandstone and pale wood, they were certainly "Within Walls" as the gathering of buildings were encircled by tall stone battlements. The second area could be considered "Lands Afar" compared to the starting zone in the forest.

"We just need to find the broken ground," she said, filling in the continuation of his thoughts. "Even if the reward is trash, I figure this would be neat to tick off before we headed on to the perils of the jungle."

He nodded and gestured for her to lead the way.

Sally spun the STAR up as she walked around, bringing up her chat with Theo.

Sally: Thanks for the special delivery, pup x
Theo: I don't know what you mean ;)
Theo: They were snooping about the town for info on us
Theo: *Unacceptable*

She shivered and closed the chat. Theo had always been a bit of a dweeb willing to skirt the laws of morality, but, since becoming a Vampire Lord by accident, he had embraced the main character vibes—and it worked well.

"Hey, Humps, who out of us do you think would be the most likely to turn into a proper villain and go rogue?"

"Theo," he stated without a moment of hesitation.

That would have been her guess too. "*Whaaat?* Not Lucius, with how he was going to betray us, anyway? We've only known Norah for a few weeks, technically."

The Death Knight said nothing in response, knowing that they both knew the vampire had it in him to become deranged—especially if he didn't get enough sleep. That he seemed content to follow Sally's ambitions rather than have a grand scheme of his own was probably their greatest boon.

Sally felt compelled to fill the silence. "I just don't think I'd be able to beat him in a duel if he turned on us."

"Could you defeat any of us?" Humphrey raised an eyebrow and grinned.

"You dare?" she huffed and scowled at him. "You forget your station. I have half a mind to—oh! Look over here."

Sally hopped across the warm stone of the street and into a large building with an open doorway. Shaded from the sun, it took her eyes a little while to adjust to see what was inside. "Some kind of temple," she murmured, narrowing her eyes at the floor.

Cracks ran across it, not from age or decay, but seemingly chiseled in some abstract pattern she didn't understand.

"Just need the 'Crimson Mar.'" Humphrey grinned.

"Well, I'm not bleeding on it. Remember last time?" She rubbed at her wrist in remembering the bugged *[Necroblast]* she had used in fighting the dungeon boss.

Humphrey looked around. The sides of the room had plain wooden benches between and beyond four pillars that held up balconies overlooking this middle area. "Maybe you don't have to." He raised a plated finger to point at one of the pillars.

Sally walked over to see that one of them had a red marking across it. Not even really like a splatter of blood, but perhaps paint or something chalky. Her gaze turned to the inert torch affixed to the wall. With hand outstretched, she held and pulled it—and with some resistance, it relented to clicking to the right. The sounds of gears turning proceeded with the grinding of stone as a doorway opened on the back wall.

"Neat!" She walked over and stuck her head inside the opening. A short hallway leading to some stairs was lit nicely by torches. "Funny how long these can last, huh?" Sally raised an eyebrow at the flickering flames.

Humphrey shrugged and followed her down, the edges of his armor scraping the walls as they descended.

Sally tilted her head at the small chamber at the bottom of the stairs. Perhaps expecting some sprawling subterranean dungeon, she was almost disappointed to find just a small room. Plain and unfurnished, except for a stone slab with a wooden chest atop.

"Hmm." She narrowed her eyes. "Check for traps, Humps!"

The Death Knight sighed and pushed past her into the room. He stood, waving his arms around, before grasping the wooden container. The lack of any immediate repercussions from his diligent efforts seemed like he had done a good enough job.

He popped open the lid, and Sally moved up beside him to look inside.

> Broken Shield
> One of three pieces of a legendary shield lost to time.

"Can't be that powerful if it lost to time," she grumbled. "Now we have to find two more pieces to complete it, I assume?"

The Death Knight shrugged, and then looked up at the back wall, drawing her gaze to it too. In flickering crimson, words began to appear slowly across the stone, until they formed a phrase.

> Deepest Pit, Unending Night, Between Two Worlds, Eternal Sight

"Ah, our next clue. Write that down, Humphrey." She glared at the plated figure still grasping the empty chest. "Never mind, it's gone now." The last of the letters faded away.

She began to walk back up the stairs as he placed the container back to follow her. At the top, she waited by the torch switch to flip it so that the Death Knight would have the briefest of struggles to get back through before it closed.

"Not the worst adventure." She grinned. "Better than stabbing elementals."

"Indeed. Not only did we receive part of a legendary artifact, but we also received experience."

"Huh?" She looked down at her STAR to see it glowing gold. "We'd best get to the meeting place then, while I decide what to pick!"

She ran back outside to start to gather her zombies.

Humphrey stopped to narrow his eyes at the Temple, pausing as if waiting for something to happen. His helmet flame illuminated the dark shadows on the peaked ceiling.

"*Soon*," he grumbled to himself, and strode off to rejoin the zombies.

CHAPTER FOUR

Rat Race

Sally groaned as she trudged through the sand. "I can't believe that we haven't picked up mounts yet. This is agony."

Humphrey grinned and looked out at the swirling desert. "It's not that bad."

She rolled her eyes in response. "I still can't decide on my new skill. Oh, I've seen Lucius's ultimate, where he can shadow all four of us at once, but what was Norah's?"

"It's a summon. Like the statue we had fought in the dungeon but not made of stone."

"Neat! Is it undead too?" Summons were great if they could share all their auras and buffing abilities.

"*Yes*, I believe so. Do you want to know what my ultimate is?"

She grimaced. "Is it much cooler than mine, like with flashing lights or environmental effects?" There might be a little envy there over Theo's ability to bring about pitch-black night and slow things before he used that darkness to shoot people with his finger. Actually, thinking about it too hard made it seem all the more ridiculous.

"*Yes*," the Death Knight said with a grin.

Sally groaned again. "Pass, then." Not that she liked everything being a surprise, but she knew he did—and there was some merit in having a bit of spectacle and tension in a fight. The dry sands tiring out her eyes, she relented to hitting her skill selections to pick one.

Pick One
[Skull Seeker] Remains are easier to find from corpses.

> **[Tomb Dweller]** Party Buff—Increase Resistances for a short period.
> **[Curse: Decay]** Channeled Curse—Target slowly loses health if they are over 50% HP.

[Skull Seeker] seemed a little redundant at this stage. Unless there was anything cool she could craft with body parts, she already had more skulls than she could get through. A little bit of foresight went a long way. An Inventory full of remains sounded neat in a macabre way, but it was already cluttered enough with things she didn't like to look at.

[Tomb Dweller] would make the Party briefly even more hardy than they were. Didn't affect her minions, however. Plus, there must be a point where diminishing returns kicked in and any further buffs wouldn't be worth the opportunity cost. Gross, she was starting to think of these things like Theo. In fairness, with the number of skills they were accumulating as they leveled, it was a lot to keep track of. She yawned and moved onto the next.

The new *[Curse: Decay]* had piqued her interest as it was something channeled, rather than having to cast it all the time. Only worked on pretty healthy targets—but even then, it gave her something to do from range when *[Mortis Bomb]* was on cooldown. She ground her teeth together.

[Curse: Decay]

"I went with a draining skill," she said with a shrug.

"Figures." Humphrey grinned.

Sally grumbled to herself. Despite the long rest, the fine grains of the System had started to wear at her brain again. Maybe that was just the sand. Archie wouldn't tell them much about the next area and had absconded as soon as they were settled and properly awake. New problems, as always.

A handful of figures loomed over the next dune, and she licked her lips in hopes that it might be more Player brains eager to jump inside her stomach. Only slightly disappointed, she realized it was the rest of the Party. Filled with a little renewed energy, she increased pace and caught up to them.

"Thanks again for the gift." She kicked sand at Theo when they got close enough.

"I don't know what you mean." The vampire pushed up his glasses. "Although there is somewhere I'd like to take you."

Sally narrowed her eyes but shrugged. "Sure. We already leveled up—so Humphrey can help the others?"

Agreements were murmured and nodded.

"We have a busy day ahead, so don't spend too long." The Death Knight glared at Theo.

"Of course." He smiled back and put his hands in his pockets.

Sally rolled her eyes and then the pair of them vanished in a flash of blue light. A brief moment of vertigo, and then they stumbled out into . . . more sand.

There was something familiar about the area, but it was different. Populated and less drained of life.

"You didn't get your zombie dragon," Theo began, going through his STAR, "but maybe this can be a close second?"

She tilted her head and caught the item he threw over to her.

> Mount Taming Lure

She beamed at the vampire, pointing it at him immediately. "Doesn't work," she said with a pout.

He jerked his thumb over to the side with a sigh, and she turned to see a hole in the ground. As her eyes narrowed, an even wider smile crossed her face. "Not bad, fangs." She kicked more sand at him and then ran for the Warren.

It wasn't exactly regal or imposing, but there was something about scurrying about the sands atop a giant zombie mouse that felt good. Sally's mouth ached from smiling constantly as the warm air whipped through her hair.

"We're going to meet them by the mountain," Theo yelled from his own mount. His had dark black fur, so Sally had chosen one with white fur to contrast.

In the process of turning them undead, they did both get a little dirty and bloodied, but the benefit was they could share all the Party boons. Not that she wanted to throw her new pet into a combat situation—keeping it alive was important. "Okay," she yelled in return. "Then straight to the jungle?"

"Yeah."

Teleporting would be much quicker, but taking the scenic route and giving the mice a test drive would allow the others to level up in the meantime. Theo must have gotten to Level Eighteen already, seeing as he still had the experience bonus passive. It had taken a lot to convince him to not get to Level Twenty—he was even more raring to go to the next level than she was.

Mostly because it was somewhat . . . worrying. The mouse ride actually gave her a chance to think in relative silence for a while, without having to be a manic mess around the Party. She hadn't been able to contact any of her friends through the System messages. Chuck, Dent, or Lana. The chat still worked because she could talk with the Party . . . but from their coma onward everything else had been peaceful. She was sure Chuck would have sent her something while they were asleep for a year . . .

The whole two Player factions fighting over the System seemed like a brain drain too. She would have to hear them out in person to see what their stances truly were—but killing over how to live in the world seemed backward. The irony tasted weird—though, maybe that was the sand too. What even was her stance on the System these days?

Sally furrowed her brow. It had changed over time. At first, she wanted revenge for her bugged existence. Break the System and eat the Architect. Her human side had pushed the nuance of morality upon her. Should she take her anger out on the others brought to this world, even if they were tasty? So the best option was to make the System fair for both Players and the Unique Monsters that were almost the same in this world.

With the Architect dead, there was a need to try to steer the captainless ship. The Wastelands told the story of what an empowered and unrestricted Unique could achieve, and her task was to make things fair for everyone again. All should have the same chances to live how they wanted.

So what next? Break the thumbs of whichever faction she didn't ally with, and then try to squeeze themselves to the next area? If anything, she needed to find an end point where they weren't constantly having to fix everything. She yawned, taking in grains of sand the mice were kicking up as they sprinted through the area.

One step at a time. Perhaps the constant struggle was what she needed, to not sit and panic over the fact she was stuck in this world as a sentient zombie. No use wishing for the impossible. Enemies were a lot easier to chew through than any existential crisis.

"You okay, Sally?" Theo shouted over to her. He was sitting back, relaxed, with his arms crossed as though he didn't need to hold the reins.

"Soon," she said with a grimace. Too early in the day to get too miserable. "I hate sand, it's—"

"Me too," the vampire interjected.

She deflated and looked around. Groups of Monsters roamed through the dry plains. Cacti and other vegetation had sprung up in areas. Small towns and Monster villages had been rebuilt and repopulated. It warmed her heart. As much as she was sad that they didn't get to experience the area properly. They even thundered past a couple of Player groups working on quests—their eyes wide in surprise at seeing the pair.

After a short while, the city loomed up on the horizon, the mountain palace just behind. Edward was happy to finally be able to level himself up—but didn't seem too keen on following into the next area with them. He had a position of authority here, so that made sense. It was good to have an ally that could help maintain control over the Wastelands. He was reluctant to admit he would teleport to her and perform his duty of being her bodyguard if they really needed it.

She most definitely would. Not just to see him, but trouble seemed to follow them around—especially when they chased it around and jumped in with both feet.

They caught even more eyes as they stampeded straight into the city, down the main road. System-created and some slower Players had to leap out of the way as they headed up toward the palace. As they reached the staircase, Theo snapped his fingers and his mount vanished, leaving him to slide along the floor on his boots.

"They can do that?" Sally yelled in surprise as she bounded past him onto the stairs. She snapped her fingers and her white mouse vanished, sending her bouncing into the stone steps. "Ow." She slipped down a couple before rolling back up to her feet. "That was fun, though!"

The vampire walked up beside her with his hands in his pockets, and she looped an arm around his left. "I bet the others will be jealous," she said with a grin.

"If we're going to be in a jungle, there will probably not be much chance to use them. Due to their size." Theo wrinkled up his nose in an attempt to adjust his glasses without his hands.

"Pshaw, unfair." She rolled her eyes and then brightened up at seeing the rest of the Party already waiting for them.

Humphrey stood with his arms crossed and eyes narrowed at the vampire. "Took you long enough."

Theo tutted as Sally relinquished her grip on him to go talk to Norah. "When are you going to get over it, old man?"

The flames behind the Death Knight's helmet rose higher. "You forget your place, boy."

"Are you going to show me it, then?" Crimson light flickered across the vampire's eyes.

"Hey!" Lucius stepped up beside them, a sweat drop emoji beside his hooded face. "We're leveled now. Ready to go into the jungle?"

"More than ever," Theo said with a grin, pushing his glasses up.

"*Yes*." Humphrey continued glaring with empty sockets at the vampire.

"Cool, cool." Another sweat drop emoji. "Glad we're all on the same page."

"Right then!" Sally called from the side with the Mummy. "Edward is waiting on the path. Let's roll out, corpse gang."

"*Corpse gang*," Lucius murmured to himself, an eye-rolling emoji beside his head.

Sally rubbed the back of her head and yawned. It was nice to have the gang together and all happy. It made things a lot easier when they got on so well. She turned back to the four of them, who were now following behind. Family, in a way. An odd one, but they were hers. She smiled and looked up at the pathway leading around the mountain.

It wasn't but a few minutes later that they saw the lithe demon at the side of the road looking rather impatient.

"*Outsiders*." He gave a short bow. "I, uh . . . don't die?"

"Well said." Sally grinned. "Glad you came out here for us."

"*Edward*," Theo said, narrowing his eyes.

"*Theo*," the demon responded.

Sally slowly pushed her way in between the two to break off their eye contact. "Worried about us?"

He sighed in response. "I just know I'll be seeing you soon enough . . . and Archie made it clear that you'd be getting into trouble with the factions within the hour, no doubt."

She leaned past him to see the path leading away from the amber sandstone glow of the Wastes and, at a border, moved through trees and deep green vegetation.

"Sounds like a challenge," she said with a wink.

CHAPTER FIVE

Warm Welcome

The dark trees of the jungle loomed overhead. Thick leaves of deep green plunged the abundant vegetation on the ground into a dim shadow as the sunlight fought a losing battle to shred through the canopy and illuminate the rich browns of the mud where plant life hadn't taken hold.

"Why . . ." Sally palmed at her eyes. "*Why* is it even warmer here?"

Theo shrugged and looked off into the dense trees. "You want the actual explanation?"

"I want you to make it stop." She deflated and turned to the rather heated looking undead Party. "That's an order for you all."

Their response wasn't too helpful. Aside from the vampire stripping down to his undershirt, none of them had any good plans to assist her in changing the climate of the area. Like the dragon had in the Wastes. Perhaps she shouldn't be so selfish. Rotating through her STAR, she brought up the map again. Not too much farther.

"We can take a shortcut to the first outpost if we go through the more overgrown part." She pointed an extended finger to the right.

"What do you think we'll have to fight?" Humphrey deflated, knowing the inevitable.

"Dinosaurs," Norah offered.

The Shade cupped his misty chin. "Jungle rats." A question mark appeared beside him.

"Each other," Theo said, looking off in the other direction, hands in his pockets.

"No time for tussling," Sally tutted. "Let's go find out who is correct." She hopped off the path and immediately tripped and fell over some vines into a dense bush.

The Death Knight went over and picked her up by the scruff of her shirt. "Don't rush to help the lady then, Theo."

"Hmm?" Theo turned his head to observe them. "There is someone watching us, but they are either too far away or too obscured for me to know where."

Sally spat a leaf out and dusted herself down as Humphrey grounded her. The rest of the Party began to look around the area, but other than the greens and brown of the jungle, there was little else to be noticed.

"Alright." Sally turned back and almost got her feet stuck in the same vines. "Keep focused, it might not be an enemy . . . uh, after we decide what side we're on."

With the shrug of the Death Knight, the Party followed her. Theo waited for a few more seconds, his eyes slowly looking around the canopy, before he tutted to himself and caught up.

Sally let Humphrey lead the way, his large sword cutting through any vegetation as Norah used her bandages to pull branches and broken foliage out of the way.

"Doing okay, Norah?" Sally slowed to walk beside the Mummy.

She tilted her head to the zombie. "Slightly envious that some of you can disrobe to some degree. Would be nice to cool off."

Sally frowned. "What happens when you take the bandages off? Aren't you just a bodacious zombie underneath?"

"Sort of, but not that simple, hun. At the end, they are attached—part of me like a skin. It's painful to have them out and off me." She gave a smile and returned to focusing on giving the Death Knight help.

With a hum, Sally slowed down further to walk beside Lucius. "What about you? Can you take your clothes off?"

"What?" The Shade jumped physically to the side as exclamation marks appeared beside his head. "Oh, you mean in general? Yeah, I could. I'm essentially a shadow underneath, so I could go without . . . but I feel like clothing gives me more form."

"That makes sense." She nodded slowly. It was a bit like how Humphrey was just a suit of metal with no actual functional body inside. Still had enough of a heart to be soft on the Mummy, though.

She slowed again to sync up with the vampire.

"No sand to kick at me here," he said with a grin.

"Give it some time, pup." She rolled her eyes. "Penny for your thoughts?"

Theo worked his jaw and sighed. "Mostly trying to decide if the arrow is worth dodging or not."

"What arrow—" she began, before a zip through the air slammed into the vampire, causing him to stumble forward.

He stood back up straight, an arrow protruding through his chest having impaled through his back. "Eh, not the worst." He shrugged, wincing as his muscles moved around the wound.

The Party spun around to look behind them. Sally drew a skull into her left hand and held her right out to use her new curse. There was no target that she could see.

Lucius stepped over to Theo to help him.

"No," the vampire raised his hand. "Don't touch, it's poisoned."

The Death Knight walked up as Sally continued to look for the perpetrator. "I can remove that for you, then."

Theo looked up at the skeletal face with impassive eyes, hands still in his pockets. "Sure, just pull it all the way through."

"Gladly." Humphrey pinched the metal tip of the offending projectile and pulled it slowly from the wound. With a small sucking noise, the tail end eventually emerged from the wound and the arrow was discarded to the ground. The pair maintained eye contact through the whole process.

Sally leaned back and frowned at them. "What are you two . . . do you know who shot you, Theo?"

"Not exactly." He broke his eyes away from the Death Knight. "It's a Player, I know that much, but they're being very cautious."

She rubbed her face and scowled back at the immutable jungle. Being stalked didn't make the overbearing humidity of the jungle any more fun than it already was. Perhaps this is what they got for being so under-leveled and out of their element. "How did you know they were going to fire at you?"

Theo put his hand on her shoulder. "These sorts of things are predictable. They'll be going for you next, so I'd advise walking directly in front of me."

Sally nodded, slightly intrigued by how assertive and aloof he was being since entering the jungle. Perhaps the mouse ride knocked a few things loose in his head. Still, she didn't fancy getting an unwelcome gift through the back of her head. Theo might like his chances of it hitting him in the torso, but she was slightly more risk adverse. Which was a concerning realization.

A sweat drop appeared beside the Shade. "What if they go for *me* instead, if you're blocking Sally?"

"Then just dodge," Theo said with a grin.

Sally nudged him with her elbow as she walked in front. "That a weak poison you can regenerate over?"

"No." He stretched his neck out as they started cutting their way back through the jungle. "I will die in three days."

"Ass." She rolled her eyes. "Cheer up, pup. This area won't be all bad."

Theo raised an eyebrow and looked off to the side but said nothing.

After a few minutes of tense travel through the foliage, Humphrey stopped and held a plated fist up. "Monsters ahead."

"Ooh!" Sally cooed. "Who won?" She hopped ahead of Theo to go see.

The vampire held up his hand, and it was impaled by an arrow en route to the zombie.

"Gotcha," he growled and vanished. Everyone stopped and turned to the empty space behind, as a pained scream rang out. After a few seconds of silence, a body dropped out of one of the distant trees—the dark shape of Theo following soon after. Another couple of seconds and he started walking back over to them.

"That's better," he said with a wide grin, his bloodied fangs exposed. "I hate being spied on. Sorry for being so prickly, Humphrey."

The Death Knight shrugged and grinned at the vampire. "I was egging you on. My apologies too."

Sally frowned, not understanding the conversation. The heat was obviously getting to her. She yawned again. "Ugh. Anything good on the body?"

"Some paperwork. It's nice when the pre-dead write down exposition for us, huh?"

She sighed and shook her head. "Don't call them that. We need to work on our public relations. And get that arrow out of your hand already." Her expression turned into a scowl at seeing that his hand was still impaled.

"I just didn't want the poison to get worse."

As she grabbed it and pulled it from him, she rolled her eyes. Too humid and sweaty for this.

"Two days now."

"Shush," she said as she put a finger to his lips. "No more, only Monster killing now. Okay?"

He nodded slowly as she spun back to the pensive Party. They hadn't even gotten to the Monster type reveal yet, and she had also just slid right past whatever Theo had found. The heat was turning her brain into soup, and it was violently close to lapping straight out of her ears.

"Save the reading for when we are safe," she said as she waved her hand in the air. "Humphrey, what is the Monster, and can we go kill them please?"

"*Yes,*" he said with a grin. "They are—"

An explosion rocked the tree line over to their right, the groan of trees collapsing among the clatter of vegetation causing Sally's right eye to twitch. The smell of smoke and burned wood washed across the Party as they stood waiting.

"This better be good." She ground her sharp teeth together. Or at least, full of brains that she could have. Theo hadn't even saved the would-be-assassin for her to eat—and a little head jelly would be the perfect refresher for this humid climate.

Five figures loomed out from the shadows of billowing smoke and broken jungle. A giant of a man in plated armor in the middle, two men in leather armor to his right, and a female spellcaster alongside a masked individual to his left.

Each of them wore a red tabard over their gear, a symbol of a triangle in white pointing downward on the front, and golden detailing down the edges.

"A Party of Monsters?" The man lifted up the visor on his helmet to reveal bright green eyes. "Well, that is certainly unusual." They seemed apprehensive but didn't immediately go on the offense.

Sally snapped her fingers. "Yeah, you might even say *Unique*." She beamed at them for a few seconds as they stood confused, before she deflated. "Tough crowd."

"You must be new to the area. Who are you allied with?" He tightened his grip on his large two-handed hammer. The rest of his group seemed to tense up alongside him. "What do you believe?"

"Depends." Sally scratched her chin. "What do you *want* me to believe?"

CHAPTER SIX

Red Team

The group in red tabards seemed to relax slightly at her question-posed-as-an-answer. "My name is Lenard," the plated knight introduced himself. "Perhaps I can enlighten you to what our cause leads us toward?"

"Eh, sure." She glanced at the others, who shrugged their indifference. "Double points if you have anything that can fix the humidity." She wasn't even supposed to sweat—she was dead! Out of the five of them, she seemed to be suffering the worst. Perhaps she was just complaining the most.

With a quick glance, Humphrey appeared stoic, but the air surrounding him was wavering as if he was a hot grill. Speaking of that, the pale vampire was doused in as much sweat as she was. Norah looked tired more than anything . . . but Lucius hadn't changed or mentioned anything about the heat so far. Maybe he was immune. Her eyes narrowed at him.

"Oh," Lenard continued, "you didn't do the Acclimatization Quest? It's supposed to be on the road you follow to the first outpost." His group started walking over closer.

Sally could feel the glares of the *Outsiders*, except for Lucius, bore into the sides of her head. Which made her just feel warmer. There was no winning with these guys. "No, we took a shortcut because we were being tracked by someone."

Lenard stopped and was on guard again. "Are you still being followed?"

"No." She shook her head. Perhaps not a good idea to explain that Theo was a vampire and drank their blood. That usually got people a bit itchy. Or enamored. She rolled her eyes. "We got rid of them."

"I don't think they were wearing a tabard," Theo murmured from beside her.

"Impressive." Lenard scratched at the back of his helmet. "There is a small group of assassins that like to prey on those new to the area."

At first, more Player on Player violence sounded draining—but a third neutral Party that could easily fit in her stomach without disturbing the balance of the two main factions was a decent appetizer before she decided on the main course.

"Let me know if you want me to kill them all," the vampire whispered, now even closer to her.

Maybe the Wastes weren't so bad. Even the forest at this point would be a delight. She thought of Jackie and the goblins—it had been a year. Did they even know what had happened? Always having to push forward . . . she did hate to be left behind the curve. They needed to be powerful to not die. Die again.

She slowly pushed the vampire's abs away. "How about you five lead us through this quest and we'll hear you out. We'll be much more sympathetic to your cause with being able to breathe here." Sally gave herself a handful of points for being able to get that sensible thought out of her melted brain.

Lenard shrugged. "Sounds reasonable to me."

The group then escorted them back the way they came, both sides giving each other glares and odd looks. There was something about the undead that the living had a natural inclination to abhor. Likewise, her group had nothing but a dim view of those who would sooner try to put them back in the ground. Players probably didn't attack each other that much, but the *Outsiders* were an exception to this rule more often than not.

It turned out that the quest had been just around the corner of the path from where they had split off into the wild jungle. Not only that, but it was the simple matter of talking to a System-created guard. The figure remained standing with a smile on his face as if they had vanished, just as soon as he passed over the small metal band they had apparently "earned" just by talking to him.

Sally sighed and grinned as she slipped the ring on, almost instantly feeling a lot cooler. Nice of the System to know that actual jungle conditions would be hell to fight through for days on end. She turned to see the tired glares of her Party, who weren't too impressed that they had missed the quest.

"What?" She wrinkled up her nose. "Now you'll appreciate it more, knowing how terrible it is without it."

They grumbled some reluctant agreements, and she turned back to the humans.

"We really appreciate your help," she said with a grin. "If you'd like to give us your sales pitch for consideration now, we're all ears."

All of them except Theo, maybe. He hadn't said anything, but she could sense that he was back on edge again. Even now that they were acclimated to the temperature of the jungle and he had hidden away his sparkling abs, he seemed ready to make a few Players dead in a moment's notice. Currently, he stood leaning against a tree with his hands in his pockets, eyes watching the leader of the group.

"Fantastic," Lenard said with a grin. "I'm sure you have had your share of issues with the System in your time here. It is unfair and expects us to live a life scraping for power against uncaring violence and constant conflict."

She nodded her head. That would quite succinctly sum up the majority of her experiences since awaking in this body in the sleepy zombie village. Immediately assailed and then it just continued from there.

"Therefore, the goal of our group is to take control of the System and destroy it so that no new Players may arrive, and conflict is no longer necessary."

So this was the "destroy" faction. Handy that they chose a red tabard—that made it easier to remember. She rubbed her right eye. "So, how would conflict be no longer necessary?"

The man shifted in his plated armor. "We intend to remove all System-created, and the leveling process, so that everyone is equal and there is no danger."

Sally bit her tongue as some anger began to bubble within her. They had her in the first half, she wasn't going to lie. No System-created meant no Uniques, surely? She worked her jaw in trying to find a pleasant way of getting the clarifications she sought.

"Isn't that us?" Theo asked, as he tilted his head to the side. "Aren't we part of the System?"

Even without the rings, the already tense atmosphere between the two groups had cooled. While she and the vampire were probably Player enough to skirt by on the rules, the rest of the *Outsiders* weren't. She gave Theo a few points for the camaraderie.

Lenard scratched at the back of his helmet. "I'm not sure what the stance on Uniques is . . . ah, you might want to talk to someone higher up the chain."

Sally could perhaps assume. A dangerous thing, to fill in the gaps of a plot promising violence. If it wasn't clear that Uniques had a place in their post-System world, then that probably led to the obvious conclusion. Monsters weren't welcome. She would need to put ice on this potential inferno before something flared up with the others. Points to them for holding steady.

"Well . . ." Her smile was more of a grimace as she spoke through clenched teeth. "I suppose we should hear the other side's point of view before making our choice."

"I'm not sure that—" Lenard paused as the female spellcaster leaned forward and whispered something in his ear. "Really?" His eyes went back up to Sally. "I suppose that is reasonable. However, I am sure you will come around to our way of thinking soon enough. Allow me to give you my contact information?"

Sally rolled her eyes. "Fine."

Humphrey rubbed at his metallic chin, deep in thought. Norah was a mirror of the zombie's disdain, her arms crossed and yellow eyes glaring at the humans. Lucius had his hands on his hips but a rather blank expression on his face—perhaps not entirely grasping the history behind Sally's current ire. Theo remained leaning against a tree, glowering at his potential next meals.

All in all, team red wasn't that great, Sally decided. She waved them off as they thankfully went a different direction than the outpost. As soon as they were out of sight, she deflated and spun around to the gang.

"Thoughts?"

"Should have killed them," Theo murmured first.

Norah nodded. "I agree."

"They seemed okay, but perhaps misguided." Lucius shrugged. "Maybe they'd see sense if we put the right way of thinking into their heads?"

The vampire exhaled. "Yeah, with my sword."

Sally waved them to shush. Perhaps it would have been more pragmatic to kill them now, but until they had their feet on solid ground in the new area, it was better to not step on too many toes. A little leveling and a more nuanced understanding of the area, and then they could eat everything in sight.

She frowned. "Everything okay, Humphrey? What's your take?"

"Hmm? Oh." He turned his gaze away from his thoughts and over to her. "Whatever Norah said."

Sally rolled her eyes at Theo as the Mummy grinned. As much as she was happy for the plated ex-Observer, delegating his thoughts was unacceptable, especially when he so obviously had something on his mind. "Humps. I need your thoughts. That's an order."

He stood straighter and nodded toward her. She didn't have to push the tough love button often, but it was helpful to remind them who was the boss around here when they started getting loose with their shared brain cell.

"Apologies. The rogue Observer I had absorbed had some information about the jungle."

"Spill it then." She tapped her foot on the floor. "I've no patience for your secrets now, tin can."

The Death Knight opened and closed his skeletal mouth, slightly taken aback by the sudden dress down. "In honesty . . . I find it odd that they are so focused on this issue in area three. By my understanding, I would have assumed Players would wait until the last level and sort things out at the end."

Sally wrinkled up her nose. "So you're saying they are jumping the gun, but there might also be something pressuring them to act?"

"Astute, as always." Humphrey grinned.

She sighed and waved him away. "Get down to the outpost, guys. I'm already tired of this place. I just want a word with Mr. Brooding over there and I'll catch up."

The three nodded and started off down the road as she walked over to the tree-leaning vampire.

"What's up, pup? You look like you're ready to run off and solo the whole area." She crossed her arms as she stood in front of him.

He raised his eyebrows and gave her a slight smile. "If only. There was something I wanted to tell you, but not while the others were here."

"Oh, yeah?" She beamed at him.

"No, nothing like that." He shuffled and stood up straight, looking out to the surrounding jungle. "The Ranger I killed, she had . . . a strange STAR."

"Strange STAR," she repeated. "Like . . . ?"

"Like Marius, the Cleric." His eyes shined with a red glow. "Yes."

CHAPTER SEVEN

Blue Team

Sally kicked up dirt as they followed along behind the rest of the *Outsiders*. They held back to continue the conversation but didn't want to let them get too far ahead. She knew they'd get lost somehow, and it'd be like chasing headless chickens around.

"We'll call it corrupted STAR for now, okay?" She linked her arm around Theo's, as concern covered her face.

"Sure." Theo ran his tongue across his fangs. "Someone or something must be able to create them . . . or whatever it is doing."

"Why would people even want to?" Sally sighed. As if the world didn't have enough problems to overcome, people were trying to break the System—and for what?

"It explains the poison, I suppose. Though not why they were targeting you."

She narrowed her eyes. "What do you mean *the poison*?"

"Forty-seven hours and twenty-three minutes until I die." He looked down at her impassively.

Sally wasn't too sure what to make of that. Was he still doing a bit? It wasn't exactly like him to continue past the point of being funny. Not with something like this. "You're being for real?"

He nodded.

"Ass! Take an antidote, or whatever we have that gets rid of that sort of thing."

"Already tried." He looked away from her and into the mess of deep green vegetation they were passing. "Nothing worked."

Nerves worked up inside her, and she let go of his arm. "This is serious, then? You don't seem worried. I'm worried."

They continued in silence for a moment, but the vampire finally responded. "I've lived a good life here. Well, not really *good*, and I'm no longer alive . . ." He stopped, and she turned to pause with him. "I'm not saying I want to leave the System . . . to leave you . . . but there's some calm to having a timer on my mortality."

Sally pouted and tried to read his face. "I honestly don't know how to process that, Theo."

"It's a lot, I know. My stats are completely broken, and I feel like a pup that has caught the van it was chasing. What now? I'm mostly just here for you." He put his cold hand up to the dead flesh of her cheek.

"Aw, bud." She smiled as she looked into his eyes. "Are you just working through the dialogue choices to find the romance option?"

"Yeah." He grinned, exposing his sharp fangs.

She rolled her eyes and adjusted the collar of his suit jacket. "I'm an uncaring Monster, but you've had my heart since we met by Hillan." With a sigh, she gave him a glum smile. "Honestly, I'd feel a lot more lost without you here—but if you're ready to go . . ."

"Not yet. I just need some time to process things."

"Well, you have less than two days, dummy." She gave him a brief hug and then punched him in the arm. "We'll find you a cure and rule the world together, okay?"

Theo grinned. "Only time will tell."

"Ass!" She grabbed him by the arm and dragged him toward the Party, who had stopped ahead. "We'll continue this later. The conversation, I mean." She glared at him.

Humphrey stood grinning as he watched them approach. Norah was discussing something with Lucius, emojis appearing beside his head. The Death Knight tilted his head. "Everything okay?"

"Other than Theo is actually going to die in two days? Yeah, just peachy." She let go of the vampire and gave him a half-hearted scowl.

"Troublesome," Humphrey said, as he nodded. "It was nice knowing you."

"Can you two just kiss and get it over with?" she growled and pushed Theo across the ground toward the Death Knight.

The vampire bumped up against Humphrey's crossed arms. "It's just that we are your sword and shield. We are bound to clash."

"Until we duel, of course," the Death Knight said with a wide grin.

Sally deflated and caught the gaze of Norah, the Mummy rolling her eyes at their antics. Lucius looked to have gotten his hands stuck to some manner of wild plant and was struggling to remove it from his glove without it getting stuck to the other. Perhaps she was being too hard on them. Despite no longer feeling like they were melting, the exhaustion had already done enough damage, and she was being a grouch. New area blues.

"Alright, *Outsiders*." She stood up tall and waved her hands to get their attention. "I'm calling for a time-out. Let's get somewhere safe and chill and recover." She exhaled through her nose before continuing. "If we cure Theo, then you two can have your duel. But! Not to the death." She held a finger up and glared at them.

Humphrey grinned. "Acceptable."

"Sure, sounds good." Theo pushed his glasses up to hide his excitement.

Sometimes you had to use the carrot rather than the stick. The result of the duel might have Party dynamic drama in the future, but if she could herd the cats along the right path for a while longer, then future Sally could deal with that aftermath. After all, what was the worst they could do? Other than accidentally die, perhaps.

"Norah, you're an absolute icon. Lucius . . . here, let me help." She stepped over and pulled the sticky flower from his gloves and threw it off to the side.

They needed her more than she cared to admit. Why she had settled into a leadership position, she wasn't exactly sure. Ambition was part of it. She had the big goals to push them forward . . . but she didn't exactly feel qualified for the position. Well, perhaps that was a valid excuse back in the forest, but now she had the experience of dragging the empty-headed undead through all the barriers the System had set up.

Something wasn't sitting right with her, though. She looked around, as if there could be more enemies lying in wait. There probably were, but that—oh, that was it.

"Theo?" She grabbed and pulled him back over as the group started walking once more. "What was the Ranger like?"

"Aside from the . . ." He raised an eyebrow, not wanting to repeat "poison" in front of everyone. "Uh, dark skin, curly brown hair. Her clothing was a mix of deep greens and dark grays." He shrugged. "Tasted a little odd, but I figured that was just because of the . . ."

"Okay." She tilted her head and frowned. That didn't really tell her too much . . . not without jumping to conclusions—and her legs were tired. She doubted she could pull that off. Her clothes, either, with how the sweat had glued them to her dead flesh. Too distracted.

"We are here," Humphrey announced from the front.

She assumed he meant the outpost, rather than just a general statement about existence. Although, with how she was feeling, she wasn't too sure.

A miniature fortress loomed out just ahead of them at the end of the path, which now split off in two other directions into the deeper jungle. Made of dark wooden trunks, the arched open gate was flanked by two watchtowers. Two guards in each, and two flanking the gate. All System-created and dressed in the same dull gray plate armor, bright yellow detailing, and white tabards. A brave choice for such a mucky environment.

"Welcome Adventurers. Arberg needs your assistance, should you be able?" The line from the closest guard as they approached seemed stilted and lacking context.

"Anyone read the lore?" Sally wrinkled up her face.

"It's the area to the north of us," Humphrey filled in the exposition. "Researchers and Monsters, the usual."

"Neat."

They passed through the gate and into the outpost proper. It was muddy and drab. Not exactly a great break from the rest of the jungle, but at least they should be able to avoid most danger and annoyance for the rest of the day. Perhaps if she hadn't tempted fate by thinking that.

The insides of the wooden walls had a gathering of buildings, short and stocky, made of the same dark wood. A forge, tavern, dorms, and a couple of houses for the System-created to live. Or pretend to. With a click, a small dial turned a notch in her head, and intrusive thoughts wanted to destroy and consume this little slice of civilization. The elation she had felt when she had caused the zombie apocalypse in the previous area rose up before she shook it away. She must be tired.

"Are we going to find some proper quests?" Theo narrowed his eyes and adjusted his glasses.

There was a bulletin board over on the side that looked as though it had a number of pages pinned to it. Offering rewards for services, perhaps. Hopefully, none of them were Wanted posters for the *Outsiders*—it had been a year. Surely they'd have gotten bored with chasing shadows by now?

Sally rubbed her face. "I think first we should look for—"

"*Outsiders*," a voice came from behind them.

They spun to look back at the road. A group of five figures stood, all wearing blue tabards. This Party was led by a woman in a long purple robe, flanked by a man and woman in fighter gear with shields at the ready. What looked to be two Rangers stood at both ends of the group and were dressed identically—a mirror image of each other, their faces obscured by dark green hoods.

Sally took a deep breath, not entirely mentally. "You're the other faction, and you've heard there is a new Party in town and want to delight our ears with your stance on the whole fight in hopes that we will join your side and not eat you?"

The pale woman with long black hair stepped forward and gave them a brief bow. Their blue tabards had a white arrow facing upward, and silver detailing along the edges. They really did make this easy.

"Correct, Sally. It is a pleasure to finally meet you all. My name is Rachel."

Sally raised an eyebrow. That was unexpected. "You know us already?"

"Of course." The woman smiled warmly. "Our leader has been telling us so much about you. We have been awaiting the return of the dragonslayers."

CHAPTER EIGHT

Time Out

Chuck stared, his eyes narrowing slowly. He exhaled through his nose and drummed his fingers on the arm of his chair. It was no use. He'd have to act and say something.

"Dent, feet off the table." He glared at the swordsman.

Dent rolled his eyes but dragged them back off onto the ground. "You're stressed, Chuck."

"You think?" The Druid clutched at his wooden staff. "The reports said the *Outsiders* are finally back and have entered the jungle."

"Rachel is down that way. She is more than capable." The man tilted the edge of his blade-arm in the air, watching it catch the light. "I would have thought you'd be happier to see your friends back after so long."

Chuck clucked his tongue. "Lots of things have changed."

"You worried they won't take our side?"

He didn't reply at first and just looked out toward the sky outside of the tent. "Either way . . ." he eventually said, softly. "I know what they will do when they get here."

"Chuck!" Sally threw her arms up in surprise. "The *leader* of blue team?" Her eyebrows were as high as they could physically get on her face, and she hopped around to wave her disbelief in front of the others.

"We're . . . not called 'blue team,'" Rachel began, looked like she was not used to dealing with such overt displays of mania. "But yes, Chuck is our leader. He and Dent have—"

"Dent too?" Sally beamed. It was like the greatest hits of the Wastelands but in the new area. "I'm glad they're both okay," she said as she calmed down and stood still. "They didn't reply to my messages. Oh, when you say 'he and Dent' . . . ?" She leaned her head forward and raised her eyebrows again.

Rachel returned a blank stare. "Dent is in charge of security and our second-in-command."

Theo shrugged toward the Death Knight. "I can see that ship."

Humphrey nodded in return.

"Down to business then," Sally said as she crossed her arms. "Just because Chuck was one of our greatest pals, it doesn't mean we'll blindly follow whatever it is you guys believe."

Chuck was a pacifist, to a degree. Didn't like the violence of the System. She expected his view would be to erase conflict as well, but hopefully in a less detrimental way than the red team had wanted.

"Of course." The woman nodded, with a smile. "He told us you would be shrewd. Would sooner 'eat both factions than bend the knee.' His words."

"He knows us well," the zombie said with a grin. "Shall we go occupy this tavern and sit to chat?"

With a nod, the two groups moved off toward the building. It was by no means large, but aside from a handful of System-created, it was empty and devoid of any Players. They had their pick of the tables, but they were only made to seat four. Sally tagged in Theo, and Rachel sat with the female Fighter. Shoulder length red hair and thick leather armor made it awkward for her to sit down. Humphrey only pouted a little.

"This is Tifa," Rachel gestured as she sat down too. The Fighter nodded but didn't look to want to be a verbal participant in the proceedings. "From your greeting, it sounds like you have already met with the other faction?"

Sally nodded as she shuffled in beside the vampire. The rest of the Party mingled awkwardly at the next nearest table behind them, while Rachel's group did the same behind her.

"They certainly had some *thoughts* on *things*," she said diplomatically.

Rachel smiled softly. "You can imagine why we are so at odds. While they wish to break down the System and remove parts of it—fine people such as yourselves included—our goal is quite different."

Theo tilted his head to the side, eager to hear more. Sally was waiting for the reveal that they were both kind of flawed and there wouldn't be an easy answer.

"The System is flawed, and we intend to fix it. Make it equal for all who live here, but make it so that there is more to life than progression through conflict." She continued to smile at them both.

"*But* . . . ?" Sally narrowed her eyes.

Rachel tilted her head. "There's no 'buts' as such . . . Chuck said we could be honest with you . . ." She looked around the room to check that they were the only Players here. "Somebody is making a move for the Architect's position."

"*What?*" Sally hissed, exchanging glances with Theo. "How do you know? And who?"

The woman drummed her fingers on the tabletop. "Even with the trust he has for you, I cannot tell you more without you joining us."

Sally deflated. "You haven't even told us the catch that makes you secretly terrible yet."

Theo rubbed his chin. "So you want Players and Uniques to be able to live in peace?"

"Yes, in our ideal world, violence would only be able to be inflicted on the System-created but would still be optional. You could live without fighting, should you choose so."

They sat in silence for a moment as this sank in. On the surface, it sounded perfect. No Players or Uniques could fight among themselves. But . . .

Sally licked her lips. That meant no more tasty brains. It seemed like a selfish thing to get hung up on in the grand scheme of the world. The part of her not governed by her stomach melted at the thought, however. A world where you wouldn't need to fear for your life constantly, where you didn't have to level and get stronger to make sure someone couldn't punch down at you. Her dietary requirements seemed to pale in comparison.

She wrinkled up her face. "We will . . . need time to discuss."

"Of course," Rachel said with a smile. "You need to level up too." She raised her hand and one of the cloaked Rangers brought forth a book, out of which a scroll was taken. "Chuck said you were powerful, so we can give you a teleport farther into the area. The jungle here is especially oppressive."

"And filled with assassins." Sally rolled her eyes.

The woman paused and furrowed her brow. "You've had a run-in with the *Last Word*?"

"If that's what they're called," Theo shrugged as he grumbled. "We had one tracking us until we stopped them from doing so."

"Yeah," Sally added, "who are they?"

"Doomsday cult that just sprung out of nowhere. They want the System to fail in its entirety. Plunge us all into . . . nothingness? I'm not sure, but they have been targeting powerful Players in the area, so I'd be wary." Rachel grimaced and passed over the teleportation scroll.

"Theo already has a poison that will kill him in two days." Sally took the scroll and rolled her eyes. "Can't take him *anywhere*."

"I am a walking calamity." The vampire grinned, exposing his fangs.

Rachel paused, either put off guard by the casual nature they had toward the deadly malady, or perhaps other notions derailed her train of thought in seeing Theo's true nature. Sally narrowed her eyes at the woman either way, just to be sure.

"That's . . . not good. I'm not aware of a cure." She exhaled and curled her upper lip up. "I will need to talk to Chuck."

"We can't see him yet?" Sally pouted. Ignoring her messages and refusing to see them was pretty rude—after all this time too.

"He requested . . . only when you get to Level Twenty-five. I apologize." She did seem to understand their frustration, even if she couldn't do anything about it. "The scroll will take you to the area for Level Twenty-four and up, so you'll be the underdogs."

"Suits us," Theo said with a grin.

Sally nodded. "Better than being over, dogs. What do we do once we have made a decision?"

Rachel held out her wrist, her STAR ready to trade contact information. "Send me a message. We'll take it from there. If you've had the spiel from the others, you should know they have a dim view of Uniques . . ." Her eyes unfocused to look past the pair to the rest of the *Outsiders*. "I'm not sure how they'd treat you even if you joined them. Not that I'm trying to tip the scales." She gave them another warm smile that reached her eyes.

"Our pleasant interactions with Players are few and far between," Sally said with a shrug. "Being allied with Chuck puts you a couple of steps further away from our stomachs . . . but we're not above villainy, should you cross us."

"Villainy, meaning we kill and eat you all," Theo clarified.

The woman couldn't meet the vampire's glare but nodded toward the pair. "Of course. We are well aware of what you are, and what you have accomplished in the world despite your . . . questionable methods."

Murdering was certainly that. Sally couldn't fault the woman for her ability to lead a pleasant meeting. It took more than sweet words to sway her desires, though. If possible, she wanted to meet Chuck and hear it from his own mouth before she signed up for what he had planned. Part of her felt that it should be *her* plan they were following, but if she was honest—she didn't have one yet.

The world had moved on without them for a year, and what were they now? Relics of a harder time when the System was more of a mess. She felt older. It might as well have been twenty years for how out of place she felt.

"As such, that is all I have to say." Rachel nodded and stood from the table. "We wish you good luck in whatever your future entails."

"You too." Sally waved them off as their Party left the tavern, not wanting to hang about awkwardly now that their pitch had been heard.

Lucius and Norah shuffled into the empty chairs, and Humphrey stood at the end of the table with his arms crossed. A brief silence followed as they waited for everything to sink in.

Sally clucked her tongue to break the silence. "Well . . . this is pretty exhausting, huh?"

Humphrey nodded. "What are your thoughts?"

"I'll leave it up to the floor first." She deflated and sank into the uncomfortable chair.

"Chuck seemed pretty nice," Lucius began, a lightbulb appearing beside his head—which was something odd that Sally didn't care to think about right now. "Unless something terrible happened in the last year, he should still have a good head on his shoulders."

"*Yes*," Humphrey agreed. "He might be useless for fighting, but he had generally a decent view of life."

Norah tilted her head. "Rachel and her group seemed okay too, for Adventurers. I'd hate to think that was an act."

Sally narrowed her eyes at the vampire. "What did *you* think of Rachel, fangs?"

"Hmm? Oh, she seemed genuine enough." He absentmindedly looked out through the window at the tree-laden horizon.

She exhaled through her nose. What a dweeb. That was his "thinking of power-leveling look." "So we're all in agreement that the blue team are temporary pals until we make a decision and red team are walking meals?"

They nodded and murmured their agreement. Seemed a little callous, but they had to get their villain points before people started calling them anti-heroes.

"Doesn't that mean we've basically made the decision?" Lucius asked as a question mark popped up.

"I'm not signing anything this soon." Sally shook her head. "We can be friends until we know what's really going on in the jungle."

"After that," Theo said as he pushed his glasses up, "it gets difficult."

CHAPTER NINE

Chomp

Sally tapped her finger on the table as the *Outsiders* languished around the tavern. While they had almost decided on which faction to join, the whole atmosphere of the third area was a bit of a gloomy cloud over their joyous victory lap of the Wastes.

"You're twitchy, Theo." She turned a tired gaze toward him. "You want to go somewhere?"

"Yeah." He sighed and looked out of the window. "You know what I'm going to ask."

She rolled her eyes. "Again? I can't stop you if that's what you want. It's just that you only have two days . . ."

"I just need one." He wrinkled up his nose. "Maybe one and a half."

"How are we supposed to heal you if you're off being a goof?" She pressed a finger against his shoulder as if she was pinning him in place. "You leave this to the last minute and you're getting your coffin rights taken away."

Lucius shuffled on the stool beside the bar and leaned over to Humphrey. "What does that mean? Doesn't he need that to sleep in?" A question mark appeared beside his head.

Humphrey exhaled, his empty eye sockets facing the System-created barman who seemed to be ignoring him. "*Yes*. That's not what she means."

"So then—"

Norah put her hand on his shoulder. "Best not to overthink things, Lucy." A bandage moved around in the air to wrap around two bottles of alcohol from behind the bar.

"Isn't that stealing?" Humphrey said with a wide grin.

The Mummy winked and hovered one over to him. "We're villains, aren't we?"

Sally deflated. "Fine. Go solo level and meet us at . . ." She scrunched her eyes up at the scroll. "*Heavy Logs.* Wow, that's a really inspired name. Or I guess we might not be there forever, so find us your own way."

Theo glazed over as he went through his STAR menus. "Alright. I want to find out more about this *Last Word* group and try to put a stop to them if possible. While leveling. And finding new gear."

"In one day?" Sally put her hand on his leg. "Don't push yourself too hard, pup."

He smiled, exposing his fangs. "You'll barely miss me."

Sally stared at him for a moment, silence filling the tavern. "Oh. Sorry. I was expecting you to teleport after that one-liner."

"That would have been cooler, huh?" The vampire tilted his head. "But *I'm* staying here—you'll need to teleport to . . . Heavy Logs."

"Heavy Logs," Humphrey repeated from across the room.

Sally raised an eyebrow. "You know much about it, Humps?"

"No. I just like saying the name."

Lucius cupped his misty chin. "*Heavy Logs.*"

"Heavy . . . Logs." Norah nodded her head slowly.

With a blank expression on her face, she turned back to Theo. "I think it's the brain cell that you share with us that I'll miss most."

He grinned and gave her a light kick under the table. "Let me get going then. I don't have long left."

"Ugh, this isn't going to be a thing, is it?" She shuffled out from the table to allow him to exit.

"Not for very long," he said with a smirk.

"Ass. Serves you right if you die. It should have been me." She crossed her arms as he stood up straight.

"I'd say don't be envious, but green does suit you." Theo gave her a pat on the head before looking at the rest of them. "Stay safe. I'll be back before you know it. It's . . . inevitable."

With a brief bow, he then spun around and walked out of the tavern, into the day beyond.

"I'm not green," Sally said with a sulk.

Lucius shrugged. "You're greenish."

She deflated further and turned to the Death Knight, who was now holding the open bottle but had made no attempt to drink it. "He seemed fine with leaving me to be assassinated while he was gone."

"No," Humphrey said as he shook his head. "He sent me a message while you were talking. He trusts me to protect you at all costs."

Sally rolled her eyes and sat back down at the table. All the talking today had ruined her appetite for adventure. Not even the prospect of slightly more acceptable brain meals caused her to shift from the chair. She didn't want to lose any of the gang, but especially not Theo. He was a dweeb, but with him around, she could remember her previous life, and it gave her some hope that there was something after this.

Too many stakes in the jungle. It was easier to punch the bullies, but now they were stepping into something that needed a few more thoughts to figure out. She grumbled to herself as she stared at the worn wooden table in front of her.

Norah shuffled in opposite, putting her full bottle to the side. "There's a lot going on, hun. You doing okay?"

"Yeah," she replied with a glum smile. "It's just new area blues. Once we get on the trail of destruction, then things will sort themselves into order."

If only Chuck wasn't screening their calls. It was unfair he wasn't his usual chummy self, but maybe something happened in the last year. Perhaps if they started to—

The doors to the tavern opened, and the *Outsiders* looked over, expecting to see Theo return.

"Yeah, I must have left it in here, I was just—" the first man began, before the pair of them stopped.

Their eyes looked around the tavern at the present undead, while Sally's group was more focused on the tabards that they wore.

Red.

"*Villainy?*" Norah murmured.

Sally licked her lips. "Anything we can help you gentlemen with?"

"You haven't joined anyone yet," the second man began, slightly less full of panic than the first. "Care to hear more on . . ."

"No," she shook her head, interrupting.

"I think this is them, the *Outsiders*," the first man whispered louder than he hoped. Sweat had started to run down the sides of his round face.

The second man didn't reply, but his eyes glazed over, as if he was accessing his chat messages.

Bandages shot out and wrapped around his arms, yanking him immediately toward the table where the two undead women were sitting. Sally stood and leveled her Skeleton Key into his eye socket as he stumbled toward them. *[Eat Brains]*.

The other man turned to run but dropped suddenly as the planks of wood beneath him turned into shadow, and he fell into the basement below.

With a grin and blazing crimson light blaring from her eyes, Sally hopped down onto the floor and then jumped down after him. In the earlier areas, she might have expected the Player to have broken a leg or at least been injured enough to be easy prey. No such luck in this area, apparently.

Blue light illuminated the brickwork of the small basement, the stacked barrels and wine racks reflecting the glow of the spear raised and readied toward her. The man seemed prepared.

[Escape Fate]

Sally vanished and appeared on the other side of the underground room beside the stairs, four zombies crawling from the dusty floor where she had been. The Player was already swinging the long weapon around, easily slicing through two of the rising dead as she stepped closer. A blue circle of carved runes started to build around his feet.

She was starting to consider whether they should have killed this one first. Then again, they often got lucky with Players who died before really getting into their stances to use their skills effectively. Most were used to fighting the simple System-created Monsters who followed a set routine. It seemed the third area Players had more experience in PvP.

The brick wall pressed up against her back as she ran out of space and the man dove toward her, lashing forward with the glowing spear tip with one hand. Pain flared down her left arm as it split through her collarbone and pinned her to the wall. With a grin, she grabbed the weapon with her off hand and held it there in place.

"Now what?" she hissed as he struggled to remove it.

He let go and withdrew a sword from his side, another flash of blue as a shockwave blew dust around the enclosed space. The two remaining zombies stumbled back, slightly stunned, and he spun to slash through them with his blade.

Sally pulled the offending weapon out of her as the shadowed floor above filled back in, plunging them into darkness, aside from the blue glow of the Player's skills.

[Curse: Decay]

A dark green tether slunk from her hand before it latched onto the man, sparkles of crimson flickering around where it touched him. She wasn't absorbing the health as her own, but she could feel his life draining away. So could he.

"Monster!" he growled, lashing forward with his sword.

Sally grinned and stepped to the side, shoulder barging him as his attack missed. He stumbled away, but an afterimage of him blurred through the space.

"I am!" She chuckled. "You don't even know that you never had a chance."

He spat, and a white sheen enveloped him. "That's where you're wrong." His feet scraped against loose gravel as he got into a stance.

The crimson eyes of the zombie lit up in the darkness. "Drown in your inevitable future, mortal."

[Endless Dead]

"Do you think we should go and help?" A question mark appeared by the Shade.

"No." Humphrey shook his head. "It's just one Player. She would—"

The entire tavern shook briefly, bottles and glass mugs clinking together before the vibration settled.

Before any of them could make a note about it, the door behind the bar swung open and Sally stomped out, coughing up dust.

"You okay, hun?" A bandage went around to support the zombie as she stepped around the bar back to them.

"Yeah, aah." She popped out a Healing Potion and downed it. "Turns out the System doesn't really plan where it is going to stick forty zombies when you summon them in a small room."

"Crushed and eaten?" Humphrey grinned.

"Sucks because they got in my way, and I couldn't eat him." She yawned and watched her shoulder heal up under the effects of the Healing Potion. Was never long until her clothes were ruined and covered in blood or filth. Part and parcel of zombie life.

Lucius kicked his feet back and forth as he sat on the stool. "So I guess we're killing red team on sight, then?"

Sally flexed her neck from side to side with a crack. "They knew who we were. Usually, that's a bad sign."

Humphrey nodded. "Especially after we have been away for so long. Unless Lenard told others about us, of course."

"Probably did," she agreed. "I think they could see that we weren't on board with potentially erasing all others like us."

They stood in thoughtful silence for a moment while Sally went over to loot the man she had eaten. There were no useful documents on him, and no items worth celebrating. "Rats!" She stood and spun back to Humphrey.

"Mice?"

"No. Theo went off with that information from the assassin and didn't tell us what it said." She rolled her eyes and glared at the door.

Norah stood and stretched out her back. "Perhaps that's why he wanted to go off alone, to deal with something before it's a problem for all of us. He tends to be thoughtful like that, hun."

Sally deflated. The vampire liked to showboat as if he was the star of the narrative occasionally, but he always did what was best for the team. When he had enough sleep, anyway. His portable coffin had been a lifesaver, literally.

"No use fussing about that now," she said with a grin, shuffling those thoughts away.

From her pouch she withdrew the teleport scroll. "Let's go level!"

CHAPTER TEN

Beachside

A wave of blue teleportation energy flooded around the four of them, and a sense of vertigo shifted them deeper into the third area.

Sally blinked away the blur in her eyes as she tried to adjust to the new lighting. There was always the lingering thought that it could have all been a trap—there was no way of knowing whether the blue team truly knew Chuck or was just trying to ply some trust onto the *Outsiders* for the reveal that they wanted to kill them off too. Theo had said Rachel seemed genuine though, and she trusted his judgment.

She furrowed her brow at the surroundings as the other three got their bearings. It certainly wasn't a trap, but it was unexpected. No longer was a dense jungle surrounding them on all sides, but instead, something more tropical in appearance blocked the horizon. Taller palm trees, and more sparse vegetation on sandy dirt. There was even the sound of lapping waves in the background.

Three wooden houses stood on stilts to their right, the pale wood bleached by the warm sun that sat overhead in the blue sky.

"Well," she eventually said, "this is a lot more pleasant."

Humphrey grinned. "*Yes*. To think we were so excited about jungle warfare that we have now avoided."

"*Excited*." Sally rolled her eyes. It was tropical enough, with no need to drown them in thick leaves and tripping-hazard vines. "I'm sure there's plenty of mishap and malady we can smother over ourselves in this area."

Lucius had his hands on his hips and was staring out behind them. "I feel good about this area already."

She turned her head around and looked to where he was indicating. There were Monsters. They slowly clambered around an area of damp sand where it looked as though the tide had gone out some time recently. Four legs and squat bodies. She would have thought they were crocodiles if not for the gray scales and short, round seal-like faces.

"They almost look too cute to kill," Norah said as she tilted her head to the side.

Humphrey grinned. "Almost."

Sally wasn't too convinced. Were they supposed to just kill the first thing they saw, or was there a quest . . . or . . . whatever Players were actually meant to do in this world? It had been so long since they had a normal adventure that the whole process felt foreign. She brought up the map and wrinkled her nose up.

"Let's mop these up to get our footing," she started, "and then move closer inland. Just try to get as much experience before nightfall as we can."

The Death Knight withdrew his sword and nodded to her. "Agreed. Seeing as we are under-leveled for this area, we should have no issue gaining levels."

"Don't jinx it, Humps." She rolled her eyes, and a screaming face appeared beside Lucius.

She withdrew her dagger and dropped down from the wooden platform they were on, landing on the soft sand. "More sand," she murmured. The breeze from the coastline washed away some of the heat from the sun overhead, so she couldn't complain too much. It *was* almost pleasant.

In her left hand, she plucked a skull from her belt, and it burst into green flame. As the other three dropped down beside her, she lobbed the attack into the air at the closest animal. With a burst of light, it struck them, leaving a scarred patch across their thick neck and shoulders. As four zombies began to rise from the ground, it turned and immediately mulched one with wide jaws, lashing a tail around to brain a second.

Sally pouted. Her zombies didn't do too well with the level difference, even buffed with all their auras. As the weird Monster bit through the head of the last zombie, a sarcophagus smashed down into its skull, the bandages that had swung it going limp and returning to the Mummy.

"Sorry, hun. Hate to see a good underling go to waste."

She smiled up at Norah. "No problem at all. It's more fun when we fight together!" Turning her eyes back to the creature, it hadn't moved, still laying with its head stuck into the bloodied sand. The handful of groups of other Monsters didn't seem to mind the murder of one of their own.

"Humps, what are these called? I can't keep using generic terms in my inner monologue, and you *do not* want me to name them."

"Snubtaurs."

Sally exhaled through her nose. That was worse than what she was thinking, but it was too late in the day to question whether the Death Knight was pulling her leg. Either that or the Architect truly didn't know what they were doing. She turned to Norah. "Launch me."

Bandages wrapped around her and drew her in closer, before she was lifted into the air. The rush of sudden vertigo washed over her as she was flung overhead and above the group of Monsters. As she went to land, she cast *[Endless Dead]* again to bring up her horde of zombies. They may be weak, but they served well as a distraction and bogged down the Snubtaurs to make them easy pickings.

Humphrey stomped through the sand in his heavy plated boots, illuminating through different shades of his combat buffs. His greatsword flickered with a crimson flame as he barged through the throng of zombies to sever the head of a Monster. Lucius vanished as he shadowed Norah, and the Mummy weaved her bandages through the horde to tie up and slow down their opponents.

Within a short minute, they had destroyed the packs. Although Sally had lost a dozen zombies, half of them had been replaced by undead versions of the Snubtaurs. It didn't do much to improve their appearance, but she wondered if she could use them to travel across water like skis. Probably not.

"There are some more packs farther down the beach," the Death Knight said as he tilted his head. "Or we can head farther east and into the more difficult parts of the area."

"These were pretty easy." Sally wiped the blood off her dagger. "Perhaps we can just be a mini apocalypse and kill our way through everything with the horde?"

Humphrey scratched his chin as Lucius popped back out from the Mummy's shadow. "*Yes*. That does seem quite efficient now that we are in an area more populated."

While she had been sad that *[Endless Dead]* had an apparent cap of fifty zombies, that was still plenty to get the ball rolling. There wasn't actually a limit to how many she could create, only store away. The Wastelands had been so devoid of anything living that it hadn't been worth keeping the shamblers around for the most part. But now . . . they ran the risk of becoming a threat to everyone.

And that made her smile.

"Onward!" she commanded the undead, and they started walking slowly toward the east.

She would save *[Quick Death]* for a time when it was more important. Slow zombies were a chore, but she didn't want to get caught unawares with her ultimate on cooldown. Not until they knew how threatening everyone around here was.

With a short stumble, she paused and spun around to look past her horde. Her eyes narrowed in a glare. She scoured the tree line before the shore.

"We are being watched." Humphrey nodded as he came up beside her. "Care to investigate?"

Norah followed their gaze. "I could bring the trees down, but it wouldn't be quick."

Sally shook her head. She couldn't see anyone there. Perhaps it was someone from *Last Word*, but perhaps not. "No, just be wary. I don't want anyone else with a death counter."

"About that . . ." the Death Knight said as they turned to continue with the shambling undead. "Are you sure he is not making that up?"

"I am sure. It's not his kind of humor . . . and we discussed it before the outpost." She gave the sand a glum expression as they walked.

"There's still something I feel you're not telling me."

Sally looked up at his empty eye sockets. "I can't lie when you give me those eyes." She sighed. "Remember Marius?"

"The Cleric . . . there are more like him?" Flames flickered around the back of his helmet.

She shrugged. "Seems so. At least that would-be assassin was."

They walked on in silence for a moment while Norah and Lucius exchanged looks.

"Is there something we should know, Humphrey?" The Mummy placed her hand on his arm.

"*Yes*. It is probably ideal that we are all on the same page?" He raised an eyebrow toward the zombie to see if she approved. After she gave him a quick nod, he continued. "In the first area there was a Player who had somehow corrupted their STAR System to allow them access to things that Players shouldn't."

Lucius rubbed his misty chin. "Not like how Sally and Theo are part Monster, though?"

Humphrey exhaled. "It is similar, I will admit. The method to get there is different. Sally and Theo got that way through . . . honest mistakes of the System, where it has smoothed off the edges of their odd existence. The corrupted have forced the change against what the System would normally allow."

Sally nodded. There were similarities, but ultimately her zombieness and the vampire were accidents that they had to live with. The corrupted were making the choice to steal some kind of power from the System. Usually, that sort of thing didn't end too well.

With a shrug, the Death Knight continued. "It's likely the poison that Theo has was part of that corruption—there isn't supposed to be anything that deadly. Not at this stage."

The horde ran into a group of Monsters. Large bird-like creatures with long necks and sharp beaks. While the first zombie into the fray immediately had its brains blown out by the darting mouth of the first Monster, the bird was then surrounded by four others.

Ultimately, it wasn't that difficult for the group. Even with the level difference, they shredded through three packs of the animals. Zombies were lost but soon topped up with *[Mortis Bomb]* or the fallen Monsters. Sally was growing quite the menagerie now. They swung through the last pack and then came to the mouth of a valley that led downward. Different Monsters moved around down at the bottom, but the sign just at the mouth of the decline caught her attention.

> Quest: Clear the Valley of Gnolls

"Ooh, quests—I remember these. We used to do things like this for a whole five minutes, huh?" She turned to grin at the Death Knight.

"*Yes*. The experience gained should put us over to the next level."

"Great." She returned a wide grin. "I don't have any good gnoll puns to use as a one-liner, so, uh . . ."She wrinkled up her nose and shrugged. "Let's go kill things?"

Lucius paused as the other three started down the slope. Turning slowly, he narrowed his crimson eyes at the surrounding trees. Ellipses trailed beside his head before he turned and went to catch up with the others.

CHAPTER ELEVEN

Gnoll Pun

Sally shook her hand out as the gnoll clattered back into some loose furniture. She might have hurt herself with that punch more than her target. Though, considering the creature wasn't getting back up, she might be mistaken about that. Things were going pretty much as expected. After the tide of undead washed down into the valley, the gnolls were easy enough to pick off even as tough as they were.

As Humphrey lopped the head off one of the Monsters, she hummed to herself and brought up the Party chat, just in case the direct messages weren't working.

> Sally: how's things?
> Sally: fans
> Theo: good
> Theo: currently living
> Theo: killed another LW… will meet u tonight to discuss

Sounded reasonable enough. He must have gotten more information from the second assassin. Despite her mixed feelings on the System, it seemed short-sighted to want to destroy it without a known way out. Looking at her reflection in a discarded shield, she raised her eyebrows at herself.

"Everything okay, Sally?" Lucius popped out of Humphrey's shadow and slipped over some gnoll corpses to stand near her.

She smiled. "Yeah. Theo is going to meet us later." The skull in her hand burst into green flame, and she lobbed it into the fray.

"Did he find the cure yet?" A sweat drop emoji appeared beside the Shade's head.

"He didn't say." She frowned and rubbed her hair. Should they be looking for the cure, or was he going to sort it himself? Where would they even look? If the assassins didn't have the antidote, then her next port of call would have been Chuck—the Druid might have gotten something useful from leveling up. Thinking about it, he was probably reasonably powerful now, depending on what skills he chose.

She twirled her dagger around. "I'm sure it will get sorted in time; don't you worry. Wanna team up?"

"Sure." A grinning emoji popped up. "But first . . ." He held out his gloved hand toward the horde fighting the gnolls. A crackle of monochrome lightning arced between his fingers, before a group of the Monsters grew less vibrant in hue.

With a grin, Sally jumped out toward them, and the Shade became her shadow. Slipping in between all the undead, it was simple to sneak up and stab or eat the brains of those otherwise engaged. It was always the bigger plan going on in the background that was their headache, just like in the Wastes.

First the System was in the way, and then a Unique, but now it seemed like Players were the cause of strife. Too busy trying to run the world instead of fattening themselves up for her stomach. Maybe she needed to give them something to actually worry about. She yawned and watched as Norah twisted the neck of a gnoll with her wrappings. The rough *snap* of its neck heard over the battle before she dropped the body.

Lucius stabbed the nearby enemy as she took a break to look about. Humphrey was moving slowly and methodically through the remaining Monsters. Occasionally flaring up in blue light as *[Decimate]* became active. Zombie gnolls clamored around with her own to drag their brethren to the floor to consume. It was calming in a way, melodic. Perhaps Rachel should have given them a teleport to even farther through the zone. She had underestimated how tough the *Outsiders* were, and Theo wasn't even here.

Around 80 percent of the way through the valley now, the other side that rose upward into a slope was close by. The quest hand in was up this side, which seemed mighty convenient. Although the mass of zombies made the process rather carefree, they did also slow things down—where the four of them alone could have gotten through the camp quicker but at more potential detriment to themselves. It was kind of nice being queen of the zombies for a little while again, though.

She yawned. There was something quaint about the forest area life that she missed. Things had seemed so rough then, but so simple in retrospect. With the abilities they had now, they could easily go back and sack the Capital, or murder their way through all the low-level Players. It was a wonder nobody had done something similar—or perhaps they had, and she just hadn't heard of it. Part of her daydreamed about becoming a dungeon boss, having their own lair for Players to throw themselves at. Tasty ones.

"Almost done, Sally," Humphrey said with a wide grin from the front, his blade almost hewing a gnoll in half. "Then we'll have another level to consider. I'm sure Edward would be pleased."

Up until the point where he teleported to her to save her life and ate a blade, losing a level again. At least he could respawn back in the Wastes. It was a good thing he didn't have her ambition, otherwise his Unique bug would be a huge problem. If she could come back to life, well, she'd be even more reckless than she was already.

She placed her blade into the furred head of the last gnoll and kicked them to the floor. No more brains, lest she throw them up. They tasted okay but kind of plain and bitter. Certainly not as good as a Player's. Not that there were any at the table, currently . . .

Her eyes narrowed, and she looked up at the road ahead of them just as five figures rose from the horizon to walk down. Then another five beside them. Maybe she did get what she wished for. *Abs*, she thought to herself.

"Sally." Humphrey nudged her from the side.

Behind them, coming down the cleared side of the valley, were another ten Players. They all had blue tabards on. Her STAR *bloiped*.

> Chuck: Sally.
> Chuck: I'm sorry it has to be this way

She closed it and growled up at the gathered figures. They were a good eighty feet away on either side, more if you accounted for the dead bodies in the way. Lucius popped out of her shadow and backed up into her, sweat drop emojis running beside his head.

"Looks like we've caught ourselves a little System error." A man called down from behind her.

"They're not as tough as they look," a second voice crooned.

"Dragonslayers, ha!"

Norah scowled and crossed her arms. "Aren't these guys supposed to be our friends, hun?"

"*Friends*." Sally pouted. "I suppose only the family truly matters."

"Twenty higher level Players," Humphrey noted. "What is your call?"

The current terrain wasn't very advantageous. The Death Knight might be able to block attacks for ten seconds, but if they were still stuck in this valley afterward, then they'd have trouble avoiding all the potential ranged attacks from both sides.

"I don't suppose absorbing Archie gave you any superpowers?" She grimaced toward Humphrey while the Players jeered on.

"Oh. Of course, although I can only use it in my ultimate form."

Sally exhaled. "Your ultimate is a new form? What do you think our chances are?"

"*Yes.*" The Death Knight grinned. "One hundred percent."

A question mark appeared beside Lucius's head. "Of success or death?"

"Oh, that was the question?" Humphrey raised an eyebrow and scratched the side of his head. "In that case—"

"*Outsiders!*" The first voice called out again, silencing the murmured plotting of the Players. "Any last words?"

"Pancakes!" Sally yelled, before punching the Death Knight. "Hit it, Humps!"

[Soul Knight]

The plated figure burst into bright red flame for a second before it was quickly extinguished with a hiss. His dark crimson and black armor was now replaced by bright ivory and silver as if he was made of polished bone. He took one step forward toward the northern group of Players before tilting his head backward. From his eye sockets, emerald light blossomed.

"If I die, Norah . . ."

"You're a big softie considering you're all metal." The Mummy smiled. "Just *don't* die."

He nodded and smiled. "I won't need shadowing. You three focus on the others."

Sally frowned but nodded. His new form might be visually stunning, but taking on a full ten Players was some other level of hubris. Plus, she might want those brains they were holding safe for her. She knew he was as tough as Theo was powerful, but he might be trying to overcompensate a little. Ah well, either he would be fine or they'd all die.

"*Die!*" The loud Player signaled. It had been nice of them to give the group a few moments to talk before attacking. Perhaps even with the faction war, they were still too used to pulling the attention of a boss after some prep time.

"Can you throw me, Norah?" Sally narrowed her eyes at the group ahead. Two of them looked to be some manner of holy classes, based on the ridiculously bright white garb they wore. Some of them were chanting or casting skills. Some of those might even be ultimates.

Bandage wrapped around her, and she slid backward along the ground before being flung into the air.

As one, they activated their abilities.

[Quick Death]. After a brief pause, the horde of zombies below Sally turned and began to run toward the Players. Sprinting past each other, she could see the surprise in the eyes of her opponents as the skull in her hand blazed green flame.

[True Shadow]. Lucius flickered as he became a shadow for each of the *Outsiders*. Crimson hue waved behind each of them as he readied the shadowed version of their main weapons, ready to strike.

[Royal Guard]. From beneath Norah, as the zombies rushed past her, a large figure rose out of the ground. Thirty feet tall and wrapped in bandages just like a mummy, the undead creature with a bird head had golden bands encrusted with jewels around its wrists and ankles. Norah stood atop its shoulders and gave it the command to move forward.

From behind them, Humphrey activated *[Impenetrable Defense]* and slowly walked toward his group as their skills and attacks were rebuffed by his flickering blue shield.

Sally threw out the skull just before she landed, an arrow sticking her in the leg and a spray of fire just missing her as she landed atop the most priestly looking figure. Just as she knocked him to the ground, her horde of sprinting zombies clashed into the group. Half of the Players focused on clearing the undead, either their ultimates or powerful skills ripping wide holes through the fast corpses in flashes of different light.

She rolled across the body to not break her legs, slashing out with her dagger as her shadow mimicked the action, drawing deep lines of crimson through the bright white robes of the Player.

"Turn on us, would you?" She seethed as she stood among them, her eyes blazing bright red.

Humphrey's shield dropped, and he ran to cover the rest of the distance. Heavy plated boots thudded on the ground as arrows ricocheted from his gleaming body and spells left hardly a scratch. Several ultimates started to charge as he closed in.

[Endless Knight]

A dozen green arrows struck him, embedding into his metal. A dragon's head of pure ice rose above him and sprayed him with a cone of freezing air. The surrounding ground turned into a mire of roots and thick mud, but he kept on moving.

With a flourish of his sword, the Death Knight's eyes burned a bright green. "Now you will know why you should fear the knight," he growled.

CHAPTER TWELVE

Ghosted

Sally stumbled backward as blood ran down the side of her face. The knight was a blur of blue and white light as he spun his blade around, shield covering most of his side. She jumped toward him and stabbed Skeleton Key straight through the metal and into his arm holding it.

"The hells?" he growled and bashed her away.

A second Fighter swung from her side before his arm stopped, the wrapping of a bandage darting in at the last second to restrain him. As two more shadowed ones circled around the man, he was jerked into the air toward the large bird-mummy. Sally hopped back away from the knight, holding *[Curse: Decay]* on him as her shadow stabbed him through his plated ankles.

This had been a tiring fight. Two brains eaten and almost lost her own twice over. Only a handful of Players left, but only a handful of zombies too. Many of them had been lost when she needed to *[Share Burden]* to avoid being run through with a holy lance. Norah had surrounded that woman with bandages, and under the glow of the yellow eye, turned her to sand.

Slightly more insidious when used against Players rather than Monsters, but Sally wasn't exactly one to judge. Mostly, she was saddened that the potential brain was taken off the table. She hadn't checked the stats she was getting from all these area three Players, but it was a substantial gain. The knight seemed to be regenerating health, or perhaps one of those remaining was a Healer. It was hard to gauge as she tried to use what remaining corpses there were to stay out of sight.

The man glowed with white light as he charged up an attack, and Sally tensed to brace herself. A sarcophagus suddenly enclosed the knight, and she leaped forward instead, bringing her dagger through the air in a blaze. The trap vanished just as the point met his helmet, carving through it like butter and straight into his skull. *[Eat Brains]*.

Number advantage was now in their court. She looked up to see the thirty-foot summon crunch through the wrapped Fighter with its zombie beak as Norah's eyes glowed brightly. Her beast had taken some beating, but Sally had given it the occasional *[Living Dead]* to keep it going. It drew attention, and when her horde was still large it was almost untouchable, allowing the Mummy the perfect platform to buff and entangle foes from above.

Norah had been a good fit for the *Outsiders* in more ways than one, Sally grinned to herself.

She buckled as weakness hit her legs. Adrenaline was wearing off, and the wounds she had earned now burned at her senses. It was hard to see which blood was hers, but most of her clothing was torn, showing patches of green flesh bright red and wet. Next *[Living Dead]* should be for herself. She rolled to the side on aching muscles as a Cleric with a mace swung for her, clocking one of the zombies instead. The burst of radiant light and now headless zombie told her that was a good call. She wondered how the Death Knight was holding up on the other side on his own.

Humphrey grinned as bright flame encircled him. His gleaming armor was filled with silvered holes and dents. Arcs of pale electricity rolled around his plated form as he breathed heavily—not that he was required to. These Players had been slightly smarter than most. Instead of standing in formation and getting all muddled, they had immediately arranged into groups. The Healers and casters retreated away from the melee Fighters who had held him back.

His first action had been to cause a Rogue to *[Kneel]* and removing his head hadn't been something they were able to heal. They had two knights with shields that had been hard to shift and left him open to the shots of the ranged Players. *[Compelled Duel]* hit, and they had been confused at their opponent now being untargetable. Skeletons up to force *[Decimate]* and he made short work of the Healer, who had been unprepared for a one-on-one duel.

Taking on the rest had been a slow process. He couldn't catch up to the lightly armored Players while the knights were constantly on him. Any time he knocked one of them back, the other would step in. If he managed to wound one, the second avoidant Healer would keep them up. It was both aggravating and tiring, and exactly what he deserved for his hubris.

The Mage, standing beside the Healer, cast a circle of fire around him so that they may have a moment's breathing room to recover. They didn't know he was almost immune to fire damage. He stepped through and flourished his sword. The two knights started to circle around to waylay him. Exhausting little bugs.

A sarcophagus flew in from the side, hitting the Healer in the head and knocking the pair of casters to the floor. Humphrey turned to see Norah a way off, giving a fist pump toward the accurate shot.

The two knights paused in seeing their backup clobbered to the floor—at least one of the two was knocked out, if not dead.

"Now we can have some fun," the Death Knight said as he flourished his sword.

[Expert Duelist]

The first knight lashed out at him with a long blade of green metal. Humphrey blocked it and then immediately made a counterattack at blinding speed, denting the man's armor and pushing him back. The second tried the same, but as soon as the Death Knight blocked the blow, there was a split-second response, almost disarming the shield with how unexpected the strike was.

"This lasts until you can strike me." He grinned, his own helmet flame lapping in the air. "How lucky do you feel?"

Sally rolled across the floor and growled, standing to her feet on shaky legs. The Cleric had some manner of aura that made it painful to get close to him. She had retreated and used the trusty crossbow ploy, but they had a reflective shield that knocked the bolts away.

"You are very annoying," she admonished the man.

His pale eyes just stared her down. "Your awakening was foretold. I have prepared for this moment for almost a year."

She glanced around at his dead companions. "Did a pretty shitty job of preparing then, huh?" The sound of a body being torn in half by the bandages of the Mummy punctuated the brief silence.

"Then allow me to use my ultimate." He smiled sadly, raising his hand. A radiant glow began forming in a swirl around the man.

Sally could feel the power of it. Pure, holy energy designed to eradicate the undead from this plane. He really did go all in on wanting to kill her. She didn't even know his name.

Lucius popped out of her shadow to stand beside her. With the snap of his fingers, the patch of ground the Cleric was standing on became shadow—a rough five-foot cube of dirt suddenly missing from the terrain. The man dropped abruptly into the pit and then the Shade undid the skill.

"That's kind of broken, Lucy," she said with a grimace. The man was now entombed up to his shoulders, his head looking around wildly in panic.

"My ultimate wore off, so good thing I chose you to continue helping." A smiling emoji appeared beside his hooded face.

The large foot of the behemoth stomped down on the exposed head, shattering the shield and aura, and pulping the man into the dirt.

"Sorry, hun!" Norah called down from the shoulder of the creature. "I kept this one for questioning, though." The large hand of the bird-mummy gestured forward to show a wrapped individual.

Although she had ruined the meal, that seemed like a decent enough peace offering to make up for it. The handful of remaining zombies milled around her, now slow again since the speed-up had worn off. Aside from the captive, their group of Players had been dealt with, surprised expressions on their faces and dirt and blood marring their blue tabards.

They looked over at Humphrey to see his shadowed figure lift up one of the knights, impaled on the end of his sword, before he slung them to the ground. With the quick flick of his blade, he finished off the remaining few, stabbing through the downed spellcasters. With a flourish of his greatsword, a mist pulsed from his body, obscuring him before waving away. Now he returned to his black and crimson armor, though it was silver in many places due to his wounds. He kneeled and lowered his head.

Lucius shadowed into Sally as Norah bandaged her up to the behemoth's other shoulder, and they stomped over to the resting Death Knight.

Sliding down the outstretched arms, the Mummy clapped her hands as they all reached the ground and the large summon started to sink back into the ground.

[Living Dead]. Sally cast her healing spell as they ran up to him. "Everything okay, Humps?"

He grinned as Norah helped him back to his feet. "*Yes*. Of course."

Lucius popped out of her shadow and looked around at the dead bodies. "Ten against one, very impressive." A thumbs-up emoji emerged beside him.

"I won out due to my immense defensive capability and single target stuns." He flexed out his neck as the silvered and bent pieces of his armor began to reshape.

"Yeah, yeah," Sally said as she waved her hand. "Tell Norah all about it if you want to impress someone." She narrowed her eyes back at the bound captive. "I'm too annoyed at Chuck right now."

She stomped off away from them to recover the bandaged figure, removing some of the wrappings from their face to reveal a woman with tied back auburn hair. A long gash ran up the side of her face and green eyes full of malice glared at the zombie atop cheeks sprinkled with freckles.

"Why did he do this?" Sally clenched her teeth as she lifted the woman up.

"Fuck you, undead scum," the woman spat in return.

"Fine, I'll ask him myself. But you're not off the hook." Sally dropped the captive to the ground and put a boot atop her so she couldn't squirm away. The rest of the Party walked over as she loaded up her STAR, ready to spout vitriol at the supposed Druid.

> Chuck: Sally.
> Chuck: I'm sorry it has to be this way.
> Chuck: I wanted to see you sooner—it's been a tough year.
> Chuck: If Rachel wasn't too convincing, well, we'll meet soon anyway.
> Chuck: Don't tell the others, but I've missed you all.

She stared at the messages sent during the fight. Slowly, she turned her eyes away and narrowed them at the woman underfoot.

"Everything okay, Sally?" Humphrey put his hand on her shoulder and read through the messages still up. "Hmm, interesting."

"Chuck wasn't trying to betray us," she said quietly. "Which means there are two possibilities here."

She removed her boot and grabbed at the wrappings to lift the woman back up to face level.

Her eyes danced with crimson energy as she moved her face closer to that of the enemy. "Unfortunately for you, both answers mean I am going to eat your brains."

CHAPTER THIRTEEN

System Shock

Humphrey scratched the side of his head, adding a metallic scraping noise to their pensive silence and causing Lucius to wince.

"So," Norah said as she tilted her head, "the two options are either these blue tabard Adventurers are going against Chuck's will, or they are red faction dressed up to frame the other for what they intended to do to us."

"Precisely!" Sally raised a finger into the air. "I can't decide which makes me more angry. Betrayal? I could never accept such a thing."

"But what about—" Lucius began, before she pointed her finger at him in interruption.

"I had misread Chuck's inconveniently timed messages and thought he was feeding us to the wolves." Sally tapped the side of her head. "Not that it would have really changed the course of our venture, huh?"

She glared down at the woman, whom they had gagged once more so that she would stop seething at them. Her eyes were still ablaze with hatred. It wasn't because they had killed or eaten most of her friends either. Sally knew the difference. This was disgust and disdain for what the *Outsiders* were.

"You're clearly red team," she tutted, shaking her head. "You wear your prejudice brighter than any tabard."

"That's rather poetic for you." Humphrey tilted his head at the zombie, then caught the glare of Norah.

Sally waved him off. "I ate a lot of smart brains recently. I can't remember which, but something gave me some intelligence. Or wisdom. I forgot the difference."

The Death Knight nodded slowly, his eyes narrowing.

Lucius crouched beside the bound woman. "So, are we going to kill her? Not going to do some 'good cop, bad cop'?"

"It doesn't really work if you tell them that's what you're doing." She rolled her eyes. "I'm not sure she'd tell us anything useful either way, and it feels so sad to murder in the cold light of day rather than in the heat of battle." With a pout, she gave a shrug to the Shade.

He looked up at her with his crimson eyes beneath the dark hood. "I have a skill I've never used before. It's uh . . . weird."

Sally furrowed her brow. "I can deal with *weird*. What does it do?"

"It's like . . ." Ellipses followed in the air as Lucius rubbed his chin. "It's like a truth potion, but a lot creepier."

"I can deal with *creepy*." Sally nodded for him to go ahead.

[Seek Answer]

Lucius pooled into mist and swirled into the nose and covered mouth of the woman. She tried to squirm away from inhaling the Shade, but after he fully vanished, she relaxed. Her eyes were now a crimson color, staring off at the horizon.

Sally withdrew the gag from the captive's mouth. "That *was* creepy and weird."

The woman's mouth opened but didn't move as the words came out. "You have three questions."

She blinked in return, before looking back at the Death Knight. "You might wanna take the call, pops. I might waste it with inane quirkiness."

"I'll leave you the last one," he said with a grin. "Though, don't call me pops."

Norah placed a hand on his shoulder. "I don't know. It suits you."

Humphrey deflated and crouched beside the possessed woman. "Are you part of the red tabard faction?"

"Yes."

Sally snapped her fingers and scowled at the surrounding valley. They might need to move soon if the respawns were short here. In the forest they were slow, but it also seemed to be based on how many Players were in the area. Things had been much quicker to come back after their coma where the Wastes were quite populated.

The Death Knight tapped his finger on his plated knee in thought. "Where is your headquarters located?"

"North of here, near an area known as Thunder Cove."

He raised his eyes to the zombie and gestured for her to continue.

"Ahhh." She bit her tongue and tried not to ask something weird or about pancakes. "Who is the leader of the red tabard faction?" She should have paid more attention to what the faction's actual names were.

"I do not know their true name. They are known as Seven."

"Seven?" Sally scrunched her face up. "What kind of name is that?"

Humphrey rubbed his chin in thought as the mist poured back out of the woman's mouth and nostrils to form the Shade. Lucius pulled his hood back up as the woman blinked a few times and looked up at the zombie with her bright green eyes.

"I'm sorry if that was traumatic or torturous," Sally said with a glum smile. "We're not barbarians, usually."

"No . . ." The woman furrowed her brow and looked over to the Shade. "It was actually . . . pleasant?"

"That was my first time." Lucius shrugged. "I wasn't sure what to expect, but it was fun. Did you want to be friends?"

The woman bit her lip. "Sure? Unless you are planning on killing and eating me?" She raised an eyebrow at the rest of the suddenly confused *Outsiders*.

Sally worked her jaw and let her brain catch up to the conversation. "We can let your transgression slide—but you have to join blue team and if you try to cross us, it won't end well for you."

She nodded eagerly.

"Charlotte. I . . . I'm sorry for thinking you were a Monster that needed destroying."

Norah raised an eyebrow at Humphrey, who gave a shrug in return.

"Alright then." Sally scratched at her hair. "Lucy, come help me loot for a sec. You two can unwrap our new pal here."

Resigned grunts from all of them, but they did as they were told. She walked up toward the dead Players with the Shade in tow.

"What did you do in there, Lucius?" She narrowed her eyes at him.

"Me?" A sweat drop appeared beside his head. "Nothing criminal. Player brains are interesting places, though. There's like a . . ." He rubbed his chin in thought.

"Sickness?" Sally asked.

"Yeah!" He snapped his gloved fingers. "Like a System sickness. Part of their brain that has trouble accepting this reality."

"So when you were in there, you cured that?" She kneeled by one of the bodies and started looking through their gear.

"Not really *cured*," he said with a brief pause, a question mark beside his head. "It was more like unclogging a blockage. Or pushing something under the rug."

Sally nodded and looked back up at him. He allowed the woman to suspend her belief and allow herself to be content with what life she now had here. Nearly all Players had zero active memory of their previous lives, but there must be parts lurking in the back of their minds, making them want to reject the status quo here. Marius had been a prime example of that. Other than herself, Theo and Chuck were the only others she knew who had past memories they could access.

It probably would have broken them if they weren't bugged or didn't have each other. She felt bad for the Druid being left without them for a year. It was time to reply to his messages.

> Sally: we missed u too
> Sally: I understand if we can't meet yet
> Sally: Reds disguised in blue tabards ambushed us.
> Sally: We have a turncoat. where can we drop them safely?

Charlotte might be thankful for the Shade unlocking the part of her brain allowing her to be satisfied with the System, but she didn't want to drag the woman around. Lucius could have pen-friends on his own time. They had a world to save. Or something.

She looked back up at the Shade again. The System was supposed to pump you full of something when you joined that made you forget the past and accept the new. It obviously wasn't working as well as intended. It was a difficult thing to shunt a mind to accepting a whole new reality without some consequence. Which made the power that Lucius had more powerful than a lot of things the rest of them had.

"Hey, Lucy." She stood and brushed her hands off on her clothes. "Don't you go dying anytime soon, okay?"

He nodded, but a confused face appeared beside him. "I'll do my best, Sally."

He'd have to. That sort of ability would help smooth over the world once she was queen of it—or whatever the plan shook out to be. While filling the populace with the Shade was hardly a step up from the System drugging people itself, there would be a way to do it that wasn't as predatory as they had just exhibited. She looked over to the woman, who was now unwrapped and looking rather sheepish between the two undead.

Her STAR *bloiped*, and she checked the messages.

> Chuck: Bastards!
> Chuck: Sorry, that's Dent rubbing off on me.

Sally narrowed her eyes.

> Chuck: Glad you're okay. There's a camp South of where you should be.
> Chuck: Stay safe, keep in touch?
> Sally: will do x

She spun the menus around and then brought up the chat with Theo.

> Sally: Humps just killed ten Players solo.
> Sally: Hope you're being just as impressive x

With a smile, she walked back over to the others with Lucius in tow. "Alright, listen up. We have permission from the head office to drop Charlie off at a nearby camp. She'll join up proper and spread the word of how great we are." She hoped anyway, although the blue faction might have a dim view of the turncoat, they seemed the more reasonable side.

"Charlie," she continued, "we will be killing anything in our path, so best to stay back. My zombies won't target you unless you annoy me."

The woman nodded. "Thank you, Sally. I'll be on my best behavior." She smiled, something earnest that was in contrast to how much fury her face had previously held. True magic. "I have some buff skills I could cast, though?"

"Be my guest." The zombie grinned in return. She could see that Humphrey was rather neutral on the Player, but Norah was still full of her own disdain for the Adventurer.

It made sense. Out of all of them, she was the more classic Monster. Defending her home from invading forces, that was the extent of her interaction with humans. Other than Chuck, she hadn't really met any "good" Players. Sally knew there was more nuance to it. *She* was part Player herself, of course.

She wondered what the Shade's ability would do to her. Perhaps a thought for a better, or worse, day.

"Onward, to the south!" She pointed more to the east, before correcting herself slowly, finger moving through the air.

"Sally is safe. I'm still worried, though." Chuck deflated in his chair as a ginger cat leaped up onto his lap.

"You think she won't like the plan? Won't accept it?"

The Druid worked his jaw. "There's a lot of moving pieces. I just want things to work out okay for everyone."

He stroked the ginger fur of the cat slowly, running his hand down their back to avoid the flaming skull it had for a head.

"Oh, things will," the cat started to purr. "Things will."

CHAPTER FOURTEEN

Be Plot

The wooden doorway burst open, and a shadowed figure silhouetted the opening briefly before being engulfed in a blazing torrent of fire.

Fabric burned and crisped away as the man continued to step into the room unhindered. The flames abated, and his bare torso smoldered as it healed over.

"So sorry," Theo said with a grin. "I'm supposed to ask for permission before entering, aren't I?"

The woman clambered backward, knocking into shelves as she drew up a crossbow. "This arrow is imbued with holy power, if I strike you in the heart—" Although most of her face was shrouded in some manner of face mask, her eyes were wide with panic.

"You won't." He stopped and looked around. "You'd think your hideout would be harder to find. Planning this for what? A year? Undone within a day."

"What kind of Monster are you?" Her finger tensed on the trigger.

"I could ask the same question. In fact, I did to the last three of you I killed." Theo took a step forward and grinned, his fangs catching the light. "No answer satisfied me, however."

"You'll get no answer from me either, *Outsider*."

The vampire tutted and shook his head. "See. That's where you're wrong."

He took another step forward as her finger let loose the bolt.

In all their excitement, Sally almost forgot to hand the gnoll quest in and receive the experience. After a quick jog back to the hand-in sign, her STAR blazed in the familiar golden shine to tell her the deed was done, and she was ready to level up.

"Nineteen," she clucked. "Feels like it'll be forever until we hit thirty here."

Lucius shrugged. "Well, we are behind by a year. If anything, I'm surprised Chuck and the others are still in this area and not the fourth one."

Sally narrowed her eyes to the horizon, or at least in the direction of it through the terrain and trees. Maybe there was something up with that area too—it wouldn't shock her. It was surprising enough that the jungle area was mostly working, if you ignored the pitched battles between Players.

She resigned to bringing up her skill choices.

Pick One
[Eager Stomach] HP threshold for Eat Brains is lower.
[Hard to Chew] Increased protection against Beasts.
[Unyielding Flesh] Maximum Absorption is increased by 2%.

If there was one thing she wanted to fix with the System, it would be that she could go back and choose all the skills she didn't get to pick earlier. Some manner of skill reset or picking system would be grand. Still, it was what it was.

It would even help if it wasn't so vague. The *[Eat Brains]* threshold could be huge if it was a good increase. Useless if it was only marginal. Still . . . the thought of getting food into her stomach sooner easily beat out the other options, and she prodded it before she could second-guess her appetite-led decision.

"What did everyone else pick?" She grinned. "I can eat brains sooner, apparently."

Lucius rubbed the back of his hood. "I can do this." He walked behind a tree to their left, and a second later, walked out from behind one on their right.

"Mine goes like this," Norah said with a smile. She placed her hands together to form a gap that looked like a triangle. Out amid the horde chewing through bandits, a miniature pyramid about a dozen feet to the peak burst out of the floor, sending bodies all over the place.

"Both very neat," Sally said diplomatically. "And you, Humphrey?"

"Nothing so interesting." He looked away, a wide grin across his skeletal face.

"Metal-ass, you just want to keep it secret." She huffed and looked back at the Player following them.

Charlotte smiled and cast a defensive buff on the group of zombies munching on some jungle bandits. "Tell the joke about the pancakes again. I love that one."

Sally grinned. "I would, but these guys might have heard it before."

Humphrey slowed down to scowl at the Shade, putting a wide, plated hand on his shoulder. "Whatever you did to the Player, please undo it."

It was a remarkable change. Even Sally could admit that. The woman had seemed a little put off by the newly raised dead, but otherwise was accepting of the group and their antics. Saw them as equals—which made her happy. That's all she ever wanted from the System. They just needed to line every Player up and have Lucius hop inside them for a moment and then all would be right with the world.

If only things could be that simple. It was hard enough to organize the *Outsiders* into a straight line without calamity or mischief making a mess of the process.

The Death Knight then walked over beside her. "I am concerned about Theo."

She raised an eyebrow in response. "*Softie*. What, his poison?"

"Not exactly, although that *is* concerning. Archie hid some memories before transferring to me, but I know they were about Theo." He tilted his head as he watched the zombie bandits rise up to join the horde.

"Why do you think he'd do that? What could he have known?" Sally frowned and cast *[Living Dead]* on her pals.

Humphrey shrugged. "Nothing good, I'm sure. There is a lot wrong with that man."

She punched him lightly on the shoulder. "Like falling for the wrong type of gal?"

He smiled and shook his head, before looking over at Norah. The Mummy was entangling the living bandits to give the zombies an easier deal of overwhelming them. "Part of me feels I should be wary of how . . . human I have become. From unerring servant of the Observer to patriarchal knight of a group of oddballs."

"You erred plenty before." She shook her head. "Remember back before the Graveyard, I asked you if you were happy?"

Humphrey nodded slowly, looking back down at her.

"And are you now?"

"*Yes*."

She grinned. "Then you're on the right path. Whatever the problem with Theo is, we'll get past it together. As a group."

"Remarkably levelheaded for you."

"Hey, *skull-head*! If there's one thing I am, I'm always—" She tripped on a tree root and landed on the thick vegetative ground. "—levelheaded."

A bandage wrapped around her arm to help her up, and she brushed down her clothes. Wasn't much point at this stage. Covered in all manner of grime and gore. Par for the course as a zombie. While thinking of these goofballs as her new family was first born of a joke, it was closer to reality than she'd like to admit. Her real family might as well not exist, for as far from them as she now was. There wasn't blood between the *Outsiders*—not their own, anyway—but they cared for each other.

She looked back at Charlotte as the woman smiled and talked animatedly with Lucius. They were Monsters, but that's all she wanted for the gang—acceptance. And maybe to eat some brains on occasion.

"Any other quests this way?" She looked up at the Death Knight.

He shrugged. "Killing our way through mobs isn't the most effective way of leveling, but it's relatively easy."

She would be inclined to agree. Between their buffs and the snowball effect of her horde, they were chewing through Monster packs with little need to intervene themselves. Norah seemed to like assisting, but that was more because she was trying to look after the flock rather than act out of necessity. Sally would put *[Living Dead]* up whenever it was off cooldown, and that kept some up too. With enough time and weak enough enemies, she could start growing her own zombie apocalypse without needing to use the skill.

"So, your ultimate? Give me the details." She pestered the Death Knight as she threw a green-flame skull into the next pack of enemies.

"It's meant to be a stat and defensive buff . . . but it also draws on the 'souls' that I have absorbed."

"So two Archies and the Observers? Thinking of that, we didn't see any in the Wastes." She tilted her head and cupped her chin.

"Edward said that Ruben had them killed off. Saw them as a threat to his eventual rise to power."

Sally snorted. How well did that work out for him? She was still salty that she never got to raise him as a zombie, due to stupid System rules. With a furrowed brow, she brought up her skill window and then switched to the passives. If it was possible, it'd be one of the screens that would have cobwebs on it for how irregularly she looked at it. Second only to the boxes with random things.

Dragonslayer

"No way, I received a passive for eating the dragon! It must have popped up while we died." She wrinkled up her face. "But it won't tell me what it does?"

Humphrey stood behind her to look. "Interesting. Probably nothing dire. You've lived this long without anything bad happening."

"So far. Don't jinx it." She sighed and closed the windows. "I'd best go loot all these mobs before someone yells at me." The zombie hopped over to find some corpses to sift through.

Norah walked over to the Death Knight and put an arm around him. "Everything okay, my dear?"

"*Yes.*" He furrowed his brow and looked out at the dense canopy of tropical trees. "Currently."

Theo hopped down from the small house hidden away in the treetops next to a large hill, hands in his pockets. He hummed to himself, his suit fully repaired and a glimmer in his eyes.

When he landed on the ground, he stretched his back out and yawned. Brought up his STAR windows and narrowed his eyes at some information. Gave it a pout and then closed it down, looking instead at his wristwatch.

The hideout above exploded, shaking the canopy and sending flaming debris clattering down to the ground around him. He paid it no attention as burning wood and shattered furniture dropped from above. Instead, he withdrew a sheet of paper and unfolded it.

Edward—? Now unlikely. Humphrey. Likely. Lucius. Very doubtful. Norah. No? Sally . . . untenable.

His right eye twitched, and he folded the paper back up with a sigh. He put it back in the inside pocket of his jacket.

Hands back in his pockets, he wandered off, humming to himself again as dark smoke from the wreckage filled the area.

CHAPTER FIFTEEN

Drop Off

Sally yawned. Not that this was *boring*, but it was low effort. Her zombie force had increased, and while scores of them died between each grouping of Monster packs, she was maintaining numbers through her other skills. She could really do with another ability that increased their base level again.

They hadn't come across any other quests yet, which slowed down their experience gain, but the amount of damage they were doing to the local wildlife population was at least moving the needle—according to Humphrey, anyway. Until they respawned.

"Once we drop the Player off, there is a good area to the north again," the Death Knight assured her.

"How do you know?" She narrowed her eyes.

He grinned in response. "Archie reasons."

That didn't exactly fill her with much confidence. Aside from the fact that they were probably stuck here for good, he hadn't labored upon them many more details about what was going on with the world. It stood to reason he might know all if there were five total cats that had been split from the Architect—but with two of them already she thought he might be able to . . . well; she didn't really know.

She wanted to bite into the System and take a bigger piece of it. Making peace with what she was had long passed, and she didn't expect a miracle cure that would turn her into a normal Player . . . and she wasn't even sure she'd want that. Not that being undead didn't have downsides, but after eating her way through scores of real people, a fully normal Sally might not be able to handle that weight.

Plus, all her friends were undead. They were kind of a package deal.

"I'm not saying you're too heavy, Humphrey—it just might not work as expected." Norah patted the Death Knight on the arm as he deflated, disappointed he wouldn't get to be flung into combat by her bandages.

Lucius was retelling the fight against Ruben to Charlotte, who looked both enraptured and partly in disbelief. He was probably embellishing some of the facts. The big dumb lizard hadn't been able to shift or escape from a handful of lunatic corpses, served him right for getting what he deserved. Greed had been his undoing.

She brought up her map. Monsters were thinning out now, and they were getting close to the camp where they could drop the Player off. Despite her definitely tasty brains being held in her skull, Sally didn't feel much like eating Charlotte. Maybe it was because she had accepted her. It was easier to eat a meal that was angry or fearful, perhaps something her Monster side adored.

"We're almost at the camp," she announced, mostly because she wanted a bit of attention. There hadn't been any sightings of the red team or the *Last Word*, so the trek through the wilderness had been pretty uneventful after the gnolls.

Not that she wished for hardship, and she was sure losing twenty Players would put a bit of a dent in the red's offensive capabilities. Humphrey had gotten the location of their base out of the woman, so it was possible they could go ruin their day for good. That said, they hadn't officially joined the blue team yet, even if it was a given. She just didn't fancy wearing the tabard that much—it would totally clash with the rest of her style.

"I just wanted to say thank you, again." The Player moved over to her. "I feel much better about everything, like a weight has been lifted from my mind."

Sally waved her hand. "It was nothing. Just try to get along with the blue team—I'm sure they'll be accommodating once they realize that you aren't going to double cross anyone."

"Yeah." The woman grimaced. "I realize that I might be hard to trust, but I can't . . . I can't go back to the others. Not just because the ambush failed—but ideology-wise it doesn't make sense."

Sally nodded. If things were pretty bad, then there would be a lot the woman would need to prove to be considered a proper blue faction member after absconding from the other. There was something more than just wanting to save her own skin, though. She had been angry enough to die right before Lucius had possessed her. It was . . . strange.

"What can you tell us about the red faction?" She raised an eyebrow at Charlie. "Some insider information might be useful if they try anything else."

"Oh! Well . . ." Charlie scrunched up her face in thought. "They know about you five. At least the leader did—and he wanted to make sure you either joined us or died. Knowing how powerful you were to defeat the dragon . . . you'd either be a boon or great threat to their progress."

"True and true," the zombie replied with a nod. "Their problem was not accepting me and the gang for what we are. They didn't even pretend to make up a plan for what to do with Uniques."

Charlie nodded slowly. "It's a bit shortsighted, now that I really think about it. Unique Monsters are . . . different, but in a way, they aren't so different from a Player."

"We're people too." Sally smiled. "Live and die the same, have thoughts and dreams." Mostly involving carving out people's brains and eating them off Theo's abs, but still.

The woman didn't respond but looked off through the tree line sheepishly.

Sally nudged her on the arm. "Best thing you can do is convince people of what we really are and stand on our side of the line when the final battle happens. The blue faction seems pretty on board—the leader is one of my oldest friends."

"I'll do my best, Sally." She gave her a warm smile.

"Looks like the camp ahead," Humphrey announced, narrowing his eye sockets.

Three figures moved from where tents had been partially obscured by the foliage. A man and two women in long robes, blue tabards atop their spellcaster clothing.

"Hail," the man called out, raising his hand. "We were told to expect you."

Sally grinned. "We have someone Chuck said you'd help look after." She crossed her arms. "In a nice way, not in a faux mobster way."

"Of course." The man smiled, a slim black mustache raising in tandem. "We have been told what will happen if we upset you in any manner."

This caused her grin to extend even farther. Chuck knew them well enough to know that crossing them was an easy route straight to her stomach, and it didn't matter how powerful the opposition was. In a way, she wondered if the Druid had been swayed on his stance with them in mind.

"Off you go then, Charlie. Here." She held out her arm to get her contact information. "Stay in touch, okay?"

The woman nodded and smiled back at them. "Thank you all again. I won't forget this."

With that, she turned and went over to the three robed figures, the man and one of the women escorting her gently back to the camp while the third continued to watch the Party.

"Everything okay?" Sally asked.

"Of course. Are you not planning to join the camp for a short spell?"

"Mmm . . ." She looked between the *Outsiders* and saw their apprehensive expressions. "Nah, we have lots of leveling to do. Maybe next time?"

"Oh, that is fine." The robed figure gave a brief bow. "I will have to send him out to meet you, then." She turned away and walked back into camp without elaborating further.

Sally shrugged and pulled a face at the rest of the group. "You sad to see Charlie go, Lucius?"

He rubbed his misty chin. "Not really. It was nice to make a new friend, but I am excited to meet even more."

She nodded with a smile. It was nice to make friends. No doubt they could find more among the blue faction—certainly more than anywhere else in the area. Just as she was wondering who their surprise guest could be, a figure walked out from the camp toward them.

"Dent!" Sally beamed.

The man stepped over closer to them. His right arm replaced by a long blade from the elbow down, he now sported a rough beard that aged him by a handful of years. Chain mail overlayed with dark gray clothing made him look like a lost wanderer more than a great swordsman.

From atop his shoulder, Archie appeared, wearing an eye patch.

"And Archie!" She hopped across the muddy floor closer to them.

"It's been awhile," Dent said with a grin as he nodded to the rest of them. "Chuck sent me as a bit of an olive branch for being so distant."

Sally nodded. "He must have a reason, I'm sure."

"He does." The swordsman rubbed the back of his head. "All in good time, though. You all close to twenty-five yet?"

She leaned back and pulled a face at Humphrey, who slowly shook his head. "Nineteen," the Death Knight added.

Dent blinked twice. "Ah."

Archie stretched out and leaned forward so that Sally could take him. "Typical that you would be so behind the curve and yet thriving."

The zombie cuddled the cat up close and turned to walk him over to the Death Knight. "I wouldn't say thriving, Arch. But we aren't dead yet. Dead, dead."

"Big brother." The cat nodded, before jumping from Sally's grasp and onto Humphrey's wide shoulder pad. "Just like old times, huh?"

"Almost." The Death Knight grinned. "I assume this is something more than just a casual visit to ply us to your side?"

Dent coughed and pulled a face. "Let's walk and talk. You all need experience and standing still too long makes me itchy."

With murmured agreement, they turned toward the north as per Humphrey's earlier suggestion, and the zombie horde moved ahead of them to clear the path of any Monsters in their way. Sally looked out at her group of walking corpses with a sigh. It was nice having Charlotte's buffs. Perhaps the System could give her something similar if she was meant to be a support necromancer or whatever.

Dent sidled along in the middle between her and the Death Knight. "It's actually a matter of grave importance—I believe Rachel mentioned it to you but wouldn't say too much."

The cogs in her brain ticked over a few notches. "Ah—she said something about someone becoming the new Architect?"

He nodded. "As far as we know, that is true."

Archie took over after yawning first. "There is a barrier stopping everyone from going to the fourth area and beyond. But it's not natural, and there are at least a handful that did cross before it was put in place."

Humphrey rubbed the side of his head. "To do that, it would either have to be a Unique or—"

"Or an ex-Observer with some remaining power." The cat's tail swished through the air.

Sally narrowed her eyes at the ground ahead to try to focus. So that's why there was such a struggle in this area. They couldn't progress and had blamed it on the broken System. So naturally, the only thing to do was war it out until they could come up with a solution. In all this meantime, some bad eggs had crossed through and leveled, and somehow made their way to wherever the Architect resided to claim his crown.

Or throne. Or however it worked. It wouldn't surprise her if it was the same group that had intended to kill off the Architect in the first place. Any Observers that had inside knowledge of how the System worked would be in prime position to enact these plots; that it had taken them this long was curious, but nothing to worry about now.

"What worries me," Dent continued, "is that we don't know when. It could be today; it could be in a week or two."

"But it is close?" Humphrey questioned, flame licking around the back of his helmet.

The swordsman exhaled through his nose. "Yeah."

"That's why we wanted you to level up," Archie said. "In case we need you to kill a god."

CHAPTER SIXTEEN

A Crack Forming

The weight of the phrase sank into Sally slowly. Sure, it had been the plan from the beginning, right? Eat the Architect, get revenge on the System . . . but now that it was an actual thing that they might be expected to do . . .

Well, she hadn't brought her best cutlery set, for one.

"How could *we* kill a god?" She was surprised to hear this questioning voice was her own. The rest of the gang shared a similar amount of apprehension about what was expected of them.

"Just fail upward," Dent said with a wry grin. "Same way you chewed through an army and killed a dragon."

"That was different." She deflated. Now that they'd set a precedent that they might be competent, there was no avoiding all these side quests.

Humphrey looked perturbed but tried to keep their moods up. "The Architect, while technically the creator of this world . . . any upstart wouldn't be exactly god-like in power should they take the mantle."

"So they could be killed?" Norah asked.

"*Yes*. Should they allow us the chance, *ha-ha*." The laugh had a little less heart in it than usual.

While the vague description of their power didn't give Sally much confidence, it also didn't surprise her. The original Architect was killed after all and didn't have a way of fixing things themselves. Maybe part of the world was just as it was, unable to be changed to such a degree she imagined a god would be able to. She clucked her tongue.

"What makes you sure they will be a villain, and not someone wanting to fix the System?"

Dent and Archie exchanged glances before the cat sighed and turned his one good eye to her. "We don't know for certain how they'd act. If it is the group that killed the Architect, then there's a chance they want to change the world to suit their own vision."

"Which means there's a chance that it's nothing good," Dent added, "and we're preparing for the worst."

Pragmatic. Sally scratched her hair. All it meant was that the worst was bound to happen. The narrative wouldn't allow it any other way. "You guys are Level Thirty though, right? What do you expect us to do?"

"We are . . . but . . ." The swordsman scratched at his chin idly with the end of his blade. "Chuck has a lot of faith in you. That's not to say that I don't, but . . ."

Archie yawned. "You not being a group of Players makes you somewhat of an anomaly. There are very few actual Uniques that care to run the same gauntlet as Players, if you can believe it."

Sally could. In their adventures so far, all the Uniques they had met had sooner gone to live a normal life rather than put their lives in danger. Present company excluded, of course. That was the crux of it, though, wasn't it? A normal life. Beyond being a Monster or having to grind out levels or quests to stay relevant. She screwed up her face in resignation.

"Unless anyone has any objections, I would like us to formally join the blue team." She paused and crossed her arms. "On one condition."

The rest of them stopped. Dent frowned. "We're not actually called—" he said before stopping, the cat resting a paw on his shoulder.

"I stand by your decision," Humphrey said, with a brief bow.

Norah tutted but gave a nod. "As much as I despise Adventurers, having a clear enemy would be appreciated."

"I'd like to make new friends," the Shade added with a thumbs-up appearing beside his head.

Dent smiled and raised his eyebrows. "Alright, Sally. What's your condition?"

"We refuse to wear the tabards!" She huffed and tried to stand taller to make her point.

Archie nodded. "That is reasonable. We accept."

The six of them stood in silence for a few moments before the zombie deflated.

"It's just a verbal agreement, then. There's no actual 'thing' to it?"

"Correct," Dent said with a grin, before gesturing them forward once more. "Just kill the . . . *red* team and assist us when you see us. Your group is too much of a wild card, so I won't bring you into the gears of the machine proper. You can still act as free agents until we have need of you." He tilted his head. "Until *the System* has need of you."

"Great." Sally sighed. Responsibilities. Not much had changed since the start of the day, except she trusted Chuck a little more and she could eat brains quicker. The fact that the System might need their help was a bit of a wet blanket over their plans. Still, without the System, what did they really have?

They'd just have to keep getting more powerful until the new Architect was crowned and then see what happened. Either way, they'd need to be as strong as possible. Especially as Chuck had already hit Level Thirty before them—unacceptable. As contemplative silence filled out the group, she narrowed her eyes at the swordsman.

"So, Dent, tell us about Chuck?" She grinned.

He raised an eyebrow in return but had an otherwise impassive expression. "What did you want to know?"

"Well . . . we haven't seen him since the big battle in the Wastes . . . so anything you can tell us?"

Dent tilted his head. "Hmm. Well, after you all rolled through to the golds to fight Ruben, Chuck and the surviving Players moved up to the battlefield. He healed me up pretty good. Saved a lot of lives that day, in fact."

Sally nodded. Enough to turn someone against Uniques after seeing what Ruben had wrought in the area. "Then what?"

"He tried to heal you all too. There's a remarkable amount of care in his heart for you, despite his disagreements with your . . . methods. Between him, Edward, and Archie, they devised the tomb to keep you safe while your souls wormed back into your bodies."

Archie yawned and stretched out atop the Death Knight. "Chuck is a lot calmer these days. More at home in this new world."

"Does he know we can't go back?" Sally furrowed her brow.

"Chuck does, yes." Archie nodded. "At first it weighed heavily on him, but in time it became motivation to get where he is now."

Humphrey tilted his head to look at the cat. "It is rather impressive what he has accomplished. He always had more . . . tact for these things."

Sally grinned. "Not hard when our default is eating or murdering our problems. You're right though, Humps. I'm proud of Chuck."

"You can tell him that when you see him," Dent said as he grinned. "I'm sure that will get him flustered. He has been melodramatic lately."

Unsurprising. The return of the dragonslayers mixed with the unknown new Architect, alongside the war between the two factions. That was a lot for the little pacifist dweeb. "Tell us how to level quicker then. It'll take forever to get to twenty-five." She gestured out at her zombie horde, who were chewing through packs of what looked like giant insects.

"Northeast of here, there are a bunch of large Elites and an area boss. You could probably farm that for a few levels before it starts to slow." Dent raised an eyebrow to Archie.

"Agreed. You should be tough enough to survive them. If not, then big brother needs to keep the other Archie fragments safe." He pawed at the side of the Death Knight's helmet.

Humphrey sighed. "I'll need to absorb all of you at some point?"

"We'll see," the cat said with a small smile.

"Alright then." Dent stopped and held his good hand out to be shaken. "We just wanted to fill you in on a bit more exposition before you got too far ahead of yourselves. Now you know the stakes . . . I'm glad to be on your side once more."

Sally beamed as she shook his hand. "Always a pleasure, Dent. You give our regards to Chucky, okay?"

The swordsman gave a brief bow and smile before both he and Archie disappeared in a blur of blue teleportation.

"Wow," she said with a sigh. "Things just don't stop, huh?"

"*Yes . . .?*" Humphrey shrugged.

Norah moved up and put her arm around the Death Knight. "What would a new Architect mean for Uniques like us?"

He slowly shook his head as he looked at the worried Mummy. "Anything from acceptance to immediate death."

"They remind me of the giant frog." Sally wrinkled up her face.

"Toad," Humphrey replied.

The creatures were definitely large—at least twenty-five-feet tall and patterned with green and orange scales. Not quite dinosaurs, although they were similar. Four stout legs and a large mouth filled with sharp teeth. Bulbous in nature, their yellow eyes lazily watched the area, and they stomped about in a pattern.

"The boss is deeper in." Humphrey scratched at the side of his head. "We'll need to be careful if these are all Elites."

Sally rolled her eyes. Like they were ever careful. The dark brown rocky ground was scoured of most vegetation, as if it was either volcanic underneath and too hot, or the Monsters had eaten it all. Given the length of their sharp teeth, she doubted the latter. "Let's pull one and find out. I'm not keen on feeding them all my zombies or getting collateral problems heading our way."

Skull in hand, she threw *[Mortis Bomb]* out over the space into the first Monster. A blaze of green left a small mark on the creature as it immediately stomped out the four zombies with the thrashing of its wide front feet.

"Mean," she huffed. "Alright, battle positions gang! The afternoon draws late. Let's level before it gets dark!"

They nodded their agreement as the Monster growled and ran toward them. Lucius shadowed into Humphrey, and the Death Knight pulsed with his buffs. Norah shot out two bandages to tie around the legs of the creature. The first snapped off underneath its power, but the second wrapped tight and the Monster stumbled.

Humphrey ran forward to meet them, his greatsword flourishing.

"Heard from Theo, hun?" Norah asked as she strained against the weight of the enemy trying to pull against her binding.

"Nah." She shook her head and held *[Curse: Decay]* on the target. "Knowing him, he's probably been killing things nonstop to level higher than us. He'll drop in at an opportune moment to steal some thunder."

"He's not a bodyguard, though?"

"No, just has a knack for knowing when I need him." She smiled to herself. "Oh, Humps did say I'd get another bodyguard slot at . . . twenty? It's about every five levels."

Norah smiled and summoned a sarcophagus to fling out at the Monster. "You thinking of asking Lucius?"

"You think Lucy would accept? He's settled in well with us, but sometimes it feels like he'd rather be off doing something instead of adventuring."

"Won't hurt to ask, hun." The Mummy shrugged. "Let's get to Level Twenty first."

Sally grinned and flipped her dagger around, as her curse could no longer take hold. The Monster growled as Humphrey blocked a stomp and his shadow sliced out at the extended leg.

"C'mon pals," she yelled back to her waiting horde. "Let's go feast!"

CHAPTER SEVENTEEN

Staff Meeting

Another Monster dropped to the floor, and Sally wiped off her mouth. *Gross.* They tasted like asphalt, which didn't make much sense. Her stomach gurgled as she slid off the side of the creature before it could raise as a zombie.

Things had gotten easier the more they killed. While most of her normal zombies had been pulped in short order, she now had a handful of these large lizard things at her beck and call. Too slow to be much offensive use, but they could body block and draw aggression from their target and allow the *Outsiders* to attack almost unabated.

They'd been through two dozen of them now. *[Curse: Decay]* helped, but it seemed to drain health slower on the giant Monsters. The System didn't care to give her a tangible reason as to why—but she just assumed it was some inane bullshit. She sighed and wiped the sweat from her brow.

"Everything alright, hun?" Norah moved up beside her as the other two took a brief break to stretch out.

"It's this hair," she said as she deflated. "Half tempted to cut it off."

"It suits you, though." Norah tilted her head. "If I may?"

"Go ahead."

The Mummy moved a bandage around behind her and wrapped the hair around, snaking through to bind it into the shape of a long ponytail. "It's too matted with gore to do anything with right now, but this should keep it out of your way." The bandage snipped off and Norah tied it off to keep it in place.

"Oh, thank you!" Sally beamed up at her. "Can already feel the breeze on my back. Maybe if we find a proper town, I can wash it up and we can get it sorted properly?"

"It would be my pleasure, hun." Between the bandages across her face, she smiled back.

Sally leaned against the body of the fallen Monster as undeath started to bring it back as a zombie. "How are you finding it with us now? It's only been a couple of weeks, technically, and we've dragged you through a lot."

"Honestly?" Norah looked away to watch the Death Knight limbering up. "It's been the best time of my unlife. I don't think I could do this forever, though."

The zombie nodded in return. "It would be nice to have a vacation, huh? Actually enjoy what we've fought for. Waking up next to abs and not have to worry about getting more powerful or some calamity trying to kill us . . ." She shifted away from the creature as it stood back up.

"Did you just call Theo 'abs,' hun?"

"*No*." Sally grinned and pulled a skull from her belt.

"Ready when you are," Humphrey called from the front, swinging his sword around as it burst into crimson flame.

Theo spat blood on the ground.

A body dropped from his grasp into the dense foliage. Crimson pulsing down their neck and soaking through their clothing and tabard.

He crouched and wrinkled his nose up at the dead body. "You are worth no experience. Waste of my time." His eyes glazed over as his STAR menu showed him what he could loot from the corpse.

"You're a hard man to track down," a female voice came from behind him.

"Intentionally," he replied, still focusing on the loot. "You move quietly."

"Intentionally."

Theo hummed to himself, weighing the options between two pieces of gear.

"Are you so overconfident and rude that you do not turn to face me, vampire?" The voice was curt but not overly aggressive.

"It must be difficult." He paused and furrowed his brow. "Believing you are the true one, the original, even though you know deep down . . . that it's a lie."

"*Face me.*"

A wide grin spread across the vampire's face, exposing his fangs. "Just how many of you are left, Lana?"

Sally sank as they stared at the boss. "I'm feelin' dino-sore at fighting all these tough Elites."

A question mark appeared beside the Shade, and his crimson eyes narrowed in confusion.

"If we kill the boss, we will level up," Humphrey tried to persuade her.

She wasn't so easily convinced. The boss of these ball-like giant lizards was one even larger, with predominantly red scales. Surrounding him were five of the Elite Monsters as his bodyguard.

Behind her, they now had ten of the zombified creatures, along with a token force of normal zombies. She'd need to top them off soon enough . . . although gathering more of these big Monsters would be fun once they moved away from this area. One step at a time.

"Alright, I'm convinced." She crossed her arms and tried to consider how to approach the group. "We might have to use our ultimates, which makes us weak if we get jumped by anything unexpected."

Lucius turned around and glared at the surroundings. "We're pretty secluded. They'd have to fight through the respawning Monsters to get to us."

"People can do all sorts of bullshit," Sally tutted. "But I think it's worth the risk. Level Twenty is right underneath our noses, and then it'll only be five more before his highness will allow us to speak with him."

"Usually something that would take months," Humphrey murmured. "When the new Architect could appear at any moment."

"Best to get moving, then." She limbered up her shoulders and picked off a skull from her belt. I'll work on getting rid of the guards if you guys focus on the boss?"

[Quick Death]—She commanded her fast zombies as they thundered past her. As soon as they got the attention of the Monster group, she made them drag the Elites to the side. Before the boss could join them, the large summon from Norah's ultimate slammed into him, a blaze of golden light following the giant bird-mummy.

Sally ran in beside the Death Knight, as Lucius activated his ultimate to shadow all three of them. Five Elites for her to kill while the others beat on the boss. She held her curse on the first and lobbed the flaming skull over into it.

With a hop, bandages lifted her up from the ground so that she could jump atop the Monster. Skeleton Key had no issue burying into the thick skull of the lizard but didn't go deep enough to give her easy access to the brains. There wasn't exactly a great deal of stable footing for her to stand on either, and she slid to the side and almost fell off.

Warm air billowed past her as the boss activated some kind of ability. It wouldn't be anything Humphrey couldn't handle. The plated ex-Observer was nigh invulnerable and hadn't even activated his ultimate yet. Her shadow stabbed downward, and she did the same, using the wound as an anchor to stay atop her foe. Lucius continued to stab as she held in place until the conditional came up.

[Eat Brains]. *Gross.* She leaped through the air, shadowed wrappings zipping out to assist her to the next. Two of her zombie dinos had been shredded by the living ones, and she dropped *[Living Dead]* on the remaining. They had managed

to down one of their own, and the two fallen slowly started to rise on her side. The ground shook and the sound of grinding metal caught her attention.

Humphrey was wedged inside the mouth of the boss, his armor screaming out as the large teeth tried to chew on him. Norah had a sarcophagus wedged in beside him and was trying to pry the jaws apart with her bandages.

[Soul Knight]. Humphrey burst into flame that was quickly extinguished to reveal his ivory-bone coloration, eyes gleaming bright emerald. "Chew on this," he growled.

"What a goof," Sally murmured to herself and grinned, as she started to stab at the next lizard Monster. It tried to buck her off but was too pressed in between the zombies to really move effectively. Suited her just fine. *[Eat Brains]*.

The boss roared out, and Humphrey dropped to the floor behind her. In her peripheral she could see the flourish of his greatsword glowing bright blue with *[Decimate]*. She yawned and hopped toward the next Monster, hitting the floor as the wrappings didn't come to save her. Instead, she rolled, stabbing into the leg of the Monster, diving to the side as it tried to swipe at her. *[Mortis Bomb]* and then her curse on it again. It was weakening, but not quite good enough.

Beside her, the last Elite was enveloped by dozens of bandages, assisted by the shadowed versions provided by Lucius. As the beast became fully wrapped up, the flash of yellow from behind her signaled the skill was cast and the Monster turned to sand.

"Sorry for interfering, hun." Norah turned to focus on the boss. "We need you here."

Her zombie Elites took down the last lizard, so she turned to run at the boss. It looked like it had regenerated some of the damage already inflicted and was slightly too large for Norah to do much to it. Her bird-giant punched it in the side of the head, but other than snarling and starting to charge up an ability, the boss didn't have much of a reaction.

The Death Knight fell to a knee as the Monster tried to crush him underfoot, the flat of his sword held up to defend against the attack.

"Need a hand, Humps?" She held up her curse against the boss, even if it might not do much due to his regeneration.

"Don't tell anyone, but I miss Theo being here." The flames at the back of his helmet flickered wildly.

"Oh, I'm definitely telling him that." Sally grinned and put her hands on her hips. "*Hey!* Big Monster? Don't you know I'm the only boss allowed around here?"

It turned to her and narrowed its large eyes. Steam blew through its nostrils and a glow of red and orange began to pulse around the four large feet.

"Don't get mad." Sally grinned and prepared herself, raising her dagger. "You'll meet your friends in my stomach soon enough."

The boss burst forward, waves of heat billowing behind it as it passed

Humphrey. The moment of impact drew close as it snapped forward to strike her with a heavy charge.

[Escape Fate]. She popped into the air as the zombies took the brunt of the strike, bursting to pieces in a spray across the dried stone ground. Feet landing on the boss's back, she slammed the dagger down into it. The Death Knight had caught up and slashed away at the rear legs, while Norah weaved her bandages all around the underside of the Monster to trip it as it tried to turn. All the forms of Lucius assisted, causing additional damage as the three wailed away at the creature.

This was where the skill to eat brains sooner helped out. On a large boss, especially one with regeneration, getting that instant kill quicker was huge. She couldn't use *[Curse: Decay]* on it, so it must be getting low.

She slid off its back as it bucked around, landing on the floor with a roll. Flames burst around it, shredding all the entangled wrappings, and it charged through a couple of the large zombie lizards brought back from the dead. It was a lot stronger than them, but now it had surrounded themselves with bodies. *[Living Dead]*.

Stuck between the thick presence of its own dead kind, and the constant force of the Death Knight slashing from behind, eventually it sank to the ground. Lethargic and too injured to continue.

Norah flung Sally over to it. *[Eat Brains]*.

"Ay, boss brains aren't so bad." She grinned and crossed her arms. Still not as good as Players, but it was a step up at least. Not only did her STAR light up a golden color, their Level Twenty skills ready to be chosen—but something caught her eye in the loot window of the creature.

She gasped. "A *legendary* item!"

Humphrey returned to his usual armor, his ultimate form wearing off. "Interesting. What is it?"

"You wouldn't believe me even if I told you." She winked at him and jumped down from the corpse.

Even Lucius popped out to glare at her.

"Oh, fine." She rolled her eyes. "The System must have a thing for me. It's a staff called Corpseboon."

"For necromancy then?" Humphrey raised an eyebrow.

She removed it from her Inventory and held it in her off hand. A twirling dark wood with rough twine wrapped around it. The head of the staff was two sharp horns of deep red, a jawless human skull hung in the circular gap they created.

With a twitch of her eye, the skull burst into green flame.

"Now we're cookin'" she said with a wide grin.

CHAPTER EIGHTEEN

Classy

Humphrey grimaced. "I'm not sure that's how . . ."

He was interrupted as Sally struck her two weapons together before binding them with all the twine and string she could find. It wasn't exactly stable. Perhaps the Death Knight was right. She scratched the top of her head and waved her bound ponytail about.

"Hey Lucy, come shadow my dagger for a second?"

The Shade walked over to the rock she had both her weapons laid on. He rubbed at his misty chin and then shrugged, a similar emoji appearing beside him. With an outstretched finger, he cast his shadow ability on the dagger.

Sally positioned her staff, her tongue sticking out as she tried to judge the distance and positioning. "Alright, end it."

The dagger popped back into existence and tried to escape from the blocked position where the staff now sat. Immediately she was upon them both, holding them in place with her full strength. At first, they resisted and squirmed beneath her hands, but after a handful of angry seconds, they gave up and merged.

She lifted the staff, which now had her dagger sticking from the bottom. With a flourish, she spun it around, gripping it like a spear before twirling it around and jamming it into the ground. The Skeleton Key slid into the rock easily and the staff remained standing as she crossed her arms in pride to beam at the others.

"That's not supposed to do that," Humphrey said with a sigh, rubbing the side of his head.

"Story of my unlife." She continued to grin. "Watch this too." She took a dozen steps away from the staff and pointed her finger at the inert skull sitting at the head. It burst into green flame, and then with a flick of her wrist she sent the *[Mortis Bomb]* off to splash against a rock ineffectively.

"I'm almost jealous." Norah smiled as she leaned against a rock. "Players seem to get all the fun when it comes to loot."

"Maybe that's something else we can fix with the System." She went and plucked her new item from the ground. "It also increases the damage and healing of any spell I cast with it, and it makes any undead near me extra happy."

"I'm pretty sure I can feel that." Lucius nodded, a smiley face next to his head.

Humphrey rolled his empty eye sockets. "What about your level up?"

In all the excitement, she had totally forgotten about that. Not that she cared for looting at the best of times, but it wasn't every day you found a legendary item that was perfect for your class. It was almost suspicious . . . unless that was the way it worked. It would be disappointing to get an item you couldn't use. She sighed, relenting to see what the System wanted her to choose from this time.

Pick One
[Hunger for Flesh] Undead allies have +10% Lifesteal.
[Persistent Curse] Channeling a Curse for five seconds turns it into a debuff on the target.
[Construct Golem] Create an undead golem (requires body parts).

Class Upgrade: Raid Boss

"Humps, it now says I'm a Raid Boss?" Her face wrinkled up as she waved the notification away.

"A reflection of our strength." He grinned as the crimson flame behind his helmet flickered about. "A long time coming. Most dungeons and bosses are designed for groups of three to five Players. But raids are—"

"I'm aware." She waved him away. "For ten Players? Twenty?"

"Essentially, we are a group of Raid Bosses that have escaped and are running amok."

Sally pondered this. They had already been over the power curve, and in seeing the Death Knight take on ten Players on his own, perhaps he was right. They were Monsters after all, so that designation made sense. If the Players knew, they'd run a mile before trying to combat her. Or at least gather more groups and treat her like the threat she was.

She clucked her tongue as her mind went back to the upgrades. "What did everyone else get?" Perhaps she could waste some time while she decided and not feel like the whole show was about her.

"We all agreed not to tell you." Humphrey grinned widely and crossed his plated arms.

Sally gasped. "Norah, you too?"

"Sorry, hun." She shrugged apologetically. "If it's any consolation, it is something we shouldn't need. I hope."

She groaned in response. That made her more interested in what it could be if it was a last-ditch ability. Something dangerous or desperate. Part of her knew that meant they would have to use it at some point. That's how the System liked to play these games.

"Nothing from you either, Lucy?"

The Shade shook his head, and a mute symbol appeared beside him. "It's tough because it makes me really excited, and I want to share, but I promised Humphrey, and I wouldn't want to break a promise. I'm sure you understand, and it probably won't be long before I get to use it, as it's a . . ." He held up his hands over his misty face as the Death Knight glared at him.

"Well, that's fine." She narrowed her eyes back at her options. Interesting ones once more. The golem one would have been nice if she had picked up that body-part skill back in the Wastelands, but as it stood, she only really had skulls. Enough to cast *[Mortis Bomb]* forever, but she didn't want to split the stack and burn through those reserves.

The curse one would have been perfect if she had more than one curse to cast. That was a totally different playstyle than she was aiming for. Focusing for five seconds sounded terrible enough. There would be plenty of times she'd get interrupted before that and she'd get frustrated trying to apply the debuff instead of moving on to other things.

Keeping her zombies up for longer, though . . . she was growing into the horde-leader role, and it did say *allies* too. That meant everyone. Aura stacking won out in the end. Keeping her pals up and alive meant she'd be able to grow bigger hordes with less effort.

[Hunger for Flesh]

"Alright, I picked, and I'm not telling you all either." She stuck her tongue out.

"Back to fighting, then?" Humphrey looked out at the Monsters that had respawned behind them. It was getting into evening now. They wouldn't be able to get through a whole run through to the boss again before dark.

"Yeah." She followed his gaze and wrinkled her nose up. "Let's kill our way out of this area and find a place to camp for the night."

"As you wish."

She gave her staff a twirl. It would take some getting used to, but both ends were pretty pointy now—so she shouldn't have any issue fighting with it.

She just had to remember not to put the dagger end into anything she didn't mean to.

"Oh, first things first." The Death Knight stopped as Norah began taking his crimson cloak off.

Sally watched them with a raised eyebrow, as the Mummy then moved over to her and wrapped the bright red cloth around her. "Are you sure, Humps?" A hood folded back as the rest circled around her like robes.

"I feel rather exposed without it. The color clash was nice." He shuffled and cleared his throat. "But I think it suits you well now." Norah stood beside him and wrapped her arm around his.

She took her belt off and put it around the outside of the robe so she could access her skulls—even though the staff could summon them from her Inventory—it just suited the look. A wide smile crossed her face as she gave them a little spin. "Thanks, mummy and big pops. You're the best."

"Don't call me that." He deflated. "But, you're welcome."

It had been quite the day. Sally beamed as she turned to the roving Monsters. The only thing that could make it better now would be—

The flash of blue light near them revealed the suited vampire, and he hopped down from the rocks he appeared on with his hands in his pockets. "Hey, all."

"Theo!" Sally waved him over, despite being right there.

"Wow, I must have been gone longer than I thought. You look great." He grinned and exposed his fangs.

"Productive outing?" Humphrey asked, narrowing his eye sockets.

Theo tilted his head back to look at the Death Knight. "I sure hope so." His eyes flicked back to their surroundings, and he clucked his tongue. "We fighting these lizard things?"

"Just killed the boss." Sally nodded. "Killing our way back to somewhere safe to camp."

"Somewhere safe . . ." Theo clucked his tongue and turned around. "Where does the boss spawn, in that convenient circular area?"

She followed his gaze and nodded.

"Does anything spawn right here? There's like a small prep area for Parties to get ready to fight them, yeah?" The vampire licked his lips and looked at the grouping of rocks they were standing among.

"That is correct," Humphrey said.

"Camp right here then." Theo shrugged and gave the zombie a smile. "I need a bit of exercise. It'll be like the hell portal, except less stressful for you guys."

Sally raised an eyebrow and looked at the others. It didn't seem fair to let Theo have all the fun, but then again, this was his type of thing. If they could get to sleep while he was doing his thing, then that would be experience and potential levels.

They seemed conflicted, but ultimately gave her the nod. "Alright, sounds good, pup. But any sign of trouble, or if you make it too noisy, then we'll go camp elsewhere."

"Very fair." He gave her a bow. "I'll leave you to set up while I begin."

[Endless Sleep]

She put her zombies away as the vampire darted away. Wouldn't be good if the wandering dead caught aggression from the boss or any of the Elites. As she watched Theo appear above a Monster and blaze crimson lines through it, she tapped her fingers on her staff. It slowly sunk into the ground. "I suppose this is probably one of the safest places we could be, comparatively."

Norah nodded. "Theo will watch over us, and the Monsters would stop people from approaching us directly."

Sally chose to ignore the fact that the vampire had simply stated he would solo a bunch of the Monsters through the darkness of night. It wasn't that they had really struggled, but they had acted as a team. With the light of the day waning, she put down a *[Campfire]* and rolled out her bedroll.

Lucius was asleep as soon as his head hit the floor. Humphrey and Norah were a little way off and murmured to each other for a while before they were quiet. Sally pulled her cloak around herself and deflated.

"Hey."

She looked over her shoulder to see the vampire sitting on one of the rocks. With a smile, she got up and hopped up beside him. Looking out at the open ground illuminated by moonlight, she rested her head on his shoulder.

"Tell me something new, Theo."

"You first."

"We made a Player friend today. Lucius cured her of her anger against Uniques and the System." She kicked her feet back and forth.

"Huh? Really? That's pretty interesting." Theo tilted his head to rest against hers.

"Yeah. Actually made me consider Chuck's vision of the future more. Oh, I asked her about babies too."

"Hmm?"

"I told her we either didn't have genitals or they didn't work, so I asked her if Players can make babies."

Theo was silent for a moment. "Oh."

"Short answer, no."

"State-mandated infertility?"

Sally grimaced. "Sounds a lot more dystopian when put that way, huh? Your turn."

He moved his head away to look down at her. "I met one of your old friends, actually."

"Really?" She looked up at his crimson eyes and raised an eyebrow. "Which one? Werewolf boy?"

"Lana."

"No way? How is she doing?" She smiled.

Theo shuffled awkwardly and looked out toward the horizon. "Well. You want the full truth or just the sugarcoated bit?"

"All of it."

"The original Lana was killed after Ruben's influence over the Wastes was ended. It made a real mess of the tunnels she was in. Most of her clones survived and would eventually come to blame us for that . . . you especially." He paused to gauge her reaction before continuing. "Some started to delude themselves into thinking they were the original, but the dissonance caused them to hate the System."

"*They were Last Word?*" she hissed, so as not to wake the others.

"Yeah. Got themselves corrupted because they didn't care for their humanity. I met one who didn't turn, and she gave me the antidote for the poison."

"Wow. That's a lot to take in. So . . . you're not going to die tomorrow?" She grinned up at him.

He nodded slowly. "I no longer have the poison."

"Vague answer, but I'll accept it." She wrapped an arm around him and gave him a squeeze. "You coming to sleep soon?" A yawn escaped her mouth just thinking about it.

"Not quite yet." He worked his jaw and then pressed his STAR for something. "Sally . . ."

"Yeah?"

"I know you and Humphrey are worried that one day I'll be too powerful or lose control . . . so I want you to have this." From his Inventory, he withdrew a slim, rectangular box of polished wood. A metal clasp kept it closed, but there were no other markings or details on it.

"What's this . . . a special stake or something?" She grimaced and pulled a face at him.

"Just . . . you'll know when you need it. No opening it before then, okay?" He smiled, revealing his fangs.

"Melodramatic ass," she said and sighed. "Fine. But if there comes a day where I have to kill you off, then we've already lost."

He stood up and gave her a kiss atop her head. "Sleep well, my queen."

"Dweeb," she muttered under her breath, a smile across her face as she hopped down to go back to her bedroll.

Not a bad day, overall.

CHAPTER NINETEEN

Vacancy Filled

With a yawn, Sally rolled out of her bedroll and slid down the rock she had been on, her face squishing against the dry stone of the ground. "Blurf," she muttered.

"Good morning," Humphrey said with a grin as she stood up.

She adjusted her hood and looked around. Norah was sitting up against a rock reading a book, and Lucius was perched atop the tallest jutting peak of their little campground. As she stretched out, she turned to see what the Shade was looking at. A blaze of pink energy darted between several of the large lizard Monsters.

"Did that punk not sleep last night?" She scowled at the movement and crossed her arms.

"No." The Death Knight stepped over to stand beside her. "Just killing all night, I assume. I tried waving, but he didn't heed my call."

Sally looked at her STAR, which looked normal. "Either he has been slacking, or we will need to move from the area to get all the experience."

"*Yes*." Humphrey nodded. "The latter seems most likely."

"Easy enough then." She waved at the blur of vampire. "Theo!"

He stopped in place, the beast he was standing on slowly slumping over. Hands in his pockets, he hopped down and began to stroll over.

Sally tapped her foot on the ground. "Why did you not sleep, fangs?"

Theo shrugged as he got closer. "I can nap while you travel, if that's okay with Humphrey. The leveling seemed more important."

The Death Knight narrowed his eye sockets. "Isn't your coffin now made out of metal?"

With a smile, the vampire withdrew a small cube from his pocket and threw it into an empty space. It immediately expanded out to a metallic rectangle, which caught the morning light. "If you're not strong enough, it's fine."

Crimson flame flickered higher behind the Death Knight's helmet. "I'm sure I will manage."

Theo gave them all a bow. "Until we next meet, then." As the lid popped to the side, he hopped in, falling asleep as soon as his head hit the pillow. The metal cover slid back over him.

With a sigh, Humphrey stepped over and lifted the coffin onto his back, with some assistance from Norah to get it secured in place.

Sally narrowed her eyes out to the horizon. "You'd think the System would consider us out of combat since pup is asleep, but he at least left us a clear path back into the jungle."

"Best hop to it!" Lucius jumped down from the rock and almost tripped as he landed. "Can't wait to see what we get next and don't tell each other."

She rolled her eyes. Not that she could complain about some easy levels. The System obviously wasn't expecting one person to solo these Elites all through the night—plus they were under-leveled, so it probably counted for more. The four of them began walking over the rocky terrain through the gap in the Monster packs.

As tempting as it was to beat up and eat some more of the lizards on the way out, she was tired of them already. Better to get their bearings and see where to head to next after their anticipated level up. It looked as though Theo had killed the boss at least once, and she wondered if he got any good loot from it. Words for later.

Eventually, the group made it to the edge of the rocky area and back under the canopy of dense tropical foliage. Sally's STAR illuminated a golden hue, and she sucked at her teeth. "Two levels! Theo really treated us, huh?"

> **Pick One**
> [Improved Escape Fate] Increased distance by 5ft.
> [Improved Eager Stomach] Eat Brains threshold is reduced further.
> [Improved Share Burden] Damage absorbed is reduced by 20%.

Some actual numbers for some of that too. The System really tried a little harder for this one. Although the damage absorption was quite a high amount, if the zombies were taking the hit anyway, then she didn't care too much if they popped in the process. A little coldhearted maybe, but she was dead so . . .

[Escape Fate] didn't really need to go much further. That did enough already. Eating brains a little more soon—that seemed almost unfair. Then again, she was probably the highest-level zombie in the world, and the System had no idea what to do with her and the skill progression. Having an instant-kill mechanic

seemed improper when she was so prolific and didn't have a lot of the downsides a zombie was supposed to have.

Improved Eager Stomach

Pick One
[Ignore Pain] Temporary shield equal to 20% Max HP.
[Strength in Numbers] Aura. Undead allies gain +1% Stats per nearby undead ally.
[Rave Review] When an undead minion kills a target, nearby undead allies gain STR and Speed boost.

The STAR faded to a normal silver color—no third level, but Theo had really excelled. Come to think of it, if they were Level Twenty-two now, then he would be at least the same and have his Level Thirty ultimate already. She narrowed her eyes at the metal case containing the vampire, wondering what it could be. Something edgy and overpowered, no doubt.

"Hey, Lucy." She turned her head back, avoiding looking at more skill choices. "I can have another bodyguard if you ever felt up to it. No pressure."

The Shade rubbed his misty chin, crimson eyes narrowed. "Let me think on it, and I'll let you know." Ellipses appeared beside him as he did so.

It would be unfair to expect him to join just because they were in a Party and everyone else had. But there were certainly a lot of benefits to becoming one. Perhaps there was even a way to opt out of being a bodyguard, but the others—even Edward—had never done so. Whatever his decision, it was fine. She might be able to find a different Unique . . . or even eye-patch Archie! She deflated and returned to the skill choice.

Something to keep herself alive, a big boost for when she had a large horde, or a temporary boost that was reliant on her pals killing things. She noted that the last one said "minions" and not just Undead allies . . . otherwise Theo would pout if she didn't pick it. *[Ignore Pain]* sounded like a lot of personal protection, but when was the last time she almost died? Died again?

[Rave Review] would be better if her zombies scaled better but would pair well with her ultimate, *[Quick Death]*. Nothing quite like a domino effect. Still . . . *[Strength in Numbers]* was another aura that was constant. Even with just the *Outsiders* that was a +5% buff to all stats, and summoning any zombies would increase that. With *[Endless Dead]* at full capacity, that would make them +55% boosted. She salivated thinking about a bigger horde—or even *[Zombie Apocalypse]* if the System allowed it.

[Strength in Numbers]

Something to make her more of a caster would have been nice, now that she had the whole staff and cloak/robe thing going on. Still, that just made appearing among the melee and eating people's brains all the more fun when they didn't expect it.

"I'm all done picking, and you're welcome." She gave them a bow.

"A new aura?" Humphrey asked, raising an eyebrow to Norah.

Sally wagged her finger. "I'm not telling."

"Oh." The Death Knight nodded in return. "I just felt several percentage points stronger is all."

She deflated. They needed to decide what they were going to do for the rest of the day. It was hard to think of anything that was more efficient than the Elites . . . unless there was another area with higher level Elites, of course. Sally rubbed her hair in thought.

"Unfortunately, I do not know the area very well," Humphrey said as he watched her think. "But generally, if we start killing toward the fourth area border, we will run into tougher mobs."

"Seems inefficient," she said and shrugged. "But we're ahead of the expected curve and things usually pick up as we go."

Lucius gave a thumbs-up, accompanied by a similar emoji beside his head. "Worst case, we can always call on one of our friends."

"Good point," Sally said with a nod. She spun up her STAR to open her chats.

> Sally: hey Rachel
> Sally: just in case you didn't hear, we joined Blue
> Sally: Dent is pretty persuasive
> Rachel: Glad to hear it!
> Rachel: : I hope to fight alongside you in the future.

Some brains could avoid her stomach, after all. Well, just because she was greedy enough to want to eat everyone, didn't mean she should. Eventually she would run out of Players, so that was a long-term problem. She pulled her hood over her head to shadow her face. How dire would that be? To be without any proper brains at all?

[Endless Dead] brought back all her zombies from the previous day, the large lizard zombies crashing through the vegetation and trees, unused to the busy terrain and uncaring how they got through it. They got the whiff of the pack of Monsters ahead and tramped through the area, destroying plant matter and the surprised creatures alike.

"Perhaps the System should have more limits on what you can zombify," Humphrey said with a wince.

"Don't give me that," Sally wagged a finger at him as she snarled. "Remember, I never got my zombie dragon—so allow me everything else I want *forever*."

A sweat drop appeared beside Lucius.

She pouted back at the terrain being mulched. If she had a dragon, she could fly about and do stuff like . . . probably fall off it mid-flight doing something goofy and breaking her head on the ground when she met it. There must be other dragons in the world . . . she would just need to pry the information out of someone and then it would be as good as done.

"If I ate Edward's brains until he died for real, would he come back as a zombie that could respawn too?" She tilted her head in thinking out in the open, rather than expecting an actual answer.

Humphrey shrugged. "Remember original Chuck?"

She shuddered. "I almost forgot. Do you think we should tell him, eventually?"

"What's this about Chuck?" Norah leaned in, keen to hear the unspoken knowledge.

Sally sucked her teeth. "Ah. I'm not sure I should say—but okay, you have to promise to take the information to your graves, though. Figuratively, uh . . ." She glanced between each of the undead.

Norah and Lucius both nodded.

"His . . . Player soul got stuck in limbo when he was brought to this world. It was partly tied to an actual zombie, and then when that zombie died . . . his soul found a place and he was reborn as actual Chuck." She grimaced.

A question mark appeared beside the Shade's head. "None of that means much to me, but that explains why he was a good friend if he used to be a zombie too."

"He was a friend in my life before here too," Sally said and sighed. "It all feels so long ago now."

"Things have certainly changed." Norah gave her a soft smile. "For all of us, hun."

Lucius crossed his arms. "Well, if you ask me, we're on the up! I have a super good feeling about today." Stars sparkled on either side of his head.

A crack of thunder rolled across the sky, and Humphrey growled as he held his face.

"Everything okay?" Norah put her hand on his shoulder.

With a deep sigh, he lowered his hand. "The new Architect has been chosen."

They each turned to glare at the Shade, as sweat drops continued to appear beside his head.

CHAPTER TWENTY

Darkening Skies

They stood in awkward silence for a few moments as it sank in. There would be no mistaking that what Humphrey said was true or not. Out of any of them, he would know.

"What does this mean?" Sally eventually asked, her zombies now standing still and looking around aimlessly while she processed.

Humphrey rubbed the side of his metal head. "It shouldn't be an immediate process. We have potentially a couple of days before they are empowered and can make changes to the world." He stopped rubbing and deflated. "But this is all new ground, so I can't say for sure."

The metal coffin on his back popped open, and Theo stumbled out. He adjusted his suit and put his glasses back on his face as he gathered himself. "What happened? I felt something dire occur."

"New Architect has been chosen." Sally filled him in and helped him fix his collar. "Short time before potential doom."

"Good thing I'm *not* dying today then." He gave a slight grin back. "Do we have a plan yet?"

They shook their heads.

Theo held his hand up to his eyes and sighed. "Alright, I have the location of some Level Thirty Elite humanoids we can go power level on."

Humphrey furrowed his brow. "Even for us, Level Thirty Elite Monsters are . . ."

"Trust me." The vampire grinned. "We don't exactly have the time to do anything but go all out."

The Death Knight nodded.

"How'd you get that information?" Sally prodded him in the arm. "And how far away is it?"

He shared the map details. Near the southeast point of the map, quite close to the fourth area. "I asked Chuck."

She pouted back at him. "Oh, he's talking with you now?"

"Well, you hardly ever check your messages, so . . ." Theo put his hands in his pockets and turned away from her glare. "We have mounts, but just two, so—"

"Actually, I have my own transport," Humphrey said with a wide grin. "I can take Norah." He stepped to the side and held out an arm.

[Nightmare Steed]

A large skeletal horse, covered in heavy metal garb, burst into being on the ground in front of him. Crimson flame flickered from the eye sockets of the undead creature—much taller and wider than any usual horse. But then, it'd need to be, considering the rider.

Sally whistled. "I hope that lasts longer than the last one." She turned to avoid the Death Knight's glare. "Lucy, you can pick me or Theo to ride with, either shadow or normal way."

"With you would be great!" Sparkling eyes appeared beside his head. "I've never ridden a mount before."

With a snap of their fingers, the giant zombie mice appeared beside the two undead Players. Sally hopped atop hers and gave it a pet, before holding a hand down to lift the Shade up.

"Straight there," Theo said. "No stopping?"

"Stop only for red team." Sally pushed her hood back so she could see them all better. "I know that it's a distraction, but it will be worth it."

Theo and Humphrey both nodded, and then they were away as soon as Sally cast *[Endless Sleep]* to put away her zombies. Her mount jumped and dodged through the dense trees and overgrown foliage, avoiding all the packs of the Monsters living in the jungle.

"There's a path to the north, about five minutes," Theo called out to her. "We can follow that halfway there."

Sally checked her map and gave him a nod. It would be much quicker along the road rather than trying to make it through the vegetation. She saw that she had messages pending from Chuck.

> Chuck: Sorry for everything.
> Chuck: I have a bad feeling about this.
> Chuck: Hopefully Theo knows what he is doing.
> Chuck: We don't have a tele there as it is… rough

Silly goose had been running an army, practically. Now he was apologizing for things he didn't need to. She missed him, and the small glimmer of hope within her considered the new Architect might be decent and then they'd all live happily ever after. Actually, now that she thought it in her head, it sounded less likely to be the case.

> Sally: no worries bud
> Sally: hold the fort, we'll meet soon okay?
> Sally: if it's bad, we stand together.
> Chuck: If it's bad, we fall together.

She smiled and closed it down. Poetic, although he might have been full of pessimism when saying it, rather than it being the motivational line she had read it as. They were all oddities in the System. It was a wonder they had made it this far. Still, that didn't mean she would go quietly into the infinite void.

"This is actually quite nauseating." Lucius groaned from behind her.

"Just hold tight, bud." She grinned as the warm air whipped through her tied-up hair. "And try not to vomit on the new cloak." Being covered in dried blood was one thing, but vomit would be beyond the pale. Not that the Shade ever ate anything . . .

The three mounts burst out from the greenery and landed on the illuminated road. Shuffling to the right, they began to bound down the clear path.

Lucius leaned against the zombie's back. "This is better, slightly."

"How is it you don't get motion sick as a shadow, but a little ride atop a giant zombie mouse has you greener than . . . uh, the jungle?"

"Oh, I should try that." He vanished and his crimson eyes appeared from her shadow.

She raised an eyebrow behind her, and her shadow gave a thumbs-up.

Riding time was a nice break to really process things. While the forest was mostly them pushing against the System, and the Wastes was ousting a problem figure ruining the area, the Architect coming back into being was something different.

They were potentially at a disadvantage and had no control over the when, where, or what. All they could do was get stronger and hope that if there were any problems with the new policies of the Architect, then they could just overpower them like usual. Of course, they could just as easily be erased from existence for being outside the norm. Then all of this would be pointless . . . but they had to try, at least.

Humphrey was vague on what actual powers a new Architect would have. A few days for them to settle into the role, but after that, what could they do? Some of the System was set in place, she was sure he had said at some point, so there were limits . . . but that's as far as his Observer knowledge could take the conversation. The parts of Archie within him surely knew more, but without all five, there were gaps.

If the Death Knight absorbed all five of the cats, would that make him the Architect? Probably not if there was already one assigned . . . but then that added the question of would the new god accept that there were little shards of the previous owner walking around? Probably not if it was the group that killed the first Architect. How could they keep Archie safe from an entity so powerful?

She missed the days where eating a bully's brain was the toughest challenge they had to face. Even taking Sanctuary from the System-created would be preferable to having to deal with the hand over between the murdered god and potential assailant.

"You alright?" Theo rode his mouse beside hers and raised an eyebrow.

"Long distance traveling lets my brain do too much thinking." She pouted at him. "That usually makes me sad."

"When we get to our destination, I might have something that'll cheer you up." He grinned, revealing his fangs.

Sally considered it was probably unlikely he had even more abs than currently. The second option of Player brains seemed like wishful thinking too. Third choice was potentially new items looted during his killing spree last night.

"I look forward to it," she said with a grin. As soon as he rode ahead a little, her smile faded, and she deflated. Not even a cool new legendary item could rouse her spirits. She'd still accept it, though.

"Contact!" The vampire took her from her thoughts, and she looked up ahead in the road.

Three figures stood just to the side, possibly arguing about something, before the approaching undead Party caught their attention.

Red tabards.

They went to run, but the *Outsiders* were too fast. A twelve-foot-tall pyramid burst up in front of them as they tried to escape into the jungle, pushing them back to the road. One of them, an archer, recovered and had an arrow burning with power just as Theo appeared behind them, sinking his fangs in. Sally sent a flaming skull out from her staff toward them, as bandages wrapped around the third.

Theo turned from his victim to stab the one struck by the *[Mortis Bomb]*, grabbing the body and throwing it up into the air as the Party thundered past. Sally leaped up from her seat. *[Eat Brains]*.

Norah threw her captive into the air toward them, as the vampire appeared in the air, striking them through the back before they fell to Sally, who ate their brains as well. Theo vanished again and appeared back in the saddle of his mount.

The last figure stood shocked and bleeding profusely from the neck as the raised zombies overpowered them.

"Two out of three isn't bad," Sally said as she wiped her mouth. It would just take three days for those zombies to catch up to her, if they didn't die before that. Nothing quite like a bit of cavalry to come save the day at the last minute, although they'd probably be stealing Theo's thunder at that point.

Perhaps she should ask him what his second ultimate was. Would he even tell her? Probably not. She glared at his back as he rode in front of her. She could understand the spectacle of leaving these things to mystery until they could come in and save the day, but it was also too convenient. They could have anything until the time came up where they exactly needed something. She knew Norah had something like that, and she was just counting the days until they found out what that was.

She yawned. The rest of the trip might be somewhat boring unless they occasionally ran across groups of the enemy faction. Then again, most were unprepared for the Party at full force. Little could be. It brought her brief comfort that together they were stronger than most things. Like a roving natural disaster, they had surpassed the best Players. Not only that, but they had been working to make the System a better place—few could stake a similar claim.

In fact, she had lived a good unlife. Carved her own place out among the ruins of a bugged System and gathered a tight-knit group of found family. A weird sense of love and companionship that went against her nature but felt right. Worries washed away, as she felt rather content with what she had achieved. Optimistic about the future.

She looked up at the sky, which was darkening further. The rumble of thunder shook the distance. Getting closer.

It was just a shame the System didn't share her positive views.

CHAPTER TWENTY-ONE

Ride or Die

The rest of the journey was just about what she expected. Boring. She was tired of the movement of the mount and was thankful for the brief handful of minutes that they took a break to give the creatures some of her *[Mount Feed]*. No other Players on the road—or really anything else of interest. At a certain point, they split from the main road to head south.

"About ten more minutes," Theo called out.

Sally brought up her map and stared at the little point denoting her position slowly move down the road. Almost as interesting as looking out at the same handful of trees and bushes they had passed a billion times. There had been some points of interest. Buildings farther into the jungle itself. Way back to the west, there had been a large tower that she wanted to investigate, when possible.

If they weren't in such a rush, it would have been a fun little jaunt—for sure. It was probably some kind of dungeon. Not that she was particularly fond of almost dying in dungeons, but something had to threaten her existence. She winced at putting that thought out into the world. Dangerous thoughts to be having when you had a potentially malicious demigod stalking the world soon enough. And she didn't mean Theo.

Not that she could ever consider using the magic stake, or whatever he had given her, against him. Even if he turned and became something destructive and uncontrollable. Did that make her weak? She exhaled through her nose. He had gotten wild a handful of times, and it had been easy enough to bring him back. Mostly, she thought Humphrey was just overindulging on melodrama to think the vampire could become a bad egg. She had even considered opening it up to see what she was dealing with . . . but he had trusted her not to.

She wasn't sure how she'd handle losing any of them, truth be told. They had gotten away pretty lightly in terms of punishment. Archie had been the closest to a loss, but that was willingly, and now they had another Archie . . . which seemed worse to put it that way when she thought about it. This was why she tried not to think too hard. Mania had painted several thick layers over the potential panic of her human side dealing with the horrors of the world. Mostly the violence she committed.

With another yawn, she stretched out her back and then adjusted her cloak. Imagine if the System had worked and people went back to their normal world when they died here. Like an actual video game. To be fair, she only had Humphrey's word that it didn't work like that—and the supposed memories of the dead Architect through the cat. What if she was going through all this and he had been wrong? She could have been brained by the Cleric in the diner and then woke up back in her ordinary job like nothing had happened.

After over a year now, it didn't really matter. This was her new life, and she would deal with the after when it came to be. Hopefully, it would just be erasure and the void, and she wouldn't have to consider what she had done, or lost, or could have done differently. Not that she was desperate for closure . . . she did enjoy her life, even with the conflict and macabre nature of her broken class.

"Are we there yet?" she whined at the vampire, tired of being alone with her thoughts for so long.

Humphrey shook his head from atop his giant steed. "You know you can just check yourself."

Norah gave him a squeeze from where she was sitting behind him. "Sometimes a girl just wants to be heard, not necessarily have a solution."

The Death Knight opened and closed his skeletal mouth before deflating. "I, too, long for the solid ground beneath my feet."

Sally grinned at the Mummy, before turning her head back to her shadow. "You good back there, Lucius?" She had to check he was still there sometimes. Although he seemed content enough to stay shadowed indefinitely, if she couldn't see his crimson eyes, then she would briefly panic that he had been left behind.

He popped out of his form and sat behind her, grabbing onto her cloak so he didn't immediately fly off the back of the bounding rodent. "Never been better." No emoji appeared beside this statement.

"Thinking of ways we can kill the Architect?" She grinned and turned back to looking ahead. Winding him up was perhaps unfair, but it should be on all their minds as a possibility. Mostly, she wondered what the Architect's brains would taste like—if they had any. Would eating them turn her into the Architect? Part of her had wanted that at one point . . . but now? Responsibility didn't sit well with her mania, and she'd only end up turning things into a mix of paradise and a factory funneling Player brains straight into her maw.

"No. I'm not sure I'm capable of that, even with my . . ." the Shade paused. "With the secret skills I'm definitely not telling you about."

As much as she rolled her eyes, Sally also grinned. Bunch of misfits, primed and ready to fail upward. Or die trying. *Die again.*

"We're here," Theo called from the front, popping off his mount as it vanished. He hit the ground and slid across the smooth dirt, hands in his pockets, before friction won over and he came to a stop.

"Not trying that again," Sally murmured to herself. She slowed her mouse and gave it a pet before it vanished away, Lucius and herself landing on the floor.

Humphrey's horse whinnied and shuffled to a stop, and he helped Norah down before dismounting himself. He gave the steed a pat on the side, and it vanished with a pop of dark smoke.

"Did you give it a suitable edgy name?" Sally asked, raising her eyebrow and smiling.

The Death Knight deflated. "No . . . Norah named it."

"I think *Peaches* is a perfectly good name." The Mummy grinned and gave Sally a wink.

"Very fitting, I agree." She nodded in return. Allowing the plated figure to simmer in that, she turned to walk over to Theo, where he had stopped to peer off down into the scenery to the left.

"Hmm," he said, then turned to greet her. "This will be tough."

Sally narrowed her eyes to see a sparse woodland. The trees weren't exactly tropical and resembled part of the woodland from the starting area. Dry ground, reddish trunks, and a high canopy. In the midst of all these trees and scant foliage were people.

System-created, and possibly human. They looked similar to the barbarians from the Wastes but more rugged. Thicker muscles, more armor, and their weapons glowed a dim green color.

"Looks . . . bad," she eventually said. "Level Thirty Elites . . . I'm not sure I could even damage them." Even having Skeleton Key at the end of her staff, it wouldn't take much for her to be overpowered in melee.

"You'd have to leech at first." Theo tilted his head to the side and looked at her. "Let me do the heavy lifting again. A couple more levels and the whole Party can join in."

Her nose wrinkled up. "Alright, tough guy. You certain you can even kill them?"

"There's nothing I can't do."

She rolled her eyes. "The less I dig into that statement, the better for both of us."

The vampire opened and closed his mouth before grimacing. He turned as the rest of the Party moved over after having murmured about the horse's name enough.

Humphrey looked out at the enemies and then back to Theo. "Are you certain about this?"

"Don't feign worry on my account." The vampire gave him a wink. "Just be ready to carry my coffin again soon."

The Death Knight narrowed his eyes, flame licking at the back of his helmet, but just nodded in return.

Theo stood at the edge of the area and flexed his fingers. Limbered up his shoulders and then tilted his neck from side to side. The pitch-black punch-blades appeared in his hands, and he hopped on the spot to get some energy built up.

Sally narrowed her eyes as she watched him burn time. Surely he didn't need to make such a show of it?

[Lord of Crimson]

His suit burst away to be replaced by a set of thick leather armor, bright red in color and buzzing with energy. The full helmet turned toward them, and he nodded. Around him, the ground dented and a wave of air buffeted the area before he flexed and then burst away.

A crimson trail was left behind him as he zipped straight into the first enemy like a magnet. *[Sanguine Weapon]* appeared behind him, and he stabbed out multiple times as the pink energy of *[Novice Strike]* blurred around the enemy.

As soon as the first Monster fell, *[Blood Shift]* took him over to the next one and the process repeated.

"Impressive, as always." Humphrey relented with a shrug. "I would guess he is already Level Twenty-five since he has the experience bonus, and that means has the number of skills a Level Thirty-five has."

Norah whistled. "Plus his stats . . . ?"

"You can assume that they are maxed." The Death Knight shook his head. "It is more convoluted than that, but it is safe to say if anyone could win a fight, it would be Theo."

Sally wrinkled up her face. Not because she thought herself capable enough, but because of what she was reading between the lines. "Are you saying we'll need Theo to kill the Architect?"

Humphrey tilted his head and regarded her with his impassive empty eye sockets. "No. It may not even come to that. But if it does, it will be a great boon to have the vampire on our side."

She shivered. There was something she didn't like about this conversation. The clouds overhead had darkened, although most of the daylight still made it through—and there was no hint of precipitation to cool her mood off. It was as if it was just a malaise that hung over the world, rather than actual clouds.

There was apprehension in her bones, and she hoped to get stuck into fighting these Monsters as soon as possible so she could push any worry out of her mind. Half-focused on the blur of red and pink darting around ahead of her, she brought up the STAR chat.

> Sally: hey, Lana?
>
> Your message could not be delivered.

Although she was half hoping it would go to one of the living clones, that made enough sense.

"Let's try pulling one." She sighed and looked at the group. "I need some violence in the present to distract me from . . ."

"Violence from the past," Humphrey said with a nod.

"Potential violence in the future," the Shade added, shivering as a panicked emoji appeared.

She gave them a glum smile as the skull on her staff burst into green flame.

"Yeah," she said.

CHAPTER TWENTY-TWO

The Widest Smile

Humphrey staggered backward as the enemy charged into him. A bandage broke off from the leg of the assailant, and the armored barbarian smashed through the head of a zombie.

"They're a little overtuned, huh?" Sally pouted and spun her staff.

Norah burst a small pyramid up from the ground, pushing the attacker toward the slashing blade of the Death Knight. A wide gash coursed through thick leather and into flesh, before a shadowed version of the greatsword followed the movement and split through their organs.

"So are we, hun." The Mummy smiled and retrieved her spent bandages like homing snakes.

Sally watched the figure slump over on the floor, guts spilling out but brain uneaten. It took all four of them to take down one of the measly human-looking barbarians. Usually they'd *mow* through Monsters like these. Eight levels higher and Elite, though. Humphrey had mentioned that Elite upped the effective level by a handful or something, but that was some time ago, and now that she thought about it, she might be making that up.

She turned to the side to watch the blur of the vampire streak through a handful of the enemy. They weren't all dying in one hit, but Theo would quickly [Blood Shift] back over to any that he needed to finish off. As impressive as it was, she didn't want to just be a passive observer while he got them all experience. She needed to do something.

Plus, the goof had said he had something special for her, and then immediately forgotten as he went off to kill things. It better be something worthy of the wait.

"Perhaps we are going about this all wrong?" She tapped a finger on the edge of her staff. They *were* overtuned and shouldn't be on the back foot just because the Monster had more health or defense.

"I apologize." Humphrey turned his head back to look at her. "I am not feeling my best."

"It's not you." Sally waved her hand and frowned at him. "But are you okay?"

"*Yes*. I am sure it is just the pressure of the current situation." The Death Knight turned back to looking out at the bandits.

More likely, it was a sign of something bad about to happen. He never really got ill or was off his game unless something terrible was afoot. It was enough to make her slightly worried. The new Architect was an unknown, and it had everyone in the know on edge.

"Lucius, you should shadow me," she said as she rubbed at her chin. The Shade popped down into her shadow. "My dagger can pierce all defenses, near enough. If I can stab them in the soft parts, we might be able to kill them off quicker."

"You're not really built for taking damage," Humphrey interjected, before she waved him off.

"I best be careful then, huh?" With a grin, she spun around her staff to hold like a spear. Her shadow did the same, pointing the sharp end forward.

[Summon Zombies]

Four undead rose up out of the ground in front of her. Her eyes narrowed in thought. With a twirl, she turned behind them and used *[Endless Dead]* along with the other two charges of *[Summon Zombies]* to create a small army. They'd die quickly to these Monsters, but that's not why they were here.

"Stay put!" she commanded them, leaving just the four between her and the roving humanoid targets. With a grin, she turned back to the Death Knight. "*That* feel like a bit more of a percentage increase?"

[Strength in Numbers] raised all of their stats, which should make killing off the Elites a little easier. More the fool her for not thinking of that before, but she had been distracted by the whole end of the world thing.

"Norah, if you could try to restrain their arms? I'm going to stab them in the face."

"Sure, hun." The Mummy stepped back a little farther to get a better view of the small group.

"What would you like me to do?" Humphrey asked, resting his sword across the back of his shoulders.

"Pull my ass out of the fire when I mess this up," Sally said with a grin. "I'll only have a few jabs before they mush my zombies, and I don't intend to follow them." She spun the staff around and the skull blazed a bright green.

With a twist, she flung it out at the next bandit. Another muscled man in thick hides and coarse fur armor. It struck him, and the fire burned a dark mark across his chest. Axe glowing green, he cleaved through two of the emerging zombies and ran toward Sally to leave the last one in the dust.

Bandages shot out and wrapped around his arms, slowing his attacks but not restricting them. The axe cleaved halfway through one of the zombies protecting Sally but couldn't make it all the way through.

She jumped forward, jabbing out with the merged Skeleton Key. The Monster attempted to dodge to the side but was caught by the shadowed version of her attack, piercing him straight through the middle of the head.

"Aha!" she said and beamed as the figure dropped to the floor. "Can't dodge a shadow."

"I feel like being able to instantly kill things is something we should utilize more often," the Death Knight grumbled, his skeletal face somehow deflated.

Sally rolled her eyes. "Alright, pops. Go tank them for me, and I'll stab them."

They were never much for questing or leveling the traditional way. Grinding Monsters was a means to an end, to climb over the gate that was keeping them from being more powerful. Players and Uniques were usually their biggest hurdles—but even then—working together, they'd been able to crumble through any opposition that had stood in their way so far.

With the stat-boosting zombies, and their new plan of stabbing things with Sally's broken weapon, they started to get into the swing of things. Nowhere near as fast as the vampire, but gradually they picked up the pace that could get the extra experience at little risk to themselves. Much better than sitting around and twiddling their thumbs.

[Eat Brains]. Sally wiped her mouth off and yawned. She crouched and looked at the loot on this fallen enemy while Humphrey readied to pull the next.

"Oh, shame I can't eat normal food." She stood and then frowned at the rest of the Party. "Do any of you eat normal food?" Her shadow shook his head.

"I probably could," Norah tilted her head, "but prefer not to. Humphrey doesn't eat at all."

Sally nodded. "Theo's diet is pretty restrictive, as is mine. Can't stand anything other than fresh brains. These chumps have a food item that increases health regeneration and some stats—would have been neat if we could use them."

Humphrey lowered his sword. "We could try?"

She smiled. "Sure thing, pops, be my guest." In her extended hand, she held what looked to be a rather packed sandwich.

He narrowed his eyes and took it from her slowly. Lucius popped out beside Sally, and all eyes except for the rampaging vampire's watched the Death Knight bring the foodstuff up to his skeletal maw.

Silence, except for the sounds of combat in the background, as he took a bite and began to chew. After a few awkward moments, the mashed sandwich vanished from his mouth and the Death Knight tilted his head to the side.

"I do not have a tongue, so am unable to taste the sandwich. The texture was uncomfortable. I also do not have a digestive system."

Sally grinned. "But did you get the other benefits from the task?"

Humphrey pulled a face and returned the rest of the meal back to her. "*Yes.* Although I am unsure as to whether it was worth the turmoil."

Lucius rubbed his misty chin. "I don't even have a proper body, so I can't even feign the process like pops."

The Death Knight narrowed his empty eye sockets as the red flame behind his helmet rose a little higher.

"That's fair, Lucy—I suppose there's no point filling up your boot with a half-eaten sandwich, right?" Sally wagged the food toward the Mummy. "Norah?"

"I suppose it couldn't hurt." She shrugged.

There was a pulse of energy as Theo slid over to them. Crackles of crimson lightning arced around his body as streams of blood ran down his leather armor. "Hey, what's everyone up to?"

She beamed. "We're taking turns biting this sandwich I found on the dead guy."

"Okay." The fully covered head of the vampire nodded. "Oh, I forgot to give you that gift."

Sally moved up closer to him, as he looked through his Inventory. There was an aura around him, as though he was a furnace—but it was power rather than heat. She had assumed his neat new form was similar to Humphrey's but perhaps more offense orientated.

"Here." He passed her a chain with a locket of some kind on the end.

"How sweet," she said as she held it up. It was actually a heart on the end, made from a deep red gemstone, and encircled with golden detailing. "That's thoughtful of you, pup."

"You probably saw the tower on the way over? It's a dungeon, and that's a key." He looked over to see the odd faces the Mummy was pulling in trying to get the sandwich down.

Sally rolled her eyes. "Can't just give a gal some jewelry, huh? You didn't want to use it yourself?"

"I wouldn't have the chance." He turned back to her and shrugged. "Listen, Sally, I . . . I'll get back to grinding. You should be close to the next level."

Before she could say anything further, he was off. A blur of crimson and pink as he blazed through the respawning Elites. She looked back at the group as she put the necklace around her neck.

"It would be much better if it was made from Adventurers," Norah said as she grimaced, handing back the last of the sandwich. "I just don't have the appetite for it, hun."

"That's fine." Sally placed the remnants of the snack gently back on top of the dead body, before it shifted and stood up as a zombie, splaying the entrails of the sandwich across the ground. "Let's just get back to what we are good at."

Humphrey grinned. "Failing upward and not dying?"

"You invite malady on our fair group, pops." Sally wagged a finger at him. "Go stab something and stay out of trouble."

The Death Knight deflated and turned to the next Monster in their area. Despite his visual exhaustion at being called pops, she knew that he secretly liked it. Mostly because Norah had told her as much. It was odd in the abstract, knowing Humphrey had been a floating skull and tool of the System, but now felt comfortable enough to be the head of the found family they had cobbled together.

If anything, it just went to show the depth and vibrancy of life that Uniques could live, just like any Player.

They murdered their way through another handful of System-created baddies, and then Theo slid over to them again.

"Alright, that should be a level's worth. We'll need to get up on the ledge where we dismounted to claim it."

They nodded and headed that way immediately. Theo hadn't said how long his special form could last, but if it dropped off if he was out of combat for too long, then she wanted to go accept the experience gain so he could go back out as soon as possible.

Helping each other up, they stood upon the dried mud away from the Monsters. A golden glow flooded through the STARs of the two half-Players.

"Alright, I'm heading straight back out—" Theo began, before pausing.

A deep rumbling drew their attention, and they looked up at the darkened sky.

Sally narrowed her eyes before they widened in surprise. Above them, spanning the sky, a giant skull began to form. Deep pits where the eyes should be, miles wide. A toothed grin bigger than some of the zones. It opened gradually as a crack of lightning flashed across the clouds.

"Greetings," a voice boomed out like thunder, vibrating through the floor. "I am your new Architect."

CHAPTER TWENTY-THREE

Final Observations

Sally shivered. "A big skull *is* kind of spooky."

Humphrey looked at her with a blank expression on his face. "This is just a projection, not the actual size of the Architect."

"Skull means an ex-Observer?" Theo clucked his tongue, right before his ultimate wore off and he returned to his normal clothing. "*Ah, shit.*"

The Death Knight nodded. "It is likely."

They looked back up again. Another rumble vibrated through the air as the Architect opened the giant skeletal mouth to speak once more. "I am eager to meet all of you. However, my powers are still limited. Just as a warm-up, however... it seems nobody is using the fifth area. Such a waste of resources... well, no more."

Beneath their feet, the ground shook.

"Open your map," Humphrey demanded of the zombie.

With a spin, she brought it up and zoomed out. The Death Knight came and stood behind her. They both held their breath, as there was undeniably a large gap missing where the fifth area had just been.

"Surely not." Sally furrowed her brow. "He just said he was low on power, and he deletes a huge chunk of the world? Or at least the continent we are on." She tried to zoom out further, but it stopped when the whole of their large island was fully in view.

"It means that he was truthful when he said there was nobody there. The System has a fail-safe. If there are no Players, the whole of Othea can be . . . removed." Humphrey stepped back away from her.

Theo rubbed his forehead. "So it would just be an empty sea, or the whole reality would collapse?"

Humphrey shrugged. "It is not something I have intimate knowledge of."

Lucius looked practically petrified; his crimson eyes glued to the large, looming skull. Norah just looked annoyed; her jaw clenched. They could feel the power, maybe even more than Sally and Theo could. Probably fear it more, being constructs of the System now under control of this unknown entity.

"Pragmatic," Sally eventually said with a sigh, "but doesn't exactly paint him in the best of lights. Especially with the whole skull-face thing."

The Death Knight deflated.

"Until I have a proper grip on things," the voice continued to shake the air around them, "I am disabling experience gain. So sit tight and enjoy the life you currently have."

"Ass!" Sally kicked dirt. "Also, very ominous."

Theo groaned. "Just when we were getting caught up too. But at least Chuck can change his terms?"

"Of course, I'll message him now." Sally nodded. Perhaps it made sense to put a stop to some of the System, especially if you were looking to fix it or find out where things were going wrong. Still, it didn't settle very well with her, and she wasn't too hopeful that this new Architect had only good things in mind for anyone—especially her oddball friends.

Sally: Chuck
Sally: you seeing this??
Sally: pls advise

He didn't reply immediately, so she closed it down. The level up was still pending, but she couldn't focus on it when being watched so intensely from above.

"So now what?" she asked, to a chorus of shrugs and murmurs. They did look to her for the way forward, usually. Without being able to level, what choice did they have now? A vacation? The Architect wouldn't allow something that easy for them, she was sure of it.

As if to answer her, the voice boomed out once more.

"While I am resting, I will put my errant workers back to use. There are many things wrong with this System, and their assistance is required."

With that, the skull started to fade away, to be replaced by the gloomy, overcast sky. Light rain began to fall, as if to signal their absence.

"Rude," Sally huffed. "Didn't even tell us his name." She turned to the gathered *Outsiders*. "Well, we'd best take a seat and think about what to do. Maybe head out back toward wherever Chuck is? Consolidate our allies."

Theo pinched the bridge of his nose. "I suppose that makes sense. As soon as we can level again though . . ."

"Yeah, yeah. I get it." She waved him off. "What do you think Humps? . . . Humps?"

The Death Knight was holding his face but moved his hand away at her verbal prodding. From behind his helmet, the crimson flame petered out and instead a blaze of light blue energy rose in its place. He stood tall and glared at the gathered Party.

"I am not *Humps*. I am Observer unit HM-3.3." His empty eyes went between each of them. "You are all out of sorts. Submit for correction or suffer the consequences." Bright blue flame ran down the length of his greatsword.

"This is no time for jokes," Sally said, narrowing her eyes at him. He wasn't usually this good of an actor, though.

Norah shook her head. "He's been reclaimed by the Architect. That's not really him anymore."

"We will not stand and be corrected." Theo stepped forward in front of the rest of them. "Leave us be until you return to your senses."

"Oh?" The flame at the back of Humphrey's helmet burned higher. "Are you so eager to jump onto the blade of judgment and perish?"

The vampire grinned, exposing his fangs. "Nah, I'd win."

"We shouldn't be fighting," Sally interrupted. "If you can't shrug off the control, then we will leave and you can go do your own thing." She crossed her arms and stared the Death Knight down.

"Your presence is untenable under the new order of things. Any bug or error must be corrected." He raised his sword in a ready position.

Theo shook his head. "Can you even see yourself? You're just as big of an oddball as the rest of us."

"*Yes*. My time of penance will come eventually, but for now, I must deal with things, as is my directive."

Lucius had just been quiet, sweat drops and panicked faces appearing beside him all the while. There was a lot of tension in the Party, as the now Observer-again Death Knight didn't seem to be able to buck off the controlling influence of the Architect.

Sally seethed through clenched teeth. "Then I guess we'll have to take you down a notch and knock some sense into you."

"No," Humphrey said with a cold grin.

[Compelled Duel]

The vampire tutted. "You know my stats are too high to . . ." His brow furrowed. "*Oh*, it did work."

"Ass, Humphrey!" The zombie threw her hands up in the air. Her plan was to wail on him until Norah could tie him up, using Theo's speed to block his attacks and tire him out.

"It seemed pertinent to remove the higher threat first," the response came.

Theo grinned. "I knew it would come down to this eventually, old man. Unstoppable attack power against the unmovable defensive abilities."

Humphrey didn't reply. Instead, he launched himself forward to swing out with the greatsword—a blazing trail of light blue following it. Only, Theo was no longer there.

He had shifted behind the Death Knight and slashed out with his sword, sparks flying from the struck metal armor but doing no damage.

"Pitiful," Humphrey growled as he spun on his heel to swipe backward.

Theo blocked the strike and slid across the ground by a dozen feet, leaving small trails through the dirt. "Well, I don't want to *kill* you. I have to use kid gloves."

"I hold no such reservation." The plated figure launched forward, his sword blazing with *[Grave Strike]*.

Norah nudged Sally, as both pairs of their eyes couldn't move from the battle. "If you kick Humphrey from the Party, he won't get all our aura benefits."

"You're right . . ." She chewed on her tongue. "Seems unfair when it's a duel, but we have a clear favorite to win, unfortunately."

Humphrey has been kicked from the Party

The greatsword struck the empty ground, blowing a cloud of mud into the nearby vicinity. Skeletons rose up around him as he used *[Lord of the Damned]*, before *[Adrenaline]* and *[Dead King's Court]* illuminated his dark armor with magical energy.

Theo hopped backward a few steps before holding his empty hand out. A ball of crimson energy grew within his palm, then he cast it out toward the Death Knight. The skeletons took the brunt of the attack, which burst into an explosion of bright white electricity that arced between them. Even as they fell, Humphrey jumped through the resulting cloud of power and swung down at the vampire.

Stepping to the side to avoid the greatsword, Theo received the plated boot follow-up to the thigh, knocking him back.

[Kneel]

The vampire stopped and dropped down; head hung low.

"Be at peace, miserable bug." Humphrey seethed as he swung his sword around.

[Dread Counter]

Theo stopped the attack and leaped forward with his sword crackling with critical energy.

[Impenetrable Defense]

Sally sighed and rubbed her eyes. "We might be here for a while. It would be less stressful if we knew what abilities they had chosen. Theo must have at least a handful I haven't seen."

Lucius shuffled awkwardly. "With only one of them trying to kill the other it's not an easy fight."

She nodded slowly in response. "Theo is testing the waters to see what he can get away with. Enough to debilitate but not destroy."

The vampire had become a blur as he slashed out at the Death Knight, the latter's defensive shield now gone. They went back to trading blows. The sky turned pitch black, and a crimson moon rose up behind Theo as he switched to his punch-blades. *[Sanguine Weapon]* went up to add a third striking weapon to his attacks.

[Expert Duelist]

Theo slid backward as his strike was blocked and the greatsword swung out at him, cutting through his suit jacket but not his skin.

"Evasive worm, you have not damaged me yet," the Death Knight growled.

The vampire grinned, the red moonlight reflecting on his fangs. "I am also unharmed. You talk too much for how little you can do. Now you can parry every block until I damage you, correct?"

"Correct." Humphrey flourished his blade around into a defensive stance.

Theo rolled out his shoulders. "Interesting." A pulse of energy washed over him, and he now had a blurred afterimage as he moved.

Flashes of light bloomed from where the Death Knight, illuminated in light blue, blocked the attacks and swung out immediately with his sword against the blur of red that was the vampire. They clashed another handful of times before the vampire slid away from the battle, rubbing the blood from the side of his mouth.

His suit was even more shredded now, some crimson soaking through his shirt. His moon skill remained, however, which meant he wasn't particularly damaged.

"Not bad, old man. I'm starting to learn the pattern of your attacks, though."

The Death Knight shook his head. "You will need far too many attacks to dent me. I only need one good strike. You know this to be true."

Theo darted forward, crimson globules hanging in the air behind him.

[Hard Parry]

As soon as the Death Knight blocked the shot, his greatsword swung out with far greater speed and strength than usual, critical energy arcing along the blade. The vampire spun and rolled across the ground, up to his feet and now sporting a long gash running up his side.

"Something new." He grinned, wincing slightly. "An automatic critical counter . . . for *three* strikes?"

"Too smart for your own good, for all that will help you."

With a snap of his fingers, the blood spheres Theo had left around congregated in one place, swirling up to form a figure made of the sloshing liquid. The crimson homunculus dove toward the Death Knight with a faux blade, attempting to attack him from behind.

As Humphrey spun around to block the attack, Theo used *[Blood Shift]* to close the distance and try to land his own attacks. With the clang of metal and bright flash of blue, the Observer slashed through the blood-person and then spun to block and leveled the sword through the vampire.

Stumbling again, the crimson mood faded and drab light of the overcast sky once again washed over the area. Theo had a second gash up his chest but a bright smile across his face. "Worth it. Now that's out of the way . . ."

His punch-blades burned bright red, hot like the sun, before he shot forward in a split second, shifting at the last moment to attack from an unexpected angle.

Only, it was expected.

"I lied." Humphrey grinned as his skill activated one more time. With a near instantaneous flash, his greatsword deflected the intense attack and jabbed out at the vampire. There was a crunch of bones as it pierced straight through his ribcage and heart. "It was *four* attacks."

"*Theo!*" Sally yelled.

Humphrey leaned forward to stare into his pale face. "One less bug in the System."

The vampire slumped forward, sliding farther down the blade, closer to the Death Knight. With his last breath, Theo whispered something as close to the skeletal face of the Observer as he could manage, before he dropped back down the sword and collapsed onto the ground.

Party member Theo has died

CHAPTER TWENTY-FOUR

Entombed

The greatsword dropped down to the ground, as Humphrey held up his hands to look at them. "*Oh no*," he whispered. The blue flames petered out to be replaced with low crimson ones.

Sally slid across the ground, panic on her face. She cupped the head of the fallen vampire and tried to lift it. "Theo? Theo?"

"Fucking hells," Norah swore through clenched teeth. "Roughhousing always ends in tears." Her hand raised up.

[Tomb of the Eternal]

Darkness surrounded the zombie as a stone structure burst from the ground and built up around them. Theo's body raised up on a plinth, pushing her away across newly formed stone flooring. There was the dull sound of a horse's movement, muffled from the thick walls, before torches burst into flame, illuminating the chamber.

A small room, no more than fifteen feet square, where the centerpiece was the dead vampire laid out on a light gray bed of stone. A throne of similar design sat raised slightly against the back wall across from Sally, where the Mummy went and sat, sighing deeply.

Sally looked around at the pointed ceiling and carvings around the walls that reminded her of the pyramids. She struggled to maintain her breathing and turned to Norah. "What is this place?"

"Remember how I said I used to be the Ever-Living? This is the process I'd have to undergo every time I died." The Mummy sighed again and rubbed her eyes. "While I remain here, watching over Theo, his body will not degrade, and his soul will not leave this space."

A pained smile crossed the zombie's face. "So we can bring him back?"

"I'm sorry, hun." She shrugged in response. "I was brought back using rituals known only to a handful of priests. This just holds him in stasis."

Sally kicked up dust and growled in frustration. Her eyes darted around the chamber. "Humphrey ran off, but where's Lucius?" A closed doorway sat against the wall behind her. "Maybe he was left outside?"

"If you leave, you can't get back in." Norah held up a hand. "It's designed to be as safe as possible."

With a sigh, Sally opened her Inventory and spun around to the box he had given her. She placed the smooth wooden container on the edge of the plinth by the vampire's feet. "He gave this to me; said I'd know when to use it." Biting her lip, she popped the clasp and opened the lid. This was as good a time as any. Hopefully, it wasn't actually a stake.

Inside was a folded note. With shaking hands, she removed it to reveal three vials of blood sitting in a line amid comfortable black velvet. "Can you read this, Norah? My eyes are super blurry for some reason."

The Mummy's expression softened. "Of course, hun."

They exchanged the note, and then the zombie went to lean against the stone bed again, wiping her eyes and staring at the vials.

"Dear Sally," Norah began, holding the note up. "If you are reading this, either I am dead or you are sneaking a look, even after I told you not to. I am hoping it's the latter."

"*Ass.*" Sally smiled.

"Most likely I am dead. In truth, I knew this day was coming. When we started off in the Wastelands, Archie sat me down and told me that I would die by the hands of an *Outsider*. That's part of the reason I was so hostile toward Edward."

She nodded slowly, as the Mummy continued to read.

"Turns out he was pretty weak, though. So it was most likely to be you or Humphrey. Maybe I went insane and needed putting down. I can see no other reason why this could happen. Forgive me for keeping this a secret from you all, but Archie assured me it was necessary. Hopefully, I didn't kill anyone important in the process. I *am* pretty powerful."

Sally rolled her eyes.

"Assuming you want to bring me back, unfortunately, normal resurrection magic will not work, because I am undead. I've already asked Chuck about it and have looked into scrolls or magic that do similar. Honestly, I'm not sure if I can come back from this."

Norah took a deep breath, the weight of his death on her expression now too. "In the case are three vials of blood that might provide a key for my rejuvenation. That is only one part, as I do not know how to put the soul back in my body. I had hoped my higher levels would reveal a skill to allow me to come back, but it seems the System has tired of me."

The zombie rolled the vials around. They had labels around the hidden sides. Her brow furrowed as she read them out. "Bella. Edward. Lana."

The Mummy lowered the note to raise an eyebrow in question.

"Bella has insanely high health regeneration. Edward can respawn at the cost of one of his levels. Lana is a clone, a split Player." These all made some sense; some key to unlocking a way he could live yet again. It was clearly a lot harder than just jamming all three into his mouth or open heart, though. How could they bind his soul back?

Norah gave her a brief nod and continued. "There is a dungeon nearby that I'm going to try to get you a key for. It might hold the answer. It might not." The Mummy bit her lip. "Just know that I love and trust you, Sally. Ah, only read the next part if I am totally dead for good, and preferably not out loud." She raised her eyebrows.

Sally wiped fresh tears from her face. "Is it a bunch of mushy stuff?"

"*So* mushy." Norah nodded, reading slightly farther down the page. "And then rather oddly erotic."

"Oh, pup." She gave the vampire a glum smile. "I'd go through anything to bring you back, rather than read through your cringe attempts at spicy fan fiction."

The Mummy tilted her head side to side, before folding the note back up. "I mean . . . I've definitely read worse."

"Damn it, Theo." Sally flicked his shoe. "Can't promise a gal a good time post-postmortem. You were supposed to rule the world with me, not get murdered by my possessed father figure stand-in while trying to avoid the ire of a newly formed god." She shuddered as she deflated.

"He is a good man. His heart is in the right place."

"He *was* a good *man-child*." Sally wiped her running nose. "His whole *thing* is counting, and he died because Humps carried the one. I'm going to need to bring the dumb pup back to life just to chastise him." She shook her head and crossed her arms.

"You have a plan then, hun?"

A wide grin crossed the zombie's face. "I'm done grieving for now. Instead, I'm going to murder and destroy everything in the way of what I want. I'm done playing nice. The System has been living easy ever since I stepped away from my villain era."

Norah smiled. "Good luck, Sally. When the days are darkest, that is when Monsters grow strongest."

"You always know how to cheer me up." Sally went up to the Mummy and gave her a hug. "Thanks for looking after my dead husbando."

"Of course, hun." She returned the hug. "I knew this would come to pass as soon as the System gave me the blasted skill."

Sally moved back from behind her and furrowed her brow. "You think Humps has been keeping all your skills secret because he knew this would be coming?"

Norah shrugged. "He knew something was coming, but not . . . this exactly. He had been apprehensive about the new Architect even before we got to the jungle."

"Big lug." The zombie sighed and rubbed her face, before looking back toward the inert vampire. "I'll bring pops back home safe for you too, Norah." She turned to give her a smile. "Once he can forgive himself."

"Please do. Hopefully, all wrongs can be righted."

"System allowing." Sally snorted, before moving over to the vampire. She gave him a small kiss on the cheek. "You taste *horrible*," she whispered to him, with a sad smile. "Hang tight, pup."

Standing up straight, she cleared her throat. "Alright, I am going. I'll keep you updated via Party chat, and if I die, then . . . you're on your own, mom." She paused and pulled a face at Norah.

The Mummy smiled. "Kill and eat the weak, Sally, so that we sit upon a throne made from the bones of our detractors."

Sally stepped toward the door and went to push it open—instead, just falling straight through it as if it was incorporeal—and landed flat on the dirt beyond. The best start possible.

She stood and dusted herself off, looking back at the plain wall of the small structure, peaked like a pyramid at the top. Dark gray brickwork, and unassuming. It should be safe enough left alone. She would just have to trust Norah to protect the precious cargo.

On the ground, the greatsword of the Death Knight still lay discarded. Dark blood painted some of the grass and dried dirt. With a sigh, she put the weapon in her Inventory.

Eyes blazing crimson, she looked out at the world that caused the death of her Party. Something it would soon regret. Anger welled up within her. The uncaring, all-consuming undead part of her she often squashed away to try to be half-normal. With the tether of her found family severed, the System was about to find out what an error that would be.

As she went to check her map for the dungeon location, her eyebrow raised at the slew of pending notifications she had yet to read.

The skeletal horse thundered down the road at full sprint while the rider stared impassively at the horizon. Dust and dirt flew up in their wake, the heavy feet of the steed pounding through the mud as they left the road to travel through a lightly wooded area.

Thinner branches were snapped and torn as they continued through the vegetation, crushing bushes and trampling grass.

Eventually, they stopped and the horse vanished, leaving the Death Knight to drop to the floor. He rolled out his shoulders and looked behind him. "Why are you following me?"

Lucius popped out of his shadow, a sweat drop appearing briefly before his expression hardened. "What gives you the right to run away?"

Humphrey sighed and started to walk. As the trees thinned out, they were right before an outcropping. Slowly, he took a seat on the edge. They were high up, and the small cliff they were atop allowed them to gaze over a large swath of the jungle. The thick canopy of dense greens looked misty in the drab light of the day. Patches of dirt or openings between the leaves revealed structures or places Monster groups may be lurking.

"I murdered Theo. I have no place in the *Outsiders*."

The Shade moved up and stood beside him, crossing his arms. "Don't you think Sally would need you now, more than ever?" His foot began to tap, no emojis accompanying this line of questioning.

The Death Knight shook his head and lowered his gaze. "No. I am not safe to be around. What if I turned again? Killed you or Norah? Sally?"

Lucius sat down on the edge beside the plated figure. "You're back now, though? Theo used his whispering skill on you to take you out of it?"

Humphrey didn't move and continued to stare at his own feet. A few seconds of silence passed before he spoke. "It wasn't his skill."

A question mark appeared in the air. "Then what did he say?"

The Death Knight turned his head to him, improbable tears running from his empty eye sockets.

"He said, 'I forgive you, pops.'"

CHAPTER TWENTY-FIVE

Unchained

Flickering blue flame illuminated Chuck's impassive face.
Dent hunched over beside him and threw up blood across the thick grass.
"No need to be dramatic," the Druid admonished him, before casting a healing spell on the swordsman.
"So sorry," Dent said between gasps of air, rolling his eyes. "I'll try to not get impaled next time."
Chuck bit his tongue to avoid further bickering. Instead, he looked down at the solid metal case in front of them. Rounded at the tops and sides, the dark material had a couple of thin slits along it to allow air in. "Messier than I had anticipated; casualty report?"
"Eleven dead, maybe twice that injured." The swordsman stood back up straight with a groan. "Better than expected."
The Druid looked down at his STAR, seeing that messages were coming through. He tapped it to open it up, turning away from the fire that was consuming their camp to focus on the screens.
"Sally says to tell all 'blues' to avoid her at all costs."
"What, why?" Dent turned around and stepped up to him.
Chuck grimaced, and his face wrinkled up. "Shit. Theo is dead."
"*Actually* dead this time?"
A nod was the only response.
"Fuck." The swordsman rubbed his face with his left hand. "It must have been Humphrey, right? And now she is going on a rampage for revenge?"
"That's why I keep you around, Dent. Smarter than you look." Chuck gave

him a coy smile before returning to the messages. "She's going to the Spire dungeon right now. Alone."

Dent nodded. "Then we know what we need to do."

Sally closed the chat. Chuck was updated now, and she felt a little better to have another person to vent to. She meant what she had said, though. Everyone was kill on sight now, whatever faction. She hit *[Endless Sleep]* on the zombies who were still standing around patiently, totally unaware of what had been going on.

The Party had kept her grounded, given her a reason to make do with her bugged existence. Strive for greater strength so they could all be safe. With Theo dead and the rest of them scattered and threatened with being erased by the new Architect, the gloves were truly off. She walked to the road as she dealt with the other notifications.

> **[Quest Error]** Distributing Lost Quest Items
> **[Error]** Broken Shield 3/3 Pieces Found

She narrowed her eyes. It wasn't like the System to error in her favor, so she was suspicious about the quest getting completed so easily. With the fifth area destroyed, it looked as though it wanted the task to succeed rather than fail, so she had lucked out.

> Shield Repairing… 0.0%

Her crimson eyes blinked slowly as she stood and waited.

> Shield Repairing… 0.1%

"*There we go*, more System bullshit." She rolled her eyes and turned around, forgetting that there was nobody else to talk to. "This is going to be weird." As she deflated, she brought up the last notification—the golden glow of her level up.

> Error

She seethed and jabbed it again.

> **Pick One.on.ne**
> Error
> Restricted
> Error

Restricted
Error
Restricted
Overflow
Stack Error

"*Neat.*" She jabbed at the "overflow" one, as it didn't say it was restricted.

[**Meat Hook**] Draws you toward struck target.

Oh—that didn't actually look too bad, and the System didn't break because of it. Perhaps she *was* getting lucky. Although for a necromancer, you'd usually want to draw the target to yourself rather than the other way around . . . but as a zombie, she could see the use.

With the snap of her fingers, her large mouse appeared. "Time to bathe the world in blood," she said as she smiled sadly and gave it a pat on the side. She hopped up into the saddle, and then they were off.

Her mount scrabbled back along the road, the way that they had come. Sally opened her map and put a little marker where the Tomb was, so that she could find Norah if she found a way to bring Theo back. *When* she found a way, she corrected herself. It seemed pretty sappy to want to burn the world down just because her crush was dead, but he was more than just washboard abs and an affable dork.

No time for that sort of thinking, though. The small handful of hope could rest at the back of her mind as she ripped and tore her way through the System. As her ride bounded into the tree line to head straight for the dungeon, she brought up the Party chat.

Sally: en route to dungeon, report in.
Norah: No change here, hun. Good luck.
Lucius: What dungeon?
Lucius: I'm here with Humphrey… :(

Sally wrinkled up her face. She wasn't sure how the Shade made that happen when he could only shadow Party members, but that was the least important question on her mind right now. Thoughts roving around in her mind, she bit her tongue.

Sally: How is he?
Lucius: Miserable, regretful
Norah: Tell him I miss him.

> Sally: Tell him that_

She narrowed her eyes and sighed, ducking beneath some branches as the mouse leaped through the foliage.

> Sally: tell him that he has a duty to uphold.

STAR spun down as she closed the menus. If he wasn't going to help her now, then she was done with him. They didn't have the time for anything but pushing forward as quickly as possible. Not only was Theo's existence on the line, but all of them faced the same fate if the Architect continued to crack down on problems within the System. More than anything, she was worried about the goblins and Jackie too—not to mention . . .

A flash of blue illuminated the surrounding trees as she slid to a stop.

"Edward?"

The demon stumbled across the ground, clutching at his blood-soaked suit. "Ah! Sally, I was hoping you were okay." He stretched out straight, pain causing him to wince as his blazing blue eyes focused on her.

"Hop on, we don't have the time." She gestured, and he did so without further delay. The mouse set off again, and the zombie tilted her head back. "You're injured; Observers?"

"Correct. We didn't even know of them, but they just showed up in the city and started hunting down Uniques."

Sally growled and clenched her teeth together.

"I escaped, but . . . what's going on here?"

"Humphrey turned. Killed Theo. He ran off, and now I'm alone."

The demon opened and closed his mouth a few times, before looking off toward the horizon past the tree line. "*Dead?*" There was an unexpected layer of disbelief, or sadness, in his voice.

"He is being kept in stasis, but we don't know of a way to put his soul back. I'm heading to the Spire dungeon to see if it has answers."

> Edward has joined the Party

"The others?"

"Lucius followed Humphrey, who is sulking even though he is back to normal now. Norah is guarding Theo's body."

Edward was silent for a while as they thundered through the jungle. There wasn't a lot that could be said, and the weight of the situation kept them both quiet.

They burst out of a hedge way to land beside a group of surprised Players wearing red tabards.

[Meat Hook]

Sally leaped from the mount and zipped straight toward the first, a knight, via a beam of swirling pink energy. Her staff spun in her hand as she collided with the plated figure—the dagger end going straight through their metal armor and into their heart. *[Eat Brains]*.

She then turned as the skull atop her necromancer weapon burst into green fire, before she launched off into the next Player who looked like a Healer. As a shield flickered over them, she snapped her fingers and used *[Endless Dead]*, flooding the area with zombies, including several of the large lizard Monsters.

A red beam of energy burst from one of the opponents, coring two normal zombies, the leg of a lizard, and slicing through the side of Sally's torso. She gnashed her teeth and cast *[Living Dead]* on herself. Using the other dead as cover, she slunk up into melee with the assailant and jammed her staff down, the Skeleton Key at the end piercing their foot and pinning them to the ground.

As another Player came in to assist, she ducked away and withdrew one of her other daggers, blocking the blow and sliding back behind another zombie. With her left hand she commanded the skull atop the staff to turn into a *[Mortis Bomb]*, and she fired it point blank into the struggling Fighter.

[Eat Brains] on a target crushed by the Elite zombie lizards. *[Eat Brains]* on the overwhelmed Player she had pinned and surrounded by zombies. *[Eat Brains]* on the last one, lost and without hope.

[Endless Sleep]

She turned and stomped back toward the mouse; her face caked in gore and eyes burning a bright red. Edward was still on the mount, looking rather sheepish.

"Sorry, I'm still injured, and it looked like you had a hold on things."

"I need more Players to eat." She licked her lips. "No mercy until I get what I want." She climbed up in front of him into the saddle. After a brief pause, she turned her head back to him. "You're Level Twenty-three now, better start acting like it. Here's a Healing Potion." She extended her hand back to him.

"Rough day, huh?" he murmured, taking the potion with a nod of thanks.

"You'll soon see why I prefer to keep people around me and not be alone." The mouse jerked forward as they set back off, causing the demon to spill some of the healing liquid down himself.

He bit his tongue before making a snappy response. There was something about the zombie that was different, an anger in her that he didn't particularly want to invoke toward himself more than necessary.

Sally seethed as she glared at their destination. At this distance, she could now see the tower looming ahead of them again. Killing the Players hadn't made her feel any better about how things were progressing. If anything, it made her feel angrier. Clearly, she just needed to kill more Players.

Maybe if the dungeon was a wash, she could turn her focus on wherever the red team had their base. Listen to the soft tune of their death screams before the Architect could put a stop to her. Maybe a defeatist attitude, but it was time to temper the positivity into something sharper that she could jam between the ribs of the System and hope to find some heart.

"If you have any bright ideas for bringing Theo back, I'm all ears," she called back to the demon. "When I tear this world in half, I want the dumbass to bear witness."

Edward grimaced. It was bad enough when she had wild aspirations of defeating the dragon, but the fact that she had made her threats of destroying the world have some weight to them. "Nothing at the top of my mind. I will think about it."

She grunted a reply before looking at the notifications popping up on her STAR.

> Chuck: Red team holding dungeon entrance.
> Chuck: Two Parties.

Closed that down without responding, and opened up Party chat.

There were no new messages.

She was going to say something, but bouncing around on her mount was making it awkward. After they reached the dungeon, she would.

The building loomed into their view quickly; the mouse making short work of the cluttered jungle. Easily twenty stories tall, she estimated. Almost circular, but flat edges picked up the light of the day—so maybe a hexagon or similar.

As they burst from the tree line, ten figures standing in the clearing before the structure turned to face her. Their red tabards were much dimmer in color than the blazing fury in her own crimson eyes.

Her sharp teeth formed a wild grin as the Players began to ready their spells and attacks.

Too slow. Too weak.

CHAPTER TWENTY-SIX

Tower Team

Fifty zombies rose from the ground as Sally leaped from the mount, casting *[Endless Dead]*. She landed among the rising corpses who shielded her from the volley of skills leveled toward her. A dozen zombies fell, which did nothing but anger her further.

[Quick Death]

Her ultimate shook the area with a wave of cold air, before all the undead twisted from their positions to sprint at the now surprised Players. A *[Mortis Bomb]* flung from her staff already burst among the figures, raising more zombies.

She no longer cared to differentiate between the Players. Didn't matter what they looked like. Their class or level was no concern to her. They had two states. Dead, or in her way. Snaking behind one of the large undead lizard Monsters, she shot out *[Meat Hook]* at a robed figure moving away from the melee.

They tried to bring up some manner of shield to protect themselves. Not enough. Dagger to their neck, brains now hers to consume. Sally turned, blocking a sword in between the prongs of the top of her staff, twisting it to disarm the weapon.

[Greater Demon]

An eruption of green flame came from farther back, as Edward had grown to twice his size—now sporting an exaggerated muscled figure, his horns had extended and curled around the side of his head. While green fire continued to lap around his body, his piercing blue eyes were now ablaze with power.

As her disarmed opponent stumbled away from her and into the grasping hands of her zombie pals, she held a hand up to cast *[Curse: Decay]* at the figure

Greater-Edward was stomping his way toward. His thin rapier had now been replaced by a large sword that almost put Humphrey's to shame—on fire with a similar color to his eyes.

The elation in her dulled when thinking of the Death Knight. He should be here; they *all* should be here. An arrow struck her in the shoulder, followed by a volley of three that peppered her back. She sighed and looked over her shoulder, her dead eyes meeting the culprit of the assault. "Fuck you," she said plainly, as the skull atop her staff burst into green fire.

Edward slashed forward, knocking an armored Player across the floor. His strike continued and cut into the ground—gouging a twelve-foot mark where the figure had been standing. The larger body moved as if he was animated and there were frames missing. Odd jolts in his appearance as he gained ground on the Player, flickering and pulsing around him as the power surged through his ascended form.

Their spellcasters got their act together and bubbled shields popped up around those that remained, healing spells surging with green and radiant energy throughout.

[Domain: The Inevitable]

The demon held up a hand as the area became awash with color, as if the vibrancy and contrast of everything had been turned up a notch. The garish green of the grass and undead contrasted against his large body, which now appeared luminous purple and blue.

"You are weaker," his voice both boomed and sank through the area like a constant whisper. "Thus, you will perish." Like a power cut, the protective shields and buffs around the Players flickered and went away.

Sally bit through the brains of one Player, before using *[Meat Hook]* to dive into the midst of the spellcasters, her staff spinning around and spraying the ground with bright red blood that almost glowed under this strange spell.

Edward slammed his sword down into the armored Player, splitting them straight in half, twisting the blade to send the two parts slopping over to the floor. A spell of bright yellow coursed through the air, striking him in the chest and leaving a dark mark—before Sally leaped atop the caster. The remainder of the forces were overwhelmed by the presence of so many zombies in short order.

The demon flickered with power as the colors in the area returned to normal and he shrunk down to his normal size. He dusted off his suit where the spell had burned a hole through to his skin and looked at the battlefield. Nothing left but the sounds of undead mouths chewing through fresh flesh and bone.

Sally stumbled out from behind the wall of zombies, wiping plenty of gore away from her own mouth. There was still ferocity in her eyes but also an uncomfortable calm to her.

"Alright, I'll admit your ultimate is sick as shit." She spat some shards of bone onto the grass. "Reminds me of Theo's spell."

Edward deflated. "Yes, well, it's different from that. All demons of sufficient power have a domain."

"Would look cool if you both did them at the same time." She licked her lips and then deflated. Instead, she turned her eyes up toward the tower.

The demon opened his mouth, as if to reassure her that they'd bring the vampire back, but at this point, he didn't know. With the Architect hunting for bugs, they might have their own lives to worry about soon enough.

[Endless Sleep]

All but a handful of zombies went back away, and then Sally spun on the spot to glare at two figures now approaching from the tree line to the side. She tensed, ready to *[Meat Hook]* over and consume the shadowed pair, before they stepped into the light to be revealed.

"Chuck?!" She gasped and ran over, dropping her staff on the floor.

"That's right, I—" The Druid was interrupted as she flung herself around him, giving him a hug.

"Holy growth spurts, Chucky." She looked up at him. "How are you taller than me now?"

He gave her a sad smile. "It's been a long year, Sally. Also, you smell like internal organs."

She stepped away and grinned. "Hey again, Dent." The swordsman stepped out to be beside them.

Chuck definitely looked older—and not just from the time having passed. Whatever war had been raging on between the factions, it had certainly added to age him. But he wasn't just taller; he held himself with the weight of the important job he held. His robes were simple, but well-made, in a mix of light brown and deep green that matched his hair and eyes.

Sally wiped her eyes with the back of her arm. "Things are pretty shitty now, huh?"

"You could say that." He nodded slowly. "We came to help you in the dungeon."

"Really?" She looked over her shoulder at it. There hadn't been a doubt in her heart that she could have soloed it or done it with Edward's help.

The demon stepped forward to greet them. "Pleasure again, after all this time. Perhaps my energies could be better spent elsewhere?"

Sally raised an eyebrow. "Sure?"

He nodded in return. "You know how I feel about dungeons, and I'd much rather be on the move and active."

Edward has left the Party

She gave him a brief hug, and then with a bow, he vanished in a pulse of blue light.

"Feels so apocalyptic." She turned to give them a sad smile. "It should be illegal to keep making me this sad. *Oh*, what's in the box?" She narrowed her eyes and crouched beside the rounded metal container Dent held in his good hand.

Chuck wrinkled up his face. "It's . . . an Archie."

"Time for the vet, huh? How'd he even lose his eye?" She tried to look closer through the air holes, but nothing other than a little blue light emanated from within.

"It's not that one," Dent answered. "This is area four Archie, who had fused with an Observer."

Sally frowned and stood back up. "Like the first Archie?"

The Druid slowly shook his head. "More like . . . Humphrey."

"Ah," she responded. They didn't need to say much more than that. Even her bloodthirsty mind could read between the lines. This Archie had turned the same as Humphrey, and they had contained it in this possibly magical container that just so happened to look like a cat carrier. "You haven't been able to change him back?"

"Correct." Chuck gestured toward the dungeon, and they started to walk. "Only contain him. We were hoping to help do the same with Humphrey."

"Oh, he turned back to normal already."

The two men exchanged glances before Dent spoke. "How'd he manage that?"

Sally shrugged. "Theo whispered something to him, his last words before he died. Which, by the way, I'm still mad at both of them for. As much as I love pops, Theo was clearly going easy on him. Otherwise, he would have won. I think he took the sword to the heart on purpose so that the fight didn't go on for hours, with how defensive they both are."

She sighed, deflating now that she was about to get that off her chest. As they walked across the trampled grass, marred with the results of the combat with the Players, she picked her staff back up. If he knew he was going to die by the hand of an *Outsider*, perhaps he even went into the fight accepting that his death was the guaranteed outcome.

Chuck raised an eyebrow at the swordsman, who just shrugged in response. "I can understand your frustration and anger, but why go off on your own?"

"Hmm? Oh, Humphrey is dealing with his guilt, and Lucius followed him. Norah has Theo's body and soul in safekeeping for if we find a way to bring him back."

"Really?" The Druid frowned. "Where?"

Sally stopped by the entrance to the dungeon and looked at them. "I trust you both, but I'm not telling you where yet. My family is already broken apart. I can't risk anything else. Not for anything."

"I understand." Chuck gave her a sad smile. "I was suspicious when Theo was asking me about resurrection magic, but that's why we started putting our plans into action."

She nodded. He seemed to have a much more level head on his taller shoulders these days. Definitely more than any of the *Outsiders* and associated goofballs. "I know that look in your eyes. Broken your pacifist run, haven't you?"

He rolled those eyes in response. "It was never that, and you know it. But yes, I've killed. To survive, to protect, to further the cause I believe in."

"See, I just do it for fun, so you still have the moral high ground." She grinned and tapped her staff against the dungeon wall. "You want to fill me in on more exposition as I eat my way through the tower?"

Chuck worked his jaw and looked up at the tall building as it reached toward the gloomy sky overhead.

"Sure." He smiled. "For old time's sake."

Dent nodded his agreement. "We'll try to keep up with you."

> Chuck has joined the Party
> Dent has joined the Party

The System fuzzed some information on the side of her vision. Twenty floors of challenges, it looked like only one Party had ever made it up to sixteen. None farther. From her Inventory, she took out a pen and paper to write something down, before returning it.

Not that it was the right season for looking forward to the future, but she allowed herself to be a little full of hope.

That and the brains of her enemies.

CHAPTER TWENTY-SEVEN

Rising Steps

Sally stretched out as they stood on the ground floor of the dungeon. It was just a plain open room of off-colored gray brickwork, with a staircase at the opposite end that rose up to join to the next floor above.

"*This* challenge must just be to make it up the stairs," she said as she nodded to herself. "Nice of them to start off pretty easy for us."

Chuck mostly ignored her statement. "Dent can solo the first five or six levels, then we'll need to assist. That'll give us time to talk."

She pouted but agreed. Unless there were some tasty brains, she could put a pause on the murder spree to get a little exposition.

The swordsman limbered up and put the case holding Observer-Archie on the floor against the wall. Chuck waved his hand, and it turned invisible. Enough to keep it safe from prying eyes without having to drag it floor to floor.

They walked over to the staircase, the dagger at the end of Sally's staff poking holes in the brick floor. She worked her jaw in thought, wondering how many stabs it would take around the walls to make the tower collapse. Not that the System would congratulate and give her the correct rewards for that—but it *might*, so it was worth the brain cell action.

"How do you . . . are you doing okay?" Chuck began, some of his old awkwardness showing through his current stoic personality. "Like, with Theo and everything?"

She screwed her face up. "It's difficult. On one side of the coin, I'm heartbroken. But on the other side, I'm essentially a mass murderer, and it seems petty to stop over a single one of my own being killed."

He nodded in response. "Both very human and very dissociated at once. Very like you."

"If there's one thing I am, it's consistent."

They circled up the staircase, neither of the men wanting to touch that statement. At the top of their ascent was a doorway with the number one engraved upon it. Chuck held out his hand and sent some buffs toward the swordsman: green, brown, and gold circles and pulses of energy flowing around his body.

"When you're ready, Dent."

The door opened and Sally stretched out onto her tiptoes to try to see what was inside. They stepped up behind the swordsman as he entered, his blade-arm illuminated by a sharp blue sheen.

Some kind of floating eel creature, with a head that looked more like a seal than a snake. It swirled and bobbed in the air, awaiting combat to start.

Dent went into a half-crouch, then a burst of air blew dust back against them as he vanished to appear at the other side of the room. After a brief moment, an orange line drew across the Monster, as it split in two.

"A little cliché," Sally said as she grinned, "but *super* badass."

"Right?" Chuck smiled.

"My turn for questions." She pushed him to start moving toward the next staircase. "So you and Dent?"

"Ah, don't." The Druid tried to wave her away. "You know how these things are. Nurse them back to health, they save your life, you start a warring faction to save the world together."

"How did that even come about? The last part." They reached the bottom of the next set of steps while Dent waited by the door. "No offense, Chucks, but you used to be a huge dweeb. Now you're like a warlord."

"Eh, none taken, I think." He nodded for the swordsman to continue. "We mostly started in response to the . . . red team . . . did you want me to start using our actual names, or?"

"Hell no. If you make this anything more that the simple blocks I have arranged in my brain, I will literally break down into a blubbering mess."

He grimaced. "Really?"

"You have no idea how much I have to dissociate to maintain this existence." She sighed and rubbed her face. "It's either the mania or the bloodshed. It keeps me grounded. The *Outsiders* keep me grounded. Did. But . . . continue with the talking, Chuck."

"Right." They stepped into the next room as Dent performed the same attack on some kind of stone-based golem. "Red team came up first, angry with the System. Without you being present, I wanted to give a voice to the Uniques, and those who weren't so full of hate."

"I'm proud of you for stepping up." She grinned and punched him in the shoulder as the golem clattered to the floor in chunks.

"Definitely wasn't easy, and Dent kept me on the right path." He returned a glum smile. "Apparently it couldn't be some democratic forum where the two sides could decide what was best for the world together. Had to go straight to violence."

"If only I was awake then." She shook her head as they walked around the room. "So many of them would be ingested by now. We'd be the winners."

Chuck tilted his head as they reached the next set of steps. "I was a little surprised you agreed to join us, if I'm honest."

"Hmm, really?"

The next door opened. "You've always been such a force of change for the System," the Druid continued, "and I didn't want to step on your toes or end up butting heads on what we wanted."

"Red team's plan for Uniques seemed to be kill us off, so you had that going for you."

Chuck grinned and looked over at the group of sheep made of blue fire. "Well, what is it *you* want, Sally?"

She exhaled and thought about it for a moment, watching the swordsman blaze through the Monsters with little issues; flashes of colored skills pulsing around the drab stone walls.

"I want my dork ass vampire boyfriend. My goofy adoptive undead parents. Whatever kind of little weirdo Lucius is. To see Bella and Jackie. Just . . . be accepted and be able to live."

Chuck nodded, some sadness across his face. "I want that for you too, Sally. I'm . . . I've been planning things for months. Trying to build that future, eventually. There's something I need to ask you . . ." He balled up his hands and relaxed them a few times as if he was trying to build strength.

They stopped by the stairs. "Go ahead," Sally said, tilting her head.

"We didn't know when you'd be back." He sighed. "So we've been planning—if it's even possible—for *me* to become the next Architect."

"Okay." She nodded and put a foot on the step.

"Just 'okay'?" Chuck furrowed his brow.

She smiled and shook her head. "What, you think I still wanted the job? I'm a complete mess, Chucky. You're much more qualified."

"*Oh*," he said, at a loss for words as he followed her up.

"You've been beating yourself up about that for ages, I can tell. Some things don't change." She shook her head. "I joined blue team because of your vision. If I have to have some god-like asshole ruling over my existence, you're the least worst on that shortlist."

The Druid smiled. "Wow, I'm definitely going to sleep better tonight. Assuming we live that long."

"Pretty dire, huh?" They went into the next room. The ghost of a large dog-like lizard rolled his tongue around as the swordsman charged up a skill. "Part of me wonders if I'm being selfish in trying to bring back fangs rather than working for the greater good."

Chuck shrugged. "You've done more than anyone else in trying to make this world a decent place to exist. If your heart wants this, then I think it's a just cause."

"Thanks." She smiled and sighed. Somehow, he had managed to temper some of the storm brewing within her. Maybe she *could* be selfish. She had earned it after all the effort she had put into fixing the System for everyone else. Everyone had a limit, and if she died in trying to bring her family back together, then she'd have no regrets. Briefly, she wondered if it was a spell the Druid had used on her to make her so calm again—or maybe talking through things actually *did* work.

She tilted her head and leaned against the wall as the swordsman zipped around, having a bit more trouble with the ghost. "What happened to eye patch?"

"In hiding, for safety." Chuck rubbed his eyes. "We might need them all, so that's why the Observer-Archie is being held."

"Then Humps has two more—where's the fifth area Archie? Was he destroyed?"

He furrowed his brow. "No. At least the others don't believe so, which is interesting. Presumably that means the last cat had moved somewhere before the fifth area was deleted. We haven't found them in this last year, however."

Something felt uncomfortable in the back of her mind, as if the hint of something was trying to push forward. An answer eager to find its way into the world. "Oh," she said, furrowing her brow and bringing out the necklace from beneath her cloak. "Where do I put the key for the dungeon?"

Chuck raised an eyebrow and looked at the heart-shaped pendant on the chain. "As far as I know, it doesn't require one. Unless it's for something higher up? A chest or special door?"

Sally didn't think so. Theo was vague about it, which usually meant it was something she didn't need to know right away, but the answer would become obvious when needed. How romantic to leave such mysterious clues for her to solve postmortem. She grimaced in remembering she left his note back with Norah. She wanted to read that mush before she died, at least.

"Hey, Chucky. You think if you become the big boss, you can turn me into a . . . normal woman? Maybe remove all the memories of killing and eating people?"

He pulled a face and shrugged. "I have no idea. But I'd do whatever I could for you and the *Outsiders*."

"You big sap." She smiled and stepped away from the wall to head to the next floor. "My friend Lana fell to evil and . . . Chuck, do you remember Marius?"

The Druid raised an eyebrow and looked off to the ceiling to dig around his memories. "Never met him, of course—but he was your antagonist in the forest, yeah? Corrupted STAR?"

She nodded. "We found another. You know the *Last Word*?"

"Yeah." He shook his head. "You saying what I think you are?"

"My assumption is that Theo has dismantled most of them, but there might still be someone out there who can corrupt the STARs. Oh, ass!"

"Huh?"

Dent walked over, stretching out his arms, ready for the buffs to be put back on. "What's up?"

"Theo. He had a poison that he said would kill him and then he conveniently died, so I don't know how much of that was bullshit or if he had cured it."

The swordsman scratched at the side of his head with the flat of his blade. "Sounds like he knew it wouldn't matter either way, probably enjoyed holding the secret."

She nodded. That *did* sound like the vampire. There were a few more questions she had stored up in her mind, but honestly, she was tired of talking and thinking—not to mention watching Dent have all the fun with killing everything. She opened Party chat.

> Sally: in the tower dungeon with chuck and dent
> Sally: edward is somewhere, on board
> Norah: things are quiet here

No update from Lucius, which made her clench her teeth. She needed that Death Knight back pronto so she could give him a piece of her mind.

"Alright," she growled. "I need to warm up. Tag me in, Dent."

He shrugged, and Chuck turned his hand to cast the buffs on her instead. "Next few floors are rougher, but we have your back."

Lucius fumed. Fire emojis flickered next to angry faces as he pulled on the armor of the Death Knight to no effect.

"You need to give up," Humphrey said with a sigh, staring out over the canopy.

"You need to *stop* giving up."

The Death Knight turned his head. "Why are you so intent on me going back to them?"

Lucius put his hands on his hips. "What is your purpose?"

"I have none."

"Really? You no longer have a connection to Norah or Sally? Your bodyguard duties?"

Humphrey turned back to the expanse beyond. "There was a time where I was just a minion of the System. Observing errors and bugs, making my reports, until I came across something odd—a Player soul that had merged with a Monster."

Lucius calmed and sat back down beside the plated figure.

"It was as if just seeing her detached me from the rails the System kept me on. I shirked my directives. Felt like I had to continue watching to see what this Unique individual could do. She needed to be nurtured like a flower. It was hardly a tough decision to join with this body and save her life."

He sighed and rubbed his skeletal face. "I tried to be what she needed in this world. A rock. A father figure, despite having no idea what that really entailed. I'm just a creation of whatever this world is, yet I have grown to know how to love and feel emotions. Become something greater than how I was designed."

"Happy?"

"More than anything. Sally is like a daughter to me. Norah lights up something within my metal chest that I never thought was possible. And Theo . . . I just can't accept what I have done."

"Fuck you, Humphrey." Lucius stood up and turned away from him.

"*What?*"

The Shade started to walk away. "Don't sit there, telling me how much you love something, while you continue to abandon it. We need you now more than ever. Theo trusted you to look after Sally." He stopped and turned back to Humphrey, his eyes burning with intensity. "Do you not understand?"

A heavy silence hung between the pair for a handful of contemplative seconds. Humphrey stood slowly to his feet. Flames burned brighter at the back of his helmet as shadow obscured his face, save for sparks of crimson light in the back of his eye sockets.

"Let's go."

CHAPTER TWENTY-EIGHT

Connections

Sally slid across the floor and flourished her staff, placing it down into the stone brickwork with a grin on her face. The armored Minotaur ahead of her slumped over, a large hole in their skull remaining where their brain had escaped and journeyed into her stomach. Her tongue rolled around her lips as she raised an eyebrow at the two men.

"I'm sure you could have soloed *that*, Dent." She winked and walked toward the next staircase.

The swordsman exchanged a glance with the Druid as a handful of zombies followed the energized woman. "You know I'm not squeamish, Chuck," he began, "but after watching her eat the last five Monster's brains in a row, it's getting unsettling."

"You get used to it," Chuck said with a shrug. "I think, anyway."

Sally hopped up the stairs to the door marked with a number ten. "Is there anything . . ." she began, before pushing some of her zombie pals out of the way. "Anything interesting about this floor?"

"It's the first reward area," Dent said, trying to look through the corpses struggling to arrange themselves on the staircase. "Most Parties stop here, as it gets much more difficult after."

She rolled her eyes. With the whole gang here, they'd be munching on the floor twenty boss already. If the System wasn't so keen on beating them down, she would be a lot more thankful that they were all overpowered compared to most Players.

"It's basically an ogre, strong physical beater," Chuck offered, from slightly lower down.

Great. She grinned. That was her favorite type, as she could usually beat them in both brute strength and survivability.

The room opened to reveal the Monster—a large humanoid of deep gray, two pits of golden eyes on their grumpy face. Muscled and clad in leather armor. A stone-headed axe in each hand.

Sally stopped and leaned to the side to see a second figure by the back staircase, leaning against the wall with their arms folded.

A plant person, if she had to describe them. Vaguely masculine form, most of their torso and lower half made of dark brown roots and bark. Around their shoulders was a cape of bright greenery, like a canopy of a handful of large leaves. Their head was a sharp triangle shape, and a much lighter brown, the only features being long slits that were possibly their eyes.

"Hi!" Sally waved. "Are you a Unique?"

"I am a defender of this tower," the voice hissed through the air from an unseen mouth. "Just seeing how much of a threat you are."

She chewed at her thoughts in response. Her pleasant nature wanted to make friends with the Unique Monster, but her grip on what she truly cared for was slipping. "What level do you usually protect?"

"Eighteen."

Chuck and Dent pushed through the shambling undead to stand beside her. The swordsman narrowed his eyes but didn't ready his weapon to attack.

"We are going straight to the top," Chuck spoke out loud. "Relinquish your position and we will not have to kill you."

A pulsing hiss wrapped around them—a laugh.

Sally tilted her head toward the pair. "I'll give them a second chance once they've seen what we can do."

"What *you* can do," Chuck murmured but nodded. "Call us if you need assistance."

"Time me." She grinned. "Less than five seconds."

Dent smiled and raised his blade-arm like a flag.

Sally tensed and her boots bit into the stone as she prepared to burst forward.

Norah hummed to herself, running her fingertips along the polished stone of the throne's armrests. Her eyes moved around the chamber. Even though nothing had changed, she had to remain vigilant.

"Such a shame." She sighed and looked toward the dead vampire. "My priests are long gone, if they even existed at all in this reality. If only I had learned the ritual."

She was used to solitude. Her undead life had been full of it. Queen of a

Wasteland that had forgotten her name. The spark of meeting the affable zombie was only beaten by the bright illumination of the Death Knight arriving in her life. She hadn't even thought love was possible.

Nor acceptance.

But they had brought her in without question or hesitation. She had become one of them and it felt as natural as if she had always known them. Now they were scattered, and an odd weight had a grip on her dead heart. Something that shouldn't be possible—yet she couldn't deny it.

Her yellow eyes sank back to Theo once more and her jaw clenched. If he couldn't be brought back, she would gladly join the zombie in tearing this world in half.

The torches in the tomb flickered wildly, as an ancient anger burned and swirled within her, waiting for an excuse to burst forth.

"Four seconds," Dent said, pulling a face that bordered between respect and disgust.

Sally dropped down from the empty head of the Monster and gave them a bow. She spun around to speak to the plant person, but they had vanished. "Ah?" Instead, she pouted.

"Probably going to prepare," Chuck said with a sigh, walking over and pushing some of the zombies out of the way.

"Or writing their will," Dent added.

Sally wrinkled up her nose. Player combat was a lot more interesting, but only barely. The problem with System-created was they were too simple and predictable. She ran at the ogre, using *[Escape Fate]* up above their head as they swung at her. While one of the zombies was turned to paste, her broken dagger went straight into the back of the head of the Monster, and their brains could be eaten.

If it wasn't for the slightly awkward cooldown period on the evasive skill, she could have done the same thing to every enemy so far. Probably all the way to the top, the odd plant person excluded. Things would be interesting then.

"What weapon is that?" Dent leaned over to inspect her staff.

"It's two that I merged together. A dagger that ignores any defense, and a staff that makes my necromancy stuff better. As well as acting as a focal point for casting magic."

The swordsman stood back up, a glum expression across his face. "And here I am with a fuckin' shard of metal for an arm."

"And you do wonders with it," Chuck said idly as he walked over to the side of the room where a treasure chest had appeared. "All yours, Sally."

"*Neat*. I love looting." She grimaced as she walked over to it. "You know what *would* be neat?"

Chuck raised an eyebrow. "Hmm?"

"If I could also summon skeletons and ghosts. Then, when someone died, I'd split them into a ghost and a zombie, and then when the zombie dies, the skeleton could come out." She paused as she placed a hand on the chest. "And then when the skeleton dies, I can take the skull for *[Mortis Bomb]*."

"Right." He nodded slowly.

"You'd better give me a skeleton skill if I let you become the Architect." She narrowed her eyes at him. "That's a conditional now."

"I'm . . ." He maintained a blank expression. "Sure, I guess."

He might be lying, but she was willing to take that risk. After all, they might be dead soon, so thinking that he could actually become the Architect seemed like more of a pipe dream than a reality. Maybe if she buttered him up enough, he could make her the most powerful necromancer that ever lived.

"Thanks, Chucky!" She gave him a wide smile.

Shield Repairing... 2.8%

Annoying message popped up in the way of her loot—and had hardly budged despite the time and violence that had passed. She sighed and closed it down.

3453 Gold
Greater Health Potion (5)
Sword of Fables
Jungle Token (5)
Vine Rope (3)
Flameblast Scroll
Nature's Wrath Scroll

She exhaled. "You guys want this? It's not . . . I'm already stacked. Seems beneath me if it isn't helping to save Theo or kill the Architect."

Chuck crouched to look at the contents. "I get what you mean. With our reality on the line, the gamification seems rather droll."

"Exactly." She narrowed her eyes at him and whispered. "Hey, Dent doesn't remember the old world, right?"

The Druid shook his head slowly.

Sally pouted, before a memory jostled its way into her head. "Oh, guess which weirdo in my group has a skill that you'll find super useful?"

"Which?" Chuck stood back up, and they started over toward the next staircase.

"Lucius can erase the part of your brain that finds your place in this world uncomfortable." She grinned.

"That sounds . . . like brainwashing?"

Sally shrugged and pushed a zombie out of her way. "Well, when the alternative is the way I erase brains, Players should be jumping at the chance. We helped that gal we dropped off with you guys."

Dent stepped forward to join them. "Charlotte? The turncoat?" He rubbed his chin as the zombie nodded. "I had a brief chat with her. She seemed earnestly happy, had nothing but good things to say about you."

"She was this close to being eaten." Sally put her fingers close together. "Seething full of anger toward us Uniques, and then after, she was our best bud."

"We'd have to see it in action, before we agree on the . . . morality of it?" Chuck furrowed his brow. "Not that 'morality' holds much weight in this world."

"I eat people." She nodded as they reached the next door. "On the regular."

Edward staggered backward, demonic blood dripping across the damp ground. His sword arm hung limply by his side, grip loose on his rapier.

"Really?" he said, with a wide grin across his face. "I'm not a fan of the new management, if this is his best."

The light blue flame of the skull-faced Observer illuminated the clearing, despite the canopy trying to shadow the area.

"Your approval is not required," the figure spoke in return, their voice hollow and deep. Wide wings of radiant white buffeted the air, causing the demon to wince. "You must submit to being corrected or perish."

Edward chuckled before coughing up a mouthful of blood. Couldn't even teleport under the aura of the Observer, and even then, his respawn point was under guard. The light blue of his eyes dimmed as he stood up straight, twitching painfully. "Killed by an angel? So cliché that it almost seems inevit—"

The Observer lifted their large hammer up into the air, radiant light blazing from the weapon, intending to cut off the rest of the demon's speech. Just before the attack swung down, the skeletal head twisted to the side.

From the tree line, a large figure of plated metal burst forth, slamming into the angel and knocking them to the floor. As they rolled around, shadowed arms held down the Observer, allowing the Death Knight to wrench the hammer into his own hands.

The radiant light of the wide hammer faded away, to be replaced by a blaze of crimson energy.

With a crunch, the blue light illuminating the area dissipated, to be enshrouded by shadows once more.

Humphrey looked over his shoulder at the demon, dark fire blooming in his eye sockets. "Need a ride?"

CHAPTER TWENTY-NINE

The Peak

Sally rolled across the stone floor, a pulse of healing flowing through her as the Monster slumped over. With a groan, she threw up the last three floors' worth of brains into a damp puddle.

"Is that . . . normal?" Chuck grimaced and recoiled even though he was already standing half the room away.

"Huh?" She wiped her mouth and looked up at him. "Oh, I mean it's *semi-regular* these days, so . . ." She shrugged.

"The stomach has a certain limit, I suppose." Dent mirrored her shrug. "Doesn't seem *healthy*, though."

Sally rolled her eyes, although the expression was ruined by all the zombies shambling around in front of her. "Would you all move, please!" she said in a sharp tone.

With zero hesitation, all the undead immediately turned to go stand by whichever side of the wall was closest to them, leaving the central area mostly free, aside from one that had lost its legs against the large insect Monster.

"Some brains are just gross like that too." She stretched out and cracked her back. "Tell me about the leader of the red team."

The other two exchanged a glance. Chuck grimaced again. "What did you want to know?"

"Who they are, for one. All I got was the name 'Seven.'" She tilted her head at their expressions. "Is it someone I already know? Is it Jackie?"

The Druid shook his head. "No, it's not—"

"The werewolf prick?"

"I'm . . . not sure who that is?" He looked toward Dent, who shook his head slowly.

The name wasn't much of a clue, unless it was one of the Lana clones, but they were either the *Last Word* or unaffiliated, according to the vampire. With their dim view of Uniques, it surely had to be a Player, but all the ones she really knew had been accounted for.

"Would it be more fun if you didn't tell me, and I found out by surprise later on?"

Chuck shrugged. "I'm not sure 'fun' really cuts it."

"Oh!" She hopped up and down. "Is it going to be like Lenard or Charlotte and a big reveal that one of the grunts was the big shot themself?"

"Sally." He rubbed his face. "We didn't say it was someone you knew."

"Why are you wasting my brain-buff time then," she huffed and stomped toward the next staircase.

Edward winced as the skeletal horse thundered through the jungle. "Just because we were at odds on occasion, it doesn't mean I don't want him back."

"*At odds.*" Lucius emoted some rolling eyes. "He killed you three and a half times, and you were sour about it."

"Yeah, well . . ." His blue eyes looked out into the thick vegetation as they careened past. "I'm here, and I'm helping, okay?"

Humphrey said nothing but kept his glare on the way ahead. After the demon had told them that Chuck and Dent were helping the zombie with the dungeon, they had changed course. No point getting there and not being needed. There were bigger fish to fry.

Sally panted as she looked up at the ceiling. "Wow, that was *quite* painful."

Chuck loomed over her, his face pale. "I've . . . never seen legs bend that way. Like noodles."

"Right? They're a little numb still." She shuffled up to a sitting position and exhaled. All the bones had snapped back into place and visually they were fine. "Gravity, huh?"

The Druid helped her to her feet and looked around at the room; the stonework scored by dark lines from the battle. Dozens of zombies lay pulped or severed in pieces.

"Perhaps that is my fault." Dent sighed from over by the wall. "I meant 'up' as in move forward, not 'jump up.'"

"We don't usually shout commands." She wobbled as the feeling returned to her legs. "Unless it's something irrelevant and comical. Shattering my legs was neither." She took a step forward and winced. "Well, in hindsight, *kinda* amusing."

Chuck held his face and rubbed his eyes. "I feel like this whole venture has been a penance for making you wait to meet me."

Sally didn't respond, but she smiled to herself as she stumbled forward. It was nice hanging the with pair after all this time, but the dungeon was getting repetitive and boring. As fun as the two were, it just made her miss being with the *Outsiders* more. She gave the Druid a side-eye, remembering he was a zombie with them at one time. Should she tell him? While it didn't seem fair to hold secrets, it wouldn't benefit him in any way to know.

She put a pin in that thought and went up to the next floor's doorway. "This is our plant person now, right?"

"Yeah," Chuck said with a nod.

"Hmm. Better stay out here and let me solo it." She crossed her arms. "Some Uniques are very against Players, especially dungeon ones. Let me talk to them."

"If . . . that's what you want. Just call us if there's any trouble."

She nodded and pushed through the door, into the chamber where the figure was sitting on a chair waiting. The room was furnished with basic household items—a bed, cupboards, somewhere to sit and read.

"Neat house." She smiled. "I'm Sally."

"You may call me . . . Fern. It is a shame you have come here to destroy it, isn't it?" They remained seated in the center of the room, branch-like arms folded.

"Unless you can just let me have the reward from the top?"

"My role here is to protect the queen above. That is all."

"*Boring.*" Sally faked yawning. "You know the System is about to try to erase all Uniques, right? I guess you don't get out much."

"My . . . duties keep me—"

"Listen, I'll cut to the chase because I've wasted enough time here. There's a new Architect who hates bugs like us and intends to crush them. One of my group is powerful but dead. I want whatever you got hidden away to help bring him back." She crossed her arms and glared at Fern.

"Your struggles are—"

"Plus, if you help me I have a cool Druid friend who you can hang with and actually leave the tower to do good in the outside world. Don't you want to be happy? Have love and acceptance?"

Fern stared blankly at her, which wasn't too surprising given they didn't really have facial features to speak of. "I feel that is an unfair question. If I say no, then you will kill me."

"Correct."

"There is no doubt in my mind that you would win. Do you know how many Players I've had to fight in protecting the tower?"

Sally shook her head.

"Zero. My existence has such a singular focus, but as of yet, I am inconsequential. It fills me with rage to know that after such a long time waiting, I could be erased by a manic meat sack only here on a whim because she thinks the tower can bring her dead lover back."

She screwed her face and pouted. "I never gave up *all* that exposition."

"It is written clearly on your face." Fern stood and stretched out their limbs. "You do not even know what you seek. You are just driven by blind anger and desperation."

"Correct," she said again and nodded.

"The invaders may follow us, but they are not to raise their hands in anger. I will escort you to the pinnacle for you to determine if your time has been well spent."

"Neat! You should have said that earlier, so I didn't have to throw up and break my legs." She spun around and inhaled. "*Chucky*, you can come in now."

The door opened and the pair entered, determination on their faces in expecting a fight, but soon mellowing as they saw combat wasn't taking place.

"Extra chill from both of you, okay?" She raised her eyebrows. "We are taking the shortcut, but no touching the chocolate machines, okay?"

Chuck nodded, but Dent didn't understand the reference.

"If you would follow me, then." Fern drew their attention and began walking toward the door.

Sally hummed to herself as she walked ahead. All the furniture looked well taken care of and didn't even have the added flair of vines or leaves she expected from a . . . dryad looking person. They must have been really bored sitting here alone for over a year.

"You are unlike most meat-bags, yet you are not quite a Monster either." Fern started up the stairs with the zombie in tow.

"The world likes to create oddballs. I have my own tower of them, right here." She pointed to where she was reasonably sure her heart was located.

"Fascinating." The plant person stopped by the next doorway. "And you all have acceptance in this world?"

"Not really?" Sally rubbed her hair. "Some do abide us." She jerked a thumb back at the two following behind. "But we get into plenty of conflict too."

Fern tilted their head to the side. "And you would have me leave to become embroiled in this conflict?"

With a grin, the zombie shrugged. "Beats sitting around here doing nothing until someone with more ambition runs you over, right?"

A couple of seconds of silence passed before Fern turned and pushed the door open. With a wave of their hand, the Monster ready for battle calmed and fell asleep. A five-headed dragon-looking Monster—much smaller than Ruben—with each head a different color. They circled around the sleeping creature, as she tried to work out if she would have to eat all the brains, or only one to turn them.

Up the stairs to the door marked twenty. Fern pushed through again and the chamber beyond was much larger—the roof was tall and peaked to a point. In the center of the room was a large Monster that looked like a humanoid bee queen. Powerful wings buffeted the air, as the golden crown glinted in the light, in contrast to her pitch-black skin.

"Forgive me, my queen." Fern bowed low, and the Monster vanished.

Dungeon Complete!
No experience gained
3453 Gold
Jungle Token (10)
Spire Medallion
Rare Vine (3)

Sally wrinkled up her face, double checking the items. None of it seemed to do anything, even the medallion was just cosmetic.

"Your verdict, odd flesh-woman?" Fern crossed their arms.

"Where's . . ." She took a deep breath, her hands shaking. None of that seemed right. "Where's the place I put this?" From beneath the cloak, she brought out the heart-shaped gemstone pendant.

Fern leaned closer and tilted their head. "I have no idea."

Sally clenched her fist around it. *No.* She hadn't just wasted time. Theo had said to come here; he wouldn't have been wrong. Maybe she misunderstood? She started to pace around the otherwise bare room. No chests. No podiums or alcoves. No indentations on the floor.

Nothing.

"Balls!" she yelled and threw the pendant to the floor. It shattered, sending shards of red across the drab stonework. "Double balls," she said with a sigh. "That was unlike me."

She rubbed the bridge of her nose before something caught her eye. A small sliver of parchment had been left among the rest of the broken item. Crouching, she lifted it up to read it.

In case of broken heart, break—oh, you did already. Theo.

"Ass." She smiled and wiped her eyes.

The smell of ozone hit her nostrils, and she stood up, clutching the note to her chest. Static hummed around the peaked ceiling before a glowing circle of deep green light started to emerge in midair. A tunneled portal etched with green lines came into focus, before the dark shape of a figure dropped out onto the floor.

Dressed in a dark suit, the woman took a draw of a cigarette as she moved her long purple ponytail from in front of her face and gave the surprised zombie a wry grin.

"Jackie!" Sally gasped; her eyes wide.

"Heard you had an open bodyguard job, yeah?" She stuck a hand in her pocket. "Oh, brought a little plus one. Hope that's good with you?"

Her hand extended to reveal the contents.

A ginger kitten yawned and looked up at Sally with bright eyes.

CHAPTER THIRTY

Back in Business

With a gasp, the zombie's eyes widened. "Archie?" Sally took him from the mobster and cradled the tiny cat in her arms. "You're so small."

"Mew," he replied.

"He ain't much for talking." Jackie shrugged, before turning around to see the others waiting in the room. "Fuck! You've grown, Chuck. Hardly recognize ya. And sword-guy. Pleasure?"

"Not that we aren't happy to see you," Chuck began, confusion clear on his face. "But how? And why?"

"And when?" Sally added, still cuddling with Archie.

"Fangs actually has some brains in him. When he came back to the forest, he did more than level. Turns out," she jerked her thumb back at the zombie, "*that's* the area one Archie. The cat that found us last year was originally from the fifth area."

Chuck furrowed his brow but nodded, exchanging a glance with Dent.

"Dumb vampire knew he was going to die; said he'd need us to bring the furball when the time was right. Had the pendant made, which gave a signal back to the goblins. Henkk has been training all year to get my ass over here."

"Had to be the top of the tower," Sally said as she shook her head. "So that he could aim you, huh?"

"I, uh, anticipated you having different company." Jackie grimaced and flicked her cigarette to the floor. "Fangs take out the others?"

"I'll update you as we leave this place." Sally swaddled the kitten up in her robes. "Is there a quick way down, Fern?"

"Back on floor eighteen, yes."

> New Bodyguard: Jackie, Level 23 Mobster

The mobster whistled, adjusting the case that was slung on her back. "Missed being *powerful*. Can tell you that. That's *a lot* of new skills."

"Fran and the goblins okay?" Sally pestered her, starting after the dryad toward the stairs.

"Henkk is doing what he can, keeping as many Uniques as safe as possible. Couple of Observer attacks, but nothing we couldn't handle. If we were talking pre-Architect death number of skulls, then . . ."

"We lucked out in a way there, then." Sally smiled but felt out of place. There was a great warmth in seeing Jackie again and having a kitten close to her, but it was something else too. The pressure of the eventual last stand. All her favorite people coming together to do or die one last time. It was remarkably cliché.

Jackie put her hand on her back. "You holding up okay, Sally?"

She pouted. How she missed the easy forest area. They should have just stayed there and not wormed their way through all these struggles to follow her ambition. "Humphrey killed Theo and ran away due to guilt."

"Oh, it wasn't Edward?" Jackie took out a fresh cigarette and put it in her mouth. "Fangs kept going on and on about some demon."

"Ed and Theo are like best buds. You'll probably meet him soon enough. He's another of my bodyguards." Sally narrowed her eyes at the mobster as she brought out a lighter. "Didn't you give up smoking for Fran?"

Jackie shrugged. "I'm probably going to die. Let a gal have a little fun. I *chose* this, by the way," she took a drag and blew the smoke out, "before you go thinking I got pressured into fang's little plan. The last year has been like a dream, and I've got your scrawny ass to thank for it."

"Thanks, Jackie." Sally gave her a wide smile. "The best is yet to come."

"Normally I'd roll my eyes," she replied, "but with you, I believe it."

They reached Fern's living floor and stood around while the plant person dealt with something to teleport them down.

Sally checked her STAR, to find there were notifications.

> Norah: everyone doing okay?
> Lucius: ij gote humphersy
> Lucius: ridifng
> Lucius: !!
> Norah: …

She sighed. It looked like the Shade was on the move and couldn't type properly while moving. It looked dangerously like he was still with Humphrey, but she didn't want to get her hopes up.

> Sally: dungeon complete
> Sally: reward was Jackie and a kitten
> Sally: lucy get me co-ords to meet up asap

Closing it down, she worked her jaw around. No closer to bringing Theo back—his little ploy was just to gather more allies to help solve the bigger problem. He had been acting weird for a while, and it actually tugged at her dead heart to know he had all this weight on his shoulders. Also explained why he was so sure that he would win fights if his death had been foretold.

She was sure to give him a kick when he awoke for keeping all those secrets, though.

"Gather around when ready," Fern told them. "This is usually a single person thing, but I can bend the rules a little."

"Are you coming with us?" Sally asked, as they circled by the dryad.

". . . If there is a place for me, I would like to see the greater world."

She nodded and tried to work out the mathematics of it, before a rush of vertigo and green light brought them down to the ground floor room once more. They all wavered and stumbled, apart from Fern. The kitten jumped out from Sally's grasp and padded over to where the case holding the other was still hidden.

Chuck snapped his fingers, and it came into view.

"Away from there," Sally admonished Archie. "Dangerous!"

Twisting energy pooled out of the empty case and down toward the smaller cat. Before any of them could step forward to interject, the process was complete.

Archie turned back around. "That's better, although I had hoped to grow to my full size."

"Awww!" Sally hopped over and scooped him back up. "That voice is only slightly concerning, coming from the tiny you. You absorbed the other Archie?"

"Let me out of this container."

"Yes. With the Observer side activated, it allowed me to separate myself from it. I just needed another me to consolidate into."

Chuck rubbed his face. "So we have two here, Humphrey has two, and then eye patch is in hiding."

The group stepped out of the tower into the jungle and overcast sky overhead. There was a figure already waiting for them outside, arms crossed.

"Lana?" Sally clenched her teeth, the skull atop her staff bursting into green flame.

"In a manner of speaking," the woman replied, brushing curly hair away from her face. "I spoke with your boyfriend recently."

The flames of her pending attack petered out. "If he left you alive, then you aren't part of *Last Word*?"

Lana shook her head. "I am not. See." She raised her arm up to show a normal STAR—albeit one that was a dimmer gray than Sally had ever seen.

Sally pouted and looked at her growing group of misfits. "He said he was my *boyfriend*?"

The group collectively deflated or rolled their eyes.

"Not as such, but he wouldn't stop talking about you." Lana frowned. "Took some of my blood, said to look after myself because he was going to die, and you needed protecting. Ah, but he told me not to tell you that part."

Sally bit her tongue. On one hand, he should have more faith in her and not go around telling everyone she needed to be saved—but also, it was sweet he had gathered so many of her pals around when he couldn't be here.

"It's not just me that needs protecting." She sighed. "You saw the big, spooky Architect, right? People like us are on the list to be erased." The zombie rubbed her face. "Let me go through everything that has happened again, but we can't keep doing this every time a new face appears."

The skeletal horse vanished, and the trio dropped to the floor—Lucius landing on his backside.

"A little warning next time," he grumbled.

Edward finished bandaging himself up now that he was on more stable ground. "Are you sure this is an efficient use of time?"

"No," Humphrey replied, drawing the large mace into his hands. "There are few ways to bring back a Player. Most of those will not work, as Theo is part undead."

"A fool's errand then?" Edward stretched out his back and grunted. "I'm sure you've thought about this a lot longer than I have."

"The only fool is one who does not try," the Death Knight replied, crimson flame rising at the back of his helmet.

Lucius nodded and dusted himself off. "Yeah, have some faith."

The demon grimaced, the hulking constructs in front of them illuminating the barren plain in a dim, red glow. "*Joy.*"

"And that's the abridged history of the last year," Sally took a deep breath and sighed.

"I see." Lana nodded slowly. "For what it's worth, I apologize for the other Lana-clones blaming you for the death of our originator. Accidents do happen."

Chuck shuffled forward. "Do you know who is corrupting the STARs?"

"Yes and no." The woman tilted her head. "Where they are, who they currently work for—yes. But I've never met them, nor know their name."

Sally flexed her hand. "Details then please. We will need the whole picture if we plan on eating the whole Architect."

"After working on the *Last Word* they got picked up by Seven."

The zombie groaned. That meant some of the red team might be corrupted too. *Just* what they needed—more problems. She held up the kitten and wrinkled up her nose. "New Architect might not like the corrupted Players, right?"

"I would assume not," the cat began, "but we don't know their full intentions."

As she exhaled through her nose, her STAR lit up with messages. Awkwardly trying to press it while the kitten squirmed around, she brought up the chat window. "Lucy has sent location . . . here." She pinged it across to Chuck and Dent.

"All the way down south?" Chuck furrowed his brow and looked at the swordsman, receiving a shrug in return. "With this many people . . ." He counted heads. "I can get us in off to the east of their location. We'd need to do the rest on foot."

"Or mouse," Sally murmured.

"Even better than that," Jackie interjected, a wry grin across her face. "You should see the ultimate I just got."

CHAPTER THIRTY-ONE

Shuffle the Deck

The wind whipped at Sally's face, drying out her wide smile. Even with the metal wheels jostling her as they rocketed over the rough terrain, this was truly quite the experience.

Jackie leaned over the side of the top of the stagecoach to glance down at her, her own wide grin across her face. "You see the weapon I get with this?"

"A big . . . crossbow?" Sally yelled back, a leaf almost choking her as her mouth opened.

"Twin-linked dual repeating crossbows! We need to find something to shoot!" Her head vanished back atop the coach.

"You really should be inside, Sally," Chuck admonished her from within.

She sank back into her seat and pouted across at the Druid squished in between Dent and Fern. "Killjoy," she murmured.

"It will be worse if we turn up to Humphrey with your head detached from your body because Jackie rode too close to a tree." He rolled his eyes and glared at her.

She wasn't even sure Jackie was driving. After they had been teleported to the nearby summoning circle, she had summoned it out of nowhere. An impressive ultimate that the mobster was unhealthily happy about getting to use. Even the two horses pulling the vehicle looked like they were wearing black pinstripe suits.

Kitten Archie was sleeping on Lana's lap beside her. They had all been relatively quiet once they had started moving. Being drawn to . . . well, they didn't really know what. Theo was no closer to coming back, but she had a couple more allies. She sank into the red leather bench seat.

"Alright, so we'll need to split into two Parties going forward. I'm going to suggest undead in one, and the others in the other."

Chuck nodded slowly. "So everyone present except for yourself?"

"Yeah." She pulled a face and looked out of the window at the trees flashing past. "The *Outsiders* are better frontline fighters, so you five can be the backup. I'll take Edward until . . ."

Sally sighed. Until Theo could replace him? Until another one of them died? Until the Architect broke something else about the System?

"Dent," she said. "Give us the details of potential enemies. My brain is fried."

"Architect, for one," he began. "Seven with potentially corrupted Players, the rest of the . . . red team. Any living *Last Word*. Observers?"

She nodded. Not too bad. Most of those were edible.

"The Architect; can we even fight them?"

Archie yawned and stretched as he woke to join the conversation. "If you're worried about them appearing and just erasing you with a thought, they aren't that powerful."

Sally narrowed her eyes. "*But . . . ?*"

He kneaded Lana's lap before continuing. "Originally, the System was designed to be mostly self-correcting. It is part of the reason it has been . . . tenable after the Architect's death. There are certain things the new one can change, but your core existence is not one of them."

She pouted. That sounded like even Chuck wouldn't be able to un-zombie her if they got to that point. It made the position of Architect sound like less of a god and more of an . . . administrator. A janitor to keep things tidy and make sure it was a pleasant experience. Well that had worked out *great* so far.

Lana shuffled to try to get some feeling back into her legs. "They'll have to kill us in the more traditional sense, then?"

"Indeed." Archie looked up at her. "They'll be able to summon equipment, cast skills, and send System-created Monsters. If they are smart, they will come nowhere near us and win out with attrition."

"If they did show up . . ." Sally had returned to watch the scenery speed past. "Would I even be able to punch them in their dumb face?"

Across from her, Dent smiled. "I've long given up underestimating what you and the *Outsiders* are capable of, Sally. If you want to do it, I'm sure you'll find a way."

She smiled, but she wasn't so convinced. The Architect was a few steps above Players or even a boosted Unique like the dragon. They were at least more grounded in reality, and their capabilities made sense. What if the new Architect turned the ground into soft cheese and she sank and suffocated in it?

"We're about here," Jackie yelled from the top of the wagon.

Sally opened her map, and her little blip was near the mark where they intended to find the others. A weight sank into her stomach. Maybe she could get the mobster to swing the stagecoach around the area a few times until she felt ready for this.

It slid to a stop, and the horses whinnied from the front. Too late.

Chuck leaned forward and placed his hand on her knee. "We are here for you. You've got this." He grimaced. "You're really cold, even through your jeans."

"I have *no idea* what the fuck is going on." Fern deflated and tried to work the handle on their side of the wagon.

"It gets easier," Sally said, almost believing it. Jackie dropped down in front of the window and opened the door as the zombie leaned against it, causing Sally to fall out onto the ground. "Gotta fall downward before falling upward, right?" She groaned and righted herself with the mobster's help.

She dusted herself off as the rest of the group dismounted and walked over to join her. A plain of barren stone went out in front of them. Ruined Monsters lay in piles for a distance until the flash of combat drew their attention farther ahead. Familiar shapes. Narrowing her eyes, she stormed toward them.

Humphrey wrenched the large maul from the body of the golem and stepped back. Before turning toward the next opponent, he froze. Lucius popped out from his shadow and stood beside Edward, both slowly moving themselves away from the Death Knight.

He turned slowly, to meet the burning glare of Sally standing nearby. Her eyes were alight in bright crimson, arms crossed as her foot tapped against the floor. Shadowed figures stood a way off behind her, but he couldn't focus on them with her taking up his full attention.

Humphrey dropped to his knee and bowed toward her. "Sally . . . I'm so sorry."

"What for?"

"For allowing myself to be controlled. Killing Theo . . . and then for running away."

"So, what are you going to do about it?" Her foot continued to tap on the ground.

"We are trying to find a way to bring him back, if you'll forgive me. If you do not, I understand." He continued to look at the dirt before him.

"Stand."

Humphrey gradually rose to his feet, his head still low and not wanting to meet her gaze.

"Killing Theo was a terrible thing," she began, her voice quiet. "But you broke my heart when you ran and left us alone. Even if you felt guilty, I needed you. Norah needs you. We all do."

"I am here now." He lifted his head. "Lucius reminded me of what truly mattered. I wish to atone for my misgivings and earn your forgiveness and be there for you once more."

"You need to forgive yourself, Humps." She shook her head and sighed. "You can ask Theo for forgiveness if you wish, but do not rest until you *get* to ask him. Good lesson teaching, Lucius. What did . . . Edward teach you, Humphrey?" She raised an eyebrow at seeing the demon part of the gang again.

"Mostly how to get beaten up by an angel." He turned with a grin as the demon rolled his eyes.

As much as she wanted to dig deeper into how cool that fight sounded, she instead ran up and threw her arms around the Death Knight. "I'm repressing everything too hard to give a genuine emotional response," she whispered, "but I'll just say *wah*."

He gave her a pat on the back. "*Wah*, indeed. I am here."

"Good." She released her grip on him. "Also, I brought some friends with me. You know most of them, but I'll introduce them anyway to set the scene."

Lucius and Edward exchanged shrugs.

"Chuck, Dent, Jackie, Fern, and a *good* Lana. But even better . . ." She bit her lip as the tiny figure moved toward them.

"Big brother," kitten Archie said.

"Very little brother." The Death Knight grinned, kneeling to pick him up.

Sally spun back to the gathered groups. "Alright, let's organize into Parties as previously discussed. Chuck, Dent, Fern, Lana, Jackie. Then pops and Edward can join me. Archie, you are too small to—"

She stopped as she turned back to see the cat turn into mist and enter the skeletal face of the Death Knight.

"*Humphrey!*"

"He started it." The Death Knight shied away from her as she deflated.

Chuck rubbed his chin. "Not that putting all our eggs in one basket is a great idea, but this was kind of the plan, eventually. Certainly easier than getting the other two *out* at present."

Chuck has left the Party
Dent has left the Party
Jackie has left the Party
Humphrey has joined the Party
Edward has joined the Party

She waved away the notifications. "Ugh, remember when we had actual class names and loot meant something?" She pouted. "Architect needs to fix that."

The druid pulled a face. "Are you sure? It's not like you liked interfacing with that side of things."

Despite the valid point, she chose to ignore him. Instead, she waved a hand toward all the Monsters being killed. "So, what are you even doing here?"

"Forgetting that we're incapable of looting," Edward grumbled, his eyes avoiding the glare of the Death Knight.

"There's an item that can be crafted . . ." Humphrey rubbed at the back of his helmet as he looked down at the zombie. "It's not so much a resurrect, as it can rewind time."

Sally snapped her fingers. "That's thinking outside the box, since we can't use the usual methods."

Chuck came over to join them while Dent and Lana went to loot the corpses already on the ground. "Still not guaranteed, correct?" He grimaced.

"No." The Death Knight shook his head. "With his soul in place, we have a greater chance, but I do not know whether it would reset him back an hour . . . or longer."

"System damn it, Humps. If you bring my pup back at Level One again, I will personally make you power level him twenty-four seven. I still can't believe you just vacuumed up that Archie without saying anything."

"It is too dangerous for them to go alone." Humphrey shrugged and picked up the mace to rest on his shoulders. "They'll need to take this chance to be safe within me."

She waved him away. "Alright, what do we need from these Monsters? I need to grind my teeth on something that I won't have to apologize to after."

"An item called *[Chrono Juice]*. We need one hundred of them to start with."

Dent stood up from a little way away. "I have four."

"Two here," Lana added.

Sally deflated and opened her Inventory to retrieve Humphrey's greatsword. "Better get going then, we don't have much t—"

"Opportunity," Lucius finished, helpfully.

Chuck hummed to himself; his eyes focused on STAR menus. "Is the *[Timesworn Key of Echoes]* craft?"

Humphrey nodded.

The Druid murmured something that may have been several curses.

"We can look up stuff like that?" Sally furrowed her brow.

"*Yes.*" The Death Knight grinned. "You never asked."

She flexed her hand a few times. "Alright, everyone!" They all turned to pay attention. "Most importantly, Chucky, you need to change your Party name to *Insiders*. I have mandated it."

". . . Done."

"Secondly, we aren't putting all our eggs in the Theo deus ex machina. As much as it pains me to say it, we'll need to assume that he is dead for good." She wrinkled up her nose. "With the Architect growing in power by the hour, we need at least a plan B, or some reasonable plausibility for when we eventually fail upward."

They each nodded, other than Fern, who had their usual blank expression.

"So I want the *Insiders* to focus on gathering stuff for the key with the overcooked name. Since you have three Players, you can loot more effectively. The *Outsiders* will go find the last Archie." She turned to look at the Death Knight, who nodded back.

"Already notified any capable blue team Parties to assist with some of the other materials," Dent said, closing his own STAR.

Sally smiled and looked around at them. The oddest found family you could ask for, but they were hers. "Let's save the universe!" she yelled out to their medium cheers.

Fern shrugged, raising their arms awkwardly after everyone had calmed already.

CHAPTER THIRTY-TWO

Brained

Norah sank down on the throne and exhaled.

"Sorry this is so boring, Theo," she said to the inert body of the vampire. "If only my priests were still alive." It never took this long. Although, she was usually the one dead—so her view of that time might be distorted.

Knowing the System, the ability to summon the priests to complete the ritual would come at her next level up—or maybe at twenty-five. Some guilt about not leveling up quicker gnawed at her stomach, but what was done was done.

The Mummy extended out a bandage, unfurling it through the air, before curling it back and into her hand. She repeated this process another handful of times, then her brow furrowed.

As the next bandage went out, it caught the light in an odd way. Instead of being a dull gray fabric, it now appeared to be covered in gold leaf. It returned to her hand, and she raised it to see that it was normal once more.

"Curious," she said.

Her eyes went over to the side as chat messages popped up, the notifications of the Party members switching around. A warm smile emerged beneath her bandages.

"Not long now," she whispered, as vibrations through the ground caused dust to fall from the ceiling of the stone chamber. "Not long at all."

The skeletal horse and zombie mouse thundered through the undergrowth.

For all that the day had brought them, Sally was energized. The anger and panic had worn away to leave her with the determination to fix this third area. Fix the whole world. Which appeared to just be this singular continent, oddly.

She had given herself enough time to be morose about Theo, but seeing all her pals together again . . . she had to do her best for the System, no matter who fell along the way. It wasn't her *job* to do it. She was meant to be a lowly zombie stuck in a diner for the rest of her existence. But the System had let her get away with more and more—so it'd be rude to not continue to run with it. Plus, dying and being reset was Theo's thing, and he could keep it.

Edward was a decent enough stand-in for now . . . if he would stop pulling on her cloak. She glared back at him, to which he returned a sheepish grin. The skeletal horse had much more room, but he hadn't been eager to get back on it for some reason. Probably wasn't comfortable being sandwiched between the metal Death Knight and the fleshless horse. Lucius was shadowing Humphrey instead.

They were riding back deeper into the jungle, where Chuck and Dent were sure that the eye patch Archie would be hiding. With him being one of the cats, she had thought he might be able to sense that they were coming . . . and with how he could predict the vampire's demise they might know the safest place to be picked up from and that the *Outsiders* would be looking for him.

She had the feeling that there were some other things going on in the background that she hadn't been clued in on yet. Theo had to die for something else to happen, perhaps. That's why it had been kept a secret, so as to not interfere with the progression of the . . . end times. A bit melodramatic to call it that, but with the overcast sky and looming threat, it fit well enough.

Before setting off, she had asked Humphrey what joining all the five Archies together would do—especially if they were absorbed by him. He had just shrugged, which seemed like bullshit. There was no way he hadn't spoken to the cat about it or knew through their memories. Another bad surprise to be mindful of, no doubt.

She looked at the map again as they bounded over fallen trees and grassy patches. There was a dungeon in the nearby vicinity. It seemed like a good bet. With the world going crazy, people weren't likely to want to stand around and plan out a dungeon run. The only people who would be trying would be those hunting down something specific . . .

Her jaw clenched. There had been two Parties of reds outside the Spire dungeon. Were they waiting for her specifically? What did they know that she didn't? Other than how to work most parts of the System she had been intentionally avoiding. She had a feeling that the identity of Seven, their leader, might play some part of it.

Nobody seemed to have seen them or could describe them. Given that their doctrine was especially hostile, those sorts of leaders were usually at the forefront. The big bullies hoping to crush things to rule over the dust. Acting from the shadows . . . just meant that there was something else at play. Another reason for the formation of the faction and mess in this third area.

It couldn't be any of the *Outsiders*, as they were all in a coma. Edward spent all his time doing his part in leading the Wastelands. What about the *Insiders*? Jackie was safe. She was too low a level to be around here and had made her peace with living a quiet life up until being called upon. Fern was suspicious, but also completely overwhelmed with life outside of their dungeon.

Part of her believed that Chuck could have masterminded leading both factions. Either to ensure he remained on top of the food chain in this area, or . . . no, there was no real benefit for him. His plans seemed to click with how he felt about the System way back in the forest area. The fact that he had killed now proved how far he was willing to go for the blue team's worldview. Dent had only wanted to be the best swordsman in the world. Would he have chosen red if not for the connection to Chuck?

Lana was the oddest one out, which was saying a lot. Not really a Player or Monster. A clone of the real one, but seemingly as pleasant as the originator. Currently, anyway. She had helped Theo, where the other clones were part of *Last Word* and wanted an end to the System.

It was very convenient that all these friendly faces were together at the right time, to the point that it was hard for her to trust it. And trusting people was one of her key facets. That and being fine with murder and eating brains.

"Contact ahead," Humphrey called out. "Reds."

She narrowed her eyes and gathered her focus on what lay in front. They had reached the dungeon already, her internal monologue making the time pass by quicker than expected. A semicircle of stone sat among bushes, a gated doorway on the flat side already wide open.

Two Parties of reds, these ones not just standing around awaiting their demise, however. They had dug in, used logs and rocks to create low fortifications for their casters and ranged attackers to fire from while the melee classes stood ready at the front with shields up. Either they were camping every dungeon and landmark in this area, or there really was something up.

No matter, perhaps a little eating would help calm her mind.

It was times like these that she missed the Mummy and the ability to be flung into the middle of bad guys. Badder guys? The skull on her staff burst into green flame as she hopped up into a standing position on the mount's saddle.

[Quick Reversal]

Edward cast a buff on her as the *[Mortis Bomb]* flew off toward the crowd.

The lights of the Player's attacks blazed through the area like a terrible disco. *[Impenetrable Defense]* flared up as Humphrey dropped from the horse as it vanished, his arms wide to attract all leveled attacks.

Lucius popped out from the Death Knight and immediately hopped over and into Sally's shadow as she jumped from the vanished mouse and shot out *[Meat Hook]* over the heads of the waiting melee and into a Ranger near the back.

The beam of pink energy drew her over their heads, and she stuck her tongue out at them. *[Endless Dead]*. Dozens of stored zombies began to crawl up around the reds as she bounced off some kind of spherical shield that was protecting the ranged attackers. Sally fell to her back and rolled away to avoid an attack bursting up earth from where she had been. She slunk behind a normal zombie that dropped from a follow-up attack, a wide grin on her face.

[Desecrate Life]

She flourished the staff around, jabbing out on occasion to put holes into random enemies—whether they were heavily armored or not. All the while moving away and putting undead between her and whoever tried to attack.

At the last moment, she felt the presence of a rogue class appear behind her, the slight vertigo of their abilities wearing on her before it faded off and the demon's enchantment activated. She spun near instantly and the intended attack against her was rebuffed. Instead, she hit them with the skull end of her staff, twirling it around to slice them with Skeleton Key at the base. First slash caught their arm, disarming them, second twirl caught them across the collarbone and dug in deep.

"Why are you here?" she growled at them, pulling the dagger free from the wound, a shadowed version stabbing the opponent in their legs.

Humphrey radiated with energy as his buffs pulsed over him. With slow, methodical steps, he had worked his way in among the crowd, blocking and riposting. Every strike perfectly calculated and deliberate. From his side, Edward would dart in to take advantage of every time he would put an enemy on the back foot, making up for the Death Knight's slower speed by weaving in high spikes of damage as he struck out at vital points.

The red didn't answer her question and was even less talkative once she had eaten the brain from their skull. Anger in their eyes, though, which reminded her of Charlotte. A brief wave of guilt rode through her, and she wondered whether she should try to save some of these misguided souls.

"Lucy!" she began, turning toward her shadow. Before she could finish that thought something weighty struck the side of her head, and the world tipped to the side. Briefly, she panicked that someone was about to eat her brains—either the pent-up guilt and horror she repressed from her own actions—or something had been knocked loose in her head.

System messages flared up in her eyes as she struggled to get the strength to right herself, and without thinking about it, she selected *[Yes]* to get it out of the way.

The sounds of battle vanished, and a cold feeling washed over her. Raising her head, she blinked away the brief pain in her skull and observed the inky darkness around her. The STAR, illuminating plain stone beneath her, *bloiped* as a message came in.

> Ruben: Hey Sally?
> Ruben: Do you want to go bowling?

CHAPTER THIRTY-THREE

Calm and Collected

She groaned and rolled into a sitting position. Clearly she had died, and this was some manner of penance for all the evil she had brought to the world. The chat window closed, and she palmed at her eyes. She didn't even like bowling and was still lukewarm on the dragon. They weren't even real notifications; they felt like she had dreamed them.

Opening her eyes to glare at the empty darkness surrounding her, she now saw another pop-up that was behind the faux-chat.

> Dungeon
> Solo—Difficulty: Hard

That started to make some sense. She had accepted entrance to the dungeon in trying to escape getting her skull further broken in. Hand up, she massaged where she had been struck. Bruised, but any other damage had been healed up. Must have been some ability to have hit her so hard.

Her eyes narrowed in trying to see where the exit was, but after a dozen feet or so, there was just pitch-black gloom in all directions. Nothing in her STAR allowed her an easy escape, either.

"What's the point?" she asked the empty expanse and sighed. "I've already done solo stuff recently, and it's pretty boring."

It only ended up with her amassing a bunch of zombies and chewing through any problem until one of her friends showed up to temper her runaway mania. A dungeon would be no different.

The squeal of a door came from behind her, and she spun around, the green flames of a prepared *[Mortis Bomb]* illuminating the surrounding fog. There was a doorway there now, but it wasn't open.

She rolled her eyes and went over to it. "Spooky stuff won't bother me. You really don't know who you're dealing with." Might be odd to talk to the dungeon, but somebody had to hear her.

Grumbling, she pushed open the door and stepped into a brightly lit room, causing her to cover her eyes with the back of her arm. Sounds started to filter into her ears as her eyes adjusted.

"You're late for your shift, Sally." A voice came from the side.

Wide-eyed, she lowered her arm to see the diner where she used to work. "Miss Doris?"

"Who else?" The woman shook her head. "Get into uniform and take orders. It's about to get busy."

Sally nodded slowly in disbelief. The tables already had several people sitting and eating or drinking coffee. Warm daylight came in through the windows, illuminating the place so familiar to her. Absentmindedly, she changed her current outfit back to the white blouse and red skirt. Gradually, she shuffled around to her place behind the counter.

"Not bad, System," she murmured. Next to the counter beside the till was a piece of paper. A character sheet for necromancer, a doodle of a very angry looking cloaked zombie at the top. Looked a little like her.

The door opened, and a figure was silhouetted against the bright light, barely any other details of the world visible beyond the entrance.

By instinct, a smile rose up on her face. "How can I help you today?"

As the figure stepped forward, she could see that it was a man, younger than the usual clientele. Maybe around her age. Handsome, but looked like he could recite half of the script of . . . that fantasy movie . . . by heart. She couldn't think of the right reference, which made her brow furrow.

"Coffee, please."

"Sure thing, Theo." She smiled again, despite the confusion. "Not dead anymore?"

"Not here," he replied, as she turned to find the coffee pot. "I can be alive forever, here."

"Must be nice," she murmured as she picked up the container of coffee granules. *RatJuice*, it said. Disgusting.

"You can stay here with me, if you like." His voice was calm . . . soothing, almost. "Be alive forever too."

She rolled her eyes and turned back around, a mug in hand. "You must really underestimate me. Here's your coffee."

"Oh?" Theo tilted his head. "It's not tempting?"

"I'm only playing along for my own amusement." She glared at him. "You think I give a fuck about the diner anymore? I'm the Queen of the Undead you hacky excuse for mental manipulation." Her hands clenched against the edge of the counter, splitting the wood under her tight grip. "Either maintain the illusion or let me proceed with your dumbass dungeon challenges."

Theo pulled a face, before fading away, the whole diner following suit—blowing away like dust in a breeze she didn't feel to leave nothing but an empty, stone room lit by a lantern.

Sally deflated and looked over to the side, where a large treasure chest sat beside a closed door. "If that is a mimic, I will become *untenable*."

The treasure chest faded away like dust.

She stomped forward into the next room, pushing through the door. Her feet squelched on soft flooring, as lanterns lit up. A chamber made of writhing and bloodied flesh. Figures sat up against the walls, their heads cracked open and brains missing.

"Pass." She waved her hand and yawned. "I've got better things to do today if you could just hurry this along."

A few seconds of silence passed before this illusion vanished away too. She had spent every waking minute of her existence in this world trying to come to terms with what she was, what she had lost, and the effect her actions had on the System. Some cheap party tricks weren't going to dazzle her or shake her to the core.

No door appeared.

"If you're struggling for ideas . . . how about the time that Theo and I tried to smooch under the crimson moon—but now he's dead! What about reliving the time Humps killed Theo, and I was unable to stop it! All the loot I never looked at that was secretly useful stuff! Show me that the world would have been better if I hadn't killed the people that I have!"

She clenched her jaw and relented to the silence.

"You are no fun." A voice hissed from outside her peripheral vision.

Sally turned, but there was nobody there. "I'm loads of fun, just not in this specific type of dungeon."

"Well," the voice continued, now seemingly on the other side of her, "if you don't complete it properly, then how can I give you the reward at the end?"

"I'd rather just leave, thanks." She glared around, but still nobody was to be seen.

"Even though it is something that will . . ." The voice cut off and faded away.

Sally rolled her eyes. "You can't decide whether to say it'll help bring Theo back or help me defeat the Architect, right? Which one is more important to me?"

"Fuck you!"

"Just let me out and I'll—" She stumbled out into the heat and smells of battle, directly into the weight of someone in heavy armor.

[Eat Brains]

She pushed the figure over and glared around. The Death Knight was withdrawing his sword from a fallen Player, while Edward was patching himself up with some bandages.

"Oh, there you are." Humphrey grinned. "We were worried that you had fallen."

"As if." She rolled her eyes. "I just went through the dungeon solo already."

Lucius popped out of the Death Knight's shadow and stretched out. "I did wonder why I was forced out of helping you. Almost ate some damage myself for a change."

"What dungeon?" Humphrey crossed his arms.

Sally jerked her thumb backward toward the empty space she had vanished from. "Got a pop-up over there."

He raised an eyebrow and stepped over the dead bodies to get closer to her. "There is nothing there. The *actual* dungeon you have to enter physically, over there." He leveled a plated finger over toward the clear doorway leading down into something underground.

She shrugged. Either that Player had a weird skill that stuck her into a space where her mental faculties were tested, or something else was keen to prod around inside her empty skull.

"Are you okay? What happened?" He put a hand on her shoulder, concern in his skeletal face.

"It was somewhere with a lot of illusion magic, to either trap me or cause me trauma, perhaps." She rubbed the side of her head with the staff. "The diner from the old world, bodies of people I had killed. Then I broke it, so it let me out."

"That doesn't surprise me," Edward murmured, as he walked over. He was soaked with sweat and had rips through his bloodied suit.

Humphrey scratched at the side of his head. "Hmm, I am not aware of such a thing. Even with the memories I have absorbed."

Sally pouted. "So that was some kind of bespoke shenanigan? Someone targeting me to take me out?" She glared around the area.

"Yes. Shame that they underestimated you."

She waved him off. "I have plenty of issues, but I'm aware of them. Prodding at my last life, my morals, or what is troubling me at present just makes me angry. And hungry. But I couldn't see them to eat them." Her head tilted to the side and pouted. "Think it was Seven or the Architect?"

Humphrey opened and closed his mouth a few times. "It is too beyond me to say. I could imagine cases where that could be possible, but it is unlike anything I am aware of."

The zombie deflated. Architect could probably do something similar with little issue. Seven could only do it if they had some kind of Unique ability, or their STAR had been corrupted. Those should be the only two currently targeting her specifically.

She turned her head toward the dungeon. "So I guess we still need to do this, then?"

"Yes. There might be more reds in there as well. It is not a 'closed door' dungeon." The Death Knight looked over at the other two, the Shade helping to patch up the demon. "We can't rule it out as a hiding place for eye patch."

Sally nodded. She was glad that the three had no issue finishing the Players off, even if they did look a little more damaged than usual. *[Living Dead]* wouldn't help Edward, but she threw it up for the rest of them. She ground her sharp teeth together. There was something stuck in the back of her mind.

A choice to be made. Some weakness to be erased. The illusion dungeon put it all into perspective—helped her instead of breaking her. With the weight of everything happening in the System, there was a moment of clarity in her aching head.

"Lucius," she gestured the Shade over. "I want you . . . nah, I can't even make that joke with you." She sighed and shook her head from side to side.

"What is it?" He slipped over some gore as he tried to get closer.

"I want you to use *[Seek Answers]* on me."

CHAPTER THIRTY-FOUR

Already Perfect

The gathered three stared at her blankly, although Edward didn't know what she was asking. She crossed her arms and wrinkled up her face. "What?"

"Are you . . . sure about that?" Lucius winced away, a sweat drop emoji appearing behind him.

"What's the worst that could happen?" She shrugged.

Humphrey shook his head. "It's not like we really know what it does. What if it erases the memories of your old world?"

"Good. If anything, those memories are a weight on my shoulders. I can't return there. All it does is make me miss something I can't have. If Theo is gone, perhaps it will stop the ache over that too." She rubbed her forehead. "It would be hypocritical to put others through this if I wouldn't do it to myself, right?"

"True. But I'm . . . still not seeing the benefit."

Edward squirmed; his brow furrowed. "Can someone fill me in?"

Humphrey turned his head. "Lucius has a skill that forces the target to answer three questions truthfully. It also seems to erase any disbelief and hate they have for the System."

The demon nodded slowly. "Isn't your burning hatred of the System what drives you?"

"Used to be." She shrugged. "But this is my home . . . you are my family and friends. I need to be undivided in that. If I'm too hell-bent on bringing the System down, then I'll lose sight of what truly matters."

Humphrey deflated and rubbed his eye sockets. "I cannot stop you, but I do not know what the ramifications may be."

"I'm on board if we get to ask the questions," Edward said with a wide grin.

"One each." She wagged her finger. "I realize what I'm asking could be dangerous, especially at the final hour, but I have faith."

The Death Knight just relented with a gesture, and the Shade stepped closer to her.

"Ready?" Lucius asked calmly.

She returned a nod.

[Seek Answers]

For a moment, there was a cooling sensation. Like settling into a bed of fresh sheets. Calming and comforting. She could hear her heartbeat, like it was banging on the window on the outside, wanting to get in. Her teeth clenched, but before she needed to act, it was over.

The drab daylight filtered into her eyes, and she took a deep gasp of the warm jungle air. In front of her, the three still stood, Humphrey glaring at the demon, who looked sheepish.

"Hey," she said, furrowing her brow.

"How do you feel?" The Shade put his hand on her shoulder. "Everything okay?"

Sally raised up her hands to view them, pouting as her brow furrowed. "I don't . . . feel any different."

A smiling emoji appeared in front of her vision. "Maybe you were perfect all along?"

"Yeah," she said as she grinned. "Now let's go into the dungeon and stop wasting what time we have."

They gathered up, and she put away her undead with a wave of her hands. Being able to drop a horde right among people was perhaps her strongest skill, on reflection. Something about suddenly being surrounded by hungry undead spooked most Players, even discounting how much the zombies would get in the way or add their own damage to the battle.

Humphrey stomped up to the open doorway of the dungeon and paused. "You're sure that you're fine?"

Sally nodded. "I still have all my memories. There's just no . . . I don't feel angry at the System for bringing me here. You remember back at the start, how I felt like the *Last Word*? Now I'm just . . . this is my home, and I need to protect it. I feel reinforced. Validated."

He nodded in response and started walking into the dungeon.

She followed behind him, pulling the hood over her head. Sure, it had been a risk—not knowing how it would affect her mind—but she knew she needed it. Her human side had been in a panic since day one, and as much as she had been able to drown it out with the zombie side taking the reins . . . things had gotten a bit much as of late.

Now? She felt calmer. More focused. She grinned, before turning a scowl toward the two lurking at the back. "So, what did you guys ask me?"

They winced at the question, but the demon and Shade exchanged a quick glance. "You didn't hear or weren't aware?" Edward raised an eyebrow.

"No?" She narrowed her eyes further.

"Nothing weird, then." The Shade shook his head, a sweat drop appearing.

Humphrey grunted and turned a glare back at them. "If we could focus on the dungeon, please."

The pair nodded, and Sally shrugged, turning back to watch where they were going with her eyes only slowly moving away from the suspicious two. Dimly lit by lanterns, the chamber they were entering had the broken bodies of whatever Monsters were supposed to be guarding here.

"Set dressing, or reds ahead?" She crouched beside one of the dead. Some kind of bipedal lizard, armor made of bones, and a feathered headdress on their bloodied head.

"The latter," Humphrey replied, flames starting to curl down his greatsword. "No experience to be gained here, so their intentions are . . ." He stopped and furrowed his brow over his empty eye sockets. There was an open doorway ahead of them, but his head turned slowly to the left.

Sally frowned, following his gaze to the plain brickwork wall. "What—" she began.

A beam of light shot from the wall, spiking across the room toward them. Catching through the peak of her hood, it slammed into the Death Knight's shoulder armor, stopping about an inch into him.

"Ouch," he growled, crimson flame dancing behind his helmet.

It wasn't an energy attack though, and Sally looked up at it as it retracted. It looked like a sword, flat and silver—but weaved through the air, stretched out as it had come from the wall, wiggling as if it was a snake.

Lucius struck a pose and held his hands out to form a triangle. With the hiss of air being released, the whole side of that wall vanished to appear as a soft shadow. In another room just past it, a man and a woman stood, both wearing red tabards. Surprise illuminated their faces in being found, as the wavy sword snaked back to the man.

[Compelled Duel]

Humphrey immediately strode toward the man, the duel intending to stop the odd attacker from getting to any of the squishier Party members.

"I have to hold this one," Lucius groaned, his hands still extended. It was larger than what he could usually shadow away, so that made sense to Sally.

As she gestured for the demon to follow her, the woman in the room pulsed with purple energy. "You're on your own Lambert," she said, before sinking away through the floor, bubbles pooling around her.

"Damnit!" the man growled and thrust his sword toward the looming Death Knight. It shimmered and flowed through the air like a ribbon, almost circling the plated figure before darting down—striking Humphrey on the side of the head.

He stopped and glared at the man. "You corrupted your STAR for something so pitiful?"

Sally slid toward the side of them to see—and the Death Knight was right; on the man's wrist was a glow of unmistakable red. At a guess, it had allowed him to use his sword like a wiggly worm that could go through walls. She nodded to herself at this astute observation.

Humphrey swung his greatsword around, the snake-like weapon of the Player wrapping around it but doing little to absorb the force.

"We do what we need to. The world needs rid of filth like yourselves." He was sweating, and his eyes were full of anger.

"Incorrect," Humphrey interrupted, fire blazing along his weapon. With a jolt forward, it tore through the ribbon sword and cleaved straight through the chest and neck of the man. "Giving into desperate power makes you weaker, not stronger."

He looked over at the nearby staircase as the Player slumped over onto the floor. "That makes me the winner." With a shrug, he gestured for the others to come through the shadowed wall. "This might be a good shortcut."

Sally nodded and led the others through, allowing the Shade to let go of his spell once they were all through. The Players must have known that they would be on the way—otherwise they wouldn't be waiting to stick the sword through the wall. A couple of inches lower, and it would have been quite the assassination attempt.

"The other Player probably went to warn the others," she said as they went to the stairwell leading downward. "My assumption is a full Party of corrupted STARs."

Edward rubbed the back of his head and looked back at the wall now blocking their escape. "What's all this about? If you explained it previously, I probably wasn't listening."

She narrowed her eyes at him and stopped at the top of the stairs. "We're all bugged as Uniques, right? Which often comes with an ability. Something the System has given you that it probably shouldn't have but knows how to work with it."

Humphrey nodded. "Corrupted STARs are from Players stealing some ability from the System without its consent. There are usually unintended consequences from the usage."

"We fought against one in the first area," the zombie continued, "who turned into a fallen angel or something really edgy. Some of the evil Lana's have a potentially incurable poison. This dude had a wiggly worm sword."

They looked down at the corpse. His STAR was now colorless, just a shadow of whatever it was before, and his sword looked regular.

Lucius kneeled to pick it up and check. He swung it side to side to confirm, and it was indeed regular now. "The lady sunk through the floor. Some sort of teleportation?" A question mark appeared beside his head.

Sally shrugged. "Just some way of delaying the . . ." She glanced over at the demon. ". . . one-way trip into my stomach."

Humphrey started off down the stairs, and they followed suit. With potentially unknown powers expecting them, they were slightly more on guard than they usually cared to be. The Death Knight led the way down into a long hallway, torches illuminating the walls, with the demon in the back to keep an eye out to make sure the bubble-woman didn't try to surprise them.

"You think I could fix them?" Lucius asked, whispering from behind her.

She shook her head. "Don't want you touching the corrupt stuff, Lucy. We don't know if it could spread or anything." She wrinkled up her nose. "If you're going to be fixing people, we'll want you in top form, right?"

The Shade agreed. A thumbs-up emoji appeared beside his head.

Humphrey stopped and raised his hand up, and the rest of them halted. It looked as though there was a doorway ahead of them leading to a wider room.

Sally strained her ears in an attempt to pick out any noise. At first—nothing—but then there was a grumbling voice.

"Told you we should just kill the animal."

"You can't even catch the blasted thing," a deeper voice boomed out.

"Well now the undead are here." This one, the woman from before. "What do you plan now? Your skill didn't work, and Lambert is dead. They might already be upon us."

"Then Mus here can kill them off, right? Your arrows loaded up, big guy?"

"Yeah," the deeper voice sounded out.

Sally leaned forward, as close to the Death Knight's head as she could manage. "Humps! Humps!" she whispered.

He turned his head slowly and narrowed his eye sockets at her.

"We have to save the cat."

CHAPTER THIRTY-FIVE

Falling STARs

A bulky man holding an overly large crossbow grunted as he aimed at the doorway raised at the top of the set of stairs. The lowered room they were in held no information about where the supposed cat had gotten to. Radiant light swirled around the thick bolt, ready to be fired. Once the undead Party stepped through, they'd get a taste of his corrupted skill.

If only Janie and Grant would stop bickering. He rolled his eyes and tried to tune them out. More the fool Lambert if he got picked off and killed after Grant's skill hadn't gotten rid of the zombie. Seven might be mad about it, because it took awhile to get a new corrupt STAR sorted, but it wasn't really any trouble for him. Once he killed the undead group, he was sure to be lavished with praise from their leader.

A cloaked figure stepped out from the shadowed hall to the top of the stairs. Crimson eyes and a long staff in their hands.

His finger clicked the trigger, and the bolt went out, detonating at the top of the stairs into a burst of divine fire. Lowering his crossbow, he held his hand up, causing the fire to persist and block the passageway beyond.

"There we go." He grinned. "I'll just keep this up as long as needed."

"You want us to go ahead and catch Neil up, or assist?" Grant asked.

"Nah, you—"

"That was rather rude," a voice whispered from behind his ear.

Lucius rammed the dagger end of his shadowed staff into the back of the man, who stumbled forward. The focus on holding the fire wall up dropped, and it petered out quickly.

From the top of the stairs, the large figure of the Death Knight burst forth, leaping from the higher platform down to the wounded man. As his sword blazed bright crimson, he landed, skewering the bulky Player straight through.

"Damn!" Grant growled. "We need to—" He turned to the woman, but only a handful of purple bubbles were in the place she was just standing.

He turned back to see that the room was totally empty, as if everyone else had vanished. As his brow furrowed and his hammer shook in his hand, his boots started to take him down to the exit. Then, the shock of pain and a quick death—not even time to register what happened before he dropped to the floor.

"Ha!" Edward grinned. "Even your eyes betrayed you." He withdrew his thin sword from the slain Player.

Sally slouched against the wall and rolled her eyes. "On one hand, it's pretty weak that you all have these abilities you've never told me about. But there's also no way I'm going to learn and remember like . . . way over a hundred skills."

"You at least know the basics of what we regularly use, though?" Humphrey wiped his sword off and grinned.

"The basics, sure." She rolled her eyes again. "You're invincible, Lucy is invisible, and Edward is inevitable."

"That's not . . ." The Death Knight narrowed his eye sockets. "What does that make you?"

"*Impatient*. Let's go eat the rest of these Players." She pushed off from the wall and started off toward the door out. "This one didn't even get to use his broken ability. How mean of you, Edward."

"I'm a demon, and it's not my fault he can't pass a basic blindness check." He folded his arms and let her go past.

"Don't start talking like that's a thing. Any excuse to stab a man through the eye socket." She shook her head as the rest of them followed.

"That's not something I'm known for." He furrowed his brow and then looked back at the others. "Is it?"

The Shade twirled his shadowed staff. "I didn't think I'd get much use out of it, but I can store the last three weapons I've shadowed to draw from as my own."

"You have my sword, then?" Humphrey asked, ignoring the demon.

"And Norah's bandages." A thumbs-up emoji appeared. "Those seemed like the most useful three. It uses a Shadow charge to bring out, and opening up that wall used a bunch too, but since I've never fully explained or expanded on that mechanic, we'll continue on as normal."

Sally sighed. When was the last time she got to be meta about her skills or how the System did things? She couldn't remember, because she wasn't good at remembering. If only she could remember why that was . . .

The next passage took them to a split in three directions, stone doorways that led to three rooms. From the one straight ahead, amber light pooled out into the open space. The doorway on the left was closed, while the third on the right looked as though it had some kind of lock on it.

"Normally, I'd say that was our best bet." She jabbed her staff toward the locked door. "But bubble-girl could probably go through it."

Lucius stepped up beside her and put his gloved hand on the door. It vanished and allowed them to see inside.

Dead Monsters, in some kind of storage room that had been looted already. She gave him a nod, and he removed his hand; the door turning back to solid stone.

Sally tapped her chin in thought. "Second guess would be the boss area, right? That's where I'd go and hide in plain sight, as the boss."

Humphrey nodded and then put his hand up to his forehead, the flame behind his helmet flickering wildly. "To the left, then."

"You have a map inside that head of yours?" She grinned and turned to that door. Before entering, she paused and furrowed her brow at it.

"Archie has memories of the layout. It is imperfect but will lead us to the right path." He stopped behind her. "Everything okay?"

She tilted her head backward to look up at him. "Usually we aren't *expected* in a dungeon, so we are at a disadvantage this time. If Theo was here, he would say we need to develop a door breaching routine for safety."

"Are you sure he wouldn't just push through and solo everything?" Edward murmured to himself at the back, still loud enough for everyone to hear.

"Here's my plan," Sally started. "We'll do it as I explain it, so it's like one of those . . . no, you wouldn't get the reference. How sad is it that there's only two people in this world I can make pop culture references with? And one of them is double-dead, and the other wants to ascend and become god?"

Lucius flexed his fingers, his whole body tensed and ready. "Is this part of the routine?"

"No . . . no, it's not." She pulled a face at him. "Humps, you're going to block the majority of the door, because you do. Have something defensive ready for if we are immediately attacked. Lucius, you'll shadow the door, squished next to pops so that we get the jump on anyone trying to jump on us." She took a deep breath. "I'll scoot down between Humphrey's legs with *[Meat Hook]* and *[Mortis Bomb]* ready to assault any targets."

They stood in position, awaiting her word for the door to be shadowed.

"And what about me?" Edward asked.

"Ah!" Sally jolted up and turned back. "I forgot you were still there, bud. You can check our six for any betrayers."

The demon rolled his eyes but made the effort to look alert.

Rolling her tongue across her sharp teeth, green flame burst across the skull at the top of her staff. Left hand out ready to latch onto waiting enemies, she gave the signal to the Shade. "Hit it!"

In an instant, the door became nothing but dull shadow, allowing them to see in. Straight into the shallow cupboard.

"Oh," Humphrey said, his posture relaxing. "It was probably the next left, then."

The zombie growled and got back to her feet. "Good practice run. Eddy, get that smirk off your face." She stretched out her neck and began walking toward the already open door.

> Chuck: We have 80% of the time fluid.
> Chuck: One team has all the metal bars.
> Chuck: Rest of the Blues are getting the other parts.

She smiled to herself. Where was this Chuck with the army of followers back in the other areas? Would have made her life easier and perhaps she would have eventually got that crafting tutorial done if other people got her all the boring stuff.

> Sally: gr8
> Sally: we are in dungeon hunting Arch.
> Sally: killed some corrupted players - keep an eye out.

The elephant in the room was . . . what do they even do once they have all five of the cats inside the Death Knight? Does he ascend to something powerful? Even so, and if they managed to bring Theo back, how do you even go about fighting something like the Architect?

She rubbed her staff against the side of her head. In some way, she knew already. The same thing that she had been doing since the first day she came into this world. Break things and cause havoc. Eventually the big bad in charge will notice her causing a ruckus and make themselves available for her waiting maw.

They moved through the open doorway into a wider room, well lit by a burning fire in the middle.

"Some kind of ritual pyre." Edward narrowed his eyes. "It's a wonder they didn't all die from smoke inhalation."

"Maybe they're immune," Sally murmured, circling around the outside of the flickering flames. Perhaps she was supposed to be more wary of open fire, since she was a zombie. Around the other side of the room were more dead lizard people. "Dungeons are even less fun when someone has ruined all the uneaten brains already."

"Indeed," Humphrey said, stepping behind her. His armor glimmered bright amber as it reflected the fire. He held up a plated hand to his forehead and let out a long hiss.

A question mark appeared beside Lucius. "You alright, pops?"

"Yes." Humphrey withdrew his hand to glare at the Shade. "Architect just gave a new directive to the Observers."

They all turned to watch him.

"I have maintained control. Do not fret." His shadowed eye sockets sparkled with crimson light. "They are no longer able to break my spirit."

"What did Theo whisper to you with his skill?" Sally tilted her head.

Humphrey stared at her impassively for a second. "I do not recall. The Architect has told all active Observers to move to this third area for further instructions." He turned his head to see the Shade glaring at him with arms folded.

"Looks like we're running out of time." The zombie turned with a sigh. "Let's go find this silly cat."

The Death Knight nodded as they moved past him, Lucius turning and walking backward to maintain eye contact.

He then unceremoniously tripped over one of the lizard corpses and fell straight on his back.

"Oh," he said, an emoji of a bandaged head popping up. "There's something written on the ceiling."

Sally stopped and looked up. "That's not writing," she said, furrowing her brow. "That's . . ."

Her eyes opened wide.

CHAPTER THIRTY-SIX

Smooth Words

"Oh, no." Sally's hand went up to her chin. "You were right, *it is* writing. It's just not something I understand. We'd better check the stoves."

A question mark popped up beside the prone Shade.

"Never mind, only Humps would get it." She held out her hand to help him up.

The Death Knight stepped over and looked up. "Hmm." After tilting his head and rubbing his chin, he abruptly turned around and strode straight for the burning pyre in the middle of the room.

Sally raised her eyebrows but knew better than to panic over such a thing. A couple of seconds after the large plated figure vanished into the flames, he returned with something in his hand.

"Nothing like a bit of heat to clean off the muck," he said with a grin, skeletal face shadowed against the blaze.

"Yeah, yeah." She gave the righted Shade a pat on the back. "What did you grab?"

"A key hidden in the flames by Archie."

Sally nodded. Pretty smart of the cat, really. She wouldn't have expected to find anything of use in the constantly burning pyre—a Player wouldn't either. Knowing that Humphrey was near fire immune, and placing the message that only he could read, meant that they were expected. Of course, with Humphrey knowing what most of Archie thought, that all seemed to track.

"Where does it go to?" she asked. "A door? A special place in your heart to get the rest of the other Archie souls inside you out? Some treasure for a change?"

"*Yes*," he replied.

Sally narrowed her eyes and shrugged. "I'm starting to wonder if Theo got the better deal here."

The Death Knight looked a bit sheepish at that statement, some guilt still inside him over the fateful fight he had engaged in with the vampire. "It is for a door, farther in. This is the only way to open it."

She held out her hand. "Well, let me put it in my Inventory. If you walk about holding it in your hand, that bubble girl will come steal it. Or something worse, and we're not playing that sort of game today." She flexed her fingers as he slowly placed it in her grip. "Ah! It's pretty hot still." It vanished into her intangible storage.

"*Yes*. Let us continue. The doorway awaits us."

The Shade rubbed at the side of his head. "Couldn't we just shadow the doorway, anyway? And they have someone who can go through walls?"

Sally shook her head. "You're overthinking this, bud. Let's just go eat puzzles and solve brains."

With no further disagreements, they all gathered to continue to the next room. The zombie practically hopped over to the closed door in readiness to go through their prepared breaching protocol once more. This time hopefully to something more than a closet. Together, they repeated the planned actions, the demon only grumbling in the background a little as the stone door vanished.

A large room where some monstrous lizard creature had been killed already. Their body lay sprawled across the floor with dozens upon dozens of puncture wounds across their scaled form.

Humphrey went up to it and narrowed his eye sockets. "How strange. These wounds did not bleed."

"Didn't bleed . . . or the blood went elsewhere?" Sally snapped her fingers and looked around the room for any clues. She was thinking of something like vampirism, or a weapon that could draw blood, but she also didn't discount any weirder explanation.

The Death Knight prodded at the corpse. "I actually can't tell." With a shrug, he started to push the corpse to the side of the room so that they could pass through to the other side easier.

"Handy of them to clear the way," Lucius put his hands behind his back as he strolled about.

"Hmm." Sally wasn't so convinced. Not only for her selfish stomach reasons, but there was still something else that didn't sit well with her.

There was nothing immediately untoward about the room, however. Similar stonework as the rest of the dungeon, and the usual torches illuminating the walls. Maybe it would feel less weird if she needed to actually put effort into killing things. Any traps should have been disabled by the Player group too—so all they were left with was chasing shadows in hopes of running into the room where Archie was hiding.

"They have not killed the boss yet, if that is what you are thinking about." Humphrey returned to her side once the opposite doorway was clear. "Otherwise, the dungeon would make a fuss about it. Whether that is a conscious choice by them or not remains to be seen."

"I'll be seeing their remains soon enough," she grumbled to herself. An alive boss meant that they'd be able to take any loot for themselves once they killed it. If she didn't know any better, she would put money on the cat hiding behind that eventuality.

"Ready breach protocol," Humphrey ordered, turning to her and attempting to wink with his empty eye sockets.

"Hmm." Norah tilted her head to the side and wiped her bloodied hands off on her thighs. "That's much better."

She stepped away from the body of the vampire, Theo now completely wrapped in golden bandages.

Humming to herself, she went around and sat atop the small rock throne to regard him.

"That is the best I can do." She sadly smiled. "The rest is up to them."

Another vibration shook the tomb, and more dust fell from the ceiling.

Edward stumbled forward, almost bumping into the back of the Death Knight, who was preparing to breach the door. "Shit," he seethed, spinning back around.

"What are you—" Sally began, turning her head to see him looking the other way—an arrow protruding from his back. "Are you even watching our backs, you goofball?"

"Clearly not well enough," he hissed, trying to find the culprit. Over near a darkened corner, a couple of purple bubbles popped and vanished into nothing.

"Hit and run tactics don't work too well on us," Humphrey said to the empty room, although he looked back at the demon with something akin to concern on his face. "Well, on us undead, at least."

Sally clucked her tongue. "Yeah, I can't heal you, demon-man. Shoulda chosen the dead side."

Edward turned to scowl at her before seeing that she had a Healing Potion extended in her hand. "Thank you." He nodded. As he downed the liquid, the arrow worked its way out of his back and fell to the stone floor. "That Player is going to be a problem."

She shrugged. "You got a cooldown on your duel still, pops?"

"It will be a little time yet, *yes*. Perhaps we should change marching orders?"

After a suitable amount of squabbling among themselves, they arranged into a group so that the Death Knight was at the back, Edward and Lucius were in the middle, and Sally took lead at the front. It would be much harder for someone lurking in the background to drop an arrow that could do high damage to the two undead, rather than the softer pair in the middle. Not that Sally was keen to test if she could survive an arrow to the head, but there was always one of her skills to bail her out.

Into the next room, which had a handful more dead lizard people and two exits. A wider doorway to the east, and a small one to the north. It looked as though the wider doors were locked at some point, and the Players had been through and gotten it open through the method that the dungeon required—or perhaps the bubble-woman had just gone through and unlocked it from the other side. That seemed unfair, even if Lucius could do even better than that.

"Which way, Humps?" She crossed her arms and pouted at the inert corpses on the floor.

"Boss is through the wider doors," he replied, tilting his head. "I do not believe the other direction is important while this way is already open."

Edward scratched his eyes. "Why does everything here look so itchy?"

The group exchanged glances.

"Poison or a curse?" Sally furrowed her brow and put a hand on his arm. As he withdrew his hands from his face, his eyes were no longer bright blue, but a strange shade of deep purple.

"Not sure." He grimaced. "How do I look?"

"Not . . . great?" Her grip withdrew so that she could open her Inventory. She must have more antidotes or something? "How do you feel?"

The demon stood up straight and furrowed his brow. "Very strange. I'm not even sure what I am afflicted with. I want to claw my own eyes out and probably continue digging through into my brain. After that, I might be okay."

"Ick," she replied, well aware she did a lot worse. At least her skill turned it into a flash of violence rather than a drawn out and painful process. "You can resist it though?"

A sharp-toothed smile spread across his face. "Oh, no. I'm only a few seconds away from a second and most likely more fruitful attempt." He held up his rapier into the air. "However . . ."

They all tensed, expecting him to impale himself—either at the whim of the curse, or to die and respawn back in the Wastelands. Instead, the light drained from his eyes; the purple shifting back to the bright blue gradually, as a sheen of similar foul light started to appear on his weapon.

"*[Exchange Malady]*," he explained. "Any negative status effect I am afflicted by, I can transfer over to my weapon to use as an enchantment. Infrequently."

Sally rolled her eyes. "Had me worried for nothing. Just be careful where you point that thing. You're the only one who can come back from death, remember?"

"Don't worry, it will be—"

"Inevitable?" Lucius tried to finish, helpfully.

". . . safe in my hands." Edward glared at the Shade.

The zombie clapped her hands together. "Okay, now that we have those oddball antics out of the way, shall we go over to these big doors and head on through toward the boss?"

They all nodded their agreement, and she sighed, allowing a smile across her face. Nearly there.

The wider doors meant that their plan wasn't as effective—and she wondered whether that meant an ambush would be more or less likely without such a good choke point. Then again, the five of them could get through anything, more or less.

She turned her head to the man with the strange grin. "I can tell there's something on your mind, Neil."

"Caught me." He grinned. "We've known each other too long."

The *Outsiders* collectively rolled their eyes.

"Always interrupting my plans at the last minute with your own ideas, huh?" She smiled and crossed her arms. For a Player, he had fit in with them surprisingly well, all the way back when . . . some time ago? An average-looking guy on the surface, with short brown hair and sharp features, only the shark-like mouth gave him away as being different.

"I was just thinking . . ." He rubbed the back of his neck. "They'll be expecting us to go straight for the boss. We should head the other way."

"Ah, I don't know." She grimaced and the Death Knight gave her a shrug. "Sounds like it could be dangerous."

Neil grinned widely. "Nonsense. We're the *Outsiders*. If you're that worried, just let me hold on to the key to free Archie?" He held out a hand, palm open and wanting.

That made sense to her.

She brought up her STAR Inventory to track it down.

CHAPTER THIRTY-SEVEN

Unskilled

Sally held the key in her hand and furrowed her brow. One of her best friends in this strange world, Neil, stood close with his hand outstretched, ready to receive it.

Although she had no problem giving it to him—she trusted him, of course—it was just as safe in her own hands. They were all traveling together, after all. Her eyes drifted away from him and toward the rest of the *Outsiders* surrounding her. Humphrey. Lucius. Edward.

The Death Knight and Shade looked calm enough, just waiting for her to make the transaction. Edward seemed . . . off? Maybe still a little perturbed about almost digging his own eyes out.

"Why did you want to hold it again?" She raised an eyebrow at the man. Why did he smell so . . . edible, yet gross?

Neil smiled warmly. "You always have your hands busy in combat. If they've set up an ambush, maybe I can open the door while you keep them occupied."

The zombie nodded. That tracked, for the most part. She *did* usually have both hands and stomach full when fighting. Their goal was to rescue Archie, rather than kill all Players.

Edward grinned widely and leaned forward. "I can believe that, Neil. You *are* known for being sneaky." He stood back up straight. "In this instance, though, I believe the key is safer with Sally."

The Player's eye twitched, but he didn't change his expression. "Well, I disagree, but I relent to the group, as always."

"Heck yeah you do," Sally said with a nod. "Classic Neil. But now you have piqued my interest toward the second door." She tapped the end of the key in thought before putting it back in her Inventory.

Humphrey sighed. "Well, we are pretty short on time. I'd rather not hang around when there are lots of things to do."

"You three are the strongest," Edward said, a wry grin still across his face. "You take the route of danger, and our good pal Neil and I will quickly investigate the cleared side passage."

"As much as I dislike splitting the Party, you're probably the least of us I'd worry about, and Neil is practically invincible for having survived this long with us!" Sally beamed.

Neil did not look as enthused and shot a glare at the smiling demon. "I suppose that is pragmatic."

She snapped her fingers and dragged the other two toward the door, as Edward gestured toward the side entrance. The pair walked over, and Neil led them through the stone door, shutting out the rest of the *Outsiders* preparing to go through to the boss area.

A dozen steps in, the man turned suddenly and threw out a sharp spear that radiated green energy. It slammed harmlessly against the doorframe, as the demon was no longer there.

"Who are you?" Neil growled, eyes now searching throughout the otherwise featureless room.

"You can't betray the betrayer." Edward's voice hissed around the room.

"You could see through my ability. How?" The man was sweating now, another spear in his right hand as a flowing white orb began forming around his left.

"I am the king of deceit. The lie that weighs heavily in the hearts of the strongest. A mountain of ruined trust gripped tightly by the pained chains of regret."

Neil turned, flourishing his weapon and trying to gauge where the voice was coming from.

"Perhaps, worst of all . . . I am *inevitable*." Edward flashed out and caught the Player in the side with his rapier, before being knocked back away.

"That's all you had?" Neil grinned, his mouth contorting in odd angles. "Barely a scratch after all that bravado." He held up his glowing hand toward the demon.

Edward shrugged and slid his sword back into its sheath. "Nobody betrays the *Outsiders* except me."

Neil twitched as if pained, his prepared attack faltering slightly. "No, what have you done?" He looked back up in fear, his eyes glowing purple.

Edward crossed his arms and grinned, his sharp teeth illuminated among shadow as the Player dropped his weapon to the floor.

* * *

Sally pushed the Shade out of the way. "You really need to use your other skills more."

"Do not," Lucius huffed, but relented to her going in front. "My shadowing ability is the most powerful thing I have to offer."

Humphrey grinned. "So that you are under no threat of taking damage?"

"Unfair!" Next to Lucius's head, a bobbing angry face appeared.

Sally waved her hands at both of them. "Alright, settle down, you reprobates." Although she had started it, they should know better than to continue. She turned her head to see the demon walk through the wider doors to join up with them.

"Well, you didn't get very far." He tilted his head, a smile still on his face.

"Neither did you." She frowned. "Where's uh . . . where's . . . things go okay over that way?"

He nodded and his grin widened. "You could say it was an *eye-opening* experience."

"Okay, cool. Come help us breach this next door."

Edward deflated before walking over to take his position and assist them.

Sally raised her hand, kneeling behind the Death Knight to shoot ahead once the door opened. She felt that something was wrong, and it wasn't just the rumbling of a potential meal missed. By her approximation, there should only be two corrupted Players left. Or one? She wasn't sure why she thought that, though.

But there was a danger, like a vibration through the floor. A second Party.

"This is the one," she murmured, licking her lips. "Get ready gang."

Although . . . if the bubble-girl had been spying on them, she might have seen their door breaching plan and would have told any potential second Party about what to expect. In which case . . .

"Wait a sec. I think we need to switch things up."

The tall man stretched out and lowered his bow. "I thought they'd be in more of a hurry than this."

A woman dressed in purple, swirling orbs of light around in a circle, shrugged. "Maybe Neil got them."

"Wishful thinking," a third Player in full plate armor grunted as he leaned against the wall.

The other two in the room said nothing. One, a lightly armored man with a blonde beard, kept prodding his glowing red STAR. The last, a figure shadowed by a large blue hood, stared directly at the door, waiting. None of them stood in direct line of sight of the entrance once opened.

"I hear something," the first man said, bringing his weapon back up.

The woman cast the light orbs out onto the floor, and four featureless figures made of pure white light rose up to draw swords from out of the air.

"Remember," the knight said, "as soon as the door opens we need to—"

"Hit it!" Sally yelled with a wide grin.

The shadow bandage they had stretched across the hallway held her back like elastic. Humphrey kept her in place as the Shade tried to tighten it from where he stood by the wall, a dozen feet to the left of the actual door, with his hand ready to shadow it. Edward mostly looked like he didn't agree to this plan but was ready to jump in after her.

As the wall vanished, she shot forth, air flapping at her cloak for the brief change of speed. The merged weapon held like a spear, she almost immediately collided with a Player, the dagger slamming into their side and piercing their lungs.

She dropped to the floor on top of the tall man.

"Ah, *shit*! Cast it!" someone in the back shouted.

A cool feeling washed over her even as the blood from her victim soaked through her clothes and warmed her. As much as he was struggling, her attention went up to the others in the room.

Around her, a cage of white light had formed. Just about the exact size of the room. Looking quickly behind her, it had covered the shadowed wall and Edward was currently struggling to push through it.

Most curious, however, was that she was unable to use any of her skills.

With a quick hop to her feet, she spun the staff and blocked the sword swing of the knight.

"Oh?" She grinned widely. "You think I'm trapped in here with you?" She slowly pushed back against his sword, the man shaking as he gradually relented to her strength.

Her eyes blazed bright red. "You're trapped in here with me."

"Now what?" Lucius hopped up and down in a panic.

"I'm not sure what this does, other than keep us out." Humphrey strode over to the door, flame burning behind his helmet. "This is a corrupted ability. Usually Sally would just use *[Endless Dead]* and that would be a quick end for them."

He swung the door wide open to see the glowing bars of the cage blocking the way.

Edward and Lucius squeezed in beside him to watch what was going on.

Sally wasn't really a melee expert. Sure, she had been using daggers for most of her zombie career, but that was usually a short-term deal to opening up skulls to get the juicy bits inside. Still, she was a Raid Boss now. Above an Elite or Champion, and the other designations they had long forgotten about.

Something this knight was learning the hard way. Their silly cage prevented their skill use too. While the Ranger lay bleeding out on the floor, struggling for breath, the rest were somewhat hesitant to engage in melee.

The Mage, Sally would leave for last. Glowing light around her hands meant the purple-clad Player was the one holding the cage up. She could already see they were at an impasse.

Keep the shield up and try to whittle her down in melee, which wasn't exactly going their way. Or drop the shield to allow all their skills but get immediately swarmed by her stored up zombies.

She blocked another swipe and twirled the staff around, the dagger end slicing across his shin, cutting through the metal armor like butter and drawing blood. The thief now moved in to assist. Two daggers, slick with some manner of poison, perhaps. Rather rude, in her opinion, and she ground her teeth. It reminded her of Theo's poisoning.

The bearded man swung in as the knight regained his footing, but Sally had already stepped back away and used the pronged end of the staff to divert the attack. She twisted her weapon and his arm tangled in between the jutting parts. With a pull, he lurched toward her. Letting go of the staff briefly, she wound up a quick right hand to punch him straight in the face.

And the result was . . . surprising, even for her. The man flung back, dropping his daggers to clutch at a face beyond broken. Without their skills keeping them together, her strength was able to shatter bone.

The Players paused briefly, in shock and unease. A mistake on their part. Her plan changed, knowing how this would eventually end, anyway.

Rolling beneath the slow swing of the pensive knight, Sally launched the staff like a thrown spear.

The Skeleton Key found its target in the forehead of the Mage, and the cage started to crack and fade away as the figure dropped to the floor.

"Inventive," she said with a grin. "But ultimately, nowhere near enough."

[Endless Dead]

CHAPTER THIRTY-EIGHT

Key Boss Battle

[Endless Sleep]

Humphrey stepped into the quiet room. Flattened against the walls were the crushed remains of the corrupt Players, along with a handful of dead zombies. Against the side wall, Sally sat, her head in her hands.

"Everything okay?" Concerned, he stepped over to her as Edward and Lucius filtered into the room.

"Yeah." She sighed and looked up at him. With the back of her forearm, she wiped the blood away from her mouth. "It just seems like such a waste."

"Their brains?" The Death Knight glared around at the fallen to ensure they were actually dead.

"No. I mean, sure, I didn't eat any of them. Corrupt brains are icky." She stood slowly, her joints and bones clicking back into place. "It's just . . . why do they try so hard, but always fail?"

Humphrey stood for a moment, a blank expression on his skeletal face. Eventually, he shrugged. "Isn't that to our benefit?"

"Sure, it's just unrewarding. Where is their caution? One life and they throw themselves at me?" Her shoulders sank in exasperation. "I wanted to be overpowered to stay alive, but it just makes me a magnet, like . . . bugs on my windshield."

"*Yes.*" The Death Knight turned and pointed toward the exit door. "Shall we?"

She glanced over at the other two, but they didn't seem keen to weigh in on the issue. Well, one of them could come back to life, and the other could hide away to avoid damage. As much as she loved brains, she was tired of being a killer of the weak. Hopefully, the bubble-girl would have seen what happened and could tell the others on the red team not to try fighting her in an enclosed space.

It wasn't even fun. She took almost as much damage as the Players did, they just didn't have her level of damage reduction.

From her Inventory, she withdrew the key and stumbled over to the door. It was engraved with a nice pattern and stood out from all others they had come across so far.

"Are you sure I can't just shadow it?" Lucius asked from behind, a question mark appearing beside his head.

Sally turned her head and shook it slowly.

Returning to the task at hand, she pushed the key in. It didn't fit. She blinked, her energy reserves totally spent for the day at present.

"I could just shadow the wall next to the door?" The Shade offered.

The zombie groaned. "Somebody else is in charge. I tap out."

Humphrey put a hand on her shoulder and then gestured at the door, looking back at Lucius. "It's been a long day, Sally. The key is to where Archie is, not necessarily to the boss room or wherever this leads to."

She leaned her head against him, a rather painful experience given that he was made of metal plate. They waited and watched the Shade step up and put his hand on the door.

Norah wiggled her bare toes. Her legs, arms, and half of her face were now uncovered.

"Unfortunately, that's the best I can do," she said toward the golden-wrapped vampire. "You have to allow an old lady her modesty."

She smiled and looked around the chamber. The entirety of the walls, ceiling, and floor were wrapped with the dull gray bandages. A cocoon had been built around them both to reinforce the walls.

"I am absolutely itching to tear some Adventurers limb from limb." She sighed and flexed her fingers. "Let me see how Sally and the others are getting on."

As she worked her chat messages, a sound came from outside.

"This is a strange building."

"Yeah, there's no entrance. Nothing on the map."

"What do you think it could be? Treasure?"

Norah furrowed her brow and pouted. "*Tease*," she murmured.

Sally idly brought up her STAR to check the messages coming through.

> Norah: Still safe here.
> Norah: Hope everything is fine x.

> Sally: all good. Killed some ppl.
> Sally: about to rescue arch x

"I feel bad we have left Norah in the middle of nowhere, alone." She pouted as she closed her chat and looked up at the Death Knight.

"I know." Humphrey nodded. "I wish things had been different."

Unfair for her to beat him up about killing Theo, as tempting as it was. It was a sore spot for the large slab of metal, and she didn't want to push those buttons now that he had come to terms with having a figurative heart.

It was almost a relief that they couldn't level currently. While new skills were nice, it was one less pressure on them, when they already had a time limit. She *did* need new armor, but otherwise the rest of the Party was pretty on top of things. It helped that they were Monsters with scaling stats and didn't have equipment like Players did.

Briefly, she wondered if she would ever get to see her own stats.

The door became shadow, and Humphrey stepped forward to look through. "Staging area," he said. "A room to rest before the actual boss." With that said, he walked through and then broke whatever passed as a locking mechanism on the other side.

Lucius dropped the shadow and then the door opened the normal way, allowing the three of them through.

"Dungeons aren't as fun when they're already mostly cleared." She stuck her tongue out and looked around the chamber.

Pleasant and well decorated compared to some of the plainer rooms. Benches of polished sandstone around the edges for people to sit. Enough space for a campfire, to sit and eat, prepare all your buffs before you faced whatever was on the other side of some double doors.

"Did you ever have fun in dungeons?" Humphrey tilted his head.

"Sure," she said and shrugged. "When we did the thing, and I summoned the devil, who gave me the broken skill. That was neat."

Edward narrowed his eyes at her, apparently still put out that he didn't get his turn to put the coin in and get a skill reset.

"Are we just going to go in and kill the *whatever-is-in-our-way*? My zombie summoning is back off cooldown now, so unless they are going to turn the tables and have something I am actually weak against, we can just pop them and move on."

The demon shuffled, looking around. "I am still aware we have one Player lurking in the shadows waiting for us to show a moment of weakness."

Sally looked around, as if she expected to catch the corrupted woman in the act right now. "It would be a really bad idea if she tried. I would hope that she had enough brain cells to know when a battle was lost." The zombie sighed.

"I really don't want another life thrown away in vain, thinking I am so easily humbled."

"I think you're very humble," Lucius said.

She snapped her fingers. "I'm not even going to make the obvious joke there, that's how tired I am." Her eyes narrowed as if her brain wanted to reconsider. Instead, she spun on her heels and strode over to the exit door.

Edward sidled up to the Death Knight. "With all your absorbed knowledge, don't you know what the boss here will be?"

Humphrey grinned. "*Yes.*" Then he moved forward to step up behind the zombie.

She flung the doors open to reveal a bridge walkway that led to a large, square platform. Stepping out, she could see that there was a moat about a dozen feet wide all around this middle area. Filled with . . .

"Is that acid or just green apple flavor water?" Her face scrunched up.

Edward sighed. "Let's assume the former and not try the latter. I feel we'll know soon enough, anyway."

They all looked over at the figure standing in the middle of the platform, illuminated by light pouring in from the high ceiling. Sally had expected a giant lizard, or maybe even a dinosaur, given the theme. Some Monster of large size with a brain that tasted like algae.

Instead, a lizardman of relatively average size stood with his muscled arms across his chest. Two short horns protruded from his scaled head and his golden eyes glared at the empty wall, as if he hadn't seen them come in yet.

"Not a Unique then," she surmised. "We had gotten a bit too used to that being the default in this sort of situation."

"*Yes,*" Humphrey agreed, readying his blade.

As overconfident as she usually was, Sally didn't get this far by using only half of her brain. Oh, maybe that was a lie. Either way, she knew that the smaller the boss, the more dangerous they were. She was her own proof of such a thing. Still, they were bosses in their own right, so if five Players were meant to kill this lizardman, then she should have no problem.

Her eyes narrowed as they stood at the edge of the bridge before it joined the main platform. Although the boss was mostly bare-chested, he wore a large necklace that looked like . . . yes! It was a lock, with a keyhole.

"You see that, Humps?"

"*Yes.*"

"Ah. We can work it postmortem, right?"

"*Y*—hmm, no, I don't think so." With a plated hand, he rubbed the side of his head. The metal of his finger screamed out from friction, causing Lucius to wince.

Sally narrowed her eyes. "Are you just saying that to make this more of a challenge?"

Humphrey shrugged, a wide grin growing on his face.

With a sigh, the zombie stretched her shoulders out and flexed her arm to ready the staff for combat. "Alright, I've got the key, so I just have to get up close to him. How hard could it be?"

"At your command," the Death Knight said. The other two nodded their readiness as well.

Sally's boots dug into the bridge, and she launched forward, twirling the staff as the skull at the top burst into green flame. Her hand outstretched, she started to cast *[Curse: Decay]* on the boss as he turned to notice their presence.

[Mortis Bomb] went out in an arc of green light as the lizardman withdrew a pair of hand axes in the shape of crescent moons.

With a quick sweep, he knocked the necromantic projectile out of the air, and it careened down onto the platform floor ineffectively. Pulsing waves of blue energy started to build up around him as his face contorted with anger, his sharp fangs bared toward the approaching undead.

Sally growled. If the boss wanted to play it like that, then perhaps she should just go for the easy option. Now, almost in melee range, her eyes blazed bright crimson.

[Endless Dead]

Over two dozen zombies began to crawl out from the platform floor toward the lizardman channeling his skill. As Sally started approaching from an angle, she ducked and dodged through the rising zombies to give herself a cover against whatever ability the boss was about to use.

And then, just before the Death Knight could get into combat alongside her, the axes both went down and struck the floor among the spiraling blue energy. A pulse of power washed through Sally right before a wave of force pushed against her. She dug the dagger end of the staff into the platform and held on tight, gritting her teeth as she avoided being moved back.

Many of her zombies weren't so lucky, however. Turning her head as the energy whipped through her cloak, she saw a handful of her slow shamblers succumb to the force and fall off the edge of the platform. The waves continued, one after another, keeping her rooted in place.

Humphrey remained in place, unmoving, but unable to progress farther. The Shade had become a shadow for him to avoid the same fate, whereas the demon had been pushed back to the safety of the bridge.

"Acid?" Sally yelled out toward him.

Edward pushed his head forward and frowned down off the side of the bridge toward where the zombies had fallen.

He said nothing in return, but the slow nod was confirmation enough.

CHAPTER THIRTY-NINE

Acid Reign

Sally grit her teeth as she watched the last of her zombies get driven off the platform into the moat. She had expected the pushing skill of the lizardman to have ended by now, maybe only lasting five to ten seconds at most. It had not. And that was really annoying.

"Any ideas Humphrey?" she yelled out.

The Death Knight slowly shook his head. "He is immune to my duel and kneel skills."

She exhaled through her nose. More the fool them for being a mostly melee Party. Lucius couldn't use his borrowed bandage skill while shadowing Humphrey and couldn't do much else while the constant force was pushing everyone. If only they had Norah here.

The skull atop her staff burst into green flame as she sent another *[Mortis Bomb]* at the boss. Now, with his focus being on the skill, he didn't have the time to block the projectile with his axes. Instead, he took the blast; the skull striking him on the upper thigh and leaving a patch of darkened scales where it had damaged him.

With a growl, he turned his attention to the zombie and dropped his channeled push.

"Ah, I get it." Sally grinned. "He keeps on doing that to push away melee Players until he is interrupted by ranged Players. Simple but effective." It was a good thing that she had her broken dagger, otherwise she would have ended up in the moat like the rest of her pals.

"*Yes,*" the Death Knight said, right before he launched himself forward to engage with the lizardman.

Sally furrowed her brow and turned her glance to the side, just in time to see a large hand clasp at the side of the platform. From below, a creature rose out. Something of pale green skin and large, webbed hands like a frog, and two eyes that glowed a radiant gold.

She grinned. "Now, *this* could be interesting."

The clang of metal rang out through the large chamber as Humphrey brought down his greatsword upon the boss. Despite his smaller size, the lizardman was agile with his attacks and easily blocked and parried the slower strikes of the Death Knight. The shadowed version of the sword flashed out from beneath them, catching the boss on the leg and causing him to stumble backward.

Sally slid to a halt as she approached the new creature. It opened a large mouth, and she was surprised to see that it had rows of serrated teeth more like a shark than a frog. As it reared back, she could tell what it was about to do before it began. Staff digging into the platform for traction, she spun to the side and began sprinting off in a different direction.

From the Monster's mouth, a jet of corrosive acid sprayed out, vomited across the platform mere feet behind the footsteps of the zombie. Where it struck the stone, it sizzled and darkened it; the attack lasting a good five seconds before it ceased, and the creature turned its eyes to see where Sally had gotten to.

As much as she trusted in her ability to sustain damage, she didn't fancy her chances testing out how an acidic shower felt. She especially didn't want to ruin the cloak that Humphrey had given to her. As she circled around the back of the boss melee, she held out a hand and used *[Meat Hook]*.

The twisting pink beam shot out and struck the lizardman in the back, his attention fully focused on defending against the dual blades of the Death Knight and Shade combined. She slipped through the air toward him, pulled along by the magical tether, twirling her staff around to use as a spear. The boss twisted at the last moment, unable to fully block her attack but taking the defense-piercing dagger through the shoulder instead of the back of his neck.

From the side, there was a flash of purple light, as the demon struck out at the large creature, severing one of its hands. With a hideous screech it tried to swipe out at Edward, his sword piercing through the outstretched hand, but he was still taken up in the grasp of the Monster.

Just as Sally turned to think of how to assist him, Lucius had already popped out the back of the Death Knight. From his hands two shadowed bandages shot out and wrapped around the offending arm of the large frog creature. The Monster squirmed, intending to drag the demon down into the moat with it, but now unable to. Its radiant eyes turned to stare at the bandages leading over to the Shade.

As it went to yank him away, Lucius dropped his attack. Now free of the bindings, the creature then went to slam Edward into the platform to debilitate him before bringing him down into the moat. The impact vibrated through the floor. Sally could feel it through her boots. She winced and ran toward the creature to try to rescue the demon, but he was no longer there.

Confusion painted the odd face of the frog-like Monster, but instead of trying to find the escapee, it turned its attention to the approaching zombie. With tremendous speed, it lurched out and swiped with its good hand, a trail of green blood spattering behind it from where Edward had injured it. Sally watched it approach and grinned.

[*Escape Fate*]

Just as it was about to strike, she vanished up into the air, leaving a pair of zombies to take the brunt of the strike. She dropped down on top of the creature's head, its slick skin proving to be a struggle for her boots to get a grip on. Her intended stab with the staff didn't land as she wiggled to try to maintain balance. With a quick glance behind her, she realized that she could quite easily fall into the moat from here. As the creature lurched around, she only just managed to find purchase with the dagger to give her enough stability to not tumble into the acid.

In fact, this was a *terrible* idea. She crouched and went to leap back down to the platform, but her footing immediately slipped, causing her to fall onto her front atop the beast. One hand still clutched to the staff embedded into the head of the Monster like a flagpole, the other one was slick with corrosive slime and started to burn as she failed to grab hold of any leverage.

Dark bandages shot out again, wrapping around her arm and leg, dragging her off the Monster to fall onto the platform floor. Her staff cut an inch-deep gash across the head of the Monster, not enough to do it a great deal of damage but causing it pain, nonetheless. She landed in a heap and rolled across the stone.

"Ow," she groaned. Her clothing was thick with the acidic slime, sticking to her body and burning her skin. "I can regenerate against that," she spat as she stood back on her feet. "You will have to do better if you want to—"

She dove to the side to avoid being crushed by the falling frog Monster. Edward stepped over and helped her up to her feet.

"Thanks for keeping it distracted," he said with a wide grin.

It seemed as though the demon had reappeared and leveled an attack into the throat of the creature while it was busy trying to shuffle her off. A pool of bright green blood was now seeping out from the corpse, sizzling and burning the stone floor.

She turned her head back to see the combat between the Death Knight and the boss. While Humphrey had every advantage in terms of defense and attack strength, the lizardman was just too quick. Always ready with one or two of his blades to block the greatsword. She did notice, however, that he wasn't using any of his skills.

At first, that seemed like he was trying to extend the fight and have a bit of fun while they had more important things to do. But in reality, he was most likely trying to wear the boss down without killing him so that they could use the key. Before she joined them, her eyes quickly went around the chamber to make sure there was no second frog or perhaps any purple bubbles among the corners. This would be the opportune time to strike at the *Outsiders*, but she still hoped the Player was slightly smarter than that.

"Can you restrain his arms?" she called over to Lucius.

"Ah, no! I'm getting low on charges for that."

"*Convenient*," she murmured to herself. It wasn't fair to expect him to replace the Mummy, but it meant they'd have to go for plan B. "Shadow me!"

The Death Knight didn't look damaged at all, despite being overtaken in the melee. He had caused a few superficial wounds to the boss that looked like the intention was to try to slow him down rather than kill outright. Raising the greatsword high into the air, the lizardman suddenly pulsed with energy and leaped backward.

"I am slowed," Humphrey stated, his boot slowly stepping forward.

The boss began summoning the waves of blue circles around himself once more, axes near the ground.

Sally planted the staff in the ground and slid across the floor away from it so the Shade could jump into her shadow. With the flick of her hand, the skull shot forth, the green flames lapping at the air. It was difficult to control at such an angle, and her eyes went wide as it missed her target by inches. "Rats!"

A second after, a small knife glimmered in the air as it arced across the chamber to strike the boss in the arm. His channeled skill interrupted right before the first pulse.

Edward swooped by and helped her up to her feet. "I don't usually throw those. Lucky us." The splash of dripping liquid came from their right to stop his smile in its tracks, and as they turned, they saw another large frog-like Monster crawling from the moat.

Sally pulled a face but nodded. "Oh, smart. So interrupting him summons the froggies. Now we have the mechanics down. We can farm him on reset."

"What?" The demon looked back at her. "Can you just go use the key already?"

"Fine!" She rolled her eyes. "Lucy, we're up."

The slow had worn off on the Death Knight, and he had reengaged the lizardman, his five skeletons joining the fray to defend against attacks and slowly surround the boss.

Sally ran and slid between Humphrey's legs, jabbing upward with the dagger end of the staff into the left forearm of the boss. Lucius did the same with his shadowed version of her weapon, but in the right forearm.

Arms waylaid by their attacks, the Death Knight struck the lizardman on the side of his head with the flat of the greatsword, disorientating him. That was all it took to buy enough time.

The zombie hopped to her feet and slammed the key into the open lock, twisting it to the side. There was a deep click as the process was completed.

With the briefest of panicked looks at the unexpected assault, the lizardman boss then exploded.

CHAPTER FORTY

Unbroken Bond

Sally stood there, stunned, covered in boss viscera. The frog Monster had vanished, and the group of them just stood there alone, covered in blood and charred scales.

"Ah," she said. "That was slightly unexpected."

"I agree," a familiar voice from the floor piped up.

She looked down to see Archie now sitting where the remnants of the lizard-man were. Eye patch covering one eye, he looked rather amused to see them.

"Archie!" She crouched. "I'd pick you up, but I'm covered in gore *for a change*. Why'd you have to go hide somewhere silly like this?"

"Just seemed neat." He shrugged.

Humphrey walked around to stand behind the cat, eyeing up the corners of the rooms. "It is not entirely safe here still, little brother."

"I know, big brother. It is time, then."

Sally pouted. "So soon?"

Archie moved up to her and rubbed himself against her legs. "Trust that this won't be the last you'll see of me. Unless you all die, of course."

She gave him a little kiss on the head, before the Death Knight reached down and picked him up. He turned away from the rest of them to absorb the last Archie.

Lucius put his hand on her shoulder, a sad-faced emoji appearing beside his head. Edward remained indifferent but kept his eyes on the shadowed areas of the large chamber.

Sally stood and brushed off the tattered parts of her outfit. Her diner clothes were ruined now, thanks to the acid, so she changed to her Wastelands black

T-shirt and jeans. Not the same feel when wearing the cloak like a mage's robes, but she'd repair her skirt when they weren't in a such a dire position.

Humphrey turned back to them; his hands now empty. "It is done."

She worked her jaw. "*And?*"

"And we should leave."

Dungeon Complete
No Experience Gained
No Reward Gained
No Gold Gained

"Wow." She rolled her eyes. "All that avoiding the acid moat and losing all my zombies, for a cat that immediately died and no money."

A portal sprung into being, leaving them the option of teleporting back to the surface. She narrowed her eyes at it before scratching her hair. There was nothing left for them to do here. Still . . .

"Hey, Humps, I have a question . . ."

Janie held an arrow at the ready.

One that would explode and scour the area with a constant curse that stacked damage and made any affected targets go crazy. Drop to the floor and claw out their own minds. She should have used it inside the dungeon but didn't want to poison the area for the rest of them while they still needed to find the cat.

Then she had found Neil's body. Face down, fingers thick with gore, a pool of blood surrounding his face. It sickened her that these Monsters had killed her Party. They had been together for months, and now . . . they were dead.

This would be her revenge. Arrow trained on the area where the dungeon teleport would spit you out. She already had three more area damage arrows lined up. It would be simple to pin them down and drown them out.

She was smarter. The corruption made sense. Hatred for the System turned to stealing power to fight against it. Players should be in charge.

A flash of light as the first of the *Outsiders* stepped through.

Arrow went out, a grimace of determination on her face. But no expected explosion.

Her brow furrowed at the blue light, another blue flash as the attack curved toward the large, plated Monster.

A pink beam shot back and struck her. Panic ran her through right before the zombie did.

Sally dropped down to the ground and watched the body of the woman slump over and roll down the slight decline. "*Oops*, almost ate your dirty brain!" She turned and beamed at Humphrey. "So I guess the answer is *yes*. You *could* teleport with *[Impenetrable Defense]* up."

"You live and learn," he said with a grin. "Well, some of us do."

She turned and wrinkled her face up at the bubble-girl. The ambush wasn't a bad idea, but still . . . disappointing. She *wasn't* smarter. "If you weren't corrupt, we could have fixed you."

Edward wiped the sweat from his forehead. "I was expecting a bigger change with you, Humphrey, considering you have the whole Archie now."

The Death Knight grunted. "It's not that simple. You should know by now that important things don't happen until they are ready."

Sally nodded. Archie did like naps, and all the different parts probably needed to get reacquainted. "It's like my legendary shield."

Shield Repairing... 8.2%

"Shield?" Humphrey asked, tilting his head. "The one we were questing for?"

"Yeah, pops. The System pity-provided me all the parts since area five vanished. It's repairing now and taking forever."

"Curious." The Death Knight rubbed the side of his head. "Did you try assisting the repair?"

Sally clucked her tongue. "Now what makes you think I have the first clue about shield repair? It'll be done when it's most convenient, like you just said. What's our plan now that we have all the cats?"

"Assuming we are leaving the rest of the crafting gathering to Chuck's group, we should focus on personal power." Humphrey then looked back at the other two. "Although I am not sure what we can achieve when we cannot level or equip items."

She shrugged. "I could do with getting my zombies back, to start with. We can think while we eat."

They murmured their agreement, and Humphrey gestured which way to go. As she stumbled over the dead Player bodies still hanging around, she brought up the chat.

Sally: Archie rescued.
Sally: Chuck is working on something for Theo.
Sally: Hope to see u soon x
Norah: That's good. I hope so too x

She spun it around.

Sally: Chucks.

> Sally: got cats
> Chuck: 80% on materials here.
> Chuck: stay in touch.

"What do you suppose we do once they have all the parts?" she asked out loud.

Edward stepped up beside her as they walked and held out a teleport stone. "Dent gave me this. It goes to the main city of Upbranch, where there is a smith or crafting station. Whatever Players use." He stowed it back away. "They'll meet us there with the rest of the blues."

"I've got to hand it to the boys. They're certainly organized." She grinned and looked up at the tree canopy. "Could certainly do with some of that in our lives, huh?"

Luckily for her, there were groups of humanoid System-created nearby. Humans who were part of some expedition or something, based on their gear. She would have complained if it had been insects or mud Monsters, so she took what she was able to get.

Lower level too, so it was almost too easy. *[Meat Hook]* took her into the first, her dagger finding a place in their neck before she ate their brains. She was struck by a crossbow bolt, but she just pulled it out and growled at the offending Monster.

In an act that would probably seem cruel to an outside observer, the rest of the Party went through the packs of humanoids debilitating limbs and disarming weapons, to give the ever-growing zombies an easy task of chewing through or eating the brains of the victims. It was just pragmatic.

Sally stumbled and put her hands on her hips, projectile vomiting a warm stew of mangled brains onto the ground. "Ugh . . . I swear my stomach is getting smaller."

"Perhaps you are just eating too fast?" Lucius had his eyes covered, a green, sickly emoji beside his head.

She groaned and rubbed her stomach. "You guys are just lucky you don't have to eat."

"I eat," Edward said, "just not in front of everyone. Or all over the floor."

Sally hiccuped. "It was only all over the floor *after* I had eaten it. I'm not . . . I have *standards*." Placing a hand to her mouth, she was able to avoid a second burst coming up.

Humphrey stood, watching the zombies mow through the Monster packs, his arms crossed and an unimpressed look on his skeletal face.

Now out of the dungeon, it was starting to get dark, although Sally had no proper gauge on how much time they had spent doing things. It had been a long day; it was hard to believe that earlier they were all gathered around the giant lizards Theo had killed. The whole world had changed since then.

"Alright, troo-*oops*." She put her hand back up to her mouth. "Zombies are almost capped, what were your thoughts on what to do next?"

The Death Knight turned to her. "Let us get that shield ready for you." Hand outstretched, he gestured over to a flat tree stump.

"Like how?" She wrinkled her face up.

Inside her Inventory she looked around for the shield. As far as she knew, it had just been a notification, and she would receive it once it was complete. At some point, her Inventory had become a jumbled mess, despite being otherwise super organized. She didn't even remember looting most of it. "I just have half a sausage taking up one slot? Why couldn't it stack with the untouched ones?"

Eventually, at risk of boring the rest of the group, she found it—*[Broken Shield]*.

"Huh, didn't notice it pop up when it came into my hoard. Thought I was yet to receive." She shrugged and brought it out into her hands. It looked simple at this stage; a round and slightly concave disk of bronze colored metal.

"How often do you look at your notifications?" Humphrey tilted his head.

She shot him a sheepish grin. "My what now?" It had actually been awhile since she had checked on the brain bonuses she had received. It might be worth clearing those.

+1.4% Strength
+0.8% Agility
+2.2% Wisdom
+1.1% Constitution
+1.6% Intelligence
+18% Melee Damage
+3% Melee Critical Chance
+15% Physical Defense
+12% Magic Damage
+2% Magic Critical Chance
+24% Magic Defense

"Ah, heck." She winced away from the boxes. "If I knew there would be so much paperwork involved, then I . . ." She cupped her hand to her mouth again as her stomach growled in protest. She *knew* she was wiser now, even though that percentage would only be a couple of stat points even if she was maxed out—and she wasn't as buffed up as Theo.

She ignored any further introspection on that side of things and stared down into the shallow dip of the shield that was now sitting patiently on the tree stump.

Humphrey rolled out his shoulders. "Alright, gather round, children. If you all help, then this will go a lot quicker."

"Okay, pops!" Lucius said, a grinning face appearing beside his hood.

Edward rolled his eyes but stepped over so that the four of them were surrounding the broken shield.

The Death Knight finished glaring at the Shade before he turned back to the group. "It's simple. Hold your hand over it."

Sally was the first to act, her hand almost immediately hovering over her side of the object.

> Repairing…

"I'm *repairing*," she said with a wide grin, watching as the other three did the same.

They stood in silence for a dozen or so seconds before the excitement in her eyes dulled. "This is still going to take forever, right?"

Humphrey nodded slowly. "*Yes*. And when it's not in your Inventory you cannot see the progress percentage. *Haha*."

She deflated. Glad at least that her stomach had settled, and she wasn't about to fill the dish-shaped artifact with brain slurry. "Is it going to be a good shield at least? Do you know what it does?"

"It is bound to you, and the stats and effects are determined by your class. It is different for all who complete it."

That was slightly more exciting. Sounded like more broken System goodies.

The four of them stood there, staring at the inert shield for what felt like hours, as the sun slowly set.

"Well . . ." Sally deflated for the tenth time. "Who wants to share neat stories? You have a crush on anyone, Edward?"

"Ah, look, it's complete now!" The demon grimaced, trying to will the object to be done.

"Ha!" She grinned. "I'm not so easily fooled. You think I was born yes—"

> Broken Shield Repair Complete
> Receive?

CHAPTER FORTY-ONE

Against the World

> Aegis of the Fallen
> Undead raised from Summon Zombies are equal to your Level
> Nearby allied undead have Minor Regeneration
> +10% Constitution

Sally whistled as the shield went into her Inventory. She read over the description again. Then a third time, just to be sure.

"What's the level over Raid Boss?" She grinned.

"World Boss," Humphrey answered. "But those were not implemented."

She withdrew the aegis into her left hand. It looked nothing like the circular bronze shield that they had worked on. It was more oval now, a slate gray wood with a skull design on the front. Tilting her head, she got a better look at it. No, it wasn't a skull—it was a stylized zombie head, a split line showing the brain from the top. Behind it were waves of golden . . . hair? "Is that me?" She puckered her lips.

"Spitting image," Edward said with a wry grin. "Aside from the head injury."

"About time the army of the *Outsiders* had a logo." Humphrey grinned, a twinkle of red flame in his empty eye sockets.

"Army?" Sally whispered, still taken aback by the legendary item.

"We're about to go to war against the System itself, Sally." The Death Knight tilted his head. "We are at the forefront of the efforts. Are you the only one who hasn't seen that yet?"

She blinked slowly and looked at the other two.

"You're a people magnet; we're all behind you," Lucius said, a thumbs-up appearing beside him.

Edward rolled his eyes but smiled. "Theo once told me, 'save the diner waitress, save the world.'"

Sally snorted. "Don't put all your eggs in this basket, guys. I'm too full of brains. And myself." Her grin turned into a soft smile. "We'll do our best."

Humphrey nodded and then looked up at the sky. "Might be an all-nighter. The wicked never truly rest."

[Endless Sleep] put all her new pals back away. Her *[Summon Zombies]* skill now given Level Twenty-three zombies was *very* good. Hardier undead meant more uptime, more chance of conversions, and more stats from *[Strength in Numbers]*.

Sometimes she did feel like the System's favorite.

Her STAR *bloiped*, taking her away from feeling good about herself.

> Chuck: We have everything.
> Chuck: Meet at Upbranch
> Sally: what's upbranch

She closed the chat window down before he could reply. It'd only be a sensible answer, totally missing her joke. Her stomach had a weight in it, but this time it wasn't due to all that she ate. If this plan didn't work out . . . well, no point thinking about that just yet.

"Alright troops, Chuck has the goods. It's time to split—if you could do the honors, Edward."

He gave a low bow and then brought out the stone, a sinister grin across his face.

"That's not how you hold a pickax."

"Sod off, it's not really the right tool for the job. I'd like to see you do better . . . nob."

Norah sighed and rubbed her forehead. This was torture.

There were now five distinct voices outside, and they had determined that this must be some kind of treasure trove and were hell-bent on getting inside.

Their ineptitude just made it more frustrating that she couldn't twist their heads off. They had tried digging at the soil around the tomb, climbing up atop the roof to see if there was a way in, and touched every stone for the secret entrance button. Now they had finally decided to hack away with tools.

It'd be no use. It would take much greater force to unseat her from this throne and break the magical structure down.

One was coming, of course. That is why she had reinforced it with a bandage cocoon. Was it enough?

It was everything she had, so it better be.

With a flash of blue, the *Outsiders* arrived in Upbranch. Nothing like the sandstone and blocky buildings of the city in the Wastelands, everything here was made with a rich brown wood or light gray stone. System-created wandered around to make the place populated and didn't give the odd group a second glance.

Waiting for them by the teleport circle were the *Insiders*.

"Chuck!" Sally hopped over and threw her arms around him.

"Oh! *By the Earth Mother*, you smell of acid and vomit, Sally." He peeled himself away from her.

"Sure do!" She grinned. "And *blood!* Did you really just call upon the Earth Mother to curse me?"

He shook his head as Sally greeted the rest of them. Dent gestured for them to follow toward the forge. Two other groups of blue faction were present and followed behind the two Parties.

"Ay, Boss?" Jackie sidled up to her. "I know I'm not a walking stiff, but these dweebs are cramping my style a bit."

"I hear you." She looked back at Fern and Lana, who were in mid-conversation. "No promises, but I feel like some old gang action is overdue."

The mobster grinned and gave her a nod.

That might make things awkward, in terms of Party dynamics. Too many friends and the silly five-person limit. Maybe the two groups didn't need to be split up—but if they were able to get Theo back, then that's the *Outsiders* sorted. It was hard being the boss.

"Here we are." Dent gestured to the forge, an open furnace of heated amber light pooling from among dark metals where a third blue faction group was already waiting. A System-created blacksmith stood at the side, arms crossed. "We have a high-level craftsperson who can make it for you. We wouldn't want it to fail somehow and all our efforts be wasted."

Sally nodded as one of the blue-tabard women stepped forward. She was surprised to realize that it was Rachel. The woman gave her a nod, and Sally returned a wave.

Chuck turned around. "Alright, I want this area contained. Maintain a perimeter and do not let anyone else close. Kill them if you need to. We *will not* be interrupted."

With a grunt, Dent stepped away from the forge to stomp after the groups of blue now moving into position. "You heard the Arch-druid, no more than a dozen feet between each of you. Eyes peeled, otherwise I'll peel them for you. Move your ass, Russ!"

Sally whistled. "You two actually run a tight ship."

The Druid gave her a brief smile before it slipped away, his eyes looking around the area. "While I prefer to be lighthearted, the stakes are too high. We can't afford to fail at this stage."

She nodded and smiled back to Humphrey. "You really think Theo will be needed to save the System?"

Chuck raised an eyebrow, and his smile returned. "That's not why I am bringing him back."

"Sap." Sally shook her head. "And that's not a tree pun. Well, it is, but . . . thank you, Chucky."

He gave her a nod and then went to oversee the crafting.

She leaned over and rested up against the Death Knight. It was heading into night now, and the day had tired her. Too much emotional and physical exhaustion when she just wanted to eat people and make silly quips. The dream. Her eyes turned to the side, and she saw Lucius talking with another familiar face—Charlotte.

Maybe this is how Players felt all the time. The community, things being peaceful and everyone helping each other. The unfair lot she had been given no longer angered her. It just made her sad. How things could have been different. But this is what they had now . . . and looking at the Shade and the Player animatedly talking, there was a future there where everyone could get along.

"Everything fine, Sally?" Humphrey looked down at her and put his hand on her shoulder.

"Far from it, pops. But has it ever been?"

He grunted. "Have faith. Some things are written by destiny."

Sally pulled a face. "Was it destiny for all the Players I've killed? Things can't just be for my benefit."

"I can say no more."

She moved away from him and scowled. "You know something, don't you?"

"No."

"Big metal ass having ass. I'm going to go talk to a different goofball if you're going to be all cryptic." She walked off before he could respond and found Edward leaning against the side wall of the forge on his own.

"Doing alright, Mr. Sinister?" She grinned.

"Eh." His glowing blue eyes looked up toward the sky. "I am . . . filled with regrets."

"Remarkably open for you. Please share more." She placed her staff into the ground and leaned against it.

"Do you think Theo can forgive me, and we can turn a new page?"

She snorted. "What? Are you serious? You two are like best buds already."

The demon furrowed his brow. "Really? But . . . ?"

"You're as big of a sap as any of us, huh?" She shook her head and sighed.

They fell into a brief silence as the sounds of the forge went on in the background. The murmurs of conversations that she didn't care to hear a low drone in the background.

"I loved, once."

She raised her eyebrow and looked back up at him, unsure how to respond to that.

"She was . . . she changed me. The first person I never betrayed. A Unique demon. Light rosy skin, eyes like the galaxy, and the softest blue wings. Taken from me by a group of Players before Ruben took over the Wastes."

His blue eyes searched the clear night sky.

"Oh, Ed." She pulled him in for a hug. "I'm so sorry."

Hesitant at first, he then reciprocated and sighed. "The vomit doesn't really do it for me either, I'm afraid."

"Sorry, ha." She pulled away and wiped her eyes with the back of her forearm. "I probably shouldn't do *that* either, don't want to get acid or vomit in my eyes."

"Thanks for including me in your oddball family." He grinned at her and then stood up straight. "But that's my emotional allotment for the year, so now I will be off to maintain my reputation."

She beamed at him as he walked away, and then sighed. Just what she needed when she was running thin—everyone coming and giving her their . . .

Her head turned to see Lana standing nearby, looking rather sheepish.

Sally smiled softly and gestured her over. "I've been vomiting a lot and am rather dehydrated, so if you're going to make me cry, then I might literally die."

"Ah." The woman grimaced and brushed the dark curls away from her face. "That makes me feel pretty awkward about what I was going to say then."

"That you appreciate being included and accepted? Thankful and sorry for something?" Sally stuck out her bottom lip.

"Yeah, you got me. Been one of those kinda days, huh?" Lana smiled and looked over at the forge.

Sally sighed and wrinkled up her nose. "Just my whole existence, really. Aside from the odd week or two between areas, I've always been at one end of the blade or the other. I'm a force of chaos."

The clone shook her head. "You're a force of change. Most of us here have been dragged along by your strong ambition for it. I know you probably think you got the short end of the stick, but in my view, you're sitting atop the tree."

Perhaps. Sally rubbed her hair. It was itchy being bundled up, and she needed to wash it before she let it free. She was the Queen of the Undead, sure, but the leader of an army? Over by the forge, Humphrey was talking with Chuck. In catching her glance, they beckoned her over.

"Duty calls." She shrugged apologetically. "But for what it's worth, you're just Lana to me. No further qualifiers on that."

The woman nodded and smiled, moving away to allow Sally to go.

Chuck wiped the sweat from his forehead. "Almost done, Sally."

"Actually," Rachel's voice came from farther in, "it is complete. Successfully."

Bubbles of excitement rose up in her stomach as the woman brought it out, a soft smile across her sweaty face. A key of bright blue, a pulse of white light illuminating it from within.

With a shaking hand, she reached out and took it. It was warm and heavier than it looked. Straight into the Inventory so nothing terrible could happen to it. She then threw herself at Rachel and gave her a tight hug.

"Thank you so much. And sorry about how I smell. And also how it might look for a zombie to throw themselves at you suddenly."

"You're welcome." Rachel smiled despite the overpowering undead woman. "I only hope that it works."

"Let's get moving," Chuck ordered, his voice stern but soft. "Perhaps we'll sleep tonight after all."

Sally beamed as she released the Player and hopped over toward the Druid.

A pain suddenly pulsed through her head, and she gasped in surprise. Everyone around her suffered the same malady, confusion, and discomfort radiating around the gathered groups.

Then, the notification pop-ups appeared.

New Event!
Defeat the World Boss
Target: The Outsiders
Proximity Tracking Active

Teleportation is Disabled
Mounts are Disabled
Party and Guild System Frozen
Reward: Immortality

Sally rubbed her eyes and looked up to see every nearby System-created turn to her group and glare menacingly.

CHAPTER FORTY-TWO

One Eventful Day

Chuck held his hand up, his fingertips glowing a pale green light. "Everyone to me!"

Outsiders, *Insiders*, and three groups of blue faction started to pool toward the Druid, pushing back the System-created, who now had murderous intent in their eyes.

"Looks like we are finally being targeted," Humphrey growled, stepping up beside the zombie to protect her.

Sally's head swam, not just because there was now an event to kill her, but there were still a bunch of unwanted notifications pushing themselves into her vision.

> Outsiders Remaining 5/5
> Class upgrade: World Boss

"Ugh, are you seeing this?" She ground her teeth together as they became crowded by the press of other bodies.

"*Yes, ha-ha*. An unexpected outcome from their foolish plan."

She rolled her eyes. "Just after you said that World Bosses hadn't been implemented yet too."

The Death Knight scoured the surroundings as the last of the Players gathered around the forge. "Then be proud that you are the first, and probably the most powerful living Monster in this world at present."

"And most wanted," Edward said from behind them, the stress in his voice evident.

Chuck circled his hand around and a bright bubble of green light surrounded everyone present, roots growing from the ground and following the arc of the dome to encase them all.

Class Skills Unlocked
Death Aura
Ruin
Continuous Power
Brain Drain

Her mouth opened and closed. "I got new skills?"

"World Boss privileges." Humphrey nodded. "They have made you a worthy challenge to live up to the threat against you."

Chuck clapped his hands together, as Dent encouraged people to be quiet. "Alright, the plan has changed. First thing, we need to create a moving barricade to get the *Outsiders* safely out of the city with minimal destruction of the populace."

The Druid sighed before continuing. "Then I want you three groups to spread out and act as reconnaissance. I anticipate large groups gathering, so do not engage. Stay safe and stay alive. That's an order."

"Start getting ready," Dent yelled. "Move on the signal."

Sally grinned sheepishly as the Druid looked back at her. "This is a lot, Chuck. Everyone is fine with protecting me while I run my fool's errand?"

He nodded. "Our strength lies in our unity. There is little more we can do as Players to resist the new Architect at present. The *Outsiders* are . . ." he trailed off as he looked between them. "You're the antidote for what ails the System."

"I'm just full of ambition and empty of stomach." She grinned. "What are the *Insiders* going to do?"

"We're following you. You might be a boss beyond reproach now, but we don't know what will be sent after you."

Sally nodded. "*Strength in unity*. Although having nine oddballs to banter with is going to hurt my head." She tilted to the side and narrowed her eyes at Fern.

The dryad stared impassively at her in response.

"Well . . ." Chuck rubbed his face. "Clock is ticking. When you are ready, we are going to head toward the southeast exit and then on toward the tomb."

She brought up her map, furrowed her brow, and zoomed out. "Fu*hhhh*— that's a long way." The Architect really screwed them over by stopping teleports and mounts. Better get her walking legs on. Just as she turned toward her Party to ready them, her STAR *bloiped* as messages came in from Norah.

* * *

The Mummy's bare hands clutched tightly at the stone arms of her throne. Knuckles whitening to a pale shade of blue gray as her jaw worked.

"You see the messages, yeah?"

"Yeah, boss event, I can read."

"The tracker is saying we're red hot here."

". . . you mean?"

"One of the *Outsiders* must be in this stone box."

They couldn't get it open. But that didn't stop them from trying. It just meant they stood around and talked inanely about such annoying things.

Norah hoped Sally would get here soon, so that she could tear the gathered Adventurers to shreds.

"She says there are Players at the tomb, but it is secure." It didn't do much to comfort her, though. Worry painted her brow as she pouted up at the Death Knight.

"The die has been cast." He smiled sadly back at her. "Let us make do with what best we may offer this world."

Sally rolled her eyes at the melodrama of the Death Knight. The Architect had just made her more powerful. Even if there was a target on her back now, Players didn't have it in them to actually organize and make themselves a threat.

Would it change the odds against her? As much as worry rolled around in her recently emptied stomach, part of it excited her. She wasn't just a boss or a Raid Boss now . . . she was a World Boss. A challenge of unequaled strength. Now she had to raise the vampire from the dead just to gloat over him. Technically, he was no longer in the *Outsiders*, so if he came back, he wouldn't get her new bonuses, but he'd also be outside of being tracked.

"I'm ready, Chuck!" She turned and prompted the dam to be broken. While there was still plenty to try to process, she was a sitting duck currently. They'd have more chance to avoid danger on the move.

The Druid nodded to Dent, and the swordsman strode to the front to yell at the prepared Parties.

"Fifth column to the front. Eight on the right. *My* right, smart-asses. Third, you're on the left. *Insiders* will protect the rear. Maintain formation to keep the *Outsiders* central. Do not kill System-created unless absolutely necessary. Am I understood?"

A chorus of acknowledgment came from the gathered blues, and the groups started to align themselves, ready in the dome of thick vines.

It was kind of Chuck to keep the System-created safe. She gave her Party a brief smile as they gathered behind fifth column. While they could have easily killed and eaten their way through the city to reach the open wilderness, the Druid was true to his word in wanting some manner of peace to the System.

"On three!" Dent yelled, having received the nods from each Party leader as well as Chuck. "Three!"

The Druid snapped his fingers, and the vines receded, lowering the dome that covered them until nothing remained. Flares of light illuminated the dark streets as the groups marched forward. Defensive skills and wards pulsing around, stopping the attacks of the System-created or pushing them back. It was quite the trick for the Architect to turn the whole world against her. It made her feel important.

"This is probably a terrible error on their part," Humphrey added, almost able to see her inner monologue across her facial expression.

She grimaced. "Do you think there will be *grave consequences*?"

"For some." He shrugged. "This will delay their full ascension, but they are keen to get rid of you without having to bloody their own hands."

Sally nodded but didn't have anything to add. It was enough that the bad Players were foolhardy and brash in trying to oust her from this world—if the Architect themselves wanted to fall into her stomach due to their hubris, then that would be a bit anticlimactic.

"It won't just be Players and the occasional Monster group we need to worry about," Humphrey continued to fill the silence as flashes of light continued to paint their route through the rest of the city. "There will be set waves of System-created that will test you, and any remaining merged Observers will be coming straight for you."

Rolling her eyes, she then deflated. "Ugh." Sally pulled her hood lower down to her eyes. "So you're saying the next . . . however long is going to be filled with constant and gradually escalating combat again?"

"You act like that is a surprise." He grinned in return. "We have some advantage with it being night. It'd do us well to—"

Day Reset

Blinding them all, the sun started to rise, as if the whole night had been skipped. In fact, as Sally clenched her teeth together, she had no doubt that was the case.

Lucius pushed up between them, sweat drop emojis at the side of his head. "What happened?"

The Death Knight shook his head. "More foolish actions. It does not bode well that the new Architect is a gambler."

The question mark that then appeared beside the Shade just prompted Humphrey to continue.

"Another use of their scant power to reset the day to morning again. It was not likely that many would come for us right before bedtime. Now everyone has the benefit of a good rest, all their skills charged to full, and daylight—so that we may be hunted immediately."

Sally sighed again. "Joy."

They reached the gate of the city and passed through, out onto the open road. Behind them, Chuck raised both his hands into the air and a wide wall of vines and wood rose up to block the exit and prevent any System-created from following them out.

"Alright, Dent," he said. "You organize the recon routes."

The swordsman nodded and gathered up the blues while the Druid stepped up to the *Outsiders* alongside the rest of the *Insiders*.

"This is going to be a very long day, isn't it?" Sally asked him, pouting before he could respond.

Chuck shrugged, right before the mobster pushed him out of the way slightly.

"Scoot, plant boy. Guess what resetting skills means, Boss?" She wiggled her eyebrows, her lit cigarette hanging limp in her mouth.

It took a second for it to click, but then Sally's eyes opened wide. "Your stagecoach doesn't count as a mount, right?"

"Nah. It's ready and raring to go."

Humphrey grinned. "That is fortuitous. I am glad to have you on our side once more."

Jackie brushed him off. "Yeah, whatever, tin can. We'll be pushing the weight limit with your heavy ass on board; luckily the rest of you are bean poles." She glared around the gathered group as she removed the cigarette from her mouth.

"No time like the present, then." Sally clapped her hands together. "It will still be a few hours of travel, but we're much better off."

Chuck nodded his agreement, and the mobster stepped over to the side, raising her hand up with index finger outstretched like she was going to fire a gun. With a faux click of the trigger, an area of plain grass hummed as her stagecoach fizzled into being. A large thing of dark wood and black metal supports. Two horses whinnied, their dark pattern resembling pinstripe suits.

The mobster gestured for everyone to start loading up, and they moved over to the door that popped open.

Fern collared the zombie as they shuffled over. "Sally. I still do not know what is going on in this world. But this whole experience has been interesting. Thank you for taking me from the tower."

Sally tilted her head. "Of course. I knew you'd have a little more fun out here."

"Chuck is strange. I am yet to decide if his power over nature is divine or scandalous. But I am keeping an eye on him." The dryad's impassive eyeholes glared at Sally.

"We're all kinda weird in our own way," she replied, gesturing for Fern to hop on the coach before her. "But we look after each other and live the best we can."

Edward leaned his head into the doorway. "Even if that involves mass murder."

She stuck her tongue out and pushed him out of the way. Sure, she had killed more normal people than many of the actual villains in this world. Eaten because she was greedy and had gotten revenge through coldhearted bloodshed. Even made sport of it on occasion . . .

But she was pretty sure they started it first.

CHAPTER FORTY-THREE

Invasive Species

To say the inside of the stagecoach was cramped would be putting it lightly. While Jackie once again took to the roof to wield the mounted dual repeating crossbows, the rest of them didn't fancy their chances atop the thundering coach at the speed they were traveling. Well, aside from the Shade, who was shadowing the mobster up top. Jackie was extremely elated to find out that Lucius could somehow wield his own mounted weapons.

Sally rubbed at the edges of her cloak. She was somewhat nervous, and it wasn't just because she was now in the limelight. They had put a lot of effort into getting this artifact that only *might* bring Theo back. But then, it wasn't even about if he might stay dead—as sad as that may be. They were all together, which was great, but all heading to the same stationary place. Putting all their eggs into the same basket to the extreme.

If the Architect, Seven, or anyone with an axe to grind got wind of the location, that's where the end times would occur. While Humphrey might be sure the new god was shooting themselves in the foot by forcing the event, it wouldn't matter if they won out in the end. It wasn't like her desperate and half-brained ideas hadn't ever worked out.

She eyed up those in the coach. The Death Knight took up the majority of the other side, with Chuck and Dent wedged in uncomfortably beside him. Sally was next to the window on her side, with Lana, Fern, and Edward after her.

"Tell us a story, pops," she asked as she pouted toward him. More to break her train of thought rather than to fill the silence.

The Death Knight sighed, but his skeletal face relaxed. "This is the third Architect."

A silence, somehow thicker than the previous one, settled into the wagon.

"*What?*" Sally grimaced, confused.

"Hmm." He shuffled awkwardly in the seat, while everybody but Fern glared at him. "That wasn't really much of a story, was it?"

"Spill it already, otherwise you're walking."

"Very well. The Architect that died just over a year ago was put into place accidentally. There was one before him who was the true creator of this world, this System. Something went wrong when testing how to bring Players here. Instead, they swapped position with someone from your world."

Chuck clucked his tongue. "That explains all the ham-fisted pop culture references."

"And to think we are one of a handful that really gets them?" Sally shook her head. "So they got here and just tried to make the best of a bad situation?"

Humphrey nodded slowly. "Unfortunately, they didn't have the vision of the true creator, which gave rise to the number of . . . oddities and problems the System has."

The stagecoach shook and jolted.

"*Run straight, ya goons!*"

"So, it was probably just some dork like us then?" Sally grimaced and looked out of the room. A cobbled together reality. Thankfully, it had been stable enough to get this far. "You know of this because of Archie?"

The Death Knight nodded.

"So . . . is the cat actually the Architect?" Dent asked.

"The Architect had a soul, as much as any Player does. When he died, it would have left this world the same. But every Archie is a split of his memories, a recording he was able to take from himself and apply to a Monster. Not his entire being, just what he was able to save."

"Almost like me, then." Lana rubbed her forehead and sighed.

The stagecoach fell into silence once more. Sally didn't like that story very much.

Norah hummed to herself and smiled. It was nice and quiet outside now.

It had taken a lot of concentrated effort to do it—especially while maintaining her bandages—but she had managed to summon her ultimate outside. Their screams had been quite delectable. The tearing of their flesh and shattering of their armor as the giant zombie broke them into pieces.

The bloodlust had been sated for a while, but it hadn't stopped what was approaching.

Seeing the pop-up messages telling her that she was being hunted didn't even dampen her mood—that just meant more Adventurers to add to the pile.

Sally was on the way as fast as she could.

Good. Now they'd have time to prepare for the storm.

* * *

Chuck wrinkled up his face as his eyes were unfocused, reading some chat messages. "Northern team have eyes on two Parties of red en route on foot. Other two teams are clear."

"If they were smart," Edward began, "they'd all congregate somewhere and attack us as the biggest group they could."

Lana nodded. "Probably when we're distracted by another threat."

"After we've used the key," Dent said, "I have a shortlist of locations that might be beneficial to try to hold."

Sally just looked miserable as she watched the jungle go by out of the window. The first time Players were going to make an effort to actually kill her, and she didn't even feel up to the challenge. And for what, immortality? That was probably a lie. Not like she would trust the Architect to uphold that end of the bargain, even if they could make that a reality.

For the most part, the *Outsiders* had always been the aggressors. Now having to be on the defensive to stay safe . . . it felt wrong. But what was the alternative? They could keep moving with the stagecoach, but the Architect would just get stronger, and the event wasn't likely to end just because everyone got bored and couldn't keep up with them. The Players had tracking now; the *Outsiders* couldn't hide away.

Finding all the Players and eating them could work in the short term, but there would surely be some other way the Architect could put pressure on them. They were the big bad in all of this. Aside from the corrupted, the other Players could be converted to being more peaceful here.

"Holding up, Sally?" Chuck asked her, while trying to get more comfortable pressed up between the Death Knight and the coach wall.

"Meh." She shrugged her shoulders. "I'll be fine once I have something to sink my teeth into."

"*Whoa! Contact!*"

The stagecoach shuddered, and everyone shuffled to one side as it turned at an angle; the horses whinnying. As they slid to a stop, the sound of the crossbows on the roof vibrated through the whole carriage.

Sally popped the door open and fell out, pushed by the rest of them. Landing awkwardly, she rolled up to her feet, withdrawing her staff and shield at the ready. A rush of air pushed against her as a thick vine swiped through the air, aiming for the mobster firing off continuous bolts.

A flash of blue illuminated the area as a bubble shield went up around the stagecoach. Chuck stood just outside the doorway, his staff held up high and maintaining the barrier.

"Protect the coach!" he yelled, as everyone else poured from the vehicle.

Sally turned to see their assailants. Three giant flowers, their vibrant petals closed to form a faux mouth. They moved around on tentacle-like roots, each with four arm-like vines that were barbed with thorns as long as daggers.

"I've got one," Humphrey growled, hitting it with a successful *[Compelled Duel]*.

A little hasty, perhaps, without seeing what they could do—but it did lower the threat against the coach by a third. She ran, avoiding the whip of one of the protruding appendages. No brains in these bulbs. Both because they had tried to attack possibly the most powerful group of Players in the System but also literally, as they were flowers.

The green flame of *[Mortis Bomb]* was flung from her staff toward the nearest giant plant. A pleasant soft violet color, and over twenty feet tall. As the bomb struck it, the flower turned its large mouth toward her. With one action, it scooped forward and ate up the rising zombies, into whatever lurked within. That was the opposite of how these things were supposed to go.

Sally held the end of the staff out as she got closer, almost upon her target. A barrage of crossbow bolts peppered the plant before the spray moved across to the other two. From the prongs of her weapon, red light circled.

[Ruin]

Beneath the roots of the Monsters, a circle of red light emerged—twenty feet in diameter. It immediately began to tear away at the underside of the flower. The Monster writhed in pain as pulses of damage radiated up through them and flakes of its roots started to fall off.

Sally jumped into the air and shadowed bandages came up beneath her feet, pushing her higher into the air. She shot a quick glance down at the Shade below her and grinned. A thumbs-up emoji appeared beside his head as she went up higher, right before the plant launched itself forward.

The bandages tore away from her as Lucius was eaten by the bulb. She dropped, crimson energy burning in her eyes as she spun the staff around, ready to puncture the petals below her. Vines whipped through the air toward her as she fell. The first missed, swiping over her head, but the second she had to block with her shield. A thorn caught her briefly across the forehead, drawing blood, but most of the damage had been prevented.

She landed on the soft flower, jabbing the Skeleton Key side of her weapon into it as drops of her blood flecked onto the Monster. It was so large that the depth of the dagger didn't do much to it. Sally growled and pushed it across, cutting a line along it.

Another vine swung across and she rolled out of the way, the plant striking itself. In pain and frustration, it moved its mouth up higher, trying to turn vertical. Perhaps to digest the Shade. Sally ran up the increasing slope of the large petal and leaped with staff out to pin herself to the creature before she fell. Shifting her weight, she swung up to the pouting entrance to the plant, faux lips closed.

Staff jammed in, she created a small gap. "Are you okay, Lucy?" He hadn't died, that was for sure, but it was a terrible position to be in.

"I'm stuck; I can't move!"

He couldn't see her to shadow either, she assumed. Her brow furrowed as she watched a vine sway around, ready to slash out at her again. Either this would work, or it would end poorly. She liked those odds. The long, green appendage whipped out at her.

[Escape Fate]

By using the barest of gaps the dagger had allowed, the System let her vanish downward inside the plant. It was dark, and the walls were sticky, as if covered in thousands of fibrous hairs.

"Is that you, Sally?"

"Sure is, bud." Her staff burst into green flame, illuminating the inside of the flower. "You ready to get out of here?"

He nodded and then vanished, shadowing her.

"You are not assisting?" Fern turned their head toward Edward.

"Big Monsters aren't really my thing." He raised an eyebrow in return. "I am watching the stagecoach in case this is a decoy, or we are betrayed."

Fern nodded and looked back down at the combat. Dent, Lana, and Chuck had taken down the one on the left. Humphrey was finishing off the middle one. The last had eaten both Lucius and Sally, but nobody seemed to be panicking about it.

The rotating barrels of the roof-mounted dual repeating crossbows spun down, and Jackie sighed.

"Could do that all fuckin' day." She pulled out a cigarette and lit it.

There was a brief silence, as if all the sound in the area was sucked into a vacuum, and then the third plant exploded.

Parts of the flower rained down in the area in thick, sodden chunks, as the roots and vines collapsed to the floor and shriveled up.

Sally stepped out of the ruins of the Monster, covered in pink gore and radiating with energy.

"I think they made a mistake." She licked her lips. "This amount of power is . . . hard to swallow."

CHAPTER FORTY-FOUR

Pressure

Sally flexed out her extended fingers. There was still a hum of energy to them. Slowly fading, but the skill had been more than she had expected.

"What was that?" Humphrey asked, as he stepped over.

"*[Brain Drain].*" She turned her head to observe him. "Damage based on how many brains I've eaten. It scales *pretty* well."

"Pretty well," the Death Knight repeated, looking back at the remains of the giant flower.

Lucius stepped up to them, trying to rub the plant gore from his arms. "You have eaten *a lot* of brains."

"More than most," she agreed. It had a long cooldown, but it was essentially a kill move at this point. Something to keep in her back pocket, possibly as she throttled the Architect.

"Back to the wagon!" Chuck yelled out, forcing them all into action.

Sally exhaled. Despite not needing to breathe or have a pulse or do anything a living person does, she had settled into doing the motions at some point. Made her feel like a human again, maybe. The System allowed it, or at least didn't punish her. Now look at her.

A plated hand rested on her back to help her along. "That was the first invasion wave. They will increase in severity for as long as the event goes on."

She looked up into the empty eye sockets of her faux father. "How often?"

"Unknown. I estimate between twenty minutes and an hour per wave."

That wasn't terrible. Assuming they could keep the stagecoach functional, then they'd still be making better time than anyone else in the area. She looked up to see Edward and Fern drop down from the roof, while Jackie remained leaning against the dual repeating crossbows, a lit cigarette in her mouth.

"Humps, any knowledge on Observer threats?"

"Hmm." He stopped by the doorway and looked back out into the jungle. "I believe there are just under twenty remaining. Some will have moved to the other areas under the directive, but the majority might be here, somewhere."

She nodded and gestured for him to enter the stagecoach. The sooner they could get moving, the farther they could travel before getting interrupted again. She hopped in last, to be squished against the closed door once more. The faces of those inside looked more strained now.

"This plant stuff is gross," she said with a sigh, prodding at it all over her black jeans. "At least it smells nice, though."

"An upgrade to what you are usually covered in," Edward agreed, pulling a face.

She wrinkled up her face as most of the others nodded their agreement. "I still feel like we are missing someone, though."

They looked around and counted themselves. All present.

"Don't worry," Dent said. "I'm keeping an eye on everyone. Just in case there's a shape-shifter or something, you know?"

Edward tilted his head. "You'd be able to tell?"

Dent didn't say anything but nodded.

The stagecoach lurched forward again as the gangster-adjacent horses pulled them back onto the road. There was a slight breeze that rushed through the open window on Sally's side, and it calmed her. She needed to save a bit of that rage and energy for the rest of the day.

While the death of the vampire had set her off on the quest to kill and destroy everything, she had been tempered by her friends gathering. Something he had planned, knowing her well enough to keep her on the right track, apparently. If he was lost for good, then she'd rage again, but this whole event thing was so draining. Maybe it would be better if she fell, eventually.

She was an oddity, an error that had inflicted plenty of wounds on the System. If you put the faction war down to just human nature, then the world had done fine for a year without them. If she had died in the first area . . .

Things would be pretty bad for Uniques still. Ruben might still be in power and doing worse things to the Wastes. She shouldn't be so hard on herself. All that was left now was to fight until either she or the System broke.

The stagecoach shuddered as if prompted by her thoughts.

"Sorry!" Jackie called from the roof. "Think I just hit some schmuck."

They hadn't stopped moving, so it couldn't have been anyone dangerous. Or with any sort of situational awareness. Either a Player following the tracker blindly, or a System-created Monster wandering onto the path. Nothing exploded or stabbed through the walls, so the danger must have passed.

"How are you doing, Sally?" Humphrey asked.

"Meh," she said, taking her eyes away from the roving outdoors to turn toward the group inside. "I am *the* villain now. System has made sure of it. To all but those in this coach, I am the big bad evil gal."

"You're not . . . *that* evil, though." Chuck pulled a face, remembering all her achievements, good and bad.

She idly looked between each of them. "Other than Humphrey, I could kill you all."

Dent shrugged. "Hasn't that always been the case?"

"In less than five seconds," she added. Her eyes went back to the jungle as thick silence filled the stagecoach. Not that she would kill them, of course. She was powerful before and could have taken most of them individually, maybe some of the weaker ones grouped. But now . . . the System had burdened her with the capacity to be something worse.

It would be a simple case of using all of her event skills at once, then picking off the remainder. Probably dagger the Death Knight immediately, before he could use one of his many defensive skills. Drop fifty zombies among the carnage of whoever remained.

That would make her an easy target for others, though. And alone.

She smiled to herself before looking over at Chuck. "Are there many first wave Players in the blue team?"

He shook his head. "A couple. There's more in red team, but even then—not a lot of people made it through both areas."

Dent tried to adjust his sitting position but had no room to move against the Death Knight. "The ones who did were either lucky, strong, or extra patient."

"All four of us are first wave." She nodded, looking over at Lana. "What about the rest of your old Party?"

Chuck gave a sad smile. "Anyone who hasn't pushed this far or fallen is just trying to live a normal life in the other areas. After Ruben fell, they went back to the forest."

Sally could understand that, to some degree. It was something she coveted as well, some days. After being forced to adventure to line the pockets of the dragon, it was no surprise some Players wanted to give that a break. No doubt another thing that had shaped Chuck's vision of the future.

"I've never been to that area," Lana offered. "I mean, this body hasn't."

"We'll go there once this is all over." Sally smiled and sank into the seating, closing her eyes. "Big feast and party, all the goblins and all the pals we've made along the way."

She didn't open her eyes, but she could feel the mood in the coach lighten.

Although a feast didn't really mean a good thing for the *Outsiders* usually, unless there were some naughty Players on the side to munch into. Once Chuck's vision came to pass . . . there would be no such delights for her.

Well, she was sure the Druid wouldn't make her starve. Maybe he could invent fake brains for her to eat. Stock her fridge up with them. Live a normal-adjacent life with . . . no, too soon for daydreams. There would be another invasion wave coming up soon, something to sharpen her teeth on.

"Recon, Chucky?"

His eyes unfocused as he went through his chat. "Clear so far, updates are slow from one team, however. Still alive."

That could mean anything, though. The stagecoach vibrated as they went over a rockier part of the road.

"*Ah, you're fuckin' the suspension, tin can.*"

Humphrey grinned sheepishly.

Even if they lost the stagecoach now, they had saved hours of trekking through the jungle. Especially if they were meant to be assailed every twenty minutes or so. Instead of being bogged up just outside one of the major cities, they'd be close to the fourth zone. Her brow furrowed.

"Anyone know if the fourth area barrier dropped?"

They looked at each other, but with shrugs and shaking heads, they had no idea.

"Whoever the Architect is, they took someone with them who could create a barrier." Humphrey tapped a finger on his knee. "It is likely any accomplices are still in that area, since the fifth was destroyed."

"Then they might have kept it up." She pouted. Eventually, all the gathering forces would push them up against the wall of the area they couldn't move into. If it had gone and they could continue rushing past . . . well, it wasn't as though they could outrun the Architect, unfortunately.

Chuck nudged the Death Knight. "Any closer to knowing what Archie is planning? Even with us, he was cagey about some things."

"I'm afraid not." He tilted his head from side to side. "It's not that simple. You know how cats are."

"I . . . guess?" The Druid grimaced.

Sally fidgeted. "I can feel the next invasion coming. Why are they against me? Shouldn't Monsters be on my side, against Players?"

"Such a betrayal," Edward said idly, as he stared out the other side of the coach.

"Also," she continued, "can we just outrun them?"

Humphrey shrugged, pushing the two men sitting next to him against the walls more. "It is possible, but we would be delaying the . . ." His eyes narrowed at the demon. "We would have to fight them eventually, and it would be better to do so when the process is under our control, or at least expected."

"True," Dent agreed, while trying to push the Death Knight back away. "Last thing we want is to be fighting Players or worse and have a train of System-created arriving late to the party."

"*Or worse*," she repeated to herself, looking back out of the window but holding onto her staff tighter.

Norah was out of breath. The toes of her bare feet gripped at the armrests of her throne as she stood upon it, her arms extended out and fingers twitching.

Unraveled to the point of being covered by little more than a bikini's worth of bandaging, her deep gray hair draped over her face as her head hung low in concentration.

The tomb vibrated again; the wrappings cocooning the interior squirming around as if in as much pain as she was.

Small trails of dark blood ran down her arms to gather and patter against the stone floor below her.

"Aww," a deep voice boomed from outside. "Why won't you come out to play?"

Another deep vibration shook the air inside the chamber full of bandages, and the Mummy hissed from the pain.

"Just a little while . . . longer," she seethed, her yellow eyes aglow, beaming through her hair as she looked down toward the golden-wrapped vampire. "True Monsters never die, they only fade from the memories of the foolish."

She clenched her teeth together as something pounded on the outside walls.

CHAPTER FORTY-FIVE

Flying Coach

Sally rolled to the floor and needlelike shards of chitin stabbed around her, embedding almost a foot deep into the ground. The invasion had come just as she had expected it—something like a sixth sense warning her just before. Enough time for them to disembark from the stagecoach and wheel it farther away.

Chuck, Edward, and Fern remained near it for protection as Jackie pelted the enemy with long streams of bolts from the roof.

Lana seemed to be an odd mix of midrange fighting. A small crossbow in one hand and a hooked sword in the other. With Dent, Sally, and Humphrey at the front, the clone kept between them and the defending group to ensure nothing started to get ideas.

Not that they could miss the movements of the current foe. Lucius spun a shadowed staff beneath her as she readied her own, looking up to the large figure slowing them down.

Some kind of bipedal porcupine; it was larger than even the plants had been. Singular, thankfully, but it was fast despite its size. Something like this would be a Raid Boss, she assumed, based on no prior knowledge. Despite the blood running down her left shoulder where her shield hadn't been up quick enough to block one of the long projectiles, she had a wide grin across her face.

This large Monster had a brain.

Debatable, if it was fighting both the *Insiders* and *Outsiders* together—but technically—it would have something up in their head. She just needed to get up there once it was on low enough health. This had been proving difficult so far, as it didn't seem to have an issue battling all three of them in melee. Not only was it a giant creature, but it had metal armor across its stomach, and a spiked mace and a shield in their hands. Every so often, in between swings, it would shoot out the sharp spines into the air.

[Brain Drain] was still on cooldown, and she didn't want to lose all her zombies by summoning them around the Monster. They did much better against small groups or weak crowds, so hopefully the next invasion was something more to their benefit rather than a giant Monster again.

Dent had taken a bit of damage but was remarkably evasive—she had watched him parry the giant mace of the Raid Boss, where most people would have been flattened. Chuck was keeping him healed and providing the occasional shielding to one of the three in melee range. Although Jackie had been firing at the large creature almost continuously, most bolts had fallen away from the armored parts—only two dozen or so actually finding purchase somewhere that drew blood.

Still, she was used to these sorts of things taking no time at all. Every minute they spent battling this creature was one minute further from Theo, and people could be tracking them down. People *were* tracking them down.

"Grab it, Humps!" She ran toward the Monster as it swung the large mace toward the Death Knight.

He dropped his sword and instead caught the metal head that was almost equal in size to the plated figure. Blue and white light flashed over him as he slid back two feet—and as the porcupine tried to bring the weapon back up, it could not.

Sally leaped into the air and hit *[Meat Hook]*, the spiraling pink line flinging her up onto the extended arm of the Monster. She continued the momentum by running up the arm, *[Mortis Bomb]* bursting over her staff before being shot off toward the growling face of the boss.

Spines shot out in reflex. *[Escape Fate]* moved her away, right onto the long snout of the Monster. The rest was just procedure. Everyone debuffed the opponent, and she stabbed. She grinned. She ate brains.

Sliding down the falling body, her fall was broken by a landing pad made of soft fern and moss. She rolled back up to her feet and bowed low. A few seconds passed, and then up behind the zombie, the boss began to stand back on its feet.

Sally righted herself. "Back in the vehicle, stop gawking!" Turning her head back to the undead porcupine, she gave it the command to protect the road. The System wasn't likely to allow her to store away something that big, and she was full already. Slow legs meant they'd soon outpace it—so if it was able to soften up anyone following this route, that would be neat.

Running back to the stagecoach, they filtered and squeezed back in. Lucius popped out of Sally's shadow and went back up to Jackie's. With a short pause to light a new cigarette, the mobster gestured for the horses to start dragging them back onto the road. They zoomed past the confused-looking Raid Boss, their arms hanging limply at their side.

Sally hung out of the window and waved bye to them. She then sank back inside before anyone could chastise her for risking losing her head.

"Under different circumstances, this might even be fun." She tilted her head to the rest of the group, who perhaps didn't share her point of view.

"A challenge is good and all," Dent rubbed his chin, "but only if there's the option to tap out."

Chuck nodded. "There will be a point where we will be outclassed, even if you're not."

She pouted. "Eh, I'm not sure. There will be a time where the Architect will intervene if I can hold out enough, right?"

The Druid shrugged. "This is all pretty big and unexpected. Whatever happens, the world is going to be drastically changed."

Sally scrunched her eyes up. There was a connection somewhere . . . even if the Architect was bad news for Uniques and those with bugs and errors, they hadn't done anything bad toward Players. Whether that was because Players were needed to keep the System going, or the new boss just had better ideas for how to run things . . . it seemed odd.

"Dent," she asked, "what defensive options do we have near the area four border?"

"There's either a fort inhabited by neutral stone constructs, or a shallow amphitheater type space out in the open."

While a fort might be a traditionally good place to try to defend against unknown Monsters and Players, being trapped in rooms or corridors would be a detriment to them as much as it would for their assailants. The outside area would give them plenty of space for all their skills and to engage threats as they saw fit . . . but they'd also be sitting ducks for certain types of skills.

"Ah, let me think on it," she eventually decided. "I much prefer being on the offensive."

"That could be an option." Dent tilted his head to the side. "Until we lose the stagecoach."

Walking wouldn't work out too well when Players had tracking on them, otherwise it would be ambush time. "Invasions happen at night, Humps?"

He nodded slowly. "There is no rest until the event is complete."

Given that "complete" meant the *Outsiders* dying, she wasn't too keen on that. There went the plan of waiting until night and finding where the Players slept too. If only the dead could be resurrected, they could just die and then be brought back to complete the event themselves. Her brow furrowed.

"How does the whole soul thing work, Humphrey?"

The Death Knight shuffled awkwardly. "How do you mean?"

"Pretty much the whole process, right? Souls get here, in these bodies, then when people die—where do they go? Is it even a soul thing?"

His mouth opened and closed. "I'm unsure what I can tell."

At least four pairs of eyes glared at him, waiting for more information. "You *know*, then?" Sally narrowed her eyes.

"Not . . . exactly. Even the fully formed Archie does not have the full Architect's memories, and some part of what you are requesting is part of what the original creator had set up."

Her hand clutched her staff tighter as her teeth clenched. "So, what *do* you know?"

He sighed and took a few seconds to gather his thoughts. "A soul, as you imagine it, does not exist. There is no ghostly spirit inside you that leaves or was even brought into this world. It is more of a sequence of data."

"Our thoughts, the way our brains work, and the like?" Her eyes grew tired, but she still glared at him. "So we're all clones, in a way?"

"The you from the other world is dead, so it is more a transfer of consciousness." Humphrey had a sheepish look across his skeletal face.

Lana leaned back and closed her eyes. "So, for all intents and purposes, I am the *original* me. As much as any other Player is."

"Then Norah isn't stopping a soul from floating away, but the data stream that is 'Theo' from what? Being erased?" Sally tapped her foot on the floor.

"That is . . . I'm sorry," Humphrey lowered his head. "I do not know what happens after a Player dies."

She wasn't satisfied with that answer. "Chuck, resurrection magic works here, right?"

He nodded. "There are limitations, but yes."

"Then there must be some . . . temporary storage of Player data, at the least?" She pulled a face. On the surface, it still sounded like it was a soul and they were just arguing semantics. Knowing for sure might guide them into finding a way to . . . do something useful?

"At least for a week." The Druid unfocused as he brought up his STAR windows. "Under seven days, most of the body's present, some material components. Very long cooldown."

She nodded but didn't really know what to ask next.

"I don't usually tell people I have it." Chuck looked out of the window. "There's always more death than chances to use the skill. Lately I've been selfish. Saving it for if one of us fell."

It didn't take much to guess he was talking about Dent. The rest of them were undead or Unique. She couldn't blame him for it. If she had a special bring-someone-back-to-life skill, she'd only use it for the *Outsiders*. They'd probably be a lot more reckless if they did, though, not that they currently needed it.

She yawned, the conversation exhausting her emotionally. They still had a little while to go before the next invasion.

"Makin' good time, Boss!" Jackie called from above. "Might only be one more invasion before we get to bats!"

With a touch of her STAR, she brought the map up. The mobster was right. While they could have spent all day getting this far on foot, the stagecoach was making the distance a non-issue, the occasional speed bump of an invasion notwithstanding. Walking and getting into fights every twenty minutes would have been draining.

She allowed herself a little excitement. Even though she was trying to temper her expectations and know that, realistically, Theo might not come back with the key, it would be great to see Norah again. She bet the Mummy had been pretty bored just sitting there and watching the dead vampire.

Plus, even if the key didn't work, Theo's data might be in the System for a little longer. They could find another way to bring him back, she was almost sure of it.

And if he was dead for good, then she would remember him fondly as she brought the world to its knees.

A crack of thunder sounded out over increasingly darkening skies.

Assuming they all lived that long, of course.

CHAPTER FORTY-SIX

As Foreshadowed

Sally rolled across the rain-slick grass, her shoulder popping out of place as she landed in a crumbled mess of limbs.
[Living Dead]
"Ow," she said through clenched teeth. Just one more invasion, they had said. They were right, but naturally, it couldn't have been that easy.

She stood on her feet and cracked her back out. Five enemies had popped out of the ground before the stagecoach, and it was only by a miracle that Jackie had managed to bring it to a safe stop without ramming into some of the nearby trees. Why she hadn't gotten the feeling the invasion was about to happen like last time, she wasn't sure, but it sure made the start of combat rather awkward.

Both Dent and Edward had almost been crushed to death as soon as the coach emptied. Humphrey became rooted and couldn't get into melee to draw aggression. Jackie had to hold off on firing so that she didn't draw the Monsters to herself.

And as for herself, well, the creatures summoned to best her looked like bipedal rhinos, but their horns and heads were made of metal. Slightly taller than Humphrey, they were quick and strong. Apparently she couldn't eat their brains, either—something she had just learned the painful way.

Two of them were now dead, and with the Death Knight drawing them in, she raised her staff up and cast *[Ruin]*.

A red circle illuminated around Humphrey and cracks began to form around the enemies. She had tried not to look at the skill descriptions of the new abilities too much, as they made her feel ill. *[Ruin]* didn't affect allies. She knew that much, which made it great for dropping on the big metal man.

Humphrey flashed as he activated his parrying skills, blocking the attacks of the sword strikes and leveraging near-instant critical strikes right back at them. Chuck had cast a spell that slowed their reaction times, so even if they were powerful, they couldn't react quick enough to prevent the retaliation. She stood back and used *[Curse: Drain]*, occasionally shooting off *[Mortis Bomb]* when she could.

The extra zombies didn't do too well, but for the time they were alive they boosted all her undead pal's stats. There was no point getting in the way of the Death Knight in full force, and once Jackie and the others joined in, they made short work of the last three.

Even as the last Monster was still collapsing, she was running back to the stagecoach, followed by everyone else.

"Apologies for using my cooldowns so soon," Humphrey said.

"Stuff it, pops." She cast *[Living Dead]* on him. "We got through it a lot quicker."

Doors closed and they were all sardined back inside. The horses struggled for a moment to get the stagecoach out of the ditch they had fallen into, but soon enough, they were back on the trail.

After the rocky road, there was the thudding of wooden planks as they crossed a bridge. Rain continued to fall, and thunder rolled around the sky. Sally looked at the faces in the coach. They looked tired already. Apprehensive, wet, and weary. Fern looked fine, though. The dryad hadn't really provided much support during the combat, remaining part of the stagecoach defense team—which was fine. She did kinda drag them into this whole ordeal.

"Ah." Chuck pulled a face as he stared at his map. "After the bridge . . . I should have guessed where the tomb would be, if I had thought about it."

"You did know where we were going, right?" She gave him a soft smile. "But thanks for keeping it out of your brain for me. Never know who might be prying."

"Haven't had another dungeon try to snatch you up?" Edward asked, raising a tired eyebrow.

"Nah." She tilted her head against the side of the coach and felt the vibrations through her skull. "I reckon it was that chap you killed in the eyeball. We didn't see what his corrupted skill was, and it'd explain part of why they knew we were about to enter."

Humphrey grunted and nodded.

"Twelve to fifteen minutes," Chuck said, closing his map. "The invasion will come soon after we get there, but there should be enough time to prepare the area, at least."

Sally gave a brief nod but didn't say anything further. Now the knot in her stomach was weighing her thoughts down. She felt silly for the worry, but it would be a big change for the gang if they couldn't bring the goofball back. Exhaling from her nose, she brought up Party chat. Norah hadn't sent a message in awhile. Hopefully she hadn't fallen asleep from boredom.

> Sally: on our way.
> Sally: ten minutes or so x

Norah couldn't reply.

Through golden eyes that ran crimson, she saw the messages pop up from the zombie. Perhaps a bit of relief would have sunk through her body, if she could move. Instead, a brief, pained tear dropped from her face to land in the large pool of blood covering the base floor of the tomb.

"I can smell you in there. Can't wait to grind you between my teeth."

The top of the cocoon flexed slightly as the brickwork shifted under the next pounding assault. Although the tomb wasn't meant to hold up to being under constant siege, she had put her all into keeping it together. Her literal life.

Norah grinned through clenched teeth. How soon the tables would turn. She just had to hold out a little longer.

Bloodied cracks along her dry skin revealed glowing, radiant light.

Just a little longer.

Sally wrinkled up her face. "So I literally just stab him with it and turn it like I'm unlocking something?"

"It sounds a bit barbaric, huh?" Chuck shrugged. "But it's like . . . temporal or something, so it won't damage him."

"Just a jump-start then. The whole turning back time thing seems a bit reductive." She looked at the object in her Inventory, but daren't withdraw it yet in case something happened to it. Something *would* happen to it, she was sure of it.

Pulling another face, she looked out the opposite window to see the Spire dungeon in the distance past the jungle. Fern was already looking that way.

"Did you want to go home, Fern?" She leaned forward to get a proper look at the dryad.

"No. I am currently happy." They continued to stare at the dungeon as it slowly left their view.

That was a hard sell, but she took it at face value. Fern wasn't in the *Outsiders* and didn't have any reason to join them on their death-wish journey. They could opt out at any time; well, any of them could really. If Theo hadn't died, she probably wouldn't carry these guys along with her. Just send them somewhere safe and let the five undead fight until things were done. For better or worse.

But that was the crux of it, really. They wanted to rescue the System from whatever this Architect wanted and run things the way Chuck and the blue team wanted. In that way, they and hopefully most Uniques were on their side. Players were a harder sell, especially now that they had a homing pointer to come kill the *Outsiders*—to become immortal.

She tilted her head. "The reward of immortality is pretty transparently ridiculous. Cartoon villain kinda stuff. How likely is it that I am wrong?"

Humphrey tilted his head back to stare at the ceiling and exhaled. "The original intention was that death wasn't the end. Even in this world, you were supposed to be able to leave. Of course, we know how that has gone."

"So there was supposed to be something like Edward's bug but without the level loss?"

They turned their gazes toward the demon, who just shrugged.

"It's possible." The Death Knight nodded. "Again, not something I have the current details of."

Sally rolled her eyes and looked back out at the miserable weather. They were getting closer now. She could feel it. The pressure of the inevitable point where she'd be sitting there in the rain beside his body, just waiting for it to activate. The not knowing was driving her insane. And then having to deal with an invasion at the same time, unending waves of . . . she sighed, and the stagecoach lurched onto a muddier path.

"Visual!" Jackie yelled from up top, soaked from the rain. "*There's contact.*"

Growling, with eyes burning bright crimson, Sally leaned out of the open window. There it was—the tomb. Currently being assailed by a large figure and surrounded by at least two dozen smaller ones.

"Fuck them up, Jackie!" She shouted at the mobster.

Returning to the inside of the coach, she seethed with anger. "Norah is in trouble. Humps, I need you on the big guy. Everyone else, kill your way through the smaller shits and then help pops. I'm going straight for Theo."

The flames behind Humphrey's head burst with greater intensity, and he clenched his fists tight. Stoicism passed through the rest of them, nods and grunts of approval. The stagecoach rocked as the mobster took it down the embankment, heading straight for the large figure.

[Maximum Firepower]

Jackie revved up the dual repeating crossbows, beaming out bolts that burned a bright red. The figure turned as the projectiles burst up chunks of damp mud from the ground as they worked their way toward him.

"Jump!" Sally shouted, and they began to leap out from the coach as it rocketed through the gathered enemies, pulping two of them as it zoomed in a wide arc to start circling the tomb.

She rolled across the wet grass and brought her shield and staff up. The smaller Monsters were pill shaped. Dark gray with weird faces drawn on them.

Humphrey was already aflame and bursting toward the main antagonist, which she frowned at.

A large patchwork teddy bear, twenty feet tall, with a wide mouth filled with very real-looking teeth. With mismatched eyes, it looked almost gleeful to be interrupted by the gathered Parties. From her peripheral, she saw the two pulped dolls reinflate to being their normal five-foot size.

The combined *Outsider* and *Insider* teams worked through the enemy. Hardy and regenerative, but not very offensive at this stage. She didn't have the brainpower to work through this. Despite being undead, her heart was pounding in her chest.

"Norah!" she yelled out into the bad weather. "We're here, open up!"

Cracks of golden light started to appear around the brickwork of the tomb as she ran toward it. Even now, she didn't draw the key, just in case. Nothing left to chance.

[Icon of Eternity]

The tomb exploded in a flash of radiant light, blinding and stunning everyone but one. Sally. From the ruined building, a female figure made of solid gold rose up into the air as bandages swirled around her. Drawing up from inside the tomb, they wrapped around the golden figure slowly, covering up the shining radiance.

Sally had no time to stop in awe, even if everyone else was dumbstruck. She leaped over some of the ruined brickwork, almost slipping across the wet stone.

There he was. Wrapped in golden bandages, which was odd, but no other thoughts were in her head. Staff sank into the ground beside her as she hopped up atop him.

Key from her Inventory and into her hand. It was cold, translucent, powerful.

No hesitation, she brought it down into his stomach. It stopped halfway, as though it had fit into something tangible, and she twisted it with a heavy click.

From her hand, the key vanished. Consumed. The attempt made.

As swirls of bandaging slowly dimmed the area around her, she waited.

The rain continued to fall, the sound of it pattering against the stone the only thing audible as the fighters remained stunned. But she waited.

Red eyes wide, she gripped his shoulders, wanting to shake him and wake him up.

Sally . . . waited.

CHAPTER FORTY-SEVEN

Thrice Bitten

The radiant light illuminating the area faded as Norah became covered once more. With the number of bandages reducing as they spun back around her body, she sank down back to the ground. Sally had her hands gripped on the vampire, her unnecessary breath caught in her lungs. Theo didn't take a breath, nor did his heart start beating again.

Mostly because he didn't need to.

"Ugh," he groaned. "Who designs something with *four* charges?"

"Theo!" Sally pulled him up by the golden bandages to give him a hug. "It worked."

[Living Dead]

She let him go so that she could move the bandages to reveal his eyes. Norah settled down softly onto the throne and deflated into it.

"Are the bandages necessary?" Sally bit her lip as she looked over at the Mummy. "And thank you so much. Also, are *you* okay?"

"Can only use that when I'm on less than 5 percent health," Norah said with an exhausted smile. "A little while longer and I might have just died. Keep the bandages on for now. It's part of the process."

Sally nodded, confusion in her eyes before she looked down to see all the blood soaked through the broken stone of the tomb. It didn't really help her confusion, but she realized it might not have been boredom that kept the Mummy from replying.

Before she could say anything, she was lifted up as the vampire stood, carrying her in his arms.

"Thanks for bringing me back. I knew you could do it," Theo said, his smile poking through the dense bandages. "I need to stop dying, huh?"

"*Please*." She smiled. "You might want to pop me down for now, though—things are messed up. Like really."

"Oh." He placed her down gently and then looked out at the gathered Parties about to fall out of the daze that Norah had placed upon them. "Everyone is here, just as planned."

"You're kind of an ass for doing that all in secret." She nudged him. "I forgive you, though. We'll need to kill this chump before I give you the exposition."

He nodded, his sword drawing into his wrapped hand. "*Ah*, you didn't read the bottom part of the letter, right?"

"Not yet," she said, narrowing her eyes.

Norah cleared her throat. "I did."

The vampire physically winced and turned sheepishly back to the exhausted Mummy. Her attention soon washed away from teasing him as her yellow eyes caught the large shape of Humphrey.

"There's still life in this old gal yet." She smiled and stood. "Only three seconds before they recover. Not enough time for a proper reunion."

Sally looked and nodded toward the vampire. They knew what to do.

And then the ceasefire ended, and after some brief confusion, the battle resumed.

The giant-stuffed Monster slammed down onto the Death Knight, but he blocked it with the flat of his greatsword. Edward and Lana slashed through two of the pill-shaped dummies. Jackie had switched to her normal crossbow so as not to pelt everyone with bolts. Chuck supported Dent as he severed through another two of the odd Monsters.

Sally grabbed up her staff, the skull atop it bursting into green flame. Theo's sword started to glow bright red as he crouched, ready to sprint forward. *[Mortis Bomb]* went out, and the vampire followed it, striking the first stuffed creature right after the projectile did. As the zombies climbed from the ground, he vanished and appeared by the next Monster to cut them through.

With a grin toward the Mummy, Sally shot off with *[Meat Hook]* to arrive at the next opponent. The dagger end went into their painted-on face, and they started to deflate. They had no brains, which was unfortunate.

"Oh, I like that," Theo said with a wide grin as he slid up beside her.

"Right? Now I can be both ranged *and* melee." She gestured to him with her shield.

He took a step back to observe it fully. He whistled. "I like our logo. Oh, can I get into the *Outsiders*?" He looked around to see who he might be putting out.

"No luck, pup. Party System is broken." She flourished her staff and pointed it toward the teddy bear.

Norah walked up behind them, not engaging in the battle. Her skin looked sore and cracked still, and Sally scowled at the damage she had sustained just by keeping the dumb vampire safe.

The Mummy gestured back. "The little soft Monsters are coming back."

It was true. The first couple they had destroyed had now begun reinflating.

"Must just have to kill the big guy." She shrugged. "Let's go help pops."

Humphrey was managing to hold his own easily enough. His defenses not taking too much of a beating, yet he had been unable to damage his opponent at the same time. His sword would just bounce or slide off, unable to cut the patchwork pattern of the Monster.

"Maybe I need to find more chewable friends." The creature chuckled to itself.

His wide smile then turned to confusion. Pain flared up his leg, and he looked down to see a small, almost-green woman in a red cloak jabbing him with the end of her staff.

"Yes, you look crunchy." He grinned as he reached his hand down toward her.

A flash of darkness above him, and somebody landed on his head. Before he could act, the little green snack shot out a swirling pink beam up to the intruder. She then swung upward, dragged up his side by the beam and spinning her horrible dagger around inside him along the way.

"No!" he shouted, a long split running from his knee up to his rib cage before the zombie spun up to his head.

Sally grimaced as she wavered, and the golden-wrapped vampire held out an arm to keep her steady. She had expected the bear to be filled with some kind of fluff or stuffing. But it was just blood and meat. Their skin was just weirdly rubbery, which reminded her of that pigman Unique they had fought in the Wastelands. He had wanted to eat her too.

"You look kinda goofy like that." She raised an eyebrow at Theo. "What you got going on under there?"

"Wouldn't you like to know?" he replied.

She couldn't see his facial expression to judge how he intended that statement. Before she could prod him further, the bear shifted and raised his hands up to grab at them. Stitching worked up his side to repair the gash she had created. This was dragging on longer than she thought—they'd have to contend with another invasion soon.

"What even are you?" she growled, stabbing the encroaching hand with the Skeleton Key.

"I've come to eat you all for master!"

She rolled her eyes. "Let me guess, that is Seven?"

"Not telling!" The other hand grabbed Theo for a second, but almost immediately, the vampire burst out in a flurry of slashes from his black punch-blades.

The patchwork fingers of the Monster fell apart, spraying blood and odd chunks of bone down across their head.

Sally was tired of this fight already. "Everything keeps regenerating."

With a shrug, Theo glanced through his STAR menus. "Looks like dying reset all my abilities." The blood around the pair started to swirl into a spiral before gathering into a dark ball at the tip of his finger.

A grin across his face, the air cooled as he placed his finger at the top of the patchwork leather by his feet. There was a shockwave that cleared the gathered darkness, just as the blast blew a deep hole through the bear's head, burying straight down to his neck, almost. While the Monster staggered slightly, he didn't fall.

"Gosh." Sally rolled her eyes before jumping down into the large wound.

A few seconds passed as the vampire watched the head sew itself back up, now with Sally trapped inside.

The Monster grumbled. "Something feels odd."

"Now we'll see who likes being chewed!" The muffled voice of the zombie came from within.

Theo hopped down onto the damp grass as the Monster started to thrash around and claw at its own face. Hands beside his pockets as they were still wrapped, he walked over to Humphrey.

"Theo," the Death Knight said.

"Humphrey," the vampire replied.

For a handful of seconds, the pair stared at each other impassively. Then they both moved in and hugged.

"You watched over her," Theo said.

"I faltered, but together we survived."

They moved away from each other, and both grinned. "You look rather odd bandaged like that." The Death Knight tilted his head.

Norah jostled him from the side. "What does that say about me?"

"Nothing, *ha-ha*. It suits you, but I was not expecting a similar look for Theo." He shuffled awkwardly.

Everyone had stopped fighting for the most part. The strange pill-shaped Monsters didn't really attack back, just regenerated—although now that Sally was doing something to the giant patchwork bear, all the surrounding opponents seemed to be deflating to a degree.

"Must be pooled health regeneration or something," Chuck surmised. "Good to have you back, Theo."

The vampire nodded. "You've grown. I'm glad that you, Dent, and Jackie are here. Lana and the plant person are a surprise, though."

"It's been quite the day or two of surprises." The Druid grinned and rubbed the back of his head. "I suppose Sally didn't have the time to get you up to speed?"

Theo shook his head. "Dying took a lot out of me. How long was I out for?"

Humphrey looked between the others and furrowed his brow. "Technically, less than a day?"

"Oh. I thought it would have taken longer." He looked back at the writhing and slightly deflated Monster. "She did say the Party couldn't be changed. Looks like there wasn't enough time to win the final battle without me."

"Unfortunately." Chuck nodded. "Architect has started a world event to kill the *Outsiders*, Players have tracking to their location at all times. Teleportation and mounts are disabled."

Theo tilted his head and then turned back to the Druid. "Oh. Perhaps I can go and lie back in the crypt instead?" He grinned, pushing through the wrappings to expose his fangs.

"Not only that," Humphrey added, "but there are invasions of high-level Monsters every twenty minutes. We are expecting one imminently."

"Out of the frying pan . . ." the vampire murmured to himself.

Sally cut her way out of the stomach of the near-empty sack that once was the bear and gasped for air. Stumbling out onto the rain-slick grass, she then stopped and threw up.

"That's my gal," Theo said, smiling, as he walked over to her.

"Gross." Sally shook her head before standing up to greet him. "If I had known our reunion was going to work, I probably wouldn't have arrived covered in vomit and gore."

He said nothing but brought her in for a hug.

"It looks as though I left parts of him still inside," she whispered, her eyes going over to the lumpy patchwork bear, "but that's all vomit too."

"Why was he filled with meat and bones?" he whispered back.

"Right? I can bear-ly believe it."

Theo sighed and pulled himself away, a smile still on his face. "Thank you for finding a way to bring me back. I wish I could have told you that—"

He was silenced as the zombie put a slimy finger on his lips. "Let's survive the event, and then you can give me all the mush, okay?" As he started to nod, she narrowed her eyes. "And the *other* stuff."

Humphrey cleared his throat. "We'd best either move to a new area or get set up here for the next wave."

Sally nodded and prodded the vampire away from her. "Chucky, organize the troops. We'll take the next invasion here and then go to the next location."

The Druid nodded and immediately delegated the job to Dent, who then turned and started barking orders to everyone. Under the guidance of the swordsman, they started to get into a defensive formation.

"*Theo?*"

The vampire turned around to see the demon approaching him. "*Edward.*"

He gave a brief bow before holding his hand out. "Such a shame you darken our doorstep once more." Edward grinned widely. "I only wish you could take my place and be more useful."

Theo grinned back and took up the handshake. "You've been keeping them safe, so you've earned the stay of my blade."

"Quit *flirting* and get *ready*." Sally stormed in and pushed them apart. "You can be best buds after the world has stopped ending."

As if on cue, a flash of lightning lit up the glum sky. The rolling thunder soon after signaled the rise of darkened shapes coming from the nearby tree line.

Another invasion to quell, their weapons and spells were drawn at the ready.

CHAPTER FORTY-EIGHT

Time and Time Again

Cloaked in shadows that obscured their dark metal armor, the only points of light on their new assailants were their singular eyes. Large orbs of pale white light that observed the gathered groups with impassive expressions as they drew nearer. Longswords, spiked maces, and halberds held in their plated hands, all made of black metal.

"Cousins of yours, Lucius?" Sally raised an eyebrow, but the Shade just shook his head, some slight panic in his emotionless expression.

"These are Wraith Knights," Humphrey explained, adjusting his posture into a defensive stance.

"Oh," she said. "Like you, but more like a ghost. They're undead then, right?"

"Yes, but . . ." The Death Knight shrugged. "You can try."

Sally strode out in front of the rest of the resistance. They were all primed and ready for the signal. There were . . . eight Monsters. Not terrible odds, but these invasions were meant to get more difficult as time went on. Now, with Theo on their side, they had a little more power behind them—even if he wasn't part of the Party at present.

"Hey! Kneel before your undead queen!" She placed her staff into the ground and crossed her arms—a difficult thing to do while still holding her shield.

The Wraith Knights paused their advance and stood regarding her. No response came from them.

"Best choose wisely. Otherwise, we'll do this the hard way." Her grin widened, and her crimson eyes practically glowed through the light rain still pelting the area.

With the sudden pulse of gray energy, the middle wraith blew a beam of energy toward her from its central eye. The attack burned into the ground, drawing a shallow trench through the mud.

"Bad choice," she said from midair, *[Escape Fate]* taking her up at an angle toward them. Her own beam of pink energy striking one and zipping her toward the fray. "Attack!" she yelled out.

She spun her staff around as different colored lights bloomed around in the gloom. As she collided with the first one, her dagger impaling through their armor, she spun to block the attack from another. With a sword looming up behind her, Theo slid into position and parried it away from her. Just ahead of them, the wide figure of Humphrey barreled into three of the wraiths, right as bandages wrapped around their legs, knocking two to the floor.

"Reminds me of when we took the bronze district in the Wastes," Theo said as he deflected another blow before slashing out with his own attacks.

"Good memories," Sally agreed. "Our dance of death, the screams of our enemies . . ." she dodged a mace before blasting the Monster with a *[Mortis Bomb]*. "Our family all together."

The vampire vanished to appear above his opponent, a third punch-blade of pink energy appearing in the air as he dropped down onto the wraith. "Now look at the little group we have gathered." He severed the head of the Monster and dropped to the floor, his eyes going over to the gang leveling off spells and attacks toward the melee.

"Yep!" She slashed the dagger end of her staff, severing off a hand at the wrist, as the pronged end tied up the weapon aimed for her. "Everyone gathered for the end times."

"Not sure who the plant person is, though." Theo stepped to the side to avoid the heavy downswing of a two-handed axe as he rubbed his bandaged head.

"They were in the Spire dungeon." Sally's shadow slashed out, tearing a gash through her opponent's lower leg and causing them to stumble. "Guardian of one of the higher floors. You didn't know?" As the wraith dropped, she slammed it with her shield, then twisted round the staff to impale it through the neck.

He shrugged. "All I knew was that the tower was the highest point in the area, so Henkk would be able to find it."

"You didn't even know if I could make it up there?" She kicked the Monster over and struck it again in the head.

Theo grinned, his fangs only barely showing through the golden bandages. "You're *Sally Danger*, I knew you'd make it to the top."

"Aww." She feigned embarrassment. Perhaps he was right, though, even if he was trying to flatter her. Her head tilted to the side as she watched him combat the next Knight. If anyone was going to bash their head against something until they won, then it would be her.

As he flashed around in a blur of pink and crimson, she turned to the rest of the combat. Things had gone their way. A couple of other trenches had scored along the muddy grass, but nobody was too injured. Humphrey and Norah had taken out two, she had taken out three with Theo, and Dent had taken one down. The last two were still in combat—but with the assistance of the others in the back, their time was short-lived.

Theo finished off his wraith and tried to put his hands in his pockets, but the bandages were in the way. "So something like that every twenty minutes?"

She nodded. "The last ones were a little tougher, but we weren't as prepared." Her eyes narrowed. "We didn't have you either, pup."

"You want me to stick around?"

Sally puckered her lips. "I knew this question would be coming, you ass. Just brought you back from the dead and you want to run off to kill groups of reds before they can get here, right?" She placed her staff into the ground so that she could cross her arms again.

"Ah, I'm too predictable now, huh?" He shuffled awkwardly. "I wasn't even dead for twenty-four hours."

"Yeah, and you'd still be dead if it wasn't for all these goofballs coming together to help me bring you back." Her eyes narrowed. "I know you like to solve things ahead of time, but I want you here with me. With us all."

Theo tilted his head to look over at all the rest of the gathered group, now done with finishing off the last couple of enemies and regrouping. His face twitched beneath the bandaging.

"Look." She stepped up to him and prodded a finger against his chest. "I may have the ambition to take a bite from this world, but you have the practical foresight to meta-game bullshit. Things are going to get rough here, and I need you by my side."

The vampire deflated and gave a reluctant nod. "You're right, I know."

"Otherwise," she continued, "I'm going to ask Norah for your letter, and I'll read the bottom part out to everyone."

He physically recoiled from her words. "Come on, blackmail isn't necessary."

Sally snapped her fingers before grabbing her staff. "My dear Theo, you forget that I am a *villain*." With a wide grin, she turned to stride off toward the rest of the *Insiders* and *Outsiders*.

Dent rolled out his shoulders and nodded to her as she approached. "Not as bad as the metal rhino Monsters. Perhaps we got lucky."

"Or now we are cursed by something," Edward added, idly scowling at the constant rain.

Chuck rolled his eyes. "More likely, we were better positioned and prepared. Theo's resurgence is a huge boost to our front line power, and aside from a few beams, the wraiths were melee focused."

"Right." Dent wiped the rain from his forehead. "Now we need to make the decision of where to go before we are bogged down in even more combat."

"What are the options?" Theo brought up his map, his eyes frowning beneath the bandages.

"Jublia Keep or the Circle of the Sparse." Dent shrugged. "I didn't name them."

The vampire slowly nodded. "I've got an even better idea . . ." He sent the coordinates over to the other Players.

Sally brought it up and tilted her head. "Looks like the middle of nowhere?"

Humphrey had already circled behind her to look at the map over her shoulder. "Hmm. Intriguing. I could not think of a more apt place for us to either fall or rise." He grinned at Theo.

"There's no marker." Chuck frowned. "I'm not familiar with the area. What is it?"

Theo's grin was wide, his fangs catching what little light the morning offered. "It's a graveyard. A big one with lots of mausoleums, crypts, tombs, and the like. Large cathedral at the back."

"A bit of all sorts of terrain, then." Dent rubbed his chin. "Not to mention thematically appropriate."

Sally nodded. "That's the most important bit." She leaned over to ensure the stagecoach was still in one piece—which it was. "Get saddled up, Jackie. Got about a ten-minute ride to our next place of final rest." The mobster shot back a nod and ran over to the vehicle.

Chuck turned his head away, eyes unfocused. "*Shit*. One of the teams just died."

"Southern one," Dent added, before shaking his head.

Sally clenched her jaw and hoped it wasn't the one with either Rachel or Charlotte in it. Seemed silly to be playing favorites now, but perhaps if they came out on top there would be a chance to bring back to life everyone who died today—or even this week, if that was possible.

"By foot, that's still a good eight hours away from the graveyard." Chuck bit his bottom lip. "We can't assume they don't have another way of travel, though."

She pulled a face. All these unknowns weren't too fun. Once again, she preferred being on the offensive rather than defensive. "No point dawdling now. We need to get set up at the graveyard before the next invasion."

The gathered force nodded and grumbled their acknowledgement.

Just before they turned toward the stagecoach, there was a flash of blue light from the side, and they turned.

A robed figure with a high collar, spectral and glowing a bright blue. A skeletal face with a sinister scowl and odd hat atop their head.

> I really need to stop using so much energy, don't I?

"Architect!" Sally growled and her staff burst into bright green flame. Although they were speaking out loud, the messages also reflected inside her vision like notifications.

> Now, now. I am currently incorporeal, so don't waste your energy, bug. I am just here to deliver a short message.

The figure hovered around until their eyes focused on Humphrey.

> My most traitorous little pet. Full of things that need to be erased.

Shaking his head, some sadness in his empty eye sockets, the Architect then lifted his hand up toward the Death Knight.

> Goodbye.

A beam, a couple of inches wide and a foot long, burst from the skeletal hand. Made of pure light blue energy, the very air around it crackled as it shot forth.

Sally turned, the afterimage of the beam still in her eyes as she saw that it hadn't hit Humphrey. Theo stood in front of the plated figure, a burning hole through the golden bandages, right where his heart was. Now there was just a hole straight through his body. The Architect sighed.

> What a waste. Until next time, bugs.

The illuminating glow of the figure faded away, washed away by the breeze. Sally growled and spun around to the vampire.

"*Seriously*? You're impossible!"

"Sally," he said, as blood soaked through the wrappings down his torso. "Hold me close now."

She dropped her weapons and threw herself around him, squeezing him tight against her. "*Asshole*. Why you gotta do this to a gal?"

"Just a few seconds longer," he whispered, deflating into her with a long sigh. "Things will be okay."

Sally leaned her head back to look at him, a confused scowl under freshly wet eyeballs. "You've got a secret again, haven't you?"

He smiled, despite how tired his eyes looked. "And . . . *done*." He cupped her ears with his hands and gave her a brief kiss on the forehead before stepping away from her.

She continued to be confused as she saw that the previously golden bandages were now soaked through with crimson, from head to toe. Fragments of glass dropped down from his torso onto the grass as the wrappings started to decay and turn to ash, revealing his pristine suit with no sign of the previous wound on him.

"Sometimes," he said, taking his crimson glasses from inside his jacket to put back on. "My genius scares even myself."

CHAPTER FORTY-NINE

A Place to Rest

The short coach ride over to the graveyard was rather quiet. Partly due to the apprehension of the struggles that lie ahead and the sudden appearance of the Architect. The fact that he tried to assassinate Humphrey was concerning.

Mostly, however, it was quiet because Sally refused to speak to Theo.

They didn't have the time to stand around and chat. Not wanting to get caught out in the open or traveling again, they had gone full steam ahead. She had glared at him and told him he had ten minutes to come up with a good excuse for that whole event.

Sally sighed and looked out of the stagecoach window. In truth, she wasn't that mad at him. Upset that he had almost died again, perhaps. Time had become messy, and she had spent too long sinking into the pit of her feelings. Emotionally spent for the day.

The goof had done it to save Humphrey. Was it necessary? The Death Knight was full of defensive and protective skills he could have used, if fast enough. But instead, Theo had offered himself up. It might have even been to show Humphrey that he was forgiven, that the vampire didn't even hesitate to give up his life for the metal chunk.

She had some idea why. Perhaps. At least, she knew that Norah probably had a decent idea. Once this was all over, she'd really need to find a way to repay the Mummy. Not only had she watched over the dead vampire, but she'd done so almost at the cost of her own life. And it had worked. With the undead not requiring most of their insides to function, turning back time had just wound his soul back inside him instead of having to go through a resurrection that made sense.

Not that it meant that he could survive a blast straight through the heart though—especially as a vampire. Staked through with Architect energy, the vampire almost seemed pleased with the outcome, rather than being a messy pile of bloodied abs in the wet mud.

"I can see it!" Jackie called from up top. "Two minutes!"

Sally wondered why the Architect was so reckless. Already pushing their powers as much as they could. Was it important to get the Death Knight killed off as soon as possible? If they knew that he had the full Archie collection that might be the case. Humphrey hadn't been too clear on what the full cat may bring, but it couldn't be anything good for the new boss.

The stagecoach shifted as it turned off the main road and onto a rougher gravel path. Leaning out of the window, she could now see the graveyard.

And it was beautiful.

Any grumpiness she still held toward her Party melted away as she was left more breathless than usual. As much as it looked like the biggest cliché going, the graveyard was picture perfect. An eerie mist hung around the dense grays and somber greens of the stone markers in the overgrown grass. Dead trees stood guard between tombs and mausoleum entrances. Shadowed in the distance was the looming cathedral-like structure.

Sally had a difficult time keeping a smile off her face. It was a good thing the vampire was up top, so that she could regain her composure before giving him a dressing down.

She practiced her scowl and just about got it down as the stagecoach pulled up just inside the gates of the graveyard.

"Everybody out," she growled, partly just because she was so excited. "Dent, organize the troops. I just want a quick word with the *Outsiders* and then we'll join you."

He nodded in response, his eyes already darting around the scenery before he had exited the vehicle.

Sally gestured with her head to the undead Party as they hopped out after her. They all looked rather sheepish, aside from Lucius, who was just perpetually worried.

"Not *you*, Edward." She sighed and pointed him away.

"Ah." He rolled his bright blue eyes. "You said *Outsiders*, I thought, and *technically* . . ."

Theo started nodding his head before catching the glare of the zombie.

"So help me, I will crack your heads together like a pair of badgunk eggs if you don't stop the shenanigans." She flexed her fingers and watched the demon wander away.

With a deep sigh, she then put her hands on her hips and frowned at them all. As if daring them to speak up. They were silent and waited for her to ask the questions, which she was more than happy to oblige.

"First up. Why are you jumping in front of bullets for a literal tank, fangs?" She tilted her head.

Humphrey cleared his throat. "I probably would have died, actually. It was a specific beam designed to be unblockable by any ability but could disrupt what makes me . . . me."

"Like the Observer and Archie bullshit?" She crossed her arms, and he just nodded in return. "So the second question is, how did you survive a shot through the heart?"

Norah raised a hand. "That was my fault, hun. While watching Theo in the tomb, I may have messed with his corpse." She blinked her yellow eyes. "That sounded better before I said it."

"Messed with *how*?" Any faux anger she had been putting on was slowly eroding, as this was all too much to keep up with.

"I moved the position of his heart." The Mummy pulled an awkward face. "Since he doesn't really use it much, I just shuffled it around and put something else in there."

"I thought my chest felt a little weird." Theo nodded along with the explanation.

Sally closed her eyes and took a deep, unnecessary breath. "What did you put in him, and *why*?"

Norah shrugged. "Call it mother's intuition, but it seemed like a safe place to store those three vials of blood since we weren't using them at the time."

"Like I'm my own Inventory space," the vampire said with a wide grin.

The zombie clenched her teeth. "So explain then, Theo. You seemed rather happy and confident about the results."

"It's pretty simple." He snapped his fingers. "Their blood didn't mean much on its own, and I was unlikely to gain much benefit from just drinking it. However, activated with a beam of the Architect's own power . . ."

"Impressive," Humphrey concluded. "Are you sure that it has taken full effect, though? Clearly, you recovered from the wound."

Theo shrugged. "Want to try killing me and find out?"

"Enough!" Sally stepped over and prodded the vampire. "So what was the 'I'm dying again, please hug me' thing about?"

"Oh." He rubbed the back of his head sheepishly. "I was just setting my respawn point."

"*I'm* your respawn point?" While there was a hint of indignation in her tone, that didn't actually sound so bad. Assuming he could actually come back from death using Edward's bug, anyway. It would be nice not to have to test that, but in a way, it was comforting to know he had chosen her to come back to. Not that there was any better choice, but she chose to take it as a good thing.

"That way I can—"

"Yeah, yeah. Save the mush for after the apocalypse, please. We'll even ignore the parts of your story that don't make any sense. Like that you didn't know you had the vials in you, or that the Architect would strike you there, and what was with the fancy bandages, Norah?" She stomped her foot with impatience, knowing the next invasion was soon.

Norah shrugged. "I don't actually know. It made Theo's dead body look nice, though."

"Thanks, Norah." He gave her a brief bow. "I appreciate that."

"I also couldn't look you in the face, dead or not, after reading the end of that letter."

Theo pulled a face and turned away from the Mummy, placing a hand over his eyes in shame.

Humphrey narrowed his eye sockets. "Should *I* be reading this letter?"

Sally, Norah, and Theo all turned to say "No!" at him in unison.

The zombie sighed once more but felt content. While they were a constant pain in her backside, these were the *Outsiders* she knew and loved. What they were all fighting for. She turned her head to see Lucius looking rather out of it. He had been rather quiet since they had left the site of the last invasion.

"Alright," she said. "Go see Dent and get your orders sorted out. We are short on time. Lucy, walk with me a second."

They nodded and turned to go and see the swordsman as she gestured for the Shade to follow her through a line of worn gravestones.

"Talk to me. You seem a little lost, Lucius. Is it just too many cooks here?" She gave him a soft smile.

"Not exactly." The Shade looked out into the dense mist of the graveyard. "I am just not sure what my purpose is."

"Hmm?" Sally stopped and leaned against a large gray plinth. "I think you've always been a helper, right? Either through combat, your advice, or with your brain skill."

He tilted his head and put his gloved hands in his pockets. "I suppose you're right."

"You helped get pops back too, yeah?" She grinned wider. "If anything, Lucy, I'd say you have the biggest heart of us all." And certainly in the right place, unlike Theo's.

Lucius nodded and a thinking emoji appeared beside him. "I think . . . the adventuring life is not for me in the long term. I have a lot of fun with the *Outsiders*, we *are* like family . . ." He looked over at a couple of them in the distance, arguing on where to stand. "But helping people in a noncombat situation sounds less stressful."

She stepped forward and gave him a hug. "That's what we're fighting for. I want us to win so that you can have that."

"Oh!" A shy emoji beside his head. "I wasn't sure how you'd feel if I left . . . especially after not becoming your bodyguard."

"Don't sweat it." She stepped back from him with a wide grin. "What I want most for you . . . for any of you, is to have a happy and safe life. Acceptance within the world. What you choose to do with that, I support you all the way."

He nodded. "Let's go save the world, Sally."

"Heck yeah!" She gave him a playful shoulder push.

The pair walked back over to see Dent and Chuck looking worn out already. She gave them a grin to hopefully energize them. "What's the plan?"

Dent stretched out. "We're viewing it as three separate zones. We'll fight in the first and fall back to the one behind as necessary. This first area, which is mostly open, to start with. Jackie will pack the coach at the start of the second area, which is more built up with tombs and crypts. Then if things get real dicey, we'll fall back to the cathedral."

Chuck nodded. "And if things get bad there, we'll see you in the afterlife. Not that there probably is one."

"Not like I'd go anywhere good if there was," Sally agreed. "Solid plan though. We're going for the *Outsiders* up front, *Insiders* at the back again?"

"Pretty much." Dent nodded. "Edward, Lana, and I will be more in the middle to protect the three at the back."

"And I'll switch as required," Lucius added.

Sally turned to look at the entrance. It would be nice if the Monsters came that way and filtered in through the graveyard and didn't just spawn in behind them.

In saying that, it was odd that there were no System-created Monsters here. There should be hordes already prepped for her to take control and grow an army. Now that she thought about it—the place where Norah had her tomb didn't fill back up with those Elite barbarians either.

"Has anyone seen any System-created?" she asked, raising her voice.

Murmurs and shaken heads—they had not. Not since leaving Upbranch.

How odd. She furrowed her brow in thought. A screeching sound disrupted her thoughts as she turned toward the entrance gates to see them buckle and twist. The shadow of something with more claws than what was healthy rose up from the ground, dulling the scenery.

Two large orbs of fiery red opened and stared down at the gathered resistance. The red dragon opened its long mouth as the two Parties readied their skills.

[Become Ashes]

CHAPTER FIFTY

Finally

Flames licked at the edge of the graveyard, fighting to take hold of the damp grass still under assault from the inclement weather.

Sally sighed and stretched out, ash falling from her burned and cracked skin. Her fingers twitched as she maintained the grip on her staff, but her shield arm was struggling to hold the defensive item up.

The dragon roared, vibrating the ground around them. Perhaps it served her right for being ahead of the Death Knight. While Humphrey had been able to absorb or deflect most of the fire-breath of those behind him, she was closer to the gates. Just her and Theo.

She turned her head to the side, pain slowly fading as she regenerated some of the damage, to see if the vampire made it out okay. He had. In fact, other than having the top half of his suit burned away to reveal his glistening abs, he looked mostly unharmed.

Funny how he always became such a spectacle.

As the Death Knight launched past her and Jackie spun up the stagecoach crossbows, she popped a Healing Potion and drank it down. *A dragon.* So far, the invasion Monsters hadn't been very edible, but this one might be different. Unfair to request dibs on the killing blow, as that might put others at risk. But if she got the chance . . .

A flare of green light as she sent out *[Mortis Bomb]*. Her horde wouldn't do too well against a dragon, so she kept them in her back pocket. Not literally, although she hadn't questioned how the space she stored them in actually worked. Hand extended, she started working *[Curse: Decay]* on the large opponent. It would be slow, but while her body recovered from the burning, it was helping the others out.

Why Theo's clothes seemed to burn away but hers remained only singed, she wasn't sure. Perhaps the vampire had his clothing designed to do just that, a sly gift to her. That was a bit self-*abs*-orbed though. She grinned.

Theo himself hadn't begun attacking yet, and she raised an eyebrow at him. Perhaps he was more hurt than he was letting on?

He caught her glance. "Oh. I'm just, uh . . . preparing."

Sally narrowed her eyes. "The rebirth didn't reset your stuff again, did it?"

"No." His eyes focused on the large dragon. It might even be slightly bigger than Ruben had been, but this one wasn't Unique and had no inclination to berate them. "I just . . . when I held you. I felt something."

She snorted. "That'll be a first, living dead boy."

Theo rolled his eyes. "No, I mean your power. It's not just the cool new shield, right?"

Sally beamed and looked over at the dragon. Humphrey had its attention and was holding steady, Lucius providing a second sword to help block attacks. A constant barrage of bolts were mostly bouncing from the tough scales of the Monster, but the occasional one would find a way in between and into the softer flesh. Norah was trying to wrap around a foreleg, while the others were pensive—sending off minor ranged attacks to support the front line.

It felt different from the fight against Ruben. They were slightly stronger now, sure. But even with the event shadowing them, the stakes didn't feel so high.

"Humphrey said that we're as strong as Raid Bosses now." She tilted her head back toward him. "The event was against the *Outsiders*, but it also pushed me higher. I'm a World Boss."

Theo whistled and then gave her a low bow. "And here I was thinking you just did something nice with your hair."

"Ass." She rolled her eyes but smiled. "Go flirt with the dragon instead. I'm not wasting my powers on something so beneath me."

"Ooh. I just got shivers." The vampire pushed his crimson glasses up and grinned. "Although that might be my state of undress."

Before she could reply, he was off. A blur of pink and red energy as his buffs swirled around him. Black punch-blades appeared on his hands as he vanished into a cloud of dark mist.

Norah stepped up beside her, her hands clutched on the extended bandages that the dragon was trying to escape from. "I'm sorry for my deception, hun."

"Oh?" Sally tilted her head, her curse still slowly draining the Monster. "Don't worry about it. Rearranging his internal organs is kinda weird, but I spend half my days throwing up brains or pining after a future that might not be possible, so . . ."

"Things worked out okay . . . but in truth, I was trying to recreate parts of the resurrection ritual that I could remember." Norah looked down at the floor. "After I said his heart was in the right place, it jogged some memories. When I died, they moved my heart and put something in its place until I came back."

"See," Sally smiled at her, "that's slightly less weird than just desecrating his body for fun." Why everyone had to hide these things away from her, she didn't know. It's not like she couldn't be trusted with the truth.

She watched as the vampire dashed his way up the dragon, flickering around with his pink *[Novice Strike]*. "Thank you, though. You gave it your all, and I appreciate that."

Norah's face softened, and she gave the zombie a warm smile. "Say nothing of it. I'd die over and over again for any of us. It's almost a shame that things worked out. I was ready to bring the world to its knees in anger with you."

Sally gave her a wink. "There's always time for that." After all, they didn't know how they'd really get out of this situation.

The curse cut off, signaling that the dragon was below half health. She yawned and sent another *[Mortis Bomb]* off, although the zombies would only get mushed immediately or be nothing more than a nuisance for their opponent.

What she needed was a ranged magic attack that did damage based on a held weapon. Then she would have a beam attack even better than the Architect's.

"You might need to fling me soon," she said to the Mummy. Unlike Ruben, this dragon didn't have the same amount of self-preservation—which made it more difficult as it didn't have to consider running away or focusing on anyone other than the Death Knight.

Humphrey was doing an exemplary job of tanking. He had turned the Monster to the side so any errant flames missed them all, and they were safe from any potential tail swipes. Using his absorption or parrying skills meant that any ability the dragon attempted was mostly thwarted, leaving the rest of the group to level constant attacks against the enemy.

"Just say when, hun." Norah smiled. "I'm a little sore, but I can get you most of the way."

That would be perfect, and *[Meat Hook]* could take her the rest of the way. She turned her head around to the rest of the group.

Chuck and Jackie continued to support from atop the coach. While the Druid was casting heals and defensive buffs, the mobster laid out sustained damage with her mounted weaponry. There was the occasional spray of different colored bolts, as she switched between different skills. Fern was watching the rear to make sure nothing came from the cathedral side, while Dent and Edward each had an eye on the dense woods on either side of the graveyard.

Tactics. She grinned to herself. Who'd have thought?

A lot more useful if one of the invasions was a swarm or something. She was desperate to bring out her horde—the graveyard would be so nice for them. Plus, her level appropriate zombie summoning hadn't been touched. How unfair that she was made to fight and eat Players, but they found themselves against boring and inedible System-created.

Still, only a matter of time before Seven and the reds, or maybe an Observer or two, would come knocking. The question was, when would the Architect give up?

She could definitely see the invasions continuing on and on until her group started to get picked off. Even killing off most of their detractors wouldn't cause them to be the winners. The Architect just wanted someone else to do the dirty work, and if they were smart, they would just wait out the inevitable.

But they had the cats, a possible ace up their sleeves. The reason they had risked burning up their power to kill the Death Knight off quickly. If Humps knew what he needed to do, then perhaps he was the most important one to save.

Not that she would give up any of them. She watched the dragon writhe around in anger as the vampire continued to draw blood from dozens of wounds. The System-created were getting tougher, but it was hard to contend with what both the Parties brought to the fight. If they had the other three groups of blue team, they would have an easier time . . . but she wanted them away and safe.

"Ready, Sally?" Norah's eyes burned brighter as two more bandages circled out from behind her.

She nodded, and the wrappings whirled around her, drawing her closer to the Mummy. With a grunt, she was launched forward and into the air, spinning a little as the bandages unraveled. Halfway up, she shot out *[Meat Hook]*, latching onto the dragon. Staff turned in her hand as she pointed it out like a spear. She rocketed into the side of the Monster, impaling it in the side of their neck, her staff actually embedding way past the dagger.

"Darn it," she growled, "it's stuck now." Sally swung from it, trying to get a purchase with her feet on the large creature. With how the dragon was moving around and trying to dislodge her while batting away the Death Knight, she couldn't quite get hold of anything.

A flash of dark mist and Theo was above her. "Need a hand, my queen?" He reached down to her, his weapon stowed away.

"Dork." She reached up and took his hand with a smile. Using her staff as a springboard, she jumped up, using his help to stand precariously on the back of the head of the dragon.

"It's not quite low health yet," he said with a shrug, helping hold her up so that they didn't drop down the back of the Monster. "You're a little early."

"Rats." She slid in against him as the dragon tried to turn away from Humphrey. "That means you weren't doing your job."

Theo shrugged again. "I did die."

"Well . . ." They scrambled up onto the dragon's head. "If you like being alive, then you'd better step up. I have standards now."

He pouted and gave her a nod, not wanting to argue that point any longer. Punch-blades back onto his hands, they burst into sun-bright light, and with a flash he cut a large *X* along the top of the Monster's skull.

Sally slipped and fell atop it, a burst of the dragon's blood spraying all over her. Not the worst thing, and it did get her closer to her goal.

[Eat Brains]

She slid out of the hole carved from her skill, onto an extended bandage that took her safely to the ground. Theo landed beside her as Lucius popped out of Humphrey's shadow.

"Another dragon kill for the *Outsiders*, huh?" She wiped the blood from her mouth. "Now we go in for a hug and fall into a coma again."

"Pass." Theo stuck his tongue out. "Thankfully, the System isn't sending Uniques out against us."

"Don't count your chickens yet." Humphrey rubbed the side of his helmet and looked out at the space beyond the dragon. "We don't know what could happen."

Sally narrowed her eyes at him. Certainly, he probably knew more than most. They'd just have to keep their position and work through anything foolish enough to come their way.

"Anyone smart would wait until we are busy with an invasion," the vampire said, going through his STAR to fix up his suit.

"Well, then . . ." Sally grinned widely, as the shadow of the zombie dragon rose up behind her. "Perhaps we should start our own invasion?"

CHAPTER FIFTY-ONE

Unanswered

Sally watched in awe as the dragon flew up into the air, the large, leathery wings causing gusts of light rain to pelt the area. With little ceremony, it turned and began flying off over the trees.

"You sure?" Theo asked, watching it gradually vanish out of their view.

She pouted, doubting her decision for a moment, before giving him a shrug. "We both know if I tried to fly on it, I'd only end up falling off. Plus, dragons are pretty large and unwieldy. I don't want more of our scenery trampled on."

Having the dragon hang around would be a powerful ally. She had spent some time pondering her options. Second best thing was to send it away to hunt down any non-blue opponents coming this way. At best, the zombie could eat up some stragglers and thin the numbers of their enemies, and at worst, it would still slow down their approach.

Chuck stepped up to them. "Party on the road has reported incoming. Still a few hours away but moving quicker than expected."

Lucius butted in. "Are they okay?"

The Druid nodded. "Took a bit of damage, but they're alive. Now going to meet up with the northern team. Their safety is more important than what heads up they can give us, I feel."

Sally agreed and told him as such. "It's fair to say the reds aren't playing nice, and we don't want any more losses." If the Architect just didn't like the *Outsiders*, and if they got killed off, then the remaining Players might be able to live on in the world. Even if the System couldn't abide Uniques.

Theo looked around, his hands in his pockets. "So, do we just chill out for now until something comes along?"

Sally reached out and put her hand on his shoulder. "I know it's odd having to sit still for two minutes—trust me, being defensive grinds my gears too—but it's the best chance of not getting caught out."

The vampire squirmed at the thought but eventually agreed that she was probably right.

"If you want to do something useful," she continued, "you have time to go check out the cathedral."

And he was gone, like an excited child. Lucius seemed to have tagged along as well. "You know . . ." She snapped her fingers. "If it's just going to be escalating threats occasionally broken up with quirky banter in the downtime, it might get old real fast."

"We could always try to be quiet for once?" Edward suggested, a wry smile at the edge of his mouth.

Lana rubbed the back of her arm against her forehead. "I was thinking of setting up a campfire and cooking. Some of us eat normal food, right?"

"Mostly the souls of the innocent." The demon rolled his eyes. "But you can't beat a good stew, either."

The rest of the *Insiders* murmured their intention to consume normal food, which left Sally feeling a little left out. While she could no longer eat or enjoy normal food, there was a part of her old self that missed it. If Chuck couldn't turn her normal after he became the Architect, then hopefully he could at least expand her dietary options. That must be the plan if he wanted no Player vs Player combat.

"You feeling okay, hun?" Norah walked over to her and started to adjust her hair again—the bandages having now come loose after all the fighting.

"Yeah. Well, I feel like there's no driving conflict for this downtime. A new invasion will come soon, but it'll probably be rather easy. Then we'll repeat until when?"

"Worried about Observer or Seven?"

Sally sighed. "Not even that. I'm worried about after *that*. This can't go on forever, so how can we stop the event?"

Edward pulled a face. "They didn't really give us a win condition."

"It's possible . . ." Humphrey began, "that eventually the invasions would take up too many resources or meet a condition where if a Player hasn't interacted with the event for a certain amount of time, it would cancel. This is speculation, of course."

"So just kill and eat until we get what we want." Sally sighed. "Nothing truly changes, huh?"

There was a loud groan as Theo opened the large wooden door of the cathedral.

Lucius popped out of the vampire's shadow, a sweat drop beside his head. "That's pretty spooky, huh?"

Theo raised an eyebrow. "Aren't you ghost adjacent?"

"It's more nuanced than that." The shade crossed his arms. "I'm sure ghosts can get scared too."

With a nod, the vampire accepted the point. Hands back into his pockets, he stepped into the large main room of the building.

The air was slightly cooler in here, and the dim light coming in through the large stained glass windows did nothing but highlight how dusty and abandoned everything looked. Two rows of pews took up most of the floor space, aimed straight toward a tall stone statue that sat just behind a lectern.

"Odd that the graveyard is so empty," Theo thought out loud, his voice slightly echoing around the space.

"Not even a single System-created zombie or skeleton," Lucius added, but much quieter, lest they disturb something.

Theo grinned, the light slightly catching his fangs. "Oh, I'm sure Sally can fill the place with the dead relatively quickly."

The Shade cupped his misty chin. "How do you keep doing that?"

"Hmm, the fangs thing? A lot of practice in the mirror after I first turned, and then situational awareness of where light sources are coming from. You'll notice I tend to lift my chin up slightly on occasion."

"Huh, you really do think of everything, don't you?" The Shade looked down at the dusty wooden pews as they passed down the center.

"No, but I fudge the numbers enough to where I can fake it." He stopped and looked up, taking in the peaked ceiling and the gothic carvings hidden by shadow. "I don't wish for hardship on anyone, but this world . . . It's always been a comfortable fit for my personality. Perhaps I can say that because I came out on top, and not at the wrong end of someone's sword." He shrugged and leaned against one of the pews. "Or stomach."

Lucius looked around. "You were a normal Player when you met Sally, right? You didn't kill each other because you'd met in your previous world?"

Theo ran his tongue across his teeth. "Can you keep a secret?"

The Shade nodded eagerly.

"In the old world, I had seen Sally around our town a few times, going back and forth to the diner where she worked. I had a big crush on her." The vampire smiled as he looked up at the dimly lit stained glass windows. "Eventually, I gathered the courage to go into the diner."

Lucius crossed his arms. "Bothering a lady while they're working isn't romantic, you know?"

"Yeah, I know. I wasn't going to . . ." Theo wrinkled up his face. "I just wanted to see what she was like, base my infatuation on more than just the fact that she was cute." The vampire pushed himself back up and started toward the end of the cathedral again. "Of course, when I stepped inside, I totally lost my nerve. She was busy with another customer, so I just went and sat down. Didn't even order."

The Shade followed along but didn't interrupt the story.

"Clocked the character sheet on the counter as I passed. We had some things in common. Realized that not ordering anything and just sitting awkwardly was pretty creepy, so gathered myself together to leave. Paid for a meal I never asked for and brought up our shared interest."

Theo stopped as they reached the front and looked up at the statue. Rather sinister in the dim light, the head was obscured by shadows. A robed figure that held a sword in one hand, with a shield at their side.

"I couldn't tell if she was actually interested, or if I had blown it with her," he continued. "Somehow I had put on an awkward confidence when talking with her, but as soon as I left the diner, I pretty much collapsed into a pile of mush." He tilted his head and smiled. "Of course, then we got brought here."

Lucius ran a gloved finger through the dust on the lectern. "I can see why you'd think you were the main character. Got the girl and became the all-powerful vampire."

"Ah." The vampire shrugged. "It was nice being the knight in shining armor for her for a bit. Seeing her now though . . . I'm just really proud. She knows how to drive actual change and cares a lot for people, whereas I just play the System to the extent of the current rules."

"You're relatively reasonable when you're not brooding or on a warpath." A smiling face appeared beside the head of Lucius.

"Knowing you're going to die puts a bit of a strain on the senses." Theo grinned. "I feel a lot calmer now. That said—I love Sally and would die a dozen times over for her, assuming the stolen blood works. Otherwise, just once, I guess?" He turned and started to stroll around the back of the statue.

"Romantic." The Shade turned back to the cracked doorway at the start of the cathedral. Almost time to go back, he reckoned. "Theo . . . what was it like to be . . . dead?"

Theo circled around the other side of the stone plinth the statue stood upon, now with a wooden case in his hands. "Honestly? It felt as though there was no time between getting stabbed through the heart and waking up in the tomb. Like a brief sleep where I didn't dream."

"Oh." Lucius cupped his misty chin in thought as they started to walk back to the others. "Did Sally tell you I used my System disbelief powers on her?"

"No?" He raised an eyebrow. "She doesn't seem drastically different, so that's a good sign. Who asked her three questions?"

"Humphrey, Edward, and . . . myself."

Theo's eyes glowed a bright crimson. "And what did you all ask her? I'll trade you a secret for the information . . ."

* * *

Sally practiced twirling around her staff. The stew smelled . . . okay. Normally, that kind of thing should poke at her stomach, but it hardly even registered as food to her senses. There were only so many brains she could eat, even if they were slightly different flavors. Back at the start, she had eaten more than just the special thinking parts, so perhaps she should try chomping on the next meaty morsel that turned up.

"Oh, hey, Theo." She turned to see him and Lucius arriving back from their little trip. "Find anything?"

"I certainly did." The vampire gave the Shade a hearty pat on the back before he turned his glare over to the group gathered around the cooking pot. After clocking Edward, he tilted his head back to Sally. "Found a special box. No Monsters or anything, though."

"What's in the box?" she asked, with her arms extended out to receive it as the vampire walked forward. Lucius remained in place, almost statuesque.

"Hopefully nothing time consuming," Theo said with a smile. "We have a couple of minutes, right?"

She nodded and received the box. It was relatively plain in design. A light-colored wood with steel framing and . . . the design printed on it was familiar. "Aw no," she said and pouted. "This is a chance box. Feels like forever since I saw one in person. It reminds me of when I first started out in Hillan."

"What a callback," Theo said, putting his hands in his pockets. "Now look how far you've come."

Sally narrowed her eyes at him. "You planted this here, didn't you? Ass. You're just a big softy." She stepped forward and gave him a tight hug.

"What can I say?" he said quietly, his crimson eyes moving back over toward Edward. "I don't like leaving anything to chance."

CHAPTER FIFTY-TWO

Second Breakfast

Sally ran her finger along the edge of the box before putting it away in her Inventory. "I'm going to keep that as a memento, pup, if that's okay?"

"Of course." Theo nodded and pushed his glasses up. "You already have two legendary items. I doubt it would give you anything more than a basic dagger."

"My favorite." She prodded him on the chest and smiled. "I'm going to ask Chuck something. Bad guys imminent, so keep those eyes out."

Theo smiled and watched her walk away, before turning his gaze to the Shade standing at the side with his arms crossed.

"You just pulled that from your Inventory, didn't you?"

The vampire shrugged. "The value isn't in the rarity, but—"

"Yeah, yeah." A waving hand appeared beside Lucius. "I know how gifting works. It was very sweet. I meant more . . . why did you give the appearance of finding it in the cathedral to *me*?"

"Oh." Theo turned and started to walk toward the graveyard gates. "Survive the day, and I might tell you."

Lucius sighed, and his crimson eyes narrowed. He walked over to Humphrey, who appeared to be sitting cross-legged on the ground, meditating. Norah was resting against a tombstone nearby, inspecting her nails.

"Is pops trying to communicate with Archie?" he asked, stepping over beside her.

"Perhaps, hun." The Mummy turned her tired yellow eyes toward the Death Knight. "Or he is just trying to avoid small talk."

"Ah." Lucius looked over at the campfire. Sally was talking with the Druid and Fern, while the others were packing things away. He winced slightly as he felt Norah's hand press softly atop his head.

"You are worried about more than just the looming battles, aren't you, Lucy?"

He deflated and turned back to her. "And I'm supposed to be the empathetic one." A smiling face appeared beside his head.

"Mummy knows best." She gave him a soft smile. "My ears are uncovered, if you need one borrow one." She made a show of pushing back her bandages so that both her ears were free.

"It's just . . ." He shuffled around awkwardly. "I've never had to deal with loss before. Never cared about anyone enough to where it was a thing . . . and with Theo, I put all my energy into getting pops back so that I didn't have to think about it."

The Death Knight fidgeted in place but didn't act like he was paying attention. It was hard to tell because he had no eyes to keep closed.

"Isn't that wonderful, though?" Norah crossed her arms and looked out at the gathered groups. "We are not alone anymore. Death may come for us, but it is the strength of our care and how strong we fight against it that makes our lives so bright."

Lucius tilted his head from side to side but wasn't entirely convinced.

"Honestly, hun, I'm not the best person to advise." She gave him a sad smile. "If Theo was really gone, I would have turned to anger and violence. Grief and sadness are valid and healthy after loss. Do not fear those emotions. Destruction is . . . Well, just try to be true to yourself, okay?"

The Mummy gave him a pat on the shoulder as she moved away, stepping over to the patiently quiet Death Knight and putting her hand on the front of his helmet that wasn't burning.

"Come on, big guy. Let's go show these kids how it's done."

Lucius watched Humphrey sigh and get up, and the pair walked over closer to the front line. While he was deep in thought, Sally came up next to him.

"All good, Lucy? I'm getting anxious about these battles. Chuck thinks the event ends after twenty-four hours, but I think he is saying that to give me hope." She pulled a face toward the Druid, who wasn't paying attention.

"You don't have any hope?"

"I'm not *hopeless*. Although I have been called that by at least a dozen people." She grinned at him. "I just know that some of this is out of my control—and I hate that. We've always been the ones pushing forward to take a bite out of the future, but now it feels like we are just waiting around and languishing."

Lucius nodded slowly. "I understand. We need to take back control so our destiny is in our own hands. At least then, if we fall, it can be on our own terms."

Sally furrowed her brow. "Sounds like you've been doing too much thinking. Theo got you all brooding now too?"

The Shade shook his head and went to speak—but everyone now turned toward the entrance to the graveyard, all able to feel the building presence of the invasion about to occur.

"Alright, party time." Sally worked her shoulders out. "I have a bet with Jackie that these ones will have brains I can eat."

She strode forward, spinning her staff around, as everybody started getting into positions and preparing their buffs. Her feet paused, and she looked over her shoulder at the pensive *Outsider*. "You coming, Lucy? We can't do this without you."

The road leading up to the graveyard became silhouetted with figures that strode toward the group of eleven. Sally narrowed her eyes to try to pick out what they were, and as they filtered in from the gloom and closer to their combat arena, a wide grin crossed her face.

"I win!" she called back to Jackie.

Familiar figures decked out in rough leathers and furs, their tanned bodies muscular where they weren't covered. Held in their hands were weapons that glowed green. These were the same Elite barbarians that they had been trying to grind on before—and more importantly, they had brains.

Theo stepped up beside her. "They shouldn't be too difficult, but there are quite a few of them. All at once."

"Tell me," she asked, brandishing her staff forward, "what do your vampiric eyes see?"

"Approximately thirty-six, although there may be more out of view," he replied immediately.

"Thirty-seven then," she said with a grin.

"Ugh, that's not going to be a thing now, is it?" The vampire deflated as he withdrew his sword.

[Ruin]

From the end of her staff, she cast one of her World Boss abilities, splitting the larger attack into three small circles of red light—set beside each other to create a wall over the ruined entrance to the graveyard. If Humphrey could hold and fight them in there, they would be substantially weakened.

"Serves you right." She shrugged. "For holding too many secrets and for losing the duel." Sally stuck her tongue out at him as he went to disagree. "Now be a good pup and go kill things for your queen."

Her grin widened as he stood up straight before bowing. There was the hint of a smile at the edges of his mouth before he then turned and burst forward at the oncoming horde.

A crackle in the atmosphere drew her attention to behind, where Chuck held a roving circle of lightning. With a gesture of his outstretched hand, it zipped past everyone to strike among the barbarians. The blue light arced through a large swathe of them, damaging them further as they struggled to get through the red circles of pain.

The Druid tilted his head side to side as he watched Lucius shadow Sally and then the pair swung themselves into the melee using her tethering skill. "Been a while since I used that," he murmured to himself.

Dent grunted and continued to pace back and forth.

Chuck rolled his eyes. "Is the greatest swordsman in the System envious of those able to go punch Monsters in the face?"

"Not envious," the reply came as he stopped moving. "I just don't think I'm being utilized well."

"Keeping me safe isn't good enough for you?" The Druid raised an eyebrow and smiled.

Before Dent could reply, the dryad poked their head down from the stagecoach. "I may be able to assist with your quarrel." They dropped down onto the soft mud and made the movements as if they had taken a long sigh.

They gave Fern a little space and watched as their roots began to grow down from their legs to sink into the ground. They crossed their arms and tilted their impassive head to the side. "I can now communicate with the surrounding forest. The trees will tell me if anyone approaches from either side."

"Perfect," Edward called from the side. "Then I can watch our backs." A wide grin was illuminated by his glowing blue eyes.

Chuck sighed. "Fine. Jackie can defend us pretty well enough. If I die though . . ."

"That's simple . . ." Dent limbered up his legs as a blue sheen ran down his arm-blade. "Just don't die." He sprinted off toward the fight, leaving the Druid to roll his eyes.

Norah hummed to herself as the blur of the swordsman flashed past her. She'd much rather be fighting Adventurers, but this wasn't too bad so far. Her bandages intertwined and encircled one of the barbarians. With a short struggle, they then twisted and snapped their neck. As a handful began to exit the right circle of red, she brought up a dozen foot tall pyramids in front of them to knock them back into it.

Humphrey spun around as the pyramid vanished away, his greatsword blazing blue with *[Decimate]* cleaved through a handful of the Monsters. Two fell, and blood sprayed across the already damp ground. Despite struggling against just one of these Elites the previous day, they were able to stand their ground this time around. Aided in part by Sally's new aura and boss abilities, they were punching well above their weight once again. It was enough to make him grin, so he did.

Sally wiped her mouth as the empty shell of the System-created dropped to the ground. Time to start gathering temporary stat boosts and chew through the fresh buffet. Theo burst past, slashing through the neck of one enemy as he continued on to the left group. The warm arterial blood sprayed across her, and she grinned. There was plenty of hardship to come—she was sure of it.

But for now, while they were on top—she'd enjoy it.

Before she knew it, the invasion was dead. Minimal injuries, but nothing *[Living Dead]* couldn't fix. The mood of the group was on the up, despite the odds.

Chuck narrowed his eyes, unfocused, as he looked at his System windows. "Huh." He pulled a face as everyone gathered up. "I'm getting reports in from both the forest and the Wastes. Players are grouping up with the Uniques to take down the Observer threats."

Sally whistled. "Really? That's . . . amazing!" That just went to show that all that work she had put in to fixing the System was worth it.

He nodded. "Even the remaining blues have said they came across another Party of Uniques."

"Are they on target still?" Dent asked.

The Druid nodded.

"On target for what?" Sally narrowed her eyes. "What were we all supposed to learn about secrets recently?"

Chuck grinned. "I'll send you via message. We don't know if we're being watched."

She nodded and brought up the chat window. While he hadn't gone as far as to say that one of the two groups could be a double agent, it probably wasn't the worst idea to be cautious. She trusted the undead, and Chuck as much as possible . . . but—no, she shouldn't let those thoughts cloud her mind.

> Chuck: they are on their way to destroy Red base.
> Chuck: assuming Seven is on their way to us.
> Sally: neat

"Neat," she repeated out loud. That made some sense, although relying on an assumption was never a good idea. She imagined they'd stay safe though and wondered what Uniques they had with them now.

"Caution," Fern stated calmly, interrupting her thoughts. "Something approaches through the eastern forest."

CHAPTER FIFTY-THREE

A Flag Raised

Sally narrowed her eyes at the dark woods to the side. There was nothing that overtly gave away an imminent threat. With an eyebrow raised to the impassive dryad, she licked her lips. "Any more details you can provide?"

Fern nodded slowly. "The trees there are not happy."

"Okay." She blinked. "Are you communicating with them, or is it like a vibe check?"

"The trees are not able to speak or think like you and I." The dryad hissed a dry laugh. "They produce signals in reaction to stimuli. At best, I can gather the forces drawing near are ten to fifteen minutes away, and number between four and twenty."

Chuck grimaced. "That's a wide range."

Sally sighed as Fern just shrugged in response. She considered asking the Druid to talk to the trees as well, but he would have already if that was something he was capable of. "Thanks, Fern." She turned and rubbed her eyes. Corrupt Players or reds made the most sense, and they were timing their arrival for when the gang would be busy with the next invasion. They had gotten here a lot quicker than expected.

"I know you're going to say no, but . . ." Theo stood beside her and grinned.

She scowled at him. "You dare? How could you suggest that when you don't know if it works?"

He pouted like a scolded puppy.

"Ugh, fine!" She grabbed him by the shirt and pulled him in for a kiss, then pulled a face as they parted. "Blech, I forgot how disgusting that is. We'll fix that in post." Sighing, she let go of him. "If you die for real again, I'm not bringing your useless ass back."

"You will." He grinned. "This isn't just me getting itchy feet. You'll have to believe in the me that believes I'll come back."

"I don't want to hear it." She waved him off. "Died so many times and still full of hubris. Go, now, before I change my mind."

Theo nodded, and with hands in his pockets, he turned to stroll toward the woods. The mood in the camp was closer to Sally's thoughts, and Humphrey especially had his eye sockets narrowed at the vampire.

He stopped after passing Edward. Into his hand popped his *[Demonkiller Blade]*, which he placed into the soft mud. "I know what you asked Sally," Theo said in a hushed tone, before carrying on into the woods.

Edward blinked slowly, his blue eyes looking down at the placed blade, but otherwise remaining statuesque.

Sally snapped her fingers once Theo was out of view. "I'm actually just mad because I'm jealous. Standing around defending is boring as *heck*."

Norah wiped some dirt from her hands. "You want us to go take the fight to those in the woods, hun?"

The zombie rolled her tongue around her mouth. Tough question. She shook her head. "Let Theo have his fun. Either he kills them, or we get some better intel on who they are."

"Or he dies again," Humphrey said, shaking his head.

"Ah." Sally grinned. "How likely do you think that really is?"

The Death Knight shrugged. "Fifty-fifty."

While he was technically correct, she didn't believe it was close to that dire. The times that the vampire had died were always oddities rather than him biting off more than his fangs could chew. Selecting an undead class while he was still human was an easy mistake to make and partly the System's fault. Being held somewhere outside the normal world by Archie was hardly a proper death, even if he did get reset. The fight with Humphrey only went that way because he allowed himself to be sloppy and not hurt the tin can.

It was mostly the question of how far he was willing to believe that the blood had taken effect. He certainly recovered health quicker than usual, even being outside the Party. Theo had even been convinced that he had set her as his respawn point . . . but did that mean the process would succeed? He wanted to find out, and she was sure they'd all know in short order.

With a shrug, she focused on what she could get stuck into. "Jackie, move the coach around so you have an angle on both the gates and that side of the woods."

"Sure thing, Boss." The mobster crouched at the edge of the roof. "Hey, Chucky, I need your plant magic up here once I'm all situated."

Sally drummed her fingers on her staff. Something felt off. Maybe it was the next invasion preparing to darken their already gloomy doorstep. The brains she ate might have not settled well. She cast an eye over the handful of zombie barbarians. It could just be the fact that Theo was off having fun and she had to stay put.

She turned to see the vampire's sword in the ground beside Edward. The demon was deep in thought, which she felt was an invitation for her to go and interrupt.

"Hey, Ed." She sauntered over to him, and he startled from whatever was on his mind. "Feeling bored guarding the back?"

"Ah, no." He gave a sheepish smile. "In truth, I wouldn't be here if I could help it. Theo is obviously a proper *Outsider*."

"Nonsense, you paid your dues. You might not be part of the main team, but you're still one of us. We couldn't have defeated Ruben without you." She grinned.

"Alright." He rolled his eyes. "No need to butter me up. I'm not built for this sort of combat, however."

Sally nodded. "I know. Did Theo leave his sword with you for a reason?"

"No." The demon returned a blank gaze, which the zombie held for a few seconds.

Humphrey looked away from the pair talking and leaned past Norah to level a gaze at Lucius. "You told him, didn't you?"

"What!" A sweat drop ran beside his head. "Told who, what?"

The Death Knight narrowed his eye sockets at the Shade.

"Something I should know?" Norah asked.

Humphrey deflated and looked back over at the zombie and demon staring at each other. "Sally let Lucius do the mind wipe thing, and the three of us got to ask her questions."

Lucius nodded. "Oh, yeah." His crimson eyes went up to Edward and the planted sword. "*Oh, yeah.*"

The Mummy tilted her head. "I'm not sure I want to know anymore, but I take it Edward asked something weird that has gotten Theo's feathers rustled?"

Sally blinked. "Well . . . good chat . . . Edward." The demon continued to look at her with a blank expression as she slowly turned and walked away.

Chuck grunted as he tightened the last vine. "It's . . . not a permanent solution, of course."

"Yeah." Jackie took a drag of her cigarette and smiled. "I know, but ol' Betty was feeling left out, and some of my skills don't work with the coach 'bows." She ran her long fingers down the dark metal of her normal weapon, where it was now affixed between the two larger mounted ones atop the stagecoach.

The Druid gave her a nod and hopped down, vines catching him and softening his fall to the ground where the vehicle now sat. "Everything okay, Lana?" He turned to see that she was sitting in the open doorway of the stagecoach.

"Mixed bag," she said, a glum smile on her face. "I accept who I am. My peers accept me for who I am. There are friends around me who aren't just evil versions of myself. But . . . I feel like I'm in over my head."

Chuck grinned. "Welcome to the club."

"Pshaw. You're the leader of the 'blue faction,' have command over guilds and Parties. Probably one of the most powerful Players going."

The Druid leaned on his staff. "I spent most of my time in the forest area doing all the noncombat quests after ditching Sally and her group." He smiled softly. "It's funny how different she is compared to the old world. The zombie part switched off her awkwardness and self-doubt. My excuse for leaving them was due to the violence and Player-killing."

"Just an excuse?" Lana brushed some curled hair from her face.

"Well, that was an issue. I had an odd time getting placed in this world too. Awoke in a pile of corpses awhile after the first wave. Eating people aside, Sally is just very . . . full-on. Like she is overcompensating for being a Monster by trying to fix the System. But it's all in earnest. A hero for some, and a villain to others."

The clone smiled and looked over to where the zombie seemed to be browbeating the rest of her team about something. "You're saying, with her there is a chance?"

"*A chance*." Chuck followed her gaze back to Sally and the others as he repeated the phrase. "Perhaps the best and only one we'll really get."

"And third and finally," Sally wagged her finger at the group, "no showboating. Absolutely none. Unless it would be super cool. Am I understood?"

They nodded.

It was tough being stern with the *Outsiders*. Despite the fact they'd gladly sass her or wind her up at any given chance normally, once she put her bossy voice to use, they all acted like children with their hands caught in the brain jar. Cookie jar.

She sighed and spun the staff around, inadvertently splattering some mud onto the Death Knight's legs. Theo should have found the enemy by now and was either fighting or dying. Or just watching them. With a pout, she turned away from the *Outsiders* and walked back over to Fern. Lots of standing around and talking lately. The eye of the storm, no doubt.

"Hey, Fern, you still got your feelers in the forest?"

"The intruders have stopped." They looked up at the zombie with the blank slits that were probably the dryad's eyes.

"Stopped dead, or paused . . . you can't sense Theo?" She grimaced.

Fern tilted their head as if listening more intently. "I can give no further clarification. If it is any consolation, I did not sense the blood drinker when he entered the woods."

Sally stretched out her back. That was a little better, she supposed. Somehow, he could move undetected—either soft footsteps or some other vampire ability. She knew better than to expect the best, even if she hoped for it.

"About five minutes," Dent called out to them all. "Start getting into position!"

She yawned. What a day it had been already. There was the same kind of feeling she had when they had set off against Ruben. Unprepared, to a degree, but willing to put themselves through constant conflict to reach their goal.

And their goal today? Survive and ensure there was another day where the *Outsiders* lived, and the System was better.

Was it likely? She gave a nod to Fern and walked over to where Humphrey was positioning himself. Anything was possible. The odds were once against stacked against them. Getting through an unknown number of invasions would be enough of a test, without having to worry about all the Players that might want to try their luck against her group.

The group in the woods was too small. With how powerful everyone was now, nothing short of a raid of Players could threaten their position. It was something that gave her a little comfort, even though it meant more danger was headed their way.

She smiled at the Death Knight, before her eyes went back over to the woods.

Two small orbs of bright crimson bobbed among the gloom, slowly getting closer.

Appearing back in the graveyard, Theo was soaked through with blood. Hands in his pockets, he hopped over the fence, an impassive expression beneath the gore plastered around his mouth.

"Oh," he said, as everyone turned toward him. "Did you miss me?"

CHAPTER FIFTY-FOUR

Tough and Tougher

The vampire stretched his arms out and sat down on the edge of a tombstone. "It was a small group, five reds. Very red now, ha." He pulled a face, seeing that his audience wasn't too receptive.

"Scouts?" Sally asked, narrowing her eyes at him.

Theo tilted his head from side to side. "Hmm. No. Our enemies are often foolish and overconfident, but they wouldn't send a small group like that, knowing what we were capable of."

She shrugged. "How do they really know what we're capable of?"

With a humorless grin, the vampire tilted his head toward Chuck. "Forgot something in the Spire dungeon, didn't you?"

The Druid exchanged glances with Dent. "We left the Observer in containment there."

Theo nodded. "The leader of the reds isn't Seven anymore. You might want to call them . . . Eight."

Sally gasped. "They're just an amalgamation of a bunch of Observers? I was kinda hoping it would be someone more familiar." She rubbed her hair. "I suppose this was the only way they could be a credible threat, though. A normal Player like Chuck would be too easy to eat." From behind her, the Druid pulled a face.

Humphrey rolled out his shoulders. "Hmm. That many Observers in one form is concerning. I would assume that they were powerful enough to resist the Architect's call."

"Certainly," Theo added. "It didn't make sense to me at the time, but now I understand what the *Last Word* were trying to tell me. Or trying not to tell me. It was difficult when they died so quickly." His head turned toward the good Lana. "No offense." She pulled a face in response.

"Get to the point, fangs." Sally waved a hand at him. "We have a fight in a couple of minutes. We don't have time for vague exposition to be drip fed to us so you can feel smug about yourself."

He opened his mouth but deflated upon seeing her expression. "They weren't scouting but setting something up. I disabled whatever it was, but it may still have some effect. I couldn't tell what it was meant to be, however. Either a beacon or area ability. Also, at some point, Seven absorbed the power to make corrupted STARs."

She groaned. "So there will be more random bullshit abilities to deal with." Turning to the Death Knight, she pouted. "You'd think the Architect would care more about that than us."

Scratching the side of his head and causing a grating squeal, Humphrey hummed to himself in thought. "This event might not just be for us."

Theo yawned and stood back up, his suit clean once again. "Architect saw there were four problems and decided to mash them together and deal with the fallout. *Outsiders*, Seven, Uniques, and Humphrey."

Sally nodded. "Humps is a problem, I agree. Three of those things are on our side already, in a way. Shame we couldn't convince Seven to join us and take down the bigger threat."

Rubbing his head, Chuck sighed. "Seven is aiming for more of a 'hard reset' of the System, if not the destruction entirely. So we need to stop both."

There was a rumbling through the ground, signaling the next invasion was about to begin.

"Better be something edible," Sally murmured to herself. She turned her attention over to the ruined gates of the graveyard, where shapes started to emerge from darkness. If Seven had the left-behind Observer then they could be a lot closer than they first thought. She watched the Monsters come into the light.

Large salamander-looking lizards, with spines and long fins down their backs. Wide feet with long claws, and devious grins full of sharp teeth beneath eyes of bright yellow. Green and red scales, either mottled or striped with black. Around . . . two dozen of them, maybe more.

"Something moves from the woods," Fern called out. "Singular. Slow. Destructive."

Sally shot a glare at the vampire. "You didn't leave anyone behind?"

He shook his head. "I can go check?"

She sighed, looking between the woods and the lizards about to work in toward them. Humphrey was already powering himself, ready to run in. Splitting their forces at this stage might be a bad idea. Better to focus down the Monsters as quickly as possible before the unknown got to them, so they could face it together.

"No." She shook her head. "Maintain and destroy."

Theo nodded without further argument, switching to his punch-blades and summoning his *[Sanguine Weapon]* to trail behind him. Although he seemed happy enough to follow her orders, it didn't do anything to lessen her worry about what might actually be on the way.

Sally ground her teeth together. Already, she imagined the worst possible scenario. The reds had summoned something large to soften them up while they dealt with the invasion—and after struggling through that, Seven would arrive either before they could recover, or with the next wave of Monsters.

She could be wrong, of course. Maybe it was Seven himself already coming to meet them. It could be anything—but right now she had some lizards to chew.

"Keep us updated," she shouted back to Fern, as she ran toward the invasion creatures.

Humphrey was already upon them, a flare of light appearing where he struck the first lizard. A sphere of red light encircled his target, a magical shield absorbing his attack.

Sally groaned as she pointed her staff forward. What kind of shield was it? Threshold, damage, hit, or chance based? Ahead of her, the vampire was in the fray too—more spheres of shielding popped up around a handful as he darted through.

[Meat Hook] shot her toward one as she brought up *[Ruin]* again, thankful that the longer cooldown still allowed her to cast it every invasion. Also Monsters were generally not clever enough to avoid standing in the red stuff. The dagger end of the staff bounced off the red shield of her target, with the rest of her body following suit.

A bandage darted in to assist her in landing back on her feet, now in the middle of the Monsters. Her shield came up to protect against a lashed tail, and she slid backward across the slick mud. *[Mortis Bomb]* went out in retaliation but was absorbed by the magical shield and brought up no dead.

Claws came in from the side, which she hopped away from, almost landing in the wide jaws of the next lizard. With a flourish, her staff brought up the flares of shields again. A couple of them were weaker in brightness than others, but still preventing her from dealing any damage.

"Number of hits, refreshes on cooldown," Theo shouted from the side as he mashed the skull of a Monster in, his trio of blows a blur with *[Novice Strike]*.

Ah, if that was the case, then she knew the solution. The vampire might have the best attack speed by far, and so was best at dealing with the creatures one-by-one. She didn't have that kind of patience.

[Endless Dead]

Fifty zombies began to crawl up around her, protected for two seconds as part of *[Death Aura]* so that they could get their footing before being mushed. Almost immediately, the area became awash with red light, as all the undead leveled an attack at the nearest lizard.

Sally hopped forward between a couple of her pals and brought down the skull end of her staff at the closest opponent. The shield was dull now, so she spun around and attacked with the dagger end. Much to the surprise of the lizard that was trying to push away the sudden throng of zombies, a shield did not protect it, and the defense-penetrating blade lodged straight into their skull.

[Eat Brains]

She popped her shield up around her to keep her pals afloat, even if some had already been shredded by the large creatures. *[Strength in Numbers]* quickly pushed the tide in their favor, even if it was gradually decreasing as her zombies were beaten up. The improved *[Desecrate Life]* went out, pulsing around her to weaken the foes, allowing some of the undead to hang on and regain health from *[Hunger for Flesh]*.

That felt pretty good. It was nice that the System eventually found a place for her to fit and gave her skills that made sense rather than the random assortment she had started with at the beginning. She still needed a ranged magical attack that she could cast repeatedly for when she was tired of punching things in the head, but a gal had to eat.

Theo had become a torrent of energy, zipping between six different lizards and wearing the shields down with multiple blows every time he switched position. Occasionally, he'd hit one that was open to attack and shredded them with his blades, letting the zombies overpower them. Allowing her pals to get the curse over to the new corpses so they'd rise to her side. He was always thoughtful like that.

Humphrey was having less fun, being the slowest of the group. His skeletons were out and assisting with getting the shields down, but even with the help of Lucius he was getting through the Monsters at a snail's pace—mostly on the defense. Then, with a distant whirring noise, the lizards near him were pelted with a spray of crossbow bolts, their shields flaring brightly before dissipating. One of the skeletons was collateral, with a few of the projectiles also bouncing off the Death Knight.

"Sorry, tin can!" Jackie yelled from the back as her attacks abated.

He slammed his greatsword forward into the nearest lizard's head, before twisting it, splitting their head apart. A grunt was his only acknowledgment as he stepped toward his next target.

It was a shame Theo wasn't in the Party. She sidestepped a swipe of long claws, pain shooting up her side as she was caught by the tips. A zombie took the brunt of the attack and fell to the ground. With a step forward, she fired a *[Mortis Bomb]* nearly point blank and then stabbed her staff through the front foot of the distracted lizard. The rising zombies joined the others in taking down the Monster.

Sally looked around. It seemed as though this invasion was just about spent. Without Theo or her horde, they would have had a much harder time of it all. The lizards were strong, but their difficulty was due to their protective shields. Without them, they were just hardy beaters—and so far nobody could win a punch-out against the *Outsiders*.

She plucked her staff back up and started to walk back up through the graveyard. The area surrounding the gates was becoming a detriment to fight in. Already slick from the rainfall, it was now soaked with blood and corpses. They might have to move farther up the area just to avoid slipping onto the blades of the next Monster wave. Or whatever they had instead of swords.

Other than the inedible invasions, they had been pretty lucky with the Monster choices the System had thrown their way. Possibly random. But then again, when had a System-created really given them much trouble? Ignoring the fact that she almost died to that dungeon boss in the Wastes, of course. They seemed to be getting exponentially powerful compared with how Players had more linear growth. It was almost unfair.

She tilted her head to the side to watch Chuck heal up Lana. The woman was being supported by Dent, as it looked like she had taken claws or a bite to her legs. With the brief glow of radiance, she was then mostly fine and able to walk. It reminded her of the forest and what they had sought to do back there.

Theo walked up beside her, his eyes looking over at the group of humans. "I can hear your thoughts, *Sally Danger*. You want to send them away."

"Yeah." She looked up at him and pouted. "Not a fair thing for me to ask, and they'd probably refuse."

"I understand it. But what greater strength than being willing to put their life on the line to fight to the end?"

Sally rolled her eyes. "Rich coming from you, pup. I get it though."

"Attention!" Fern called from the place they had settled into. "Contact is imminent!"

CHAPTER FIFTY-FIVE

Rocked and Rolled

The two groups became tense, half expecting something giant and untoward to suddenly burst out from the tree line toward them. After a handful of seconds of silence and no immediate threat, they gathered their composure and started to prepare.

Sally snapped her fingers. "Fangs, out into the woods and flank. Do not engage until the battle has begun. Understand?"

Theo bowed briefly and then was off, not wasting any time to deliberate further.

She hadn't wanted to split him off at first, but knowing something was on the way meant they could get an advantage by having the vampire attack from behind. He wasn't being tracked, so he should be able to do that without issues.

It was a small blessing that they had finished off the invasion in good time and recovered. No matter what was approaching, it wouldn't be fun to be stuck between both threats.

"Humps, you're going up in front to absorb everything possible. We want to hit it with any slow or entangle we have. Keep it in place and pelt it from range." She glared around at everyone and received nods of acknowledgment.

Not knowing what it was bugged her, but getting it pinned in place so they could hit it with ranged damage seemed safer from the outset rather than get the melee classes into trouble. The Death Knight could weather that storm with little issue, assuming that it was a Monster or something simpleminded. If it was a Unique or something with some actual intelligence, they might have a step up over the *Outsiders*.

Worst-case scenario she could use *[Brain Drain]*, but she wasn't keen on having that on cooldown when other things could be on their way in short order. The actual worst-case scenario was that some of them could die.

There was an invisible timer on that eventuality, and she needed to think of a solution soon.

"*Insiders*, you need to keep Chuck alive, okay? No heroics. Use what you can in range, but otherwise stay safe."

Even if the *Outsiders* were the actual target, if they were looking at putting the Druid in charge of this whole mess once the dust settled, then they'd need him in one piece. She still had half a mind to send them away, but they probably wouldn't leave even if she asked.

"Figure has stopped," Fern said. "No movement."

They all stood in silence.

From within the woods there came a screeching noise, high-pitched and abrasive to the ears, right before a flash of light briefly illuminated the woods in a radiant yellow. A small gust of air wafted out and into the graveyard, carrying with it the smell of burned vegetation.

There was a pulse of energy beside Sally, before Theo burst out of nothing to collapse onto the ground.

"Theo?!" She stepped away; questions congested in her mind as they fought for an answer.

"Yeah." He stood up and dusted his suit down. "Good news and bad news."

She sighed. "You can respawn, but the enemy can detect you and kill you that easily?"

"Did I ever tell you how smart you were?" He grinned.

"Enemy back on the move," Fern signaled.

Sally clenched her teeth together, ignoring for the moment that if his blood didn't work, then he would have been dead again. "Details, Theo. Before they are here."

He nodded and raised his voice, so that all could hear. "Tall golem looking thing. Four arms, each probably with a powerful attack that charges up. Bands of light down the arms so that you can see how charged the attacks are. One of the hands is a powerful radiant beam."

Humphrey nodded. "Were the rest of the attacks charged up?"

Theo nodded. "As far as I could see, but it caught me unaware."

"I bet you're happy you came back, huh?" Sally narrowed her eyes at the vampire. His casual attitude toward his own mortality was exhausting. Plus, if something could kill him in one hit . . .

"Well, it wasn't without . . . complications." He gave her a sheepish grin. "An *error*, as I can't lose levels due to the experience lock. So I got a stack of exhaustion instead."

"You're telling me . . ." She rubbed her eyes before sighing toward the woods. "You're essentially unkillable, but you'll get more insane each time."

"Never a dull moment, huh?"

She scowled at him and turned her attention away. He'd get a piece of her mind once all this was over, and if he was really unlucky, she'd get a piece of his mind too. There were no visible countdowns, but there were too many spinning plates now, grinding away at her patience.

A big Monster about to arrive, with overpowered kill-moves. Invasions every twenty minutes that wouldn't end, just get more difficult. Seven and the reds. The Architect. Theo's sanity. She tried to think if there were any Chekhov's guns they'd left lying around.

A vibration sank through the thick mud of the graveyard. Heavy footsteps approaching as trees began to crack and fall in the distance. Her eye twitched.

"Jackie," she turned back to the stagecoach, "got anything to light up the forest?" She was normally opposed to such wanton destruction of nature—especially with Chuck and Fern here—but it might give them an advantage.

"Sure, Boss." The mobster spat out her cigarette and grabbed the handle of Betty, her crossbow, now affixed between the pair mounted to the roof of the vehicle. The barrels of all three spun as amber light encircled the bolts within.

A wave of warm air washed over the gathered Parties as a trio of flaming bolts zipped overhead in an arc, landing two dozen feet into the woods.

"Things are damp. It might not be that easy," Chuck said from the side. He looked tired and withdrawn now, the constant combat a bit more than he was used to.

Smoke began to billow out of the dense woodland, but it hadn't turned into the raging inferno as Sally had hoped. Humphrey and Theo would have to take care of the damaging attacks quickly, as they were the only ones capable of living after taking that kind of punishment. She had *[Brain Drain]* ready if required, but she wasn't about to run up into its face and get obliterated in the attempt.

Closer still, she could see the trees shuffling and buckling. "Contact," she growled. "Do not hesitate!"

A wave of dust billowed out as the nearest trees burst away from the ground, the large figure silhouetted against the smoke screen was almost as tall as the trees. A rectangular body that rounded at the top, like a semicircle, had multiple glowing runes upon it. Four arms that ended in wide human-like hands, bands of color moving down each arm to the shoulder joints. Their top left arm was dim, aside from the two bands nearest their body. Thick dome-shaped feet stomped through the vegetation and small wall of the graveyard perimeter.

As soon as it was in sight, everyone attacked.

Lights flared and flickered around the drab area as skills and abilities pulsed toward the large golem. Roots burst around its legs and a debuff slowed their movement. A dozen bandages wrapped the two right arms and pointed them toward the ground. Dozens of bolts clattered from its light stonework body.

The free arm spun forward as the two large white eyes observed the combatants.

"Target: Outsiders. Acquired."

A flash of bright white illuminated Sally as the palm faced her.

[Dread Counter]

Theo vanished and appeared in the air above the golem. Dropping down with a punch-blade blazing crimson with critical energy, he struck the shoulder of the top right charged arm. There was a crack as he chipped a dent into the stone, but little else. Immediately, he slammed his other hand into the sliver of damage.

With a terrible screech, his metal coffin expanded within the gap, wrenching the arm apart from the body. A hiss of energy pulsed from the split wound, magical power instead of any sort of traditional blood. Theo dropped to the ground and rolled as the bandages withdrew from the broken limb.

From where Sally stood, she could see the charges quite clearly. It looked like there were ten bands on each limb, so ten percent each. Although the vampire had disabled one of the attacks, it increased the recharging speed of the other two. She was about to yell this out, before the golem tugged sharply on the bandages holding the bottom arm, sending Norah onto the floor.

Theo looked up to see the arm twist away from the restraints and hover over him. He went to use *[Blood Shift]* before realizing it was out of charges. "I'm getting really bad at count—"

An intense gout of flame blew through into the ground, turning the grass into ash and scorching the area dry.

A brief pop of energy and the vampire returned beside Sally.

"Ass, try to take this seriously." She scowled but didn't look his way. Her zombies were out of the picture, hiding throughout the graveyard. Mostly to maintain their stat buff, without getting squished, but also as an early warning for anyone trying to sneak up on them.

"I am," he whined. "You try dying three or four times in a day. Takes a lot out of you." He yawned and then set off again toward the Monster.

Without any charges left, it had taken to using its large fists in melee. One foot burst from the vine restraints and it lunged down at Humphrey, slamming into the flat of his blocking blade. The Death Knight sank half a foot into the mud from the impact, waves of color moving over him as all of his buffs came up.

An explosive shot zipped across from the stagecoach and burst on the golem's face, one of its eyes now partially destroyed. It kicked Humphrey away and turned its glare toward the vehicle.

"High Threat. Eliminate."

The light and fire arms dropped in charge percentage, as the last two bands of the radiant one completed and that hand was leveled toward the coach.

[Impenetrable Defense]

Against better judgment, the Monster twisted the attack down at the Death

Knight. A loud screech pierced through the graveyard as a continuous beam of radiant energy burst out and blazed into Humphrey's blue shield. Thankfully, the protective skill lasted slightly longer than the attack.

Theo was already back upon it, his *[Novice Strike]* clattering his weapons against the stone, doing little immediate damage. He looked . . . sweaty and tired. Sally had been holding *[Curse: Drain]* on the golem, but it seemed to be working slower than normal. That was two of their get-out-of-death free skills used up. Theo might have more tricks, but he was liable to break with a couple more deaths.

The radiant arm stayed inert, trying to swat out at the vampire, as the fire and light ones recharged quicker. Fifty percent or so, and rising fast.

"Do we want to remove the arms?" Norah called out, her face an angered scowl at being dragged through the mud a little.

Sally grunted. "No, take a leg." The arms sounded good, but the more attacks came their way, the fewer chances they'd have to evade.

A pyramid bloomed up from beneath the golem's foot, putting it off balance. A yellow eye emerged from above the Mummy as multiple bandages shot out and wrapped up the leg lifted into the air. Faint arcs of white electricity flickered down the long spools of linen before the mummified leg fell away into nothing but sand.

Bandages withdrew as the golem then tilted and toppled over.

Bright sunlight encompassed the weapons of the vampire as he crossed them against the other leg. The crack of stone followed, and the golem fell fully on its face against the thick mud, the remaining leg now also severed.

[Meat Hook] sent Sally over, as vines and roots sprung up to hold the arms down against the ground. She landed on the back of its flat head, spinning her staff around before bringing it down into the stone, over and over.

Unable to right itself, there was eventually a pop of magical power, and a sizzle followed the smell of burned ozone. The runes and glowing charges faded away, as the zombie stood over a foot-wide hole in the back of the Monster.

"No brain," she panted, "but they still put the important parts in the head."

"So dumb," Theo murmured to himself, trying to chisel his name into the back of the golem.

Fern leaned down and put their roots back into the soil. "How inconvenient."

Sally tilted her head and sighed. "What now?"

"Multiple footfalls en route, close. Maybe a dozen or more."

CHAPTER FIFTY-SIX

Eight Nine

Sally wasn't a huge fan of how things were progressing. The golem was meant to be a shock troop, softening up the *Outsiders* before the main group of reds arrived. She was sure that was who was on their way. Nobody else could have devised a golem aside from either corrupted Players or maybe a Unique. They had used a few of their important skills in the fight, but other than Theo dying twice, they had come out mostly unharmed.

Each death gave him an exhaustion stack, which she was sure Humphrey told her at some point was equal to a night's missed sleep. Theo went off the deep end around the third day of lack of sleep. Last time this happened was because of the giant toad curse, which also made him lethargic, for the most part. Now he was amped up and soon to be uncontrollable.

"Everyone fall back to the middle area!" she yelled out.

Dent nodded and took over organizing people.

With a sigh, she stepped over to the crouched vampire and lifted him up by his shirt. "Listen here, pup. I don't have time to babysit you." She placed him down and pushed him to go join the others. "I know you think you can just do whatever and mush your way to victory but—*yes, grab your coffin*—but I need you with a calm head, okay?"

"Okay." Theo looked a bit sad for himself. Coffin shrunk down and back into his pocket. He jogged up beside her as they entered the area with more cover.

Mausoleums and crypts dotted the area, surrounded by dead trees and some of the taller or more ornate gravestones. Players would be a little smarter about their ability usage and tactics. Standing out in the open was fine for invasions, but they needed to play things a little safer now the stakes were increasing. The stagecoach had been moved to across the entrance of the cathedral, Jackie being possibly the most open to attack but at least the farthest from any danger.

Sally told most of her zombies to find cover. There was something amusing about hiding zombies around in all the shadows and hidden parts of the graveyard—that she would have absolutely loved in a different situation. She kept a few of the lizard and barbarian zombies out in the mushy mud starting area. The reason why became shortly apparent.

With Theo beside her, she looked up into the drab sky as something launched out from deeper in the woods. A small, dark object, which hit an apex before starting to fall.

"Take cover," Theo whispered loudly beside her. "Death approaches."

She crouched and gave a signal to the others before covering her ears. "Don't start that again, ass."

Light flashed throughout the area, blinding everyone as a deep *thunk* proceeded a loud blast. Air rushed past them as a shockwave of force through wet mud across the more built-up area of the graveyard.

Sally peered back over her cover to see those decoy zombies were now completely gone, a wide crater replacing them in the wet dirt. "Wow. I'm sure glad we moved." Even the golem had been blasted in half by the impact. Other than the patter of mud droplets falling back to the ground and the burning smoke from the center of the impact site, it was completely silent.

"Did I get them?" a female voice rang out.

"Nah, the counter didn't change." This one, a soft-spoken man.

"Fuck! I hit something."

There was a grunt, and a third voice that was much lower reverberated through the trees. "I told you not to waste it so soon."

Sally raised her eyebrows toward the vampire, but he was practically gnawing at the stone wall they were behind, his eyes bright red. "Get down, you." She whispered, pushing his head down. The last thing she needed was another tactical nuke on their location because his eyes were giving their position away.

"Aw, my frickin' golem, man." A different male voice, scratchy. "Maybe he killed some and the rest ran away?"

"Counter still hasn't changed," the smooth voice replied once more.

Assuming these were corrupt Players, it could mean that two of their abilities were now gone. She could hear footsteps across the mud coming from the woods now, but there were too many to count. Her jaw clenched. Players were usually such a walk in the park, but knowing they had corrupt powers, and possibly led by Seven, put her on edge.

"Looks like you just made a mess of the dirt."

A couple more seconds and they'd see the stagecoach. How were they going to approach this? They all had their ultimates up, but it was getting to use them without getting mulched first that counted. She tried to bring up the chat window to send a message, but it was wavy and flickered away.

"Oh! Someone is still nearby, trying to use their chat," a different female voice cooed.

Sally was tired of this now.

The deep voice grumbled. "The tracking says they are still here. Look, up by the cathedral. A vehicle."

"No wonder they got so far ahead," the scratchy voice complained.

No point in being stealthy now. She leaned over toward the patient vampire, putting her chin on his shoulder so that she could whisper into his ear. "Do me proud, pup. Go all out and fuck them up."

A wide grin spread across his face, his fangs salivating at the prospect.

She put a hand on his back. "When I let go, you are free to do as you please."

With one last deep breath, she stood.

Immediately, *[Escape Fate]* took her up into the air to land atop one of the crypts, in clear view of the twenty figures in the lower graveyard. The ability that had nearly killed her had passed through two of her zombies as collateral, before piercing straight into the cathedral walls almost a hundred feet back.

"Idiots," the taller figure with a deep voice chastised the shooter. "Two kill moves and you waste them on trash."

Sally grinned down at them, her eyes alight with crimson energy. "Seven, at last we meet."

He was tall, easily over six feet, and encased in bright red armor that almost matched Humphrey's in terms of being bulky and over-the-top. Each shoulder pad had a skull on it, while one last skull sat behind his head like a helmet.

"Sally Danger." A wry grin spread across his face. He was pale, with sunken brown eyes, his dark hair shaved close to his head. "I had hoped to get to meet you in person. The legendary dragon killer. A Queen of the Undead."

While flattery would get him nowhere, it did sound nice hearing it from someone. He was pretty transparent, though. Not only was he simply stalling for time so that all his little red friends could get ready to attack, but she could see something else as clear as day.

His corrupted ability was to enable Observers to fuse with him. Normally they couldn't with Players. What that meant for his skills and abilities, she didn't care. Now they would die.

"I'm going to hit skip on the monologue, Seven. Nice to *eat* you."

She dropped down and all hell broke loose.

Chuck was surprisingly first off the mark, perhaps eager to get the advantage over his adversary. His protective dome of thick vines grew not around any of their team, but over Seven, cutting off him and eight other Players from the rest.

Theo was gone, immediately using his ultimate to burst into the blood-red armor, snaking off straight for the reds cut off from their leader. Humphrey wasn't too far behind but only activated his normal buffs. She was surprised to see Dent and Edward heading toward the melee so soon—they were going all out for this.

She hit *[Summon Zombies]* three times to bring a group of equal level pals, before casting *[Quick Death]*. All the undead hiding away throughout the graveyard stepped out and began sprinting to where the reds had gathered.

Flares of light and crackles of energy began painting the area as the two groups clashed. To their credit, they seemed better organized than the other groups she had chewed through. A lot of them looked corrupted or were at least geared for utility. As the first wave of her zombies clashed alongside the melee fighters, she could see Theo had taken one down at least, but the rest still stood.

A wave of light passed out of the vine-dome, bisecting with a line of amber before the whole thing split apart with a pop of magical energy. Immediately after, a crypt dropped down from the sky, crushing two Players as the others dove out of the way. Behind her, Norah's giant bird-zombie had grabbed some more of the scenery to use as a projectile.

Vines burst up around the reds, pinning those now laying prone onto the floor as Fern used their rooting skill—right before Seven was pegged by the entangling shot lobbed from Jackie all the way at the back.

Red energy swirled around the plated leader, breaking the skills holding him in place. Two swords of red light flickered into being beside him, darting out and slicing down the zombies intending to snack on the Players pinned to the floor. Several started to free themselves, and Sally clenched her teeth together.

She had hoped they would be stuck for a little longer to enable the *Outsiders* to chew through the weaker Players before they could beat on Seven. Now they were outnumbered, if you excluded all the zombies. Different auras, shields, and attack skills flickered around the area, but the boss of the reds just stood calmly, staring toward her.

"You have Chuck here too. What a fortunate battle we find ourselves in. All the struggle and strife to end in one last show of strength." A wide grin crossed his face.

Sally leaped over the wall she had been behind and sent out *[Mortis Bomb]*, running toward the melee as she flourished her staff. Enough undead to give her cover as she approached. The ones at the front were getting cut down by the glowing swords of Seven with ease. She used *[Living Dead]* on Humphrey to keep everyone topped up.

As if getting into the bigger battle wasn't bad enough, if it dragged on too long, then the next invasion would happen. Even if it spawned in behind the reds, there was no guarantee that it would be in favor of the *Outsiders*.

She slid to a stop across the mud and planted her staff down, twenty feet away from the patient leader of the reds.

"Such overconfidence." He smiled.

Sally rolled her eyes. "*Fine*, have your monologue, but I won't listen."

Theo darted forth, a blur of pink and red. While these Players certainly had better defenses and uses of their skills—they were slowly being worn away. For every strike of his punch-blades that had been blocked or absorbed, another had punctured through. Small damage, some of which had been healed—but he'd taken none in return and wasn't even going all out.

Edward had used *[Greater Demon]* and moved back-to-back with the Death Knight, using him as a shield while he protected his blind side. Dent had found another sword user and was caught up in a duel.

The ranged users weren't as effective, with Sally and all the zombies blocking the way, until a couple of the reds broke away from the melee to use their own ranged attacks. Immediately, they were peppered by dozens of bolts as the stagecoach flooded the air with shots in a high arc. Lana held her ultimate ready for the right moment, while Chuck and Fern kept up heals or entangles on the messy combat.

Sally yawned as the man finished speaking. "Done yet?"

"Just the one-liner to deliver," he said with a frustrated snarl. "Your time here is futile, as you are already dead."

She rolled her eyes. "Duh, that's kind of our whole—"

Before she could say anything further, the land around her split apart, and she fell into an abyss.

CHAPTER FIFTY-SEVEN

Fragments

Rather than fall into infinity, Sally's feet landed on hard ground. In fact, it hardly felt like she had fallen for long at all. Her teeth clenched to see that Seven was still standing ahead of her. But now . . . they were no longer in the graveyard.

In something that reminded her of Henkk's ability, the pair of them now stood in a deep gray cube. The walls were near transparent, and she could see beyond into a limitless expanse of darkness that had the slight hint of dark green in the far distance. Surrounding her odd cube were a handful of other similar rooms, suspended in this nothingness at differing heights.

"Not bad." She spun her staff around before holding it like a spear. "Perhaps it's now time for my own monologue?"

"It would only be polite." The man smiled and gestured for her to continue.

Chuck grimaced. "Now what are they doing?" He received shrugs from Lana and Jackie, while Fern just looked impassive.

The Fighters ahead of them had turned bright green. Frozen in the positions they were just in, but now looked like they had been cut out of the world. He grimaced. The assumption was either a time limit or killing the right Player would bring them back . . . hopefully that would happen before the next invasion arrived.

"They can't be targeted." He turned back to the other three who had been left out. "Start setting up to be expecting their return at any moment. If the invasion comes, perhaps we'll need to kite it around with the stagecoach."

The three nodded and started bringing things together, while the Druid narrowed his eyes back into the odd fray. Dent was in there somewhere, the only *Insider* to get caught up.

In one of the cubes, the swordsman ran his tongue across his lips, and his eyes narrowed at the red Player ahead of him. "Forcing a two-on-two duel, huh? That's very risky for you."

Behind him, bandages snaked through the air as Norah's eyes blazed with anger at the two they had to fight.

The man with a long beard and blue sword chuckled, his eyes blazing a similar color to the weapon he held. "Oh, I've been waiting to fight you for a long time, Dent . . . for *I* am the greatest swordsman."

"Unlikely. But allow me to put to rest your doubts."

A woman behind the man rolled her eyes and gestured toward him. Norah nodded but wasn't too keen on making friends with an enemy. The sword wielder had a corrupted STAR, but the woman had a regular one.

With a flash, the duelists burst toward each other, the clatter of their swords flickering light and sparks as they clashed. Briefly blinded, the woman then lowered her arm that had been protecting her eyes, ready to defend against the Mummy.

"Oh, hello!" A smiling face emoji appeared in the air beside her.

Theo stretched out. "What are the chances, huh?" He grinned toward the demon.

Edward deflated. "I'd say it was *inevitable*."

The pair were in a cube with three red Players, one of them already injured and trying to heal up. One at the back was a nervous man who seemed to be holding a spell. At the front was a bulky woman with long black hair and two heavy looking maces.

Theo's ultimate form wore off, and he pouted. "That's not fair. I wonder if I get it back when I die?"

"No, you shouldn't." Edward shrugged. "It goes by day rather than life."

The vampire brought out his punch-blades and assumed a ready position. "Shame. Never thought I'd die side by side with a betrayer."

"Well," the demon said with a grin, his rapier illuminating green. "How about side by side with a . . ."

Theo looked up at him and relaxed his posture. "Can't say it, can you, until we settle the matter of the *question*?"

"It is time we shed blood and make amends." Edward's eyes burned a brighter blue as he turned to face the vampire.

The red Players exchanged glances and shrugged.

* * *

Humphrey glared out at the expanse, looking between the different boxes full of the *Outsiders*.

"Aren't you going to fight us, you big metal bucket?"

He didn't even turn or acknowledge the voice. Sally seemed to be knee-deep in a monologue with Seven, buying them all some time. Dent was in the middle of a duel—entirely respectable—while Norah, Lucius, and a red Player were having a polite conversation to the side of the battle. Theo and Edward were squaring off but hadn't started fighting each other or the reds in the room with them.

And as for himself . . . he turned to the pair of red Players. "Which one of you caused this fracture?"

"Not telling ya." A man with a scratchy voice and large backpack grinned as he waved a knife back and forth.

"Even if we did," the woman behind him jeered, "you can't get him from here."

The Death Knight took another glance around. "Well, that narrows it down to that gentleman with the demon and vampire probably maintaining the spell." The flame on his helmet rose higher as he looked back at them. "And you have used both of your corrupted abilities."

"S-so what if we have?" The man shifted uneasily. "We still have our normal skills."

Humphrey shook his head sadly. "I am afraid you are well out of your depth." He flourished his greatsword, which burst into crimson flame. "Step forward and accept the ruin you have brought unto yourselves."

". . . and then I said, 'Pancakes!'" Sally beamed at Seven.

"Right. So that wasn't really much of a monologue. You just ran your mouth with whatever came into your head, moaned about your hair, and then attempted to tell an anecdote about pancakes that didn't even make sense." He narrowed his eyes.

She shrugged. "Perhaps you had to be there."

"When I heard about the Queen of the Undead who had brought down a dragon, I had expected more of a . . . femme fatale."

"I'm both those things." She frowned at him.

"I had considered trying to get you to change sides, but now I see that you are nothing but a Monster like all the others." His two swords of red light appeared beside him. "The whole scrawny zombie thing is a huge turnoff."

"*What?*" She clenched her sharp teeth together as her eyes burned bright red. "Like you could compete with Theo, anyway. I'm surprised you had enough room in that suit for the Observers with all that ego in there."

"Theo? Oh, is that the vampire over there, who looks like he is about to French kiss the demon?"

Sally raised an eyebrow toward the pair, currently in each other's faces talking, while the reds with them stood awkwardly waiting. "System damn it, fangs." She sighed and glared back at Seven.

Dent stumbled forward, the man passing him and stopping too. Both men paused, their breath held, before a spurt of blood erupted from the red Player, and they dropped to the ground. The swordsman stood up straight and relaxed his sword arm. "A worthy attempt."

Lucius and Norah gave him some polite applause, while the woman grinned sheepishly.

"You used your skill on her?" he asked, raising an eyebrow.

"Sure did." A thumbs-up appeared by the Shade. "I'm not allowed to touch the corrupted ones, but Jane here is normal. *More* normal, now."

"I've been trying to get through these walls," Norah interjected, "but they aren't made of any material I've come across before."

"Oh, you'll want to kill Vinny," Jane offered. "Or at least interrupt him." Her finger pressed against the side wall, pointing down at the man holding a spell in the room with Edward and Theo.

"Just *stab* me then," the vampire seethed.

Edward glared at him, face-to-face. "I'll not give you the satisfaction."

One of the red Players went to step forward before the other stopped them. "Don't interrupt the enemy when they're making a mistake."

"Why else would you ask Sally what my greatest weakness is?" Theo bared his fangs. "You seek some petty vengeance just because I killed you three and a half times."

"You are not acting yourself. This is neither the time nor the place." The demon stood taller. "Plus, this is what she answered." He leaned forward to whisper in the vampire's ear.

Theo blinked. "Oh. I mean, she's not wrong." He stood back away from the demon and scratched the side of his head with the edge of his punch-blade. "That might be a little more awkward than fighting to the death, huh?"

"Especially in present company."

The vampire turned his glare back to the confused red Players, before looking to where Sally was. "Alright. If killing these three doesn't fix the weird box thing, can I trust you to kill me so I can help Sally out?"

Edward smiled. "See, now we're on the same page, blood brother."

Theo grinned, as crimson light started to flicker around him. "Blood brother," he agreed, with a brief nod. Together, they launched toward the reds.

Blood flicked from Humphrey's sword as he flourished it around. The head of the second Player bounced across the odd floor.

"You died as you lived," he announced to nobody. "Weak and inconsequential."

He sighed. Now alone and trapped in this odd box, the two corpses offered no solution to get out or move around. He turned his attention to the other cubes in this space. Norah and her lot seemed safe. Theo's cube had become a swirling flash of light as their battle had finally progressed. The fact that the Players had been content enough to sit back and watch the pair bicker proved they were too weak to succeed.

Sally and Seven were squaring up and about to duel, and he wished he could get closer to assist. There were also two other cubes, one with some reds in it but no *Outsiders*. A larger one still was actually way above them and seemed to contain all of Sally's zombies. More the fool them, as each one boosted their stats with Sally's skill.

The invasion was now but a few minutes away, he could feel it.

"We might need your help soon, little brother," he murmured to himself.

Sally spun away, a gash through her upper arm dripping warm blood down through her top. Why was her blood even warm? Why did it run when she had no pulse? Sometimes she had a pulse, or rather her heart moved just like any other muscle.

"You know he'll be coming for you next?" Bright green illuminated her face as the skull on her staff burst into flame.

"Oh? What makes you think I won't be able to stop the Architect?" Seven took a step toward her and his floating swords carved through the air.

"First," she said, leaping backward as she shot out *[Mortis Bomb]*, "I'm clearly the main character, while you're just a terribly overcooked villain."

"Are you sure?" He blurred to the side to avoid the projectile, the skull just bursting ineffectively against the far wall. "I'm not a Monster who eats people but gets a pass because I'm overly cheerful about it."

"You just kill for different reasons. So, what, you can rule the System the way you think is best?"

He rolled his eyes. "I already covered this in my monologue. Were you really not paying attention?"

Sally shrugged. "Those kinds of things usually aren't important when I'm close to eating your brains, anyway. Plus, I was watching to see when the caster of this skill would die." She gestured with her eyebrow to where Theo was now fighting.

Seven turned to glance that way, and Sally pounced.

"Nice try." He smiled, lashing out with both swords. She was no longer there, however. A sharp pain sparked in his lower back as he spun to find her there.

Three zombies started to crawl from the perfectly flat floor where she had used *[Escape Fate]* and jabbed him with her dagger. Sally twirled and deflected the floating swords, backtracking to avoid being impaled.

"Curse immune, but you're pretty stabbable," she said, sticking her tongue out at him.

"I've wasted enough time here," he growled. "Die, roach."

The swords spun together, forming a spear of bright light that immediately darted toward her.

With a pop of energy, Theo suddenly appeared in front of her, taking the brunt of the attack and slumping down to the floor.

A second pop and he landed beside the zombie again.

"Four stacks, fangs? Why you gotta come here and steal my thunder?" She scowled at him as Seven ground his teeth together.

"Just came to deliver a message," the vampire shuddered as he righted himself. With a finger outstretched, he pointed to where Edward stood alone among the corpses of the reds.

"Death approaches," he whispered.

CHAPTER FIFTY-EIGHT

The Long Game

Seven shook his head. "We still have a few minutes before the spell collapses. Plenty of time for me to kill you."

"Writing is on the wall," Sally said and tutted. "Your faction is all but dead, and you think you have a chance against all of us?"

Theo didn't add to the conversation but stood with a wide grin, saliva running from his mouth and dripping to the floor as his eyes burned bright red.

"They were a means to an end. When I am the Architect, all will become corrupt and break the shackles of the STAR System."

Sally furrowed her brow, confusion on her face.

"I covered all of this already," he sighed. "How do people put up with you?"

"Hey, Theo." She tilted her head toward the tense vampire. "Would you still love me if I was a worm?"

He twisted his head toward her, hardly able to take his gaze away from the corrupt Player. "I would carve a hole through the System until I found a way to also become a worm."

"Sweet." She grimaced. "You wouldn't find a way to turn me back into a woman instead, though?"

"I have no preference," Theo growled, his head turning back to Seven. "As long as we can be together."

Seven narrowed his eyes. "I'm not sure what that was supposed to prove . . . other than you're both kind of weird." The spear split back into two swords, and each of those then split again—four swords now hanging in the air beside the man.

"Ah." Sally shrugged. "Just wasting some time, really. You seem fine with talking more than necessary. Typical mid-tier villain shit." It was also to try to gauge how far along the vampire was with his sanity taking a hit every time he died. He looked about ready to burst into violence, but his answer was relatively on the level.

Time to put the *[Sword of the Undead]* into action. That was a working title. She snapped her fingers, and that was enough of a cue.

Warmth buffeted her as the vampire burst forward, crimson energy pulsing behind him as *[Sanguine Weapon]* brought out a floating weapon of his own. He lashed out forward before vanishing to appear behind Seven. Both attacks were blocked with little effort, and Theo slid back across the smooth floor.

"Ah, ah, ah!" He hopped from one foot to the other. "No tricky parrying skills, right? Better tell me the number of charges."

Seven didn't turn to face him, but instead raised an eyebrow at the zombie. "Is he always like this?"

"No." She was willing to let Theo tie up the odd man filled with Observers. He wouldn't stand a chance against the whole of them, and Humphrey might be able to recycle some of the skulls within him or something.

"Do you let him fight all your battles?"

"Sometimes." She yawned. "You're overthinking this, *Five*. I'm not a monolith with underlings, I'm just the shepherd of oddballs. As long as *somebody* saves the world, I'll be happy."

Seven rolled his eyes right before Theo launched back at him. The whir of swords clashed against the punch-blades, matching the vampire's speed.

Chuck rubbed his eyes. "This is stressful. Should I have prepared a speech for this?"

With a raised eyebrow, Lana just gave him a shrug.

"Like, in an ideal world," he continued, "Sally would have just killed him and then that makes things smoother for me, right? Never seeing or meeting the leader of the opposing faction made things a lot easier to compartmentalize."

Jackie yawned from atop the stagecoach. "So we just whack him and bounce. You don't have to put on a show."

"Regardless . . ." The Druid tapped the end of his staff into the mud. "I feel like a show is coming our way whether we want it to or not."

Fern looked around impassively. "Does this sort of thing happen regularly?"

The murmured chorus of indecisive acknowledgments from the group was not too reassuring.

[Curse: Drain] did not work on Seven, and Sally wasn't too keen on getting in the way of Theo as he sped up and lashed out constantly with *[Novice Strike]*. She looked up at the cube filled with her zombies, but something was preventing her

from putting them away with *[Endless Rest]*. All in all, it was a very annoying start to the fight with the red faction leader.

She had expected it to be more dramatic—or even underwhelming, perhaps. A quick brain eaten and then onto their bigger problem of the Architect. He was probably just toying with them, which was pretty boring. If he intended on becoming the big boss, then the supposed immortality reward for killing the *Outsiders* wouldn't appeal to him. He was just here to check out who might threaten his attempt at ascension.

If there was one thing she was sure of, it was that he could not become the Architect under any circumstance.

She looked to the side to see cracks forming along the glass-like walls of their current cube.

"Looks like we have had our fun here." Seven smiled. "Are you all ready for round two?"

Before she could answer, the darkness shattered away. A burst of light flooded into her eyes before the dull gloom of the outside, followed by the mucky smell of damp earth, reached her senses. Blinking away the shock, she realized they had all returned to the same positions as before—and the Players that had been killed in the cubes were alive again.

Her shield went up as Seven's swords struck out at her, knocking her back through the slick dirt.

Dent furrowed his brow, recovering a second too late to see the impending attack of the duelist he had just won against coming for him once more.

With a flash of darkness, Theo appeared in front of him, absorbing the majority of the blow. He staggered back into the swordsman, who caught him.

"No, no, no." The vampire tilted his head back at Dent. "Be careful, corrupted!" A wide gash spread across his chest and bled heavily through his ruined shirt. Theo shuffled back up to his feet and tilted his head from side to side, his crimson eyes searching the battlefield. "This isn't *perfect*, is it? No, no."

[Perfect Dark]

A crimson moon rose up as the sky darkened to near pitch black.

With the flash of blue, the demon stepped in beside him, deflecting the follow-up of the red Player before Dent gathered himself to renew their fight.

"You're bleeding," Edward said, raising an eyebrow.

"Corrupted skill. A wound that cannot regenerate." Wisps of red flame snaked away from Theo's eyes as he licked around his lips. "It is *very* rude."

"Allow me." The demon placed his hand on the vampire's shoulder, furrowing his brow in surprise at how warm he felt. A deep red glow filtered down his rapier as the injury healed up at remarkable speed.

Theo looked down and then back at the demon, his eyes wide. "Thank you, brother. Best friend. Buddy."

"Alright." Edward rolled his eyes. "Save the mania for later. How about we show them what we're made of?"

"Guts and bones!" Theo grinned widely, his fangs reflecting the red of the faux moon.

"Well . . . okay, I was thinking more . . ."

[Domain: The Inevitable]

The reds illuminating the area grew more garishly vibrant, contrasting with the shadows, which became darker. The pair darted forward toward the Players, their weapons aglow in bright light as some of the renewing buffs faded away from the reds.

Yellow light bloomed over Norah as a large eye looked down upon her target. Dozens of bandages wrapped around them, and with a pulse of power, that Player was turned to sand.

"Shit me!" Jane stepped away from the battle. "Now I'm not sure either side is the right one."

"Then move or fall like the rest." Humphrey growled and stepped forward, as multiple shots of a magical attack struck him.

"What pops means," Lucius began, ignoring the rise in flame behind the Death Knight's helmet, "is that this place isn't safe if you don't want to fight." Into his hand, he conjured up a shadowed version of Sally's staff. "All I can do is show you the right path. It's up to you to take it."

Sally spun her staff around, deflecting one of the swords and blocking another with her shield. She was at least glad that the one thing she actually got around to crafting in this world turned out to be super useful. Not that it was helping to gain her any advantage at present.

Seven still stood with hands behind his back and a smug look on his face. Perhaps intending for her to feel foolish and weak given that she couldn't get close enough to stab him while still avoiding his four-sword technique. She had commanded her zombies to ignore him and focus on the other Players, as he would just calmly cut down any that approached.

"I assume you have more skills than just looking like a giant ass," she seethed at him.

"Naturally. I have to save some energy for the Architect, however." He tilted his head. "If you manage to land another strike on me, then I might consider using something more than my basic attack."

If he was being powered by seven Observers, then her assumption was that he could delegate tasks to them. Have all of them focus on the attacks and blocking while his Player side could just stand there and gloat over her ineffectiveness. She wasn't used to having a fight be so drawn out. Usually zombies or a well-placed skull would seal her the brain-eating victory.

As three of the swords lashed out toward her, she used *[Escape Fate]* to dodge to the side, having to use her shield again as the fourth sword waited until she reappeared to attempt to strike. Some of his confidence was warranted, she relented. Seven was proving near unassailable at present.

Not that it would stop her. If anything, she was growing more determined.

Theo turned, sensing the rising attack power of someone nearby. The man with the scratchy voice that sent off the large bomb. He had now turned and was aiming the corrupted attack off to . . . off to the stagecoach and ranged allies. Unacceptable.

With a burst of dark energy, the vampire dropped down in front of the Player and grabbed him close with a bear hug.

"What are you doing? The shot is primed! Let go!"

"Hush, little one," Theo whispered. "It'll all be over soon."

The explosion rocked the area, killing three Players and a handful of zombies as the blast vaporized the attacker. Dust and fragments of bodies washed through the area, giving brief pause to the heated combat.

Theo stood there, stunned. Not dead, somehow, but the darkened sky and red moon washed away to be replaced by the dull gray clouds overhead once more. He looked down at his body, or what remained of it. He couldn't usually see his ribcage or leg bones as far as he could remember. And although he wasn't able to move or really process anything, his body clearly knew what it was doing. New muscle and tendons began to regrow, blood slowly swirling around him as he stared blankly at the damage wrought.

As she paused to scowl at the reckless behavior of the vampire, Sally caught the glow of a weapon off to the side. It was the rail gun type shot that pierced through the whole graveyard, now charged up once more and aimed right at her. *[Escape Fate]* was on cooldown, so she went to move—but her foot slipped in the mud, causing her to waver in place.

Hands grasped her shoulders from behind, and the demon loomed over her.

"At last," he whispered, as the rail shot finished powering up. "I have my opportunity."

The blast rang out through the graveyard.

Outsiders Remaining 4/5

CHAPTER FIFTY-NINE

Multiplication

Laying on the slick mud of the graveyard, Sally looked up at the demon standing above her. After two seconds that seemed to drag on forever, his lifeless body dropped to the ground—a fist-sized hole through his chest.

| Party member Edward has died. |

"Stupid ass," she growled and shook her head. Sure, he would come back, but now he was back in the Wastelands and unable to help them. The fact that he had possibly saved her life was beside the point.

"Edward!" Theo yelled, bursting into red flame and flickering over to the woman who had fired the shot.

Dent wiped his brow as a heal came in from the distant Chuck. His opponent also received a heal from one of the distant reds. As much as he enjoyed proving to be the best swordsman in the System, he was tiring, and this wasn't the ideal battleground for proving his worth. Still, he needed to persist.

Sparks flared out as Humphrey slashed across his armored opponent, before he stepped forward and slammed the pommel of his sword into them, winding the man. The Death Knight then kicked out their leg and twisted his sword around to slice through the Player's neck as he dropped.

"We need to prepare," he growled. "Invasion is imminent."

Lucius stabbed a fallen red with the end of his shadow staff to ensure they were dead. "Theo told me that he had one last favor to call in for when Seven was here, in exchange for me giving up Edward's question."

"Oh?" Humphrey cast *[Kneel]* on an approaching Player and then easily cracked their skull with the downswing of his sword. "Must he always be full of surprises?"

"He made it sound like a gift for Sally that we'd all benefit from." A question mark appeared beside his head. "But that doesn't narrow it down."

Norah smiled. "I think I have a good guess, though." She turned her gaze over to the vampire, who was finishing carving through the one who had shot the demon.

Jackie banged her foot on the top of the stagecoach, annoyed that she couldn't spray into the crowd. Any potshot at Seven was just blocked, so she had taken to tapping out the occasional bolt at the Players on the outside.

"Come on, you goons, it's time to crack some skulls." She pulled a face and lit up a cigarette.

The stagecoach door opened and a group of eight bandits clambered out, dressed in dark gray suits and armed with melee weapons. At her command, they power walked through the midsection of the graveyard toward the fight, looking threatening.

"Seems your pals are dying just as quickly as before." Sally grinned. "Even with a do-over the best in the System aren't able to take down the *Outsiders*. And assorted allies."

"True." Seven shrugged. "Despite the stories, I still underestimated you."

"Heck yeah you did." She could feel the invasion imminent now. A complication. "Now get in my belly!"

"I remember the old world."

She stopped, foot sliding in the mud. "You do?"

"I was a nobody there. Aimless. Downtrodden. This new world gave me a fresh start and a means to take control." He smiled coldly at her.

Sally raised an eyebrow. "If it's acceptance you're after, we're all about that."

"No. I think it's time your little game ends now." Seven held out his hands, a wave of energy vibrating along his arms.

[Multi-Form]

"Oh." The zombie rubbed the side of her staff against her head. "Now there's seven of you, that was . . . unexpected and *kinda sad*, actually."

Indeed, in a rough circle, the red leader had shifted into six more versions of himself. Each was as overconfident and annoying as the last. As much as she would like to have eaten his brain, knowing how weird and corrupt he was— she'd probably get a stomachache.

Through the floor, the vibration of the invasion turned all unoccupied eyes toward the start of the graveyard. From behind the gates and emerging from shadows came . . . lots of town guards. They looked like the ones from the gold area of the Wastes city. Dozens soon became close to a hundred, and yet they still didn't stop spawning.

Theo slid across the wet mud and slammed into the side of Humphrey. "Whoa! Happy birthday. *Oh*, you're not Sally." He narrowed his bright red eyes between the Death Knight and Lucius. "I got her a little surprise."

Humphrey looked between the onrushing horde and the twitching vampire. "What did you do?"

"Simple really, Sally." He scratched the side of his head, cutting himself with a punch-blade. "I tapped in the Living Bug guy we met in the forest. Had him tweak a little variable. You see, an invasion has a set power level, and it cobbles together Monsters to make up to it before releasing. So I . . ." He stopped talking.

Lucius looked at Jane, who just shrugged.

The Death Knight sighed. "So he forced it to pick a lower power Monster, causing it to generate . . . possibly hundreds. And all so that . . . ah, I see."

Theo looked back up at him. "You're not Sally."

Sally licked her lips. This couldn't be by chance—the System wasn't this nice. She could already feel the hum of power inside her. Narrowing her eyes, she scoured the battleground for the pup. Ah, Norah was currently trying to stop him from licking the blood from Humphrey.

She smiled and shook her head. "Hey, Seven?"

Three of them raised their eyebrows, while the other four were looking at the invasion force and the remaining combatants.

"Hope the stories didn't downplay this part."

A cold light bloomed in her eyes as wind whipped around the graveyard. A fresh layer of gloomy fog enclosed all within, darkening the area. Sally held her hand out and the temperature of the area dropped sharply.

[Zombie Apocalypse]

She cackled as she slowly rose into the air atop a small pyramid. This was pure joy. Not only would her zombies easily overpower the invasion force over time, adding or replacing their numbers lost, but *[Strength in Numbers]* was now working overtime to give them a stat boost that was beyond the pale.

Strength in Numbers
+174% Stat Bonus

The rest of the reds were quickly overpowered as more than one hundred zombies crawled up around them. A spray of crossbow bolts began peppering the invasion, weakening them for the hungry mouths of the undead. The *Outsiders* turned their attention to the copies of Seven.

"You really think you stand a chance?" He gnashed his teeth as all copies spoke at once. "Come at me then, useless sacks of ill-gotten power."

Sally grinned and slid down the side of the pyramid, her staff bursting into green flame. It always came down to this. "Shoulda done your homework, *Four*. Hubris always gets our enemies killed."

"Hubris?" he yelled back, raising his hand. "I'll show you hubris." The familiar energy of the rail shot started blooming down his arm.

Chuck smiled as he quickly flicked through his guild messages. The rest of the blues had just confirmed they had destroyed the red team base and taken anything important. Taken down a token force that remained there. That made them the winners, in his mind, even if they fell—

He was shoved to the ground, to land among the loose gravel covering a nearby grave. The crack of a skill punctured the air and Fern stumbled, a fist-sized hole through their chest.

"Oh." The dryad looked down at the Druid. "I have come to the conclusion that I do not enjoy adventuring and combat."

Chuck raised up his hand, and a brief heal pulsed through Fern as they sat down on the ground softly. "Are you okay? Thank you for . . ."

"I have the option of dying or going into hibernation for my existence to persist. For several reasons, I am choosing the latter."

The Druid got up and put his hand on the bark shoulder of the plant person. "Do what you need to. We will keep you safe."

"Couldn't even . . . keep yourself . . ." The end of the sentence didn't come as Fern fell asleep.

Seven pulled a face. "How strange that keeps happening. If I want to kill someone, do I have to aim at whoever is near them instead?"

"The inability of the reds to jump on the swords for their brethren is what makes us strong and you weak," Sally said with a wide grin. "We have the power of *friendship*."

"Gross." Seven spat.

Humphrey used *[Compelled Duel]* on one of the Sevens, while Norah and Lucius tried to pin one down. Theo had become a human pinball, zipping back and forth between each copy in a blur of red and pink. Each of his strikes blocked, but as he continually sped up, he was starting to keep them busier and more distracted.

The zombies nearest the Sevens were quickly ran through but were soon replenished by the addition of killed guards at the graveyard entrance.

A Seven burst toward Sally, quickly followed by another. He dodged to the side to avoid the *[Mortis Bomb]* but as the second one bore down on her, she used *[Escape Fate]* to appear just behind them, jamming her staff backward. The dagger connected with the back of his neck, severing his spine and killing the copy outright.

As they both dropped to the ground, she flourished her staff and turned to the first one, four zombies raising around the dead body as she grinned widely. "Fell for that twice now. Were your brain cells shared around too?"

The Death Knight slid backward across the mud, glowing lines of silver across his dark metal.

"Four swords seem to be better than one," Seven said with a grin. "I feel you are holding out on me, however."

"I would not waste my true capabilities on a miserable excuse for a Player," Humphrey replied, raising his sword back up to continue the duel.

"He's just cutting through my bandages," Norah seethed, her eyes bright yellow with fury. "I don't even know where my summon went."

"I can help," Jane said sheepishly, touching the Mummy on the shoulder. A blue light enriched her, leaving a gray-blue sheen across her whole body.

Norah narrowed her eyes at the Adventurer but turned and shot out a bandage. The wrapping carried the same energy with it, and a glowing red sword swung to cut it—instead, sparks flew out and the bandage spun around the weapon to cover it.

"Thank you," the Mummy said. "I will now protect you as one of my own."

Theo spun out and slid across the mud, building a small hill of thick dirt against his foot before he stopped. His left arm hung limp by his side, lacerated in multiple places to the bone. As he caught a few breaths, it regenerated back to full health in a matter of seconds. "Oh! Regeneration makes me tired tooooo."

Two of the Sevens were approaching him. He snapped his fingers, trying to start up a tune he couldn't even hum along to, despite his attempts. "How does it go, again?" His tired eyes went up to the globules of blood hovering in the air, most of them obscured by the horde of zombies thick in the area.

Seven lunged for him, a further two swords in his hands, alongside the four floating ones.

"Oh, I remember now." Theo smiled, right before the six swords pierced him through. His eyes widened as he was skewered, but his grin remained. "It was . . . like this."

A blood-soaked hand went up as time slowed, and a dark orb burned at the tip of his index finger.

"Pop!" he said, a pitch-black blast exploding Seven's head, as the vampire himself succumbed to his wounds and fell dead alongside the copy.

CHAPTER SIXTY

Carry the Remainder

Theo popped back into existence beside Sally and was immediately impaled by a couple of swords not intended for him.

"Ack!" he said as he died.

"Pup, you . . . I am totally desensitized to you dying now. I hope you're happy." She glared down at his corpse, which didn't respond.

A pulse of energy and he appeared again.

"I think," he began, slowly turning his head toward her, "I have reached the limit and circled back to being sane again."

"Really?" She furrowed her brow. "You do realize you are saying that as you are baring all your teeth as if you didn't have lips?"

"I has lips?" He jumped away from her, tripping over his own dead body.

She sighed and looked back at her opponent, who seemed just as tired of the oddball antics as she was getting. Getting the vampire immortality had seemed like an easy win condition at the start, where his power and inability to be destroyed turned any obstacle into just attrition at worst . . . but now he was being sloppy and falling down an exhaustive path that he hadn't gone down before.

"Oh! Let's play a game." The vampire spun to regain his footing and then withdrew the small metal cube from his pocket. Without a chance for either of them to respond, he pitched it like a baseball toward Seven.

"I don't know what you hope to—" the red leader began, bringing a sword in the way to deflect the small projectile. Then it expanded to the full size of Theo's metal coffin and slammed into him, knocking him to the floor dazed.

[Meat Hook] zipped Sally over pronto, and she slashed up his chest before digging Skeleton Key into Seven's heart.

"Not sure why I haven't done that before," Theo murmured, shuffling over to his coffin. He laid against it, putting his arms around it. "I miss you, sleep."

"We're not done yet, pup. Four big bads for you to mash against, okay?" She scowled at him but felt bad. It wasn't his fault. Well, part of it was.

She watched as a couple of men in suits sucker punched a distracted Seven in the kidney with knuckle-dusters. Pained by the attack, he was tripped by the zombies crowding around. As the undead chewed and bit at him, the thugs started kicking him.

Humphrey was still in a duel with one, while the rest of her group was fending off the other two, but not making much progress. She watched and winced as one wound up a rail shot, only for it to miss as Lucius vanished to become a shadow for Dent. The three of them, and apparently a red Player, would be able to take one down on their own, but two were proving too much.

"C'mon pup, the family needs us."

Chuck threw out another heal toward Dent. It was difficult getting eyes on him while so many zombies crowded the area. It did mean that he was less likely to be targeted, though, so he couldn't complain.

He did raise an eyebrow to the side. "Everything alright, Lana?"

"Yeah." She pulled a face and shrugged. "I'm not really strong ranged *or* melee, and I feel bad for not being more useful. My ultimate, I've been saving for the right moment, but what if that passes?"

"It's cliché," Chuck said, with a glum smile. "But just go with your heart. Sally won't hold it against you for staying back and keeping us safe. It's . . . this kind of thing is more of an *Outsider* experience. Just hold tight and watch them wreak havoc."

"Thanks, Chuck." She smiled. "They certainly are something else."

Humphrey grinned as he activated both his parrying abilities, stepping in close, within the range of all four swords. They came down on him, and he reacted with unnatural, almost instant speed. Blocked and then lashed out with critical energy. Two bursts of blood from Seven's torso, his arm removed, and then his head in quick succession—the Player not even having time to react to what had happened before he died.

"Four charges!" Theo called out as he ran up.

Sally grinned. For everything that had gone wrong, and for as crazy as they all were, they had whittled the Sevens down to the last two. A cautious eye out to the invasion progress and . . . the guards were still spawning, but the wall of undead were almost immediately killing them.

> Strength in Numbers
> 196% Stat Bonus

They'd even gained more than she started with, despite Seven cutting through swaths of them.

With the Fighters in front of them waylaying any progress, and the zombie and vampire running from behind, the two Sevens growled. "So far, you have proven my point that Uniques must be eradicated. Look at your uncontested power."

"Your flattery is weak compared to your hypocrisy," Sally yelled back, sliding down an embankment of mud and almost tripping on a gravestone.

It always seemed to be the way with these types. They wanted all the power and control and would do anything to get it, even becoming what they truly hated. And for what? All Sally wanted was acceptance, and the power she accumulated along the way had mostly been luck or through hard work, rather than a concerted effort to achieve something. Other than survival, of course.

"Enough!" the Sevens shouted in unison. Closest to their approach, the four swords turned bright green before slashing out at ridiculous speeds. Dent blocked them, sliding back among a shower of sparks, before the attack refreshed immediately, striking him again.

Blood bursting from his chest, he staggered a few steps before dropping to the floor.

"Dent!" Sally shouted, her teeth then clenching together.

Chuck stood with a hand extended. It shook slightly, his muscles tensing and relaxing. It wasn't allowing him to target the swordsman, which meant only one thing. Dead.

"Hold firm and focus on the target," he yelled out, voice calm despite the rising panic in his chest. They had come too far to falter now. What had started must be finished.

"How dare you?" Sally stomped toward him. "Turn and face your reckoning."

"Oh?" The Seven with the green blades turned his head to greet the pair. "Just because you have killed five out of seven of us, doesn't mean you are closer to winning."

"But that's a perfect score?" Theo furrowed his brow.

Seven's eyes dulled and he tensed, ready to burst toward them. As he launched forward, Sally withdrew a crossbow to fire at him. Swords crossed in front of his face to deflect it, and then when he lowered them, the vampire was no longer standing beside Sally.

The green swords slashed out.

On the other side, the second Seven had engaged the others. Humphrey blocked the sword swings and kept him engaged in melee. Norah weaved her imbued bandages around and tried to trip his legs. Lucius was not present, probably shadowing someone—as Jane sat near the back, only sending buffs out to the Mummy and trying to not look like a target.

Sally rolled across the floor, blood running down her legs. The shield had stopped most of it, but some of the damage made it through. Now she had even more mud in her hair and was even angrier. Theo appeared beside Seven and started flickering around with *[Novice Strike]* and *[Sanguine Weapon]*. Another two blades of dark shadow accompanied him, with the Shade causing the attacks to be a constant flurry.

This time, he was quick enough to get some strikes in.

The blades created small punctures as the red armor became dented, and the man's attention went solely to trying to deflect all of the leveled attacks. "Stay still, pesky wasp," he growled.

Sally risked a glance back at Chuck to see how he was doing. Stoic and focused. He really had grown to be strong, even if he was putting on an act. Of course, they both knew he had a resurrection save in his back pocket, which only worked on Dent, probably. It just meant doing without him for the rest of the fight, in case he died again.

[Mortis Bomb] went out and struck Seven on the legs. He was too armored for it to damage him, but it still hit and brought up a couple of zombies. The invasion looked to be petering out now; the zombies mopping up the last of the groups. If things weren't so dangerous currently, it would have been nice to join in on that buffet.

A small pyramid burst up, knocking the other Seven forward and into Humphrey's sword. It scratched along his armor and drew a line of crimson across his face before he could regain his positioning.

"Clearly I've been going about this all wrong," he grunted, his eyes darting between the *Outsiders* wildly. "I had hoped to save some trump cards for the Architect, but you all need to perish."

A burst of blue appeared around the Death Knight's legs as ethereal chains held him in place. Seven turned and a semicircle wall of flames broke contact with Norah, burning away any of the encroaching bandages. Seven turned and held out a hand toward his twin, who was struggling to keep up with the vampire.

The two remaining Sevens merged in a flash of bright light, briefly stunning everyone—especially the vampire, who hissed at the piercing illumination.

[Hell Shield]

[Reducing Pattern]

[Expanse]

Seven activated several abilities in a chain. Around his body, an oval-shaped shield of energy sprung into place. The air crackled and buzzed before the dirt surrounding him flattened and started to burn away. A couple of zombies caught in the area started to decay, turning to ash as if their atoms were being stripped off.

"You may not approach. The area will keep expanding until everything is consumed." He grinned, a drop of blood running down the side of his face.

"Nuts to this," Sally growled. She was thankful, at least, that she didn't have to tell any of her goofballs not to approach. They could see what it did to the zombies and would no doubt have the same effect on them. The fire wall had extinguished, but Humphrey appeared to be still stuck in place.

With a crack, the area of the ability increased by another foot, consuming more mushed foliage and spent corpses. It seemed to be emerging like a large donut from the man, rather than a dome. Time to test that theory.

"Norah, up!" she yelled over to the Mummy. There was more than one way to skin an avoidant Player.

Norah's bandages wrapped around Sally and flung her high into the air.

She spun up and cast *[Ruin]* directly below Seven. As the damage pulsed through the circular area of red light, his shield started to flicker and diminish.

"Fool!" He laughed. "Now you're just easier to hit."

Sally fell, headfirst, with the staff pointed like a spear.

Lana held her hand out and cast her ultimate at Seven. *[Premature End]*

Seven held his hand up and fired the rail shot straight toward her, as his floating swords raised up to catch her fall on their pointed ends.

The shot struck her shield, bursting it into fragments, as a line of blood went into the air from her left arm. Sally threw down the staff, a trail of green flame behind it. The next few steps were a blur of movement.

Her staff struck the remaining shield, the dagger piercing and bursting his defenses. *[Mortis Bomb]* went out to strike Seven in the face, blinding him. Before Sally landed, Theo used *[Blood Shift]* just below her. He struck the blades, getting run through and bending them away from her as she landed atop him, impaling him instead of herself.

With a raised fist full of anger and crackling energy, Sally punched a hole through the vampire's abdomen, reaching through his suspended body. Her open palm went against the shocked head of the dazed Seven.

[Brain Drain]

A loud burst shredded the man, pulping his skull and exploding most of his chest. Buckled and bent red armor leaked with dark crimson as the three collapsed into the mud. His held skills sparked and faded away.

Sally raised from the ground, breathing heavily and clutching her injured arm. Theo reappeared beside her and sighed, immediately sitting on the floor.

She looked around at the scores of corpses alongside the zombies still milling around. The *Outsiders* came over, with Chuck in tow.

"Looks like blue team wins," she said with an exhausted grin.

Right before a light blue glow appeared to their side.

CHAPTER SIXTY-ONE

By His Design

The glow of the fifteen-foot-tall Architect illuminated the area.

> Well. This has certainly not gone the way I had expected.

Sally bared her sharp teeth at him. "Trying to get all your problems to work themselves out because you're too weak?"

> Hello, little corpse woman. Your time has run its course.

The Architect tilted their skeletal head and snapped two bony fingers together.

> Corpse Explosion

There was a sudden wash of extreme force and a ringing in her ears.

> Strength in Numbers
> +14% Stat Bonus

Sally blinked and wiped the gore from the back of her head with her forearm. Over at her side, Theo was making exaggerated chomping motions toward the Architect. Norah's sarcophagus opened, and she stepped out. Humphrey and Lucius stood with arms crossed, unharmed, just covered in a bit more fleshy stuff than usual.

The *Insiders* looked fine. The four team members at the back were away from all the undead so weren't caught up in any damage. Fern was still sitting, but that didn't mean much.

The graveyard surrounding them was awash with mulched rotten meat and bone fragments. All her pals were dead. More dead.

> Oh. For some reason, I thought that would work on you too.

It hadn't, because she was part Player. Same for Theo. Lucius and Humphrey weren't really corpses, and Norah had been able to hide away in time. Everything else undead around them had exploded into paste.

"Still in the habit of wasting power you do not understand." Humphrey shook his head at the large figure.

> Betrayer. If I wanted your opinion, I would extract it from you.

"You and what army?"

> Funny you should say that. There are some loyal Observers who take offense to you abandoning your station.

With a grand gesture, he motioned toward the forest. The *Outsiders* stood in silence for a handful of seconds before the Architect sighed.

> Apologies. My money was on Seven, so I did not think I'd need the others right now.

"Any chance you could talk without bringing up text boxes?" Theo rubbed his eyes, thankfully without his blades present. "It's giving me a headache."

The Architect narrowed his eye sockets. "Fine. I suppose I wouldn't want to inconvenience you right before I erase you from this existence."

"Thank you," the vampire replied melodically, before flopping over backward into a pile of soft mud.

Sally crossed her arms, still sore that her legendary shield had been destroyed. "Is it your turn for a monologue now? Want to tell us why we have to die and why you want to rule the System?"

She wanted to run up and punch him in the face, actually, but she was pretty exhausted. Theo was spent. Too many deaths had him running on fumes. Behind them, the others had moved in closer, Chuck crouched beside Dent's inert body. Lana looked like she'd rather be anywhere else.

"I suppose until the Observers get here, I could fill you in on some exposition."

The Architect hovered a little closer to the ground and rubbed their skeletal chin. "But first..."

Invasion Event Ended
4/5 Outsiders Survived
Teleportation Allowed
Party and Guilds unfrozen

Edward has left the Party
Theo has joined the Party

A flash of blue, and the demon returned. He took one look at the battlefield, before turning to face the Architect. With a deep sigh, he deflated. "Shit. Shoulda stayed at home."

"Saved you a seat, buddy." Theo patted his hand against the wet mud, splashing it on himself.

Teleportation Disabled

"Ah, my mistake." The Architect shook his head. "Don't want anyone running away now that you're all in the same place. Funny how eggs come to roost in the same nest over time. Only... one normal Player among you."

"That's not a real saying." Sally sighed and looked over at Chuck.

"Oh," the Architect continued, "but he is dead."

Half of those present winced and tried to avoid the narrowed eyes of the Druid. "What does that mean?"

"Guys," Theo whispered loudly, "we never told Chuck."

"System damn it, fangs." Sally gave the vampire a light kick in the leg. "Go sleep already if you're going to make things weird." She watched him drop his coffin and then slither inside it like a snake. "Do we really have to do this now? Humps, aren't you going to start saving the day or something?"

The Death Knight shrugged. "Seems rude when he hasn't had his monologue yet."

"*Sally,*" Chuck said.

She grumbled and walked over to him, the eyes of everyone else on her. Stopping a few feet away from him, she put her hands on her hips and scowled. "Ready for your mind to be blown?"

He gave a shrug, still crouched beside the dead Swordmaster.

"You ever wonder why you woke up here in a pile of zombies?"

Chuck narrowed his eyes. "I was... undead at the start?"

"Where I was half-zombie, half-Player, you were full zombie... and then when you died protecting me, you were able to become a full Player, as intended." She pulled a face. "I'm sorry we didn't tell you before."

"Hmm." The Druid furrowed his brow. "I suppose that does explain the weird dreams. And there I was, thinking I was just traumatized by my association with you."

"I'm sure you are, in other ways." She grinned. "I just wanted you to be normal and happy after. It was a struggle for you to accept things here."

"It probably wouldn't have been very good for my mental state, I agree." He smiled at her. "Forgiven, Sally Danger."

"Boring," the Architect called out. "The lunatic has gone to bed, and the drama fizzled out to nothing. You're closer to mundane Players than I originally thought."

Humphrey worked his shoulders. "So why not let us live?"

"No." The large, robed figure shook his head. "You, out of all of us, should know better. Uniques are an error in the System, not designed for the purpose they now currently serve."

"Aren't you in charge now?" Sally crossed her arms. "You get to decide what is an error and what things can stay."

"Correct." The Architect shrugged. "If you really need the exposition to make your little Player brains feel contented, I am here to enact the original Architect's vision, not the upstart who ruined the System with their inadequacies."

Sally wrinkled up her face. Not the worst idea on the surface of things. The middle Architect had their troubles and did the best they could, but perhaps if the original one had been able to stick around then things wouldn't have been messed up. They could have even gone home. But that was beside the point at this stage.

New Architect wanted to kill off her and her friends. That was unacceptable.

"We can't come to a compromise? Accept that Uniques are part of the System now and work around it?" She gave the tall figure her best puppy eyes.

"No."

She scowled toward the Death Knight. "Dad, aren't you going to do something?"

Humphrey winced and gave her a scowl back. "Do you need a coffin too? I cannot act until the Observers are taken care of."

Norah raised an eyebrow. "And why is that?"

His expression relaxed, and he looked away, sheepishly. "Protocol reasons."

Chuck looked down at Dent as the *Outsiders* bickered among themselves. It was strange seeing him dead, when he had been so full of life not so long ago. Even knowing he could bring him back, and the resources and spell just sitting ready to be used at any moment . . . was that a selfish action? To bring him back into this world of conflict when he was now at peace?

Fern came up beside him and sat down. Some of the hole through their body had healed up, but a large indent remained. "You are troubled. Unsure whether to allow Dent to return to the ground yet."

The Druid nodded.

"Did you discuss potential resurrection, if he should fall?"

"Of course." Chuck sighed. "The reason for me holding back the ability was specifically for him, and he knew it and was fine with it."

"So, what is your issue?"

He shuffled uncomfortably. "What if he only wanted that for my sake?"

Fern tilted their head. "I think you are both idiots, then. Bring the meat sack to life when you feel it is the right time. I do not want to see your miserable face if he dies again after your spell is spent."

Lana stood behind them both. "It's kind of pleasant so far . . . which is worrying."

Chuck stood and brushed off his robe. With a sigh, he raised an eyebrow at the Architect. "It's like two gods facing off against one another. They know how powerful each other is. When they fight, it'll be the end of one side for good . . . so they aren't rushing it. A last meal must be savored."

Sally sat down on Theo's coffin. Who knew how long he'd have to be in there to sleep off the exhaustion stacks he had built up. Even a little sanity coming back to him would be nice. Lucius was trying to explain the history of the *Outsiders* to Jane, while Humphrey, Norah, and the Architect were having an argument over whether everyone should be fighting or not. Despite how domestic everything seemed, everyone was tense—she could feel it.

Edward stood beside her with his hands in his suit pockets. "Theo going to be alright?"

"Yeah, you big softie." She smiled up at him. "Thanks for saving my life back there too."

"I felt that the best way to betray you was to betray the notion that I'd betray you." He grinned and gave her a shrug. "It was *inevitable*."

"It sure was." She looked back at the Architect. "If only you were undead, huh? And Parties weren't limited to five." Her head tilted to the side. "Weird how the fate of everything is going to be decided here, isn't it?"

The rest of the *Insiders* moved over to where she was sitting.

Chuck looked back at Dent's body before going through his chat messages. "Turns out Seven was cultivating the dissatisfaction within Players. Made them more irrational and angry at the System."

"They did act against better judgment," Sally said, exhaustion settling in her face. "Compare them to the two gals Lucius has helped. Most of your blue faction were pretty sensible too."

The Druid shook his head. "Such a shortsighted plan. Hate as a motivator never works for anything other than self-destruction."

"Nerd," Sally said with a grin.

The Architect held up his skeletal hands. "Okay, enough. They are here now, although there are fewer than I had anticipated. Apparently, a dragon went rogue and has killed some of the others before they could take it down."

Sally hopped back up to her feet with a grin. Both Players and Uniques had fought back against the Observers suddenly trying to police them. An imperfect System it may be, but it was currently home to plenty who had grown to accept it.

"I'm pretty spent on supers, guys." She then pouted. "Anyone have much left?"

Short answer was everyone had used their ultimates against Seven, aside from one person. Humphrey. Given how that worked, it didn't surprise her that he had kept it for this fight. She looked past Jackie, who was taking a long drag of another cigarette, to see that her vehicle had been destroyed. A victim of the [Corpse Explosion] perhaps, although she thought it was far enough away. Her zombie skills were worn out, and the World Boss skills had been taken away.

Back to being a Raid-level threat.

They all turned and brought up their weapons, as trees began to crack and collapse from the west.

"Less than a dozen, more than five," Fern notified them, their roots buried into the mud. "I must rest further now."

The Architect grinned and turned to the Death Knight. "You will soon see the folly of your betrayal."

Humphrey shook his head. "My entire existence is to remove problems from the System. Your time is limited."

With the flash of yellow light, a figure burst up into the sky above the woods. A bird of sharp golden color in contrast to the gray skies above. With a crack of lightning, dozens of radiant bolts of energy surged down toward the gathered groups.

The fight for the future of the System had begun.

CHAPTER SIXTY-TWO

Count Theo

The ground shook as the radiant bolts fell around the scarred battlefield of the graveyard. Sparks crackled in the air like electricity where they struck the thick mud, as the gathered Parties tried to avoid the attacks.

"They're not stopping," Sally growled, before leaping to the ground, a bolt buzzing as it flared just behind her.

Theo's coffin opened, and he popped out, spinning to land back atop it. "Sally," he cooed. "What's going on?"

She narrowed her eyes at him as she picked herself up. "Observer fight before we beat up the Architect. Did you even sleep?"

"I removed two stacks of exhaustion," he replied in an odd monotone. "But plenty still remain."

A bolt dropped from the sky and struck his coffin. The glow of golden electricity pulsed across the shiny metal surface and crackled up the vampire's legs.

"Ah!" he said, jolting off the coffin and into the mud. "Now my bones are extra itchy."

"I'm too tired for this." Sally sighed. The fight against Ruben had been a protracted battle too, but at least she had an army behind her and countless brains to consume. She didn't want to eat anyone that was corrupt, and now the Observers weren't likely to have anything worth chewing on either.

"Allow me, Boss." Jackie stepped forward, her repeating crossbow aimed at the sky. Light blue energy waved around the cylinder as she fired a single bolt. It arced through the air and struck the bird-Observer, their body suddenly freezing over and turning a similar light blue.

As they dropped from the sky, the mobster continued to light it up with a continued spray of bolts, her weapon burning a bright orange as it fired at greater speed than normal.

Before Sally could lend her thanks to Jackie, the nearest trees burst apart as nine figures burst forth. Each of them with a skeletal head that burned with light blue fire. Each of them different Monsters. Each of them intent on stopping the *Outsiders* from attacking their boss.

She flourished her staff, before realizing that the end was normal again. "Shit! My dagger fell off." Hardly any time to dig around the mud for it—it must have broken off when she threw it at Seven to break his shield.

"Lucius with pops," she commanded, collaring the vampire to drag with her to the circle of scoured dirt where the red Player had been.

A green glow illuminated the area, and Dent sat up with a cough. "Oh, hells." He shook his head, trying to clear his eyes. "What happened?"

"Sorry swordsman." Chuck smiled softly as he put his hand on Dent's shoulder. "Your duty isn't over yet."

"Balls," he replied, getting to his feet. "I won't let you down this time."

The Druid rolled his eyes. "Don't be an ass. Talking time is later, killing time is now."

Sally slid across the dirt, while the vampire hopped up and down at the edge of the area that was burned out around Seven's corpse.

"I'll thank you later for cushioning my fall, pup." She narrowed her eyes around the gloomy mud for her weapons. "When you can appreciate it . . . and understand it." She briefly raised a concerned eyebrow.

"Fifty-six, fifty-six," the vampire replied.

"What?" She sighed before spotting the reflective silver of the Skeleton Key buried half in the mud. "Aha! Get ready, pup. Choose a target or something."

"Seven sevens are forty-nine, eight sevens are fifty-six."

"Perhaps you should stay in your . . ." She paused and let the words sink in. Sane Theo had said that Seven had probably absorbed the Observer they had abandoned near the Spire dungeon. Did that mean there were eight versions of him when they split?

She stepped up to the vampire, who was drooling as he stared down at the approaching Observers. "You need to do me a favor, pup."

"Anything for my queen," he said with a grin, although his eyes remained focused forward.

"Track down and kill Seven." She held up a fistful of the previous red leader's inside meat. Maybe lungs or something.

The vampire sniffed it before giving it a brief lick. "I have his taste. I'll be back, Edward."

Sally narrowed her eyes at him as the vampire sped off deeper into the graveyard. She spun her dagger in her left hand and sent *[Mortis Bomb]* off toward the Observers.

Humphrey was at the forefront, a wide grin on his face as he blocked two of the encroaching enemies. One was some kind of warrior with a large axe, and the other was a centaur with a spear. With Lucius adding in a shadowed greatsword, they had no issue in holding their own, even with their slower speed.

Some kind of octopus-Observer was currently being held up by Norah, her bandages tripping the weaker legs and holding the weapon arms together. Jackie was pinning down a spellcaster, an owl-like Observer in shimmering purple robes.

Chuck was assisting Dent and Edward as they darted into the flank, flickering their weapons through the less armored of the foes. Lana was sticking near Fern, protecting the dryad who was still recovering, but letting off a crossbow or utility skill toward the fray when she could.

Sally tilted her head toward the Architect. He was floating there, watching. Things had been oddly cordial, and she knew in her heart that the gathered Observers wouldn't really be much of a match for the *Outsiders*, even if they were tired and powered down.

While not engaging in the battle himself, there was something she didn't trust about the floating figure. With a scowl across her face, she marched toward him.

Theo slipped into the cathedral on his tiptoes, despite verbally making creaking noises every time he stepped. The spacious interior was just as gloomy and poorly lit as earlier, with a slight chill to the stale air.

There was also a shadowed figure, breathing heavily before the statue.

"Hello!" the vampire called out. "Looks like your *number* is up!"

Seven stood and turned his head toward the large doors. "Didn't think any of you were smart enough to realize I had another. Laugh it up, though, while you can. I am spent. Weak." He held up his arm to show the previously red STAR. The corruption now faded away, the System button now pale gray and inert.

"Boo-hoo," Theo said as he rolled his eyes. He snapped his fingers and the candles along the walls burst into flame, illuminating the interior softly. "You're in my house now. I'm here to judge your sins."

"Go ahead, I have nothing left to offer." The man held his arms open. "Your zombie wench all but destroyed me. I am a ghost now."

Theo grinned and started to walk toward him, hands in his pockets. "Any final words?"

Seven smirked, his eyes narrowing. "You mean any *Last Words?*"

Shadows flickered behind Theo, and his eyes widened.

Humphrey wrenched his sword out from the torso of the centaur, their skull flickering and fading away as the body dropped to the floor. "Such a shame to see my brothers turn to ruin." He grinned at the warrior who was trying to regain composure as their legs bled heavily. The empty eye sockets of the blue flaming skull narrowed.

"You know, your footwork ain't half bad." Dent slid across the ground and raised his sword arm back up as the demon slew the spellcaster.

"Don't get any ideas. I'm not in it for the bravado." Edward grinned. "Combat isn't my speciality, but when fighting for our existence . . ."

The swordsman's blade glowed bright red as they ran off toward their next target. "Fair. What is your speciality then?"

Edward's eyes narrowed. "Being an asshole. Subverting expectations."

"Being best pals with the vampire?"

The demon flashed forward, stabbing at a large elf-Observer currently healing and supporting the ones in the front. "If I gain his trust and friendship, then it will make the inevitable betrayal all the more sweet."

"Whatever you say, pal." Dent lunged forward with his own attack, a wry smile on his face.

Unable to move any longer, the octopus-Observer took the full brunt of a volley of bolts from the mobster, their skull eventually cracking and blue fire diminishing.

"Fuck yeah." Jackie grinned, spinning up the cylinder to look for the next target.

"We make quite the team," Norah said with a soft smile, bursting up a pyramid among the Observers to knock one to the side so that they could repeat the process. "You left the *Outsiders* back in the forest area?"

"Sally and the rest of the schmucks are fun enough, but I was soft on a gal." The mobster shrugged and brought up the sight on her weapon to ready her next shot. "Dropped the adventuring life to run a tavern with her."

"If not for love, what greater fight is there?"

Jackie fired off a flaming bolt which exploded on the hapless Observer trying to escape from the entangling bandages. "Don't get me wrong, it's nice to get my boots dirty again, yeah? But it's because the undead gal can keep that little dream safe that I'm here."

Sally stood before the Architect, her arms crossed. "What are you playing at here?"

He tilted his head to her. "Huh? Are you not meant to be fighting?"

"I do what I want. You're the one who is not acting as expected."

"I am a living god. I'm not about to stoop so low as to start punching my enemies because they think they can threaten me." He shook his head and turned back to the battle.

"You mean, you're having trouble accessing actual power, and you're hoping your goons will seal the deal so that you don't have to waste what little power you actually have in getting rid of the one and only threat to your ascension?"

The Architect stopped hovering, and slowly turned around to face her fully, a deep scowl under his empty eye sockets. "You know, you're really fucking annoying."

"Duh," she said with a wide grin.

Lana crouched and swore, fumbling with her crossbow reload. She was tired and stressed, sure, but this was no excuse for being sloppy.

"You know," Fern said, tilting their head toward her. "Sally wouldn't hold it against you if you left."

"I know. And I would, but . . . what would be the point?" The woman brushed the dark curls from her face. "This is a lot more than I signed up for, but there probably isn't a greater thing that I could do with my life, right?"

She narrowed her eyes back toward the cathedral. Something wasn't right.

Chuck yawned and cast another heal on Dent, before bringing up a wall of thick bark to wall off another Observer from trying to flank in his direction. Compared to some of their fights, this was comparatively easy. The enemy seemed to have a desire to pulp the Death Knight more than anyone else, and they weren't having a good time of it.

He raised an eyebrow back at the zombie. She was in conversation with the Architect and they both looked rather tense. It wasn't like her to miss out on a fight, but then again, it was going rather smoothly compared to the fight against Seven. Too well. Now *he* was suspicious too.

If Seven had the power of seven Observers, or well, eight, then he . . . Chuck furrowed his brow. And where was Theo?

The vampire looked at the floor, which wasn't too far away now that he was on his knees. It was also covered in a lot more blood than usual. *His blood*, which was unfair because he liked to keep that in his own body for the most part. He would like to chastise those responsible, but his tongue didn't feel like moving.

Mostly because it was about a dozen feet away. Which was a lot of feet, for his tongue. It would probably blush if it understood the humor of it, but it was unable to confirm that to him, unfortunately, on account of the separation.

"I'm not going to kill you," Seven said, now flanked by two figures. "Don't want you running back and telling on us."

[Blood Shift] wasn't working, despite the charges being there, eager for him to attack. His punch-blades lay on the floor, a place they shouldn't be, in his opinion.

"In fact, you'll be very useful to us once we corrupt that STAR of yours."

CHAPTER SIXTY-THREE

Something to Paint Red

The Architect gripped his skeletal fists together. "You do not understand the amount of ruin the false-Architect has brought to the System. There's a branch in the data that is labeled 'memes.' I do not know what that is."

Sally tapped her foot in the soft mud. "I'm not here to be your agony aunt."

"I don't know what that means either!"

Trying to get the big bad to see some sense had not been a worthwhile use of her time. He just wanted to complain about how it wasn't easy to gather up the power he needed to try to smite them from existence, and her insistence that he just abdicate and allow someone more competent to lead hadn't gone down well.

Over half of the summoned Observers had been slain at no real detriment to the *Outsiders* and pals . . . although several of them were either missing or she couldn't see them from where she stood. The vampire hadn't returned, which might mean an extra Seven had traveled farther away or was hidden somehow. Or Theo had gotten lost in his mania and found something else less important to do.

Knowing the vampire, it would be the latter.

Theo didn't feel too good. Or rather, he didn't feel too *Theo*, which wasn't good.

Which made his constant smile a bit worrying.

His wrist burned and was a terrible shade of red. His STAR pulsed alongside his heartbeat—which was strange, as he didn't usually have one to note.

Seven held down a hand toward him. "See, that wasn't such a bother, was it?"

The vampire took the offered help and stood on shaky legs. His regeneration had come back, a new tongue in his mouth. "What do I do now?"

"Well, I think you should start by killing the *Outsiders*, right?"

Theo ran his new tongue across his long fangs. "Kill? Is that your order, sire?"

Seven chuckled. "It certainly is."

The crimson eyes of the vampire looked around the illuminated cathedral. There were four clones of Lana still, what remained of *Last Word*. As his glare returned to Seven, he smiled. Punch-blades of dark metal burst into his grip.

"I'd best get started then."

Humphrey slid across the mud, a gash of silver across his chest. Gradually, he healed up as he regained his footing. A smile went across his skeletal face as bandages came in to waylay the continued attacks of the large Observer with six arms.

"Shame my brothers are so weak." He flourished his blade and stepped forward. It had been a concern at first that not everyone present was contributing, but after seeing what little threat the wave of Observers had presented, he didn't blame them.

He could hear Sally arguing with the Architect and keeping him busy was beneficial until the right time came up. The lack of the vampire was acceptable, as he had a terrible grip on his sanity right now and needed a break. There had been less support from the back, but he was pretty sure the *Outsiders* alone could break these opponents with little issue.

Something concerning in the grand scheme of things, compared to how tense the Invasions had been. The worst was yet to come, or the best.

Either way, some end was upon them.

"You felt it too?" Chuck moved up beside Lana as they approached the cathedral.

She nodded. "Well, I could feel some of my clones were here. You?"

"Some power, and something Theo had said, yeah."

They stopped at the slightly ajar doors and readied their weapons. With a nervous push, the large wooden door swung open silently.

Lana gasped and covered her mouth.

Blood. All over the walls, floor, and pews. Body parts littered the place as if the figures had exploded. The statue that now ran with crimson rivers in the carved grooves of the tall figure had five heads placed at its feet. Seven and four that resembled Lana.

Before the statue stood a figure soaked through in blood and gore. Theo turned his burning red eyes back toward them.

"You should both leave."

"Theo?" Chuck went to move forward before Lana stopped him.

The vampire held up his arms to show his corrupted STAR. "I don't want anyone to see me like this. Especially not Sally."

"Is there . . . can we help in any way?" Chuck's voice stumbled as a lump caught in his throat.

"No." Theo turned to look back at the statue. "I'm using all my willpower to not come to kill you both. I am broken. I have . . . fallen."

"There's always a way." Lana grit her teeth. "Don't you prepare for everything?"

The vampire chuckled to himself. "Of course. That's why I am waiting here. For the one person who has a chance to kill me. Please leave. *Please.*"

The pair exchanged glances, unsure what to say or do. Not wanting to become collateral to the vampire's bad mood, they turned to step back out of the cathedral.

Just as a figure stepped in to move past them.

"Edward?"

"Yes, Dent?" The demon lowered his sword and wiped the sweat from his brow.

"You're bleeding. You can slow down, you know?" The swordsman leaned over to get his breath back. Between the *Outsiders*, the rest of the Observers were now tied up.

"I've had worse," Edward murmured, drawing a potion bottle from inside his jacket. "We should gather with the others. I am sure the standoff with the Architect is looming now that things are working out for us."

"Almost feels orchestrated, right?" Dent rubbed the side of his head with the back of his sword arm. "Weird for things to be so calm."

The demon shrugged. "Either the Architect is confident we aren't a threat, or they are begging for us to win."

"Latter sure would be nice."

Sally threw up her arms in exasperation. "What are you even waiting for? Do you want us to win? Is this a pity fight so that you can feel you didn't do a terrible job?"

"I have been in charge for a day, and I have achieved—"

"YAWN," Sally said, exaggerating the faux motions.

A trident of crackling blue energy emerged into the Architect's hand. "Fine, you want to fuckin' go, little corpse woman? Let's GO."

Auras and Passive Abilities Disabled
Stat Bonuses Disabled

"Hey, that's not—" She brought her staff up at the last second, barely blocking the swing of the large trident. Sally bounced across the mud, rolling over a few mounds before coming to a stop. "Ow."

"How's that 'power of friendship' working out for you now?" he seethed as he floated closer, bringing back the trident to impale her.

A group of bandages shot out and wrapped around the extended weapon. He turned with a bright glare across his face.

"I'd say it'll work out quite well," Norah said with a wide smile. "Hit it, hun."

Jackie blazed amber as smoke hissed away from her held crossbow. With a flash of light, she fired off a salvo of bolts that shot forth and passed straight through the Architect as he turned translucent for a moment.

"Pitiful," he growled, the trident vanishing from one hand to appear in the other, dropping the wrappings. He lashed out toward the Mummy, but instead struck Humphrey as he slid in front of Norah.

"My hero," she purred.

"The day is still young." He buckled slightly from the pressure of the weapon, before the Architect finally relented.

Sally rubbed her head as she turned over. Without her bonuses, she was pretty . . . she looked up to see the large blue figure flicker her way and bring the prongs back down upon her.

A large wall of thick vines burst up from the mud, the sharp ends of the weapon cracking through but not reaching her. She glanced over to see Chuck and Lana running toward her.

"Back to your feet, soldier," Lana called, looking like she needed someone to tell her that rather than the other way around.

Sally wobbled back up to her feet. "You find Theo?" She watched them exchange a glance.

"There was another Seven, and Theo killed him," Chuck began. "He said he would catch us up as soon as possible."

"Is he hurt?" Her brow furrowed. Surely not, as he could regenerate or respawn?

Chuck put his hand on her shoulder as the vines started to sink away. "Trust me on this, okay? Focus on the Architect."

She nodded, but that didn't comfort the building knot in her stomach.

"Huh." Theo held his wrist where the corrupted STAR blinked back at his intense glare. "I had hoped that I'd have more control and be able to just give myself up." He turned his red eyes to the other figure. "But you knew that already, didn't you?"

A shrug was the only given response.

"Even you are tongue-tied at the sight of me." Theo lowered his head before shaking it. "To think I could have been so easily tricked and become a Monster, just like they all worried."

The opposing figure, half shadowed by the large pillars in the cathedral, drew their weapons.

"Very well. A fight to the death it is." The vampire brought up his gore-soaked punch-blades. "You'd better fucking win."

The trident carved a wide arc through the mud as Edward and Dent dove to the side. Fern thickened the earth, causing the weapon to get stuck part of the way through to the rest of the *Insiders*.

"Playing with insects is certainly tiring," the Architect growled, a glowing orb forming in his other hand.

[Mortis Bomb] struck him in the side, but he didn't even flinch. Instead, he glared down at the handful of zombies rising from the dirt, and instead they wiggled themselves back away.

"Unfair," Sally growled. Her curse didn't work on him either, which left her with little to attempt. She had gone for a *[Meat Hook]*, but he had vanished again, letting the skill miss. He wasn't evading everything, but most of their attempts didn't seem to even scratch him when they did hit.

"Oh, you expected this to be fair?" The Architect lobbed out the glowing orb toward her. "You are just lucky I am not at full power."

She went to leap away, and the mud surrounding her suddenly turned into sand. Her feet dug into it, and she toppled over onto her face just before the attack landed.

An uncomfortable heal ran through her, sent over by the Druid. She stepped back up on her feet, most of the sand now turned to glass from the impact. The last shreds of the smoldering red cloak fell from her to land in a pile on the ground.

"Oh, now you've done it," she seethed. With a motion, she swapped back to a refreshed version of her diner outfit and threw her staff on the ground to flip her knife into her right hand. It was time to go back to basics.

"Healers are such pains." The Architect spun the trident around, turning it into a double-ended glaive. With a crack like lightning, he jabbed it out toward Chuck.

Dent was there, sparks flaring from his sword arm as he deflected the blow into the mud beside the Druid. With the arm of the Architect extended, Sally hit it with *[Meat Hook]* and spun in toward him.

"Bug!" he yelled, bringing his free hand to swat her away—before bandages wrapped around his raised arm.

Sally jabbed Skeleton Key into the torso of the robed skeleton before he vanished to appear a dozen feet back. Bandages then caught her as she dropped to the ground, avoiding the spikes that had risen up to meet her.

The Architect felt himself and raised his hand up to see dark blue blood ran from the wound. "How is this possible?"

"With friendship, anything is possible," Humphrey said, stepping forward.

"Betrayer, your use here is limited. Do not bother me while I crush the others." He rose up, a pair of axes appearing in his hands.

A wide grin appeared across the skeletal face of the Death Knight.

"Limited? This isn't even my final form."

[Soul Knight]

CHAPTER SIXTY-FOUR

Said It from the Start

The sounds of combat were muted from back in the cathedral. While the candles had all been extinguished, the occasional flash of blue light or powerful ability shone brief illumination inside the gray interior.

Atop the base of the statue, four heads continued to stare in shocked awe at the fate that had met them. A macabre display of what someone so powerful could accomplish if truly separated from any chains tethering them to normal morality.

A body, among all the blood and gore, lay broken in the middle of the floor. Rivers of crimson ran from two puncture wounds in the neck of the corpse. Broken glasses lay among rubble, as some of the structure had not been able to escape becoming collateral in the intense fight.

Despite the calm now settled in the building, slow footsteps echoed out away from the body, toward the door and outside world. Blood dripped down to the floor, decorating the stone among red shoe prints trailing behind the victor.

As the wooden door opened silently, a wide grin was illuminated by a flash of blue. Long fangs picking up the light with practiced precision.

Humphrey hummed with power. The flames of his ability engulfed him briefly before being washed away by a gust of energy.

Now, no longer in his dark crimson and black suit of armor, he radiated despite the lack of light. He was taller, each of his limbs thicker and gleaming in a reflective white. His new appearance was blockier, and his helmet no longer had the skeletal grin, but instead a flat plate angled into a triangle. Two eyes of flaming green energy blazed brighter than his usual crimson flame ever had.

He flourished his sword and stood to oppose the Architect.

"See, told you he was a mecha," Chuck murmured to the zombie.

Sally had been waiting for this. The big metal lug had been keeping his ultimate to fight against the Architect, and now that he had the full Archie in him . . . well, she didn't really know what it meant. Only that the cat was the key to winning this battle.

Still, something was not right. She scowled at Chuck again. "Do you know what is going on?"

He raised an eyebrow back at her as he prepared a spell. "Like, in the grand scheme of things, or more specific?"

"You made plans with Archie, right?" She winced as Jackie burst out an attack through the air. "What's actually happening here?" She turned and watched the Death Knight burst forward to engage the Architect in melee. "I suppose I feel like I'm a little useless right now."

"Nah." Chuck shook his head and smiled. "Everything here is because of you. Anytime one of us attacks or heals, it's an extension of everything you've fought for and put together."

Sally tried to consider this. She had said before that Theo and Humphrey were like her sword and shield, and that being queen meant she didn't always need to dirty her hands. This was like that, but bigger. Over time, she had gathered all the pieces of the puzzle to *hopefully* take down the Architect and fix the System.

"I guess you're right. I wouldn't be here without all of you, either." She smiled as she watched the Death Knight.

"Even me?" a voice came from behind them.

They turned to see Theo standing there, his clothing and most of his chest in bloody tatters.

Humphrey flashed out with his sword, green light following the blade as it burst into flame. He ducked and spun around, knocking back both axes of the Architect and causing him to vanish and appear nearby.

"Perhaps I was a fool to not take you more seriously," the Architect growled, his axes switching to maces. "I had hoped you'd get the hint after I tried to assassinate you."

"That just renewed my ambition," Humphrey replied, leaping into a downward swing. "Knowing that you were afraid of me."

"Afraid?"

"Theo!" Sally grinned at him before her expression sank away. "You look . . . *bad*."

He withdrew his hands from his pockets and shrugged, exposing his normal STAR to the extremely tense Chuck and Lana.

"Oh, thank fuck," the Druid said and sighed deeply.

Lana nodded along eagerly with this assessment but still didn't feel safe enough to say anything.

The vampire stumbled down the mud and collapsed into the waiting hug from the zombie. "Got some good and bad news, my queen."

"What is it, pup?" She ran her fingers through the back of his hair to find it was matted with fresh blood.

"Killed Seven and the rest of the *Last Word*. Lost all my special blood powers, though."

"Oh, pup." She gave him a squeeze. "Architect just disabled passives, that's all."

Theo gave a tired look over to Chuck and Lana. "No, it's not."

Sally gave him a pat on the back. "Here, take a Healing Potion. Pops has just gone super mode. You good to fight?" She narrowed her eyes back to the group fighting. "Wait, Lucy hasn't used his ultimate either, the little sneak."

"I'll do what I can. Not quite feeling myself." He worked his jaw. "Or . . . feeling too much of myself. It's hard to tell." With a shrug, he walked over to retrieve his coffin.

Chuck rubbed his face. "Can't wait to have to address that later."

Lana shuddered. "I suppose he *did* have my blood, right?"

"What are you two murmuring about?" Sally scowled. "Let's go kill the Architect! Hit it, Lucy!"

Without waiting for a response, she leaped down from the ridge they had been populating and ran toward the battle where Humphrey was exchanging blows with the large blue figure. *[Meat Hook]* struck the Architect near the bottom of their robes, and she dug her heels into the soft mud, spraying up a wave of dirt on approach to obscure herself.

Lucius popped out of Norah's shadow to use his ultimate, a shadowed version of himself appearing under each of the *Outsiders*.

Another two arms extended out of the Architect, large spikes at the end instead of hands. One darted in toward the zombie, striking just beside her before she was upon him. Her dagger went into where his leg would be, more dark blue blood spurting from the wound as a shadowed version repeated the action. As the second spiked appendage stabbed out at her, a flash of darkness had Theo in the way, blocking the attack with his punch-blades crossed against him, assisted by those granted by the Shade.

The vampire hit the dirt and slid through the mud. Bright red light had given life back to his eyes, a heal from the Druid running through him where his passive regeneration could no longer do the job.

"More worms wriggle out from the soil," the Architect seethed at the vampire, before turning his focus back to the Death Knight.

Bandages flung Sally through the air, and with a fist raised back, she threw a punch out—connecting with the skeletal face of the Architect.

As Humphrey charged up a powerful upswing, a pyramid burst up from beneath him, popping him up into the air so that his slash went over the prepared defenses of the two axes, a shadowed version of the attack ensuring the first went through unhindered.

The Architect flashed away from the combat, appearing a short distance away to examine the long line of dark blue up his chest. "It seems this is not working. I will return when you—"

[Compelled Duel]

"Fool, I'm not going to . . ." The skeletal face of the Architect contorted in weird ways. "No! But how?"

Humphrey grinned beneath his mask and held up his free hand to beckon the large figure closer. "I have the power of the old god and found family on my side."

"*Fool!*"

Sally rolled her eyes and walked back up to the ridge with Theo. "Necessary evil," she grumbled. "Stops the big boss from running away and blah blah."

Theo shrugged. "I ever tell you that I love you, Sally?"

"Of course, who doesn't?" She smiled and punched him on the shoulder. "All that death and exhaustion got you feeling sappy?"

He looked over at the pensive Druid and Lana. "Ah, I'll tell you later."

Edward stepped over and narrowed his eyes at the vampire. "*Theo.*"

"*Edward.*" He narrowed his eyes in return before they went in for a hug.

"For some reason, I feared something dire had happened to you."

The vampire stepped back away and smiled. "Nah. The only person powerful enough to stop me would be another me." His eyes darted briefly back to the pair of humans, who both held an uncomfortable grimace.

Humphrey danced beneath the blades, twisting away from the attacks to dart in himself. Another brief line of dark blue against the robes of the angered Architect.

"How can you even damage me? You are infuriating! It is *his* power, isn't it?"

The Death Knight activated his parrying ability, blocking the flurry of blows leveled at him. "I do not know what you mean."

"Of course you do, betrayer! The false Architect split themselves into fragments after I poisoned them. You hold the powers of the cat." He grew another two arms, these ones also pointed spikes.

"Scared of a cat? Such folly unbecoming of the Architect!"

Sally rolled her eyes, before looking over at the rest of the group arranging themselves in certain positions. "What's going on?"

Norah paused. "It's part of the plan, hun."

"Told you that she doesn't read her messages," Chuck murmured, before shooting her a sheepish grin.

Theo put his hand on her confused shoulder. "Don't worry, Humphrey and I had this planned out. Just do what comes natural to you." The vampire took the end of an offered bandage and walked to the other side of her.

The Death Knight dropped his sword, the weapon spinning away to stick into the dirt as he clutched at his injured arm. Green fire bloomed in his eyes as the Architect loomed over him. As one, all six arms turned into large hands, and they grabbed up Humphrey to lift him into the air.

"Such a curious waste of resources. All that power, just to be squished like an insect?" The skeletal face grinned toward the plated figure as his hands squeezed tighter.

Humphrey winced as his form started to buckle and squeal. "You do not have the strength or conviction to crush me, let alone run the System."

"Wrong." The Architect buzzed with energy as he pooled his power into his hands. Sparks and steam hissed out from the joints of the empowered Death Knight as he was crushed further.

"*Ha-ha*," he laughed. "I lose. Making me the winner."

With one last push, the Death Knight broke. The power left him, returning his armor to the small black and crimson design, albeit now twisted and silver in several places. His helmet hung limp, shadowed in the grip of the Architect.

Then, his chest burst open, and a rail of orange energy shot through the air, striking the Architect through his forehead.

He dropped the spent armor to the floor and clutched at the wound with a pair of his hands—a split going straight through his head. He turned his eyes to see a ginger cat drop to the floor on the other side.

"*You*. I am not so easily . . ." he hissed, before the rush of air caught his attention too late.

[Eat Brains]

Sally bounced off the empty head of the Architect and fell to the ground, landing uncomfortably on the wet mud. "Archie!" She immediately sat up and vomited, light blue liquid flooding over her hands until a crown was painfully expelled.

"How . . . dare . . . you," the tall figured hissed, as he sank to the floor.

With the flick of her brain and vomit soaked hand, Sally threw the crown across the battlefield like a frisbee, to land straight into the hands of the Druid. With no hesitation, he lifted it up and put it upon his head.

So much had just happened that it was hard to properly parse through it all. Sally looked over at the crushed body of Humphrey, her eyes filling with tears at the sacrifice he had made to allow her that opportunity to attack.

"There's no need to cry. Everything is well."

She looked up at the familiar voice, to see the floating purple skull grinning down at her. "You *lump*." She sniffed. "Had me worried for nothing." Her eyes turned over to everyone else, all of them currently looking at the Druid with apprehension across their faces.

Chuck flickered, his normal appearance turning fully blue before going back to his usual look. Back and forth a handful of times, until he slumped over to the ground as a Player.

"Everything okay, Chuck?" Sally slid over and crouched beside him, concern on her face.

"I really hate wearing robes," he complained.

Dent stood over him and scowled. "You've been wearing them all year?"

Chuck smiled. "Dress for the job that you want, right?" He held a hand in the air. "Things are pretty confusing, but how about this for now?"

All combat is disabled

"Enjoy your pacifist run," he murmured, before passing out.

CHAPTER SIXTY-FIVE

Death of the Party 3

Sally and Dent propped the tired Druid up against an embankment of mud and tried to give him some air.

Norah tilted her head. "That's a new look for you, Humphrey."

The floating skull smiled sheepishly. "I will find a new body in due course, I am certain."

"You're still the big softie I adore even without the shining knight exterior." She smiled. "Do not fret."

Theo snapped his fingers and withdrew something from his Inventory. Into his hands, a flare gun appeared, along with a case of different colored flares. "Gold first," he murmured to himself, before loading it into the sky and firing it.

A streak of radiant light followed the projectile before it burst into a ball of bright light.

"Goblins have eyes on the area, so they know the day was won." He grinned before loading a second one. As this went up into the air, a trail of purple shot up before blooming like a flower.

"What does purple mean?" Lucius asked, a question mark appearing beside his head.

Theo winked and stepped a few feet over to the side. Above them, a wide circle of dark green appeared, before a dark object fell out, crashing into the dirt and spraying mud and pulped zombie parts over everyone congregated.

Humphrey hovered beside him. "I was going to ask how you knew, but I should know better than that by now."

An almost picture-perfect replica of the original Death Knight armor now sat inert in the mud. A smoother metal, constructed to the same precision as the vampire's coffin, deep black with areas highlighted in a dark crimson.

With a flash of red light, Humphrey fused with it. The crimson areas glowing bright red as a flame flickered up behind his skeletal head.

"Ah, I feel like a brand-new man, *ha-ha*." He grinned and turned as the Mummy looped her arm around his. "Your foresight is still slightly concerning, however."

"I know." Theo snapped his fingers before putting his hands in his trouser pockets and walking over to Chuck.

Edward was already there, his hands also in his pockets. "*Theo*. Apparently the System does not allow any kind of combat."

"Yeah? Want to try punching me to see if it works?"

The demon narrowed his eyes. "No."

"No, because you can't . . . or no, because *you can't?*"

Sally scowled up at them both. "Quit bickering for five minutes, you two. Theo, you have some explaining to do."

He nodded. "I agree, although you'll have to be more specific about what parts exactly."

"Killing Seven and taking ages to come back."

Theo raised an eyebrow at Lana, who avoided his gaze. "Well, you know how Bella's blood gave me super regeneration? And Edward's blood allowed me to respawn?"

"Yeah?" She narrowed her eyes further, before they opened wide. "You had a clone? Where are they now?"

"Dead." He shrugged. "Seven captured him and forced him to have a corrupted STAR."

Her mouth hung open. "What? When? *What?*"

"When the other me went up to the Cathedral. There were four *Last Word* members. Corrupted Theo couldn't be controlled, however, and he killed all five of them before I got there."

"And then you killed the bad version of you." She shook her head and sighed. "I don't even want to know how or when the clone came to be, when you switched, or whether you're the original or not. Okay?"

"Okay." He gave her a low bow and rose to find that she was smiling at him.

"You did whatever bullshit you had to for us to win, thank you."

Archie yawned and stretched out. "Not quite the reunion I had imagined. I am glad to see everyone is well, however."

Humphrey leaned down to pick the cat up. "And what of you, little brother? Your eyes are still emerald."

"I liked this version best. Now that I am whole once more, I feel . . . like I am not as much of the Architect as he would have liked to have saved. While it may have looked like I just cannonballed through the head of the other Architect, it was actually more akin to a key and lock situation."

"Using what you knew, you made it so that he had a vulnerable 'brain' that I could eat, and the crown that gives the powers comes with it?" Sally pulled a face.

"Correct. When Humphrey sacrificed his Death Knight life, it left them open for the only one who could immediately extract it."

"It tasted like carbonated blueberry." She nodded in agreement.

Chuck groaned and opened his eyes.

"You did it bud; you're the boss now." She prodded his shoulder.

"Ah, Doris retired?" He shook a daze from his head. "Oh, hmm. I'm still *here*." With a raised eyebrow, he looked up at the swordsman and his face relaxed.

Sally prodded him again. "How's the process? You feel powerful? Can you fix the System?"

"Ugh." With a grunt, the new Architect stood up on his feet. "Let me have a look."

They stood around and watched him as he closed his eyes and put a hand up to his forehead. The former Druid hummed to himself for a handful of seconds before opening his eyes again—a light blue glow fading from them.

"I can see why the other guy had so much trouble." He looked over at the cat and furrowed his brow. "Your naming convention and passwords are all pop-culture references."

Archie grinned and waved his tail about. "A last act of rebellion against those that killed me."

"It's interesting, though." Chuck rolled his shoulders out. "It's a bit like a STAR menu but different. And it's not really code or magic, something in the middle." He turned to Dent and gestured him over.

The swordsman stepped in front of the Architect, somewhat awkwardly, as if he was about to be presented with a knighthood.

"Calm yourself." Chuck grinned, before putting his hand on the man's chest. "Hmm. There's . . . unfortunately, I can't replace your arm." He gave Dent a glum smile. "It's like a part of your data has been deleted."

"I'm used to it now." He shrugged. "At least it gives me an excuse to try to be the strongest swordsman in the System."

Chuck grinned. "Oh, you're definitely the strongest." His eyes then went over to the demon, and he gestured for him to replace where Dent was standing.

Hand upon his chest, the Architect furrowed his brow. "Okay . . . I think I see it. This will be useful, thank you. Lana next."

Edward shrugged and moved away, slightly confused.

"Is this where you can tell me that I'm definitely a copy?" she asked, tilting her head.

Chuck shook his head. "No, there's . . . your existence isn't defined like that. This is early days, but your importance to this world cannot be understated." He gave her a pat, and she moved in to give him a hug. "You *are* Lana."

"Thank you," she whispered, before moving away.

Sally was nothing but smiles. It still hadn't really settled in yet. They had *won*. Chuck was the Architect, and they didn't need to struggle anymore. Things literally couldn't get any better.

Chuck swiveled around to face her. "Alright, you and Theo."

They both stood in front of him. He closed his eyes and hummed to himself. "Well . . . bad news is that I can't turn you back into normal humans. Even knowing *how* Theo got this way . . . there isn't a clear reversal or even a way to duplicate it."

Sally pouted but gave him a nod.

"However . . ." His eyes glowed bright blue. "You can now eat normal food, and . . . well, thank me in the morning." His eyes went back to normal, but he paused before he turned away from them. "Actually, *do not* do that. Pretend I didn't do anything." With a grimace, he moved over to look at who was next.

Sally frowned. "I don't get it. I don't feel any different, really."

Theo leaned over and whispered in her ear.

"Oh . . . *oh*." Her eyes widened.

Lucius was next up.

"Another one of the most important members of our little gathering." Chuck smiled as he put his hand on the Shade. "I think this should give me enough homework to start putting the System back together in a better shape."

"Eh, what? Rest of us don't have anything useful for you?" Jackie grinned and took a drag of her cigarette.

He raised an eyebrow. "Fight is over mobster. Want me to have a chat with Fran about making smoking illegal?"

"Asshole." She shook her head but smiled wider.

"It's been awhile since I saw my home," Archie said. "Perhaps we can go there soon."

"It would be nice to see my new home," Chuck said. "But one thing first." He then smiled before vanishing.

A few awkward seconds of silence passed, before he returned to the exact same position, earning plenty of raised eyebrows.

"Just had to lower the area four barrier and slay the rest of the betrayers who were part of the usurper's group." Chuck nodded toward Archie. "Perhaps Sally can give us a speech and then we'll head off to celebrate our win? Sally?"

"Huh?" She shook her head. "Sorry, miles away. What the what now?"

"Speech!" The Architect grinned, as everyone else started to join in chanting the request.

"Alright, alright." She cleared her throat, suddenly feeling very put on the spot. "Where to begin? I started in this world as a humble zombie, full of anger and violence toward the System. I guess nothing really changed, huh?" She grinned before she continued. "Making morally questionable decisions along the way, I happened upon at least a dozen really amazing people. My found family. From my adoptive pops, Humphrey, right at the start, all the way up to Fern, who is probably very traumatized from our interactions."

"I am," the dryad noted, still sitting on the ground.

"You're all a piece of the puzzle that makes up my life here. Each of you has done your best and followed me through hell and back, even though I am literally a violent criminal. I've done a lot of bad things in the System, but it's all been working toward making this a better world for all of you goofballs, and any goofballs behind our trail of blood and destruction."

She rubbed the back of her hair, now running out of pleasantries. "So, to sum up, thank you all for believing in me, helping me along the way, and putting your lives on the line. We've . . . we did it. We won."

Theo started the clapping, and they all joined in. One of them might have even yelled, "Pancakes," though Sally might just have imagined that. She felt like a dog that had caught the van, and although victory was sweet, the speech had made it real and overpowering.

Teleportation is enabled
Mounts are enabled
All Skills are enabled
Stat Bonuses are enabled

Chuck cracked his knuckles. "I'm keeping combat off for now. Monsters and Players alike can have a holiday until I have some things worked out."

"What do you have planned?" Sally asked him.

"A way everyone can live here and be happy." He smiled. "But for now, we need to celebrate, surely?"

"Hell yeah." She shot a glance over at Jackie. "I'd love to go back to the tavern and see Fran and the goblins!"

The mobster shrugged. "I would sure like to see Fran, and we definitely deserve a drink or two."

Sally gasped and put her hands over her mouth. "I can *drink* now."

Chuck hovered up into the air atop waves of blue energy. "Alright, everyone gather around then. I haven't done this before, so . . . if we all die or something, then that would be amusing, right?"

"One second." Sally held up a finger and dragged Theo over to the rest of the *Outsiders*. "I started this because we needed to struggle and strive to rise against all the odds stacked against us . . . so, I am doing this as our first step into our new future."

Humphrey grinned and nodded, as they all came in for a hug.

"I love you guys."

Party "*Outsiders*" has been disbanded

CHAPTER SIXTY-SIX

Life after Death

Sally groaned and stretched out, hissing as the morning light burned into her waking eyes. She rolled to her side in the bed to move away from the glare and frowned at the figure standing on the other side of the room.

"It's *how* early, and you're already leaving me?" She pouted.

Theo grinned, exposing his fangs, as he buttoned up his dress shirt. "Big dungeon day today, wanted to get a bit more practice in."

She exhaled and sank into the bed. "Which one was it again?"

"Dark Cathedral." His smile widened.

She whistled. "The Level Forty dungeon? You get all the fun."

"You know I live for it. They're trying hard mode too, but just the east wing. Three bosses, and pops is up first."

"Humphrey *hates* going first in the dungeons. After that one time with the all Paladin raid." She brought the duvet up over her mouth to hide the grin.

"*Don't.*" The vampire shook his head. "He complained about it for two weeks. I'm going to work with him to do all this dramatic goading stuff—I'll stand in the background and make fun of the Players while he fights. Try and put them off or at least make my fight a bigger payoff."

"You're up last then?"

"As usual." He nodded. "We have Curtis as the middle boss."

"The skull golem? He's a doll, such a gentle giant. When he bursts out into a dozen flaming skeletons it gives me goosebumps. Wish I could be there to watch you fight, pup."

He pulled on his suit jacket and worked the sleeves to be comfortable. "You're on day five of the zombie event later, yeah?"

"Yeah. Still low level, but it's fun getting to play about with my pals for a bit. Oh!" She scooted up into a sitting position. "There's this Player, Kenny. First three nights he died to my hands, and I ate his brains each time. Fourth night, he's got something fierce in his eyes. I could see he'd gotten new equipment and leveled—and he managed to bash my head in, caught me right off guard!"

"Hey, good on him." He walked around the bed to where she was sitting. "Drop me a message later and let me know how it goes?"

She held his face as he leaned in, and they shared a slow kiss before he moved back away.

"You too, pup." She grinned and looked into his eyes. "But if you don't wash off and soak the bed with Player blood *again*, I won't be as amused as the first two times it happened."

"I'll wash off and brush my teeth, promise." He gave her another quick peck before moving away. "Naturally, I'm hoping for a wipe, but perhaps tonight I'll take the loss."

"First time for everything," she said and rolled her eyes. "I'm surprised Chuck hasn't given you something low level to humble you."

"Ah, I have a reputation to uphold." He gave her a bow and flourished his hand. "Until we meet again, my queen."

She stuck her tongue out at him as he vanished in a flash of blue that caught the edges of the simple wooden furniture around the room.

With the place to herself, she deflated and smiled. The event wasn't until the night, so she had the day to burn away. It wasn't like she needed to practice anything either. She had the whole shambling and eating brains thing down pretty well—even if she had to hold herself back a little. Well, a lot.

Relenting to greeting the day proper, she slid out from the bed onto the cool floor and switched into a red T-shirt and black jeans. The nice thing about the event was that it was in the forest area, so she got to spend time around the places in the world that brought her the most comfort. Not so far from home, which made stumbling back full of Player brains easier.

It did make the visit to Jackie and Fran's place a little awkward when Kenny had turned up, but he was a good kid. Thankfully, the System took the trauma of dying away now, so his anger against her had been just a healthy determination. She even gave him some more tips for fighting the undead. Secretly she hoped to foster him into being a vampire hunter to take Theo down a few pegs.

She hummed to herself and tied her long hair back. Chuck had clued her in that the odd growth was due to a bug linking it to her natural progression. It hadn't grown an inch since they had won. For their part in saving the world, Chuck moved their stats and abilities about when needed for whatever job they were doing. Which was fine—it was nice to no longer have to struggle for levels or grasp at power to survive.

Humphrey, with his Observer insight, had taken up a Head of Security role in charge of a new batch of Observers. He still liked to do a dungeon or event on occasion, however, just to keep himself sharp. Lucius had become something of a therapist for Uniques and Players alike. It suited him; he loved to help people and was happy to be outside of a combat role. Norah had little interest in fighting but had taken up a place on the Wastelands Council alongside Edward.

As the Architect, Chuck had taken the power of Lucius's skill to allow all Players to have the comfort of being happy within the System. Then, with a mix of Lana's and Edward's powers, he made everyone able to respawn. Apparently, it was the simple matter of making a recording of someone's "soul" to come back when the originator died. It worked for both Uniques and Players. Everyone had the chance to live, fight, and die if they wanted, or just hang about and enjoy their time here.

Combat was only allowed against Monsters, unless in a set event or dungeon. It was just what the little snot said he was going to do. She knew he could be trusted and was doubly glad she hadn't put the crown on herself. Half the reason she had thrown it at him was to avoid the temptation. Queen of a whole world would just go to her head.

She checked her watch and cursed at herself.

Sally: running late, sorry!
Norah: as always, I knew and planned to arrive late myself
Norah: ;)

Without the pressure of conflict, she had become even closer to the Mummy. The struggle had brought the found family together, but this era of peace had allowed them to settle and grow stronger emotionally. Without the need to grind or overplan, the time spent with Theo had been a joy too. Any worries that they were just together out of convenience for the bad times had washed away within the first week.

Now it was what, two months? Things were getting better by the week.

She left the bedroom and hopped down the stairs of their house, into the living room, to see a familiar ball of ginger fluff sitting on the couch.

"Oh, Archie! I didn't know you were sleeping here."

He stretched out and narrowed his emerald eyes. "No, I don't usually stay, because of the noise. I came over this morning. Shall we walk and talk?"

"Of course. I'm off to meet Norah and the gals for coffee."

"Acceptable. The weather is nice, at least."

They left the building and stepped out into what was indeed a pleasant day.

Despite having the whole world at their fingertips, she wanted their house to be in the goblin village. If they wanted to go down to see Jackie and Fran, there was always a room available—and the rest of the world was just a teleport away.

"Tell me, Sally, are you happy?"

She looked down at the cat. "That's an easy question. I've never been happier in all my unlife."

"Okay then." Archie tilted his head. "Are you satiated?"

"Hmm? I get to fight and eat brains and the stakes are low."

"Do you like low stakes?"

She stopped and put a hand over her eyes to block out the sun as she glared down at the ginger interrogator. "What's this all leading to, Arch?"

He sat down on the warm cobblestones. "Nothing. Go enjoy your lunch, Sally. I just wanted to make sure you were fine with the status quo."

"Well, thanks? Lucy already does that." She narrowed her eyes at him before turning away. "Adios, Archie. You should go along on the next guy's night, maybe try to keep Theo and Eddy in line. They need more babysitting than I can provide."

Archie didn't respond but continued to watch her leave, a slight smile on his fluffy face.

The door to the round chamber slid open with a hiss, and the blue light that illuminated the edges of furniture faded under the presence of the daylight coming through the opening.

A figure stepped in and sighed.

"We were going to go out for lunch, Chuck." Dent entered the room and the door hissed shut behind him.

The Architect looked up from the screens glowing blue and grimaced toward the approaching man. "Ah, crap. Sorry, Dent—lost track of time again."

"Of course." The swordsman smiled. "That's why I brought it here." Held by his mechanical hand, he gently placed a tray down on the desk.

A waft of the warm meat and pastry hit Chuck's senses, and he melted. He rubbed his eyes and yawned, trying to separate himself from staring at screens all morning.

Dent sat on the edge of the smooth desk. "*Outsiders* been behaving?"

Chuck nodded. "Pretty happy. I think Sally and Theo might be getting bored soon enough, though."

"Oh? Not content with paradise?"

He grimaced. "They came to me the other week to request I make their constitution the max possible."

Dent tilted his head. "Why's that?"

"Same reason that you did."

"Ah." The swordsman pulled a face and looked away. "That aside, they've always been the type to rise up to a challenge and defeat the odds. They are having fun now . . . but I suppose I could imagine they'd eventually want something more."

"Exactly." Chuck picked one of the pastries up and gestured toward the screens. "Look at this, though. It's something . . . big."

Dent grimaced. "Big? How big are we talking?"

"Well, you know how it's super odd that the world is just this one continent, nothing further? Like we are in a bubble?" He brought up a screen showing the continent in blue lines, zoomed out to sit inside a sphere. The fifth area restored; it resembled a croissant shape once more.

"Yeah. It is odd." He furrowed his brow at the shape. It didn't even make sense in terms of physics, as far as he understood them.

"I've been trying to . . ." Chuck clucked his tongue. "Zoom out?"

He gestured with his fingers, and the small globe that showed their world shrank down. While keeping the size set, he then tried to make it smaller still.

"Oh." Dent tilted his head. "What are those?"

His mechanical hand raised, and his index finger pointed toward what looked to be the boundaries of other spheres, just on the edges of the perimeter of the screen.

Chuck smiled. "I think we should find out."

About the Author

Kleggt is the author of the Death of the Party series, originally released on Royal Road. Upon clawing his way out of the depths of Scheduling Hell as a Forever DM, he began writing web novels, channeling his love of world-building and oddball characters into his own LitRPG and progression fantasy stories.

Podium

DISCOVER MORE
STORIES UNBOUND

PodiumEntertainment.com